Volume 3

Amy DuBoff
C.C. Ekeke
Zen DiPietro
S.E. Anderson
Michael Anderle
Chris J. Pike
L.A. Johnson
Drew Avera
Andrew Lawston

Cover Design by Christian Kallias

www.pewpewbooks.com

ISBN-10: 197957314X
ISBN-13: 978-1979573146

0 9 8 7 6 5 4 3 2 1

Produced in the United States of America

CONTENTS

STEALING TROUBLE

by Amy DuBoff

A life of crime passes the time—if you don't mind getting in a few firefights along the way.

After trading in a life of crime to run a successful coffee chain, the crew of the *Little Princess II* realize that legitimate business is their own personal form of hell. All paperwork, no thrill.

To fill the void in their lives, they decide to take from the rich to give to the poor. It's a nice sentiment, even though they'll probably just end up using the procedes to upgrade their own spaceship.

With a sleazeball businessman in their sights, they set out to steal some high-value artwork to turn around and sell on black market for a profit. In their usual fashion of leaping without looking, nothing goes according to plan. Old nemeses, incorrect assumptions, and bad luck are just the beginning of their problems.

CHAPTER ONE:
Auspicious Beginnings

Jack Tressler threw his left shoe against the wall, causing a rainbow of lights around the sole to flash on impact. "I'm bored."

Alissa's tawny eyes narrowed as she glared at him from across the spaceship's living area. "Did you seriously just throw your shoe?"

"Yeah, why?" Jack replied with a shrug.

"And where did you get light-up shoes?"

"From the *SpaceMall* catalogue."

"Didn't we cancel that subscription?" Triss chimed in from next to Alissa.

"Yeah, Finn had acquired way too many toasters," the other woman confirmed.

"It was exactly the right number of toasters to meet my copious toasting needs," Finn replied without looking up from his tablet.

"Well, you wouldn't let me leave my room, and those were the only shoes in the catalogue." Jack crossed his arms. Mid-thirties or not, he was firm in his conviction that one was never too old for shoes that illuminated with every step.

Triss sighed. "But gold with rainbow lights… Honestly, Jack."

"They're awesome and you know it."

"Someone can pull them off, I'm sure," Alissa said, "but I'm not sure that person is you. The gold kind of clashes with the silver of your cybernetic eye."

Jack itched above his ill-fitting mod. "Not like I had a choice about the model."

Alissa brushed her dark bands from her eyes. "Fashion choices aside, I hear ya. I'm bored, too."

The mood on the *Little Princess II* had been trending toward restless for some time, and shoe-throwing was certainly enough to tip the scales toward chaos. Jack knew it, and he was counting on it.

"I think it's time we took on a new mission," Finn declared as he rose from the couch next to Jack.

"Oh, stars, here we go…" Triss breathed.

Jack couldn't keep the smirk off his face as his crewmates began reverting to their old ways. "So, I was thinking we could go after some art."

"Whoa, let's back up a minute." Alissa spread her hands palm down in the air in an attempt to rein in her crew. "We have enough money to last us for our whole lives. Stealing art to sell on the black market would be—"

"Who said anything about selling it?" Jack interjected. "That's why I suggested art. It has no innate value other than the emotional attachment a person is willing to pay for. We find some pieces we like, and… appropriate them."

"But, Jack," Alissa shot back in her most condescending tone, "that would be *illegal*."

"And since when did we decide to stop flirting with the boundaries of legality?"

Alissa raised an eyebrow. "Around the time when we became legitimate business partners?"

"Was that a question?" Jack asked. "I think I heard a question mark at the end."

"This isn't up for discussion."

Jack tilted his head. "The use of a question mark, or the art heist?"

"I think both matters deserve some time on the floor," Finn suggested.

"Don't start…" Alissa warned the other man.

"Question marks aside," Jack continued, "owning a chain of coffee shops isn't quite the same thrill level as a life of crime."

Triss chuckled. "That's overselling your past a bit, isn't it, Jack? Before us, you could barely snap the clasps on your shoes without finding yourself in trouble."

"Even tying shoes can be a thrilling endeavor under the right circumstances," he replied.

"So, have we dropped the issue of that question mark?" Finn cut in.

Alissa groaned. "I don't know why I stay on this ship!" She

threw her hands in the air.

"You love us and you know it." Jack grinned.

"But back to the matter at hand." Triss rose from her favorite chair and clasped her hands behind her back. "Monetary circumstances aside, we do need to find a way to occupy our time. We can't just sit around here watching vids and throwing shoes at the wall all day."

"Speak for yourself," Jack muttered.

"You were the one who started this discussion in the first place!" Triss exclaimed.

Jack shrank back into the couch. "Sorry, I was just being contrary. I'm not used to you agreeing with me."

"See? This is our problem." Alissa returned to her seat and propped up her feet on the acrylic coffee table. "We've been cooped up here for too long. We need some common objective to get us focused and working together again."

"Like an art heist." Finn flashed a winning smile.

Alissa frowned. "Can't we think of something a little less risky? We *are* supposed to be legitimate business professionals now, after all."

"Right, like 'legitimate business people' all follow the law," Jack scoffed.

"He does bring up a valid point," Triss agreed.

Finn leaned forward with his hands on his knees. "What if we stole the art from rich people and donated it to a worthy cause?"

"You can't donate stolen merchandise, Finn," Alissa objected.

Triss nodded. "Yeah, obviously we'd have to sell it for cash on the back market and then donate that *money* to the worthy cause."

"Again, there's still the issue of the whole *theft* and then *black market dealings* thing with this plan..." Alissa protested. "What if we—"

Jack interlaced his fingers. "I don't know about you, Finn, but this is sounding like a pretty great plan to me."

"This isn't a plan! It's the kernel of an idea, at best." Alissa crossed her arms.

"All right. So we can't rule out a plan if there isn't even a plan yet to rule out." Jack eyed her. "So, tell us, Alissa, why won't this plan work?"

As he expected, Alissa took the bait. "Well, to pull off something like this, you'd need to first research wealthy individuals who weren't quite on the up-and-up with their dealings. Filter for those with decent enough aesthetic tastes to maintain a salable art collection, and then maybe you'd have a decent target list. But then you'd need to identify where they kept that art, and then figure out a way to get access to the structure. Assuming you were able to do that and procure the art, it'd then be a matter of having the correct black market contacts to unload the paintings while securing untraceable credit payments."

Finn shook his head. "No, you could never get credit payments. You'd need to trade the art for a legitimate commodity and then sell *that* for credits."

Alissa nodded. "Okay, so then you'd need a transport ship for a legitimate business to handle the distribution of those goods."

"Which we have," Jack pointed out.

"But there's still the matter of the black market contacts," Alissa protested.

"I know a few people..." Finn offered.

Alissa sighed. "But you can't just go robbing any old person."

"I've had a naughty business person list in my back pocket for years," Triss said.

"So, in what way is this an unreasonable plan?" Jack asked Alissa.

"You're going to get us all arrested," she replied with a scowl.

Finn grinned. "Not if we don't get caught."

"I place those odds at less than ten percent," Alissa said.

"We've overcome worse." Jack rose to his feet and stretched. "So, how do we get started?" A chill seeped into his left foot. He looked down and realized the limb was only covered in a sock. "You know, I think we need a heated floor."

"Now that you mention it," Finn said, "I have noticed a few things about the ship that I'd change."

"Really, the layout is all wrong," Triss admitted.

"No, we're not having this discussion!" Alissa glared at her shipmates. "We *just* got this ship last month. We're not wasting money trading it in for a new one."

"I get not spending *our* money on it, but what if we were to come into some excess funds from an individual with exceptional aesthetic taste?" questioned Jack.

"No, we are *not* stealing art from wealthy, corrupt business people so we can buy ourselves a new ship." Alissa stamped her foot.

"You know, that actually sounds like a pretty good idea..."

Triss said.

"I'm inclined to agree." Finn nodded.

Jack shrugged. "Sorry, Alissa. Overruled."

"Let the record show that I was against this," she muttered.

"Perfect. Now, who's our target, Triss?" Jack asked.

She smiled. "I have just the person in mind."

The group headed from the lounge area into the dining room that doubled as their planning space. Of course, having not actually gone on a mission since acquiring the ship, the secondary function had yet to be utilized.

"Why am I suddenly hungry?" Jack pondered aloud as he stepped into the room.

"Gah, me too." Triss rubbed her tummy. "I could really go for some pizza."

"There are leftovers in the fridge," Alissa said. "If you'd rather eat than share this target of yours, then by all means proceed. You know where I stand on this."

Triss eyed her suspiciously. "You're trying to distract me with food again."

"Me? No." Alissa shook her head.

"You know, it's this room!" Finn exclaimed. "We always eat in here."

"See? *This* is why we need a new ship!" Jack sighed. "We can't have food and business meetings in the same space."

"But what about snacks?" asked Triss.

"Oh, that's a good question." Jack stroked his chin. "Maybe we have to draw a line between bite-sized foods that don't require a napkin versus those that do."

Finn screwed up his face. "Think about it, though. With something like a buttery cookie, you really do need a napkin. Yet, I would consider that to be solidly in the business-meeting-snack-food category."

"He does bring up a valid point." Triss nodded.

Jack looked around at his colleagues and noticed that Alissa was trying to back away from the table. "I think we can revisit this issue at another time. We should go over the heist target while the overall plan is still fresh."

"Right." Triss placed her hand on the tabletop and activated the holoprojector. The image of a bald, squat man in a black business jacket appeared. "Meet Vincent Ordello."

CHAPTER TWO:
BLAST FROM THE PAST

Finn's mouth fell open as he took in the holographic representation of the businessman. "Triss, you can't be serious!"

The woman's lips curled into a predatory grin. "Oh, quite."

"That's way too high-profile a target, Triss," Alissa stated. "No way that this'll work."

"Oh, come on! When have we turned down a challenge?" Triss asked. "I mean, just look at the guy! He's practically asking to be robbed."

Jack did have to acknowledge that Vincent's T-shirt read, 'Go ahead and try'. He wasn't sure the context was quite the same, but he chose to take it as a sign. "Not entirely sure who he is, but looks good to me."

Alissa groaned and rolled her eyes. "Vincent is a Class-A sleazeball, surely, but what about his taste in art?"

"That's where his wife Merica comes in," Triss continued. "Apparently, Vincent's reputation of being an uncultured dirtbag was starting to hurt business, so he decided to try to buy himself some class—much like anyone with too much money and too little common decency. He found himself an impressionable young Art History major with an exotic accent to be both his arm candy and personal stylist. She's recently completed a remodel of his estate on Estrada, complete with seventy million credits' worth of new art installations."

Jack scowled. "What a stupid amount of money to spend on art."

"Can you think of some better way to spend it?" Alissa asked.

"Um… a spaceship?" he ventured.

"Think of the luxury yacht we could have for seventy million..." Finn said with a wistful look in his eyes.

"No, this whole plan is based on us taking the art to sell on the black market, which we'll trade for goods to sell for credits to donate to the needy," Alissa said firmly.

"Yeah, that was the original plan," Jack replied, "but I like ship upgrades much better."

"I think we're all in agreement on that." Triss returned her attention to the holographic image. "So, anyway, the remodel is complete, but Vincent hasn't yet moved into the property. That means his full security detail won't be there."

"And when's the move-in date?" Jack questioned.

"Two days from now."

"That's no preparation time at all!" Alissa exclaimed.

Finn raised an eyebrow. "Since when do we prepare properly for *anything?*"

Alissa took a deep breath. "Fair point."

"I'm thinking we raid our old equipment stash and have at it," Triss suggested.

Jack cocked his head. "Wait, *what* equipment stash?"

"Oh, you know, just some... stuff," Triss faltered.

Jack's one good eye narrowed. The heat signature on his cybernetic eye revealed that her face was flushed. "What aren't you telling me?"

"We maybe kinda didn't need you to have that eye mod," Triss admitted.

"Truth be told, we completely forgot about the tech we had hidden down there," Alissa added. "It was only *after* you already had the eye that I remembered."

Jack took a step back. "So, let me get this straight... You barely even used me on the op that you modded me for, and you didn't even need those mods to accomplish what little use you did get out of me?"

Triss looked down. "Yeah..."

Alissa placed a soothing hand on Jack's shoulder. "But remember, the eye adds character."

"You're all unbelievable." Jack shook his head.

"On the flip side, though," Finn said in the ensuing silence, "we will need those mods to complete this heist, I expect."

"Yes, we can definitely figure out some way in which you're absolutely necessary," Triss affirmed.

"Aw, you'd do that for me?" Jack asked with a tear in his eye.

"Absolutely." Triss patted his hand. "Now, we'll need to get the stealth suits out of storage, and some high-res projectors."

"Plus the laser pistols," Alissa added.

"Well, *obviously*." Triss smirked. "Finn, can you reach out to your contacts and get them warmed up to the idea of fencing some expensive paintings?"

"Can and will do." He saluted.

"What should I do?" Jack questioned.

"You can carry the gear once we have it," Alissa replied. "In the meantime, try to stay out of trouble."

He frowned at her. "What have I done in the past month to possibly warrant that statement?"

"There was the time when you got your hand stuck in the peanut butter jar," Finn supplied.

"Or when you decided that the air ducts looked funny in the corner of the lounge room and you replumbed everything so the cooking hood vented directly into my bedroom," Triss added.

"Which, incidentally, is also my bedroom," Alissa grumbled.

"And yet you resist our request for a new ship. This one needs a total remodel," Jack insisted.

Alissa glared at him. "We didn't *need* a remodel until you decided to paint the lounge room lime green right after you knocked down the partition wall."

"I thought it would make it more airy—like we were laying in a meadow."

"Then why did you paint the ceiling?" Alissa pressed.

"I just really like green, okay?" Jack's cheeks burned.

Triss smiled. "Needless to say, we will not be relying on Jack to pick out the good art from the estate."

"I may surprise you." Jack waited for Triss to continue her explanation.

"Okay, so with Jack staying out of the way, the rest of us will get everything prepped. We can be at the supply cache in about two hours, right Alissa?"

The captain nodded. "An easy jump from here."

"Great. We'll grab what we need and then bust into the estate before they know what hit them," Triss concluded. "Any questions?"

Jack tentatively raised his hand.

Triss swore under her breath. "Yes?"

"Do I get a stealth suit, too?"

Alissa massaged the bridge of her nose. "Yes, you'll get a stealth suit."

"Okay, just checking, because the last time we went on a job, you stuck me in that awful pink hazmat onesie."

"Don't try to deny that you loved that suit," Triss said.

"I—"

"Any questions from someone other than Jack?" Alissa asked. No one spoke up. "All right, get to work."

Jack let out an exaggerated sigh and walked back to his spot on the couch in the lounge room. He waited for everyone to be busy with their tasks before he kicked back to relax. It was so much easier for the others to think he was incompetent so they'd do all the work and he could just go along for the ride.

While Finn was busy making video calls to potential fences, Jack took the opportunity to level up his rival character in a game they'd had going for the past month. All in all, it wasn't a bad deal to be the manual labor punching bag on the team when there was no hard work to be done—certainly better than having genuine responsibility. He didn't know how Alissa could keep her sanity.

True to the estimation, the *Little Princess II* arrived at the destination planet in just under two hours. Jack gazed out the window as the ship made the final approach and settled into a geosynchronous orbit.

"What is this place?" he asked Triss when she came to retrieve him.

"Doesn't have a colloquial name," she replied. "We just know it as RT-317."

He took in the brown ground and minimal cloud cover. "Is it habitable?"

"Oh, no. Not even remotely. The gravity is just about the only thing that falls within tolerable limits for us frail humans."

"So… EVA suit?" Jack asked.

"Yep. We'll take the landing shuttle down and bring back what we need."

"We're not landing the *Little Princess II*?"

"The air is too acidic. The shuttle has better shielding."

Jack frowned. "But the EVA suits—"

"They'll be fine for the few minutes we'll be down there. Come on." Triss led the way to the hold in the belly of the ship.

It was the place where Jack had spent the least time over the past month, since they'd mostly just hung around in the lounge room playing video games and drinking too much of Alissa's delicious coffee. So, it came as a particularly great surprise to Jack when he entered the hold and was confronted by a two-meter-tall column of white feathers.

"Hello, Jack," the feathers greeted.

"Um, Triss...?" Jack jumped backward.

"Oh, you haven't met Morey?" she asked. "He's our mechanic."

"Th—the feathers?" Jack stammered.

"Right, sorry!" The feathers rustled. "I was in buffing mode." White feathers cascaded to the floor a moment later, revealing a bipedal metallic robot.

Jack's heart rate returned to normal. "Oh. I thought you were an alien."

Triss snickered. "Nope. Just our mechanic droid."

"And the feathers?" Jack asked.

"Easiest way to polish the chrome accents on the crawler," Morey replied.

"The crawler?"

Triss shook her head. "Stars, Jack! You know nothing about what we have on this ship, do you?"

"Apparently not..."

"The crawler is our all-terrain vehicle for when we can't land right by the destination and need to travel over rough ground. We'll use it to get to the estate, since we can't bring the whole ship right up to the entrance. I had Morey get it looking all extra shiny and fancy for us so we can blend in with the high rollers."

"I don't think an all-terrain vehicle is going to pass as a luxury towncar..." Jack pointed out.

"No, but we can look like some very sophisticated groundskeepers." Triss took a deep breath. "But we're getting ahead of ourselves. First, the equipment."

"Right."

Jack eyed Morey cautiously as he stepped around the robot and its feather suit so he could get to the landing shuttle.

"Have a safe flight!" Morey waved goodbye to them with his claw-like mechanical hand.

"We've really had a robot worker down here all this time?" Jack asked Triss once they were inside the shuttle with the door sealed.

"Yeah. Like, *every* ship in this size class has a robo mechanic."

"Then why have I never seen one?"

"Have you ever been on another ship in this size class before?"

"No."

"Well, there you go." Triss powered up the shuttle. "Honestly, Jack, sometimes I forget that you're a grown man."

"You've never given me a proper chance, if we're to be perfectly honest," Jack told her.

"I guess you have proven yourself useful here and there."

Jack buckled his flight harness. "I've come a long way. No more chewing straw, I put away the dishes..."

"Well, you *try* to put away the dishes." Triss smiled as she directed the shuttle out of the docking bay. "It's clear you don't know where the bowls go."

"There are too many sizes."

"Uh huh..."

Jack crossed his arms over the restraints. "There are seven different types of bowl, Triss. That isn't a remotely reasonable number for a ship with four humans and one robot."

"Two robots."

"Where's the other?"

"In the waste processing tank."

Jack stared straight ahead out the front window. "That one I never want to meet."

"You and me both."

The shuttle descended through the thin atmosphere and glided above the tops of rocky mountains towering twenty kilometers above seemingly bottomless canyons. There didn't appear to be a flat landing area anywhere across the barren landscape, let alone a place where people could walk safely.

"You were crazy to hide anything down here," Jack commented.

"Which is precisely what makes it such a good hiding place." Triss dove the shuttle into one of the narrow canyons.

Jack fought the urge to grip the restraints with his hands and brace for impact as the shuttle passed dangerously close to the canyon walls. "Where is everything stored, anyway?" he asked, hoping for a distraction.

"A cave," was Triss' only response.

He allowed her to focus on the flying.

Four minutes later, the canyon terminated at the maw of a mammoth cave. They passed into shadow, the shuttle's onboard lights casting an eerie blue glow on the rough walls.

Triss landed the shuttle on a wide ledge a hundred meters inside the entrance. "And here we are."

"How did you find this place?" Jack asked with wonder.

"Commandeered from an old associate of ours," she replied. "Let's get our EVA suits on."

They climbed to the back of the shuttle to suit up in the airlock. The gold EVA suit was Jack's least favorite attire, but he donned it like a pro. At least this time he'd only be facing acid air rather than transporting a container of radioactive material. Small blessings.

Once they were geared up, Triss activated the airlock and they cycled out.

The cave seemed even larger and more ominous when Jack stepped out of the comparative protection of the shuttle. The roof was at least half a kilometer overhead, with the walls a quarter kilometer to either side. Nowhere in the massive space did Jack see a stash of equipment.

"This way." Triss headed at an angle toward the right wall.

"Is it far? Maybe we should park clos—" Jack cut off when Triss extended her hand outward, causing the space in front of her to simmer.

His face lit up. "You have it cloaked."

"Sure do." She grinned inside her suit.

With a flick of her wrist, the shield dropped, revealing a dozen crates and a transparent enclosure holding six sets of armor. At the center of the grouping was a decaying corpse.

"Hmm," Jack snorted. "I'm gonna guess he's not supposed to be here."

Triss stood in silence for several seconds as she surveyed the corpse from afar. "No, that certainly should *not* be here."

She took a tentative step forward with Jack at her heels.

"Who else knows about this place?" he asked her.

"Not enough people for me to feel remotely good about who that might be." She knelt down next to the body and inspected what little remained of its clothing. "I don't think this was a he, but a her." She pointed to some feminine stud earrings and open hips. Her expression sank. "I think this was Kayla."

"I'm sorry. Where did you know her from?"

"We weren't close." Triss rose to her feet. "She worked with a crew Alissa and I used to be attached to while we were with Svetlana. Kayla was one of the associates."

"How would she have ended up here?"

"That is a very good question." Triss approached one of the nearby cases and popped the seal. She looked inside. "Damn it."

Jack jogged up next to her. "I imagine that's supposed to be full."

"Indeed it is." She resealed the half-empty crate of weapons and restored the interior vacuum.

"Why wouldn't whoever was here take everything?"

"Probably because they only took what they needed—assuming this was their stash to raid as they wished. That means that whoever was here doesn't think Alissa or I would be back for it."

"And a person who might make such an assumption would be…?

"Trent," Triss snarled.

"You said that like it's the name of a bad ex-boyfriend."

"Because he is."

"That would explain it. Care to elaborate?" Jack asked.

"Not now. Let's get this equipment loaded in the shuttle, and then we'll talk with Alissa."

As it turned out, transferring four stealth suits and a small arsenal wasn't near as straightforward as Jack had been led to believe. His first indication that he was in for a terrible afternoon came when Triss simply stood aside and pointed at one of the crates.

"That. Make it be on the ship," she said.

"I thought I was here to help you, not just be the muscle," Jack objected.

"Yeah, you're here to help me in exactly that way. Do the thing."

"It's kind of awkwardly shaped for one person to move…"

"I thought you had skills and were setting out to surprise me with your prowess?"

Jack straightened. "You want a show? Fine. I'll give you a show."

He positioned himself behind the crate and gave it a good shove. Unfortunately, the crate seemed quite happy in its present position.

Undeterred, he jogged over to the shuttle to secure a length of cabling. He looped one end around the crate and clamped the other to the hydraulic winch in the airlock. With any luck, the winch would pull the load right into place.

"Jack, this seems like a terrible idea…" Triss cautioned.

"You want me to do this? I'm going to do it my way." He activated the winch.

A whine of grinding metal rang out in the cave. Before Jack even had time to lower the volume on his external comm, the cable snapped with a sickening *twang*.

It lashed out like a whip from the shuttle, slicing off a back stabilizing fin on one end and the other embedding in an adjacent crate.

Triss stood with a stunned expression a mere meter from where the far end had cut through the four-centimeter-thick crate wall. "I told you so."

"Really? That's how you're going to play this?" Jack groaned. "You almost killed me!"

"And myself!"

"That doesn't make it any better!"

Jack took a deep breath. "I hate these crates."

"That we can agree on." Triss placed her right hand on her hip. "We'll have to unload them and transfer everything piece by piece. But it'll have to be quick or the acidity will make these weapons useless."

"The seal is broken on that crate." Jack pointed to the container with the embedded cable. "May as well start there."

CHAPTER THREE:
GETTING DOWN TO BUSINESS

Dressing up as a groundskeeper made for only a slightly more comfortable outfit than an EVA suit.

Jack tugged at the overly tight collar of his jumper, amazed how the suit could simultaneously be too tight and yet baggy. "You couldn't think of *any* other disguise?" he asked Triss.

"The interior of the manor is complete. The last project is to prune the shrubbery," she replied.

"I'll prune your shrubbery," Jack muttered.

Triss stuck out her tongue at him, but quickly composed her face when Alissa entered the cargo bay.

"Everyone ready?" the captain asked.

The four crew members were all dressed in their unflattering coveralls, which concealed the stealth suits underneath. Once they got inside the main gate, they'd go from undercover to invisible.

Jack itched above his cybernetic eye. "So… what do we do if we run into the *actual* groundskeepers?"

"We wing it, of course," Alissa replied.

"What happened to us needing a plan for everything?" Jack cocked his head.

Alissa smoothed the overalls bulging around her stomach. "Went out the airlock along with my dignity."

Jack grinned. "Just like old times!"

Triss sighed. "Jack, we did one op together, and that was only a month ago."

"It left a strong impression."

"You need to get out more," Alissa said with an eye-roll.

"You never let me leave my room."

Alissa switched into mom-voice. "That's because you get into trouble whenever you do. We've already talked about the ducting."

Jack looked at his feet. "Yeah..."

"Can we all agree that Jack requires constant supervision?" Alissa questioned.

She and the two other members of the crew raised their hands. Reluctantly, Jack raised his, as well.

"We'll figure out how to get Jack more supervised visits with the outside world after we're finished with the op," Alissa continued. "For now, the matter is closed. We all have our marching orders, so let's go."

"Go team!" Jack shouted in the ensuring silence.

His friends simply shook their heads and sighed.

"One of these days, I'll figure out proper social cues," he lamented quietly.

Triss patted his shoulder. "Just keep telling yourself that."

They loaded onto the shuttle, along with the fancied-up crawler that would serve as their ground transportation.

Jack had to admit that the robot Morey did good work when it came to making a utilitarian vehicle look like something worthy of gracing the grounds of a snooty rich person's estate. The chrome accents on the lower body frame and upper roll cage added a certain grace and elegance to the otherwise simple machine.

Jack strapped into the passenger seating near the rear of the shuttle while Alissa and Triss assumed the two chairs in the cockpit.

Finn, seated across from Jack, closed his eyes as if ready to take a nap.

"Nervous?" Jack asked him.

"Not in the slightest. Excited, more than anything. I've been wanting to go after this guy for some time."

"How do you know him?"

"More know *of* him," Finn corrected, opening his eyes. "I'm surprised that you hadn't heard of him."

"I mostly lived under a rock, when it comes to social media engagement," Jack admitted.

"Well, Vincent Ordello was known only in certain circles rather than being someone in the public spotlight. He has a legendary ability to take over a small business and suck out every last bit of profit before tossing it aside in favor of his next venture. Lots of people have lost their livelihoods thanks to him, and his appetite for a new conquests is insatiable."

Jack scowled. "What kind of business was he in?"

"A little bit of everything these days, but he started out as a butterfly farmer."

Jack gave that several seconds to sink in. "Did you say...?"

"I did."

"So wait," Jack leaned forward against the harnesses, "this legendarily evil business tycoon began as a *butterfly farmer*?"

"Well, yes," Finn confirmed, "but that was before the incident."

"Which was?"

"No one knows. The only rumors anyone has heard involve an old man and an oxygen tank."

Jack crossed his arms. "Hmm."

"It's a mystery." Finn waggled his fingers. "At any rate, that incident, whatever it was, changed Vincent. He went from a peaceable butterfly farmer to a ruthless business tycoon. The latest reports say that he owns five percent of the assets in this sector."

"You said that like it's a lot."

"It is when you consider how much there is out here. Most places, a single individual might hold a fraction of one percent. Suffice to say, this guy is powerful."

"That seems like a bad person for us to wrong," Jack pointed out.

Finn shrugged. "He'll never know it was us."

"Well, if he does find out, at least we'll go out doing what we love."

The other man nodded. "That is true."

They sat in silence for the remainder of the landing. Jack couldn't see anything from his seat in the back, but he felt the telltale bump of the craft touching down. He unstrapped his harness, then grabbed his bag full or armaments that was disguised as a carrying container for tree trimmings.

The three additional members of the team were soon geared up with their accessories—complete with Triss carrying a laser rifle cleverly outfitted to look like a rake—and they took seats on the crawler.

"If anyone asks you questions, just point to me," Alissa instructed. She started the crawler's engine. "And for star's sake, don't let anyone know you're wearing a stealth suit."

"Psh," Jack scoffed, "that would be pretty dumb to go invisible right in front of someone."

"More ridiculous things have happened," she countered.

He couldn't deny that.

The back hatch of the shuttle opened, revealing that they had set down in a grove of trees. A rough path extended through the foliage behind them, though which Alissa directed the crawler.

Jack was seated in the rear seat of the rig, and he watched off to the side as woodland creatures ran from the foreign hum of the vehicle's electric engine. While he watched, a turtle with a reflective shell ambling along on the side of the path was suddenly plucked from the ground by a dark purple bird with a wingspan of two meters.

"Holy crap! Did you see that?!" he exclaimed.

"Birds eat slow, defenseless things, yeah," Triss replied.

Jack crossed his arms and slouched down in the chair. Clearly the others weren't going to care about his nature observations.

As such, while they continued through the woods, Jack elected to keep his sightings of more of the large birds to himself. Their unblinking eyes followed the crawler as it bumped along the rugged track, silently watching from the treetops. It wasn't until the nearby trees were more purple than green that Jack couldn't contain his wonder any longer.

"That's, uh, a lot of birds."

Alissa finally lifted her gaze from the path ahead. "Whoa! Yeah, it is."

Finn pulled his left hand, which he'd been letting hang over the side wall, into the vehicle. "Is it just me, or do they look hungry?"

Alissa laughed. "Don't be silly. They're just—"

She cut off as a bird dipped down overhead, casting a shadow across their path. A moment later, a light thump sounded on the roof as something large touched down.

"Uh, guys…" Jack swallowed.

Additional thumps sounded on the roof, followed by scratches and rhythmic pings as dozens of beaks began pecking at the vehicle.

"Gun it!" Triss shouted.

Jack reached for his bag to grab his handgun, but he lurched backward when Alissa slammed on the accelerator.

Dark purple feathers swirled around the crawler as the birds took flight.

"They're going after the chrome!" Finn realized.

"That buffing did get it *really* shiny," Jack had to admit.

"Not helpful now that birds are trying to eat us!" Triss gripped the crawler's side frame as Alissa made a sharp turn on the path to avoid a tree.

Deafening squawks broke the serenity of the forest as the birds continued pecking at the vehicle in earnest.

"It. Is. Not. Food!" Alissa groaned through clenched teeth.

She accelerated the crawler once more as it finally reached the end of the forest. Beyond was an open field surrounding a walled estate, which was enveloped in a shimmering, domed security field.

"So much for a quiet arrival," Triss said through her grimace.

Alissa kept her attention on the course ahead. "I'll take being in one piece over that. We can deal with the guards."

Jack grabbed a handhold in front of him as the crawler bounced over a rock in the field. "Morey is going to be so sad the chrome got all scuffed."

"*That's* what you're worried about right now?!" Finn glared at him.

"I wouldn't say 'worried', just—"

"Shut up!" Alissa ordered.

They were almost to the entry gate. An electrical hum filled the air, and Jack identified the sound as coming from the force field over the top of the estate.

The birds around them hesitated, then turned back toward the forest.

Jack released a long breath. "That wasn't so bad." He poked his head out the window to see that the vehicle was completely covered in bird droppings, smeared with tri-point claw marks from the birds walking around. "I mean, it could have been better."

"Well, it's about to get worse."

Jack followed Alissa's line of sight out the front windshield. In front of them stood half a dozen armed guards, and they looked pissed.

CHAPTER FOUR:
INVITATION TO GARDEN

"Hey, fellas," Alissa said with her best fake smile. "Got a little bit of a bird problem in these parts, don't ya?"

One of the guards stepped forward. "The birds don't leave the trees unless they're chasing something. What were you doing out there?"

Alissa gave a guilty shrug. "Got a hankering for some truffles."

"Truffle hunting." The guard let out a guffaw. "This time of year? And without a sniffer? Can't imagine you found anything."

She chuckled awkwardly. "Yeah, silly us!"

The guard inspected the vehicle from afar. "And what brings you over here?"

"We're, uh, the landscapers," Alissa continued. She twirled a length of her dark hair around her finger. "Just thought we'd kill a little time before our shift, you know? Truffle hunting and a picnic with, uh, muffins."

"Muffins? On a picnic?" The guard gave her a skeptical look.

"They really get your appetite going for truffles."

"Huh." He considered the statement. "Have any more muffins?"

Alissa glanced back at the others. They shrugged. "We... ate them all."

The guard drooped. "That's too bad." He looked them over. "Well, we weren't expecting any new landscapers."

Alissa groaned loudly. "I *told* you to verify the appointment, Triss!"

The other woman held up her hands. "Or you could take some responsibility and do it yourself."

"Don't put this back on me!"

"Don't blame me every time you don't do *your* job!" Triss shouted back.

"Ladies, please!" the guard interrupted. "No need to argue. Let me check on the landscaping order. Maybe something was misplaced."

Triss snorted. "We're probably not even on the right planet. *Someone* doesn't know how to read an invoice."

Alissa pivoted toward Triss in her seat. "Really, you want to do this right now, in front of all these people?"

"May as well." Triss placed her hands on her hips.

While the two woman exchanged verbal blows, the guard cast a pitying look in Jack and Finn's direction, then mouthed, 'Are they always like this?'

Jack and Finn replied with slow, pained nods.

The guard breathed out through his teeth. "Look, I'm sure the issue was on our end, no need to argue. We just don't get a lot of visitors out this way."

"Oh, I wouldn't assume anything," Alissa said with an accusatory look in Triss' direction.

The guard took a step back. "Why don't you pull around the back side of the security outbuilding and we'll get this sorted out, okay?"

"Fine," Alissa said with an exasperated sigh. "At least there are still some people who try to be helpful."

Triss shook her head with disgust.

Finn mouthed a 'thank you' to the guard as Alissa drove them through the entry gate through the four-meter-tall walls.

The electronic hum ceased as soon as they were inside. Overhead, Jack could see the faintest glimmer of the shield keeping out the birds and whatever other would-be threats—like it had been a hindrance for them.

He kept his cool as Alissa directed the crawler to the far side of the guard shack. The four passengers stepped out under the watchful eye of the guards.

"Which company are you contracted through?" the lead guard asked them while consulting a holographic projection from his wrist.

"Princess Grounds Unlimited," Alissa replied without missing a beat.

Next to Jack, Finn bit his lower lip to keep from laughing.

The guard's brow furrowed slightly, but he continued. "And

what was the nature of your assignment?"

"We're supposed to prune the shrubs."

"Which ones?" the guard asked her.

"The... shrubby ones," Alissa said, expertly keeping a straight face.

The guard was unfazed by her vague and evasive response. "Ah, it must have been entered as 'King Star Stylings' by mistake. Go ahead and get to work. I'll update the system."

Finn took the opportunity to lob a tiny bundle of nanobots in the direction of the guard shack. The bots broke formation as soon as they struck the wall, working their way toward the central computer system, where they were programmed to initiate a loop of the security footage. While the team's stealth suits would be good enough for most of the activity, lifting paintings off the wall and opening doors might otherwise give them away. Since the manor was supposed to be unoccupied, the loop should go unnoticed until well after the team had departed.

Alissa flashed a winning smile. "Thank you so much!" She skipped back to the crawler. "Let's get to work, team."

They returned to their seats, and Alissa drove them past the shack along the road toward the main manor.

"Is there *any* good help left out there in the galaxy these days?" Finn whispered. "Stars! Every place we've been, you just tell people you're supposed to be there and they believe you."

"Not complaining." Jack shrugged.

Alissa chuckled. "Remind me to never bother hiring security guards."

The entry drive curved to the left, and the manor came into view. Constructed primarily of white marble, the structure rose three stories and had artistic glass atriums cantilevered on each level, providing unobstructed views of the surrounding grounds. Grass meadows were separated by exotic flowerbeds and new tree groves. Steps from the house, a triangular pool with a pyramid-shaped fountain glistened in the afternoon sun.

"Okay, so it's a nice place," Jack stated.

Finn made a dismissive wave. "I've seen better."

Jack hadn't—not up close and in person, anyway. He took it all in with reserved awe.

The meandering pathways cross-crossing the estate grounds offered a fair degree of cover from the guard shack and manor, so Alissa selected one of the offshoots that would give them the most privacy. When the crawler was reasonably well hidden behind a hedge, she parked the vehicle.

"All right, now the really tricky part begins." Alissa hopped out of the crawler, accessory bag in hand.

"The guards are going to see us in there with all that glass," Finn observed, pointing toward the manor.

Triss shook her head. "Not at this hour. The sun will be reflecting on the outside of the glass. We'll be good until sunset."

"And getting the bounty out of here?" Jack prompted. "You said you'd tell us once we got here."

"I said I'd tell you when it became relevant," Alissa replied. "Trust me, I have it all figured out."

"Except the chances of this all going to plan are virtually nil," Jack retorted.

Alissa smiled. "So, it doesn't matter in the first place. We'll get to that when we get to it. Now, take off your coveralls."

She began stripping down, and the others followed her lead. The stealth suits appeared shimmering silver while deactivated. Relatively form-fitting, the suits offered little protection from potential weapons fire, but if the suits did their job, no one would know where to aim in the first place.

Each of the accessory bags carried by the team members was lined with the same stealth material. They each inverted their bag and repacked it. Within five minutes, everyone was ready to go.

Alissa took a holographic projector from their extra supplies and placed it on the roof of the crawler. As soon as she activated it, the vehicle disappeared from view.

Jack had heard about the tech, but he'd never had access to it himself. He reached his hand out to touch the field, and it distorted where his fingertips passed through.

"Great from a distance, but not if someone runs into it," Alissa said.

"We better get going before the guards decide to do their job and walk the grounds," Triss suggested. Her composure broke, and she chuckled. "Yeah, like that's going to happen!"

Alissa smiled back, then pulled her suit's hood over her head. With a ripple, she and her bag disappeared from view.

Jack pulled up his own hood and rolled the mask over his face. He activated his suit with a touch of the wrist controls. His surroundings appeared unchanged, but he was still able to see a faint outline of his comrades thanks to a smart link between the suits.

"This is cool," he said into the integrated interior comm. The suit cancelled out the sound of his voice to outside listeners, routing the communication to earpieces inside the others' head coverings.

"Remember, the suit won't disguise anything around you," Alissa cautioned. "Footprints, bumping into an object—anything could give you away. You see someone, you freeze."

"Got it," Jack acknowledged.

"Old hat," Triss said. "Let's go steal us some art."

The group took a leisurely pace the rest of the way to the manor, taking notes on their surroundings for in case—or *when*, realistically—they'd need make a quick getaway. It'd be a jog across open ground to get back to the crawler from the manor and then reach the main gate, but it was doable. And they had laser pistols. Those always seemed to come in handy in a pinch.

Alissa was the first to reach the side door. She pressed herself against the wall next to the door and peeked in through the glass. "No sign of movement," she reported.

Triss jogged up in front of the door to inspect the biometric scanner. "For a rich guy, this dude has some pretty pathetic tech," she muttered.

She pulled several tools from her bag and began attaching them to the reader. After a minute of fiddling, a green light illuminated on the panel. The door lock clicked open.

"I'm good," Triss said, making no attempt to hide her smugness.

Alissa popped the door open before the lock had a chance to reinitialize, and she led the way inside.

Jack was the last through. He gently closed the door behind him while the others assessed the hallway.

The broad corridor extended twenty meters ahead before terminating in a set of closed doors. Several other closed doors lined the walls on both sides, and one wider opening provided access into what appeared to be a seating area overlooking the garden. Along the walls were various art installations and a handful of sculptures placed on pedestals.

One detailed painting of a lake with mountains caught Jack's eye five meters down the hall. "What about that one?"

Finn chuckled. "Oh no, not even close. The good stuff will be on the upper levels."

"I like it," Jack said.

"So it's probably worthless on the open market." Finn set a course deeper into the manor.

Thankfully, the floors were stone so the group's footsteps were invisible as they traversed the hall toward the staircase. Opposite the seating area, the stairs switch-backed up to the second level.

Alissa led them up the stairs, pausing occasionally to listen for potential occupants. Regardless of whether Vincent and his art major bride had moved in, any manner of workers or security personnel could be roaming the halls. It was bad enough knowing that the guards could discover the looping security footage at any moment, so any additional caution was worth the minimal time delays.

At the landing on the second story, Alissa gestured for Triss to take point.

"The first target painting is in the dining room," Triss explained. "I don't know why anyone in their right mind would put something like it where a person would want to eat, but I'm not the art major."

"How did you get all this intel on where the paintings would be, anyway?" Jack asked.

"The wannabe art critic wife vlogged about the whole damn thing."

"Wow." Jack shook his head.

"Sometimes, there are no words." Triss sighed.

CHAPTER FIVE:
ART APPRECIATION 101

The group slinked down the hall, following Triss' lead. Eighty meters ahead, the walkway opened into an airy space beneath one of the many glass enclosures visible from outside. On the interior side of the room, a long, white table with settings for sixteen people was arranged parallel with the back wall. It was on that expanse that the group caught sight of their prize.

"Well, that's..." Alissa trained off.

"I think I might actually throw up." Jack held a hand to his mouth. "That's not chocolate, is it?"

The 'art'—anyone present would be forced to use the term loosely—consisted of a pile of poo on the bulging stomach of a very hairy man. Much to Jack's dismay, there was no strategic arrangement of the man's limbs. Everything was out there for all the world to see. More concerning, though, was the herd of horses running across the landscape in the background, which were all various shades of blue.

"But... why?" Jack worked his mouth, trying to understand.

"Mr. Ordello himself," Triss murmured. "It is so much worse in person than the thumbnails on the Net."

"Do we want to know if he actually posed for it?" Alissa asked.

Triss shook her head. "No, we do not."

"But... this isn't art!" Jack objected.

"In what was is it not? Someone created it using painting skills and a sense of composition that make it unique. We don't have to like the subject matter, but that doesn't make it any less artistic," Triss countered.

"Except, the entire point of this mission is to get paintings we can *sell*," Jack insisted.

"Oh, there's more demand for this one than for any of the others we're picking up today."

"Why would anyone want *this*?!"

"So they can burn it," Triss explained. "The vlog had eighty-seven comments expressing a desire to buy the painting just so they could eliminate it from the multiverse."

"That's a sentiment I can agree with," Finn chimed in.

"And what drives up bid prices? Controversy. Everyone wants to be the one person to end this painting's existence," Triss concluded.

Alissa held up her hand to shield her eyes from the exaggerated portrayal of Vincent's nether regions. "That is, unless *we* burn it first."

"We most certainly will not." Triss approached the painting and inspected the frame. "We're going to get at least five million for this. We'll find a replica to burn."

"As much as I want to personally make this no longer be a thing, I can't imagine bringing another one of these atrocities into existence," Alissa said.

"I second that," Jack agreed.

"We'll sell it to the highest bidder and rejoice," Triss muttered while she gently pulled the painting from the wall to look at the mounting. The movement was sure to show up on a camera, but if the nanobots had done their job, the video feed wouldn't be showing the live footage.

"How are we getting something that big out of here, anyway?" Finn asked while eyeing the three-meter-wide atrocity.

"Cut it out of its frame, of course," Triss replied. She released the painting and it settled back flush with the wall. "It's a simple mounting—wouldn't take much to get it down, but we may as well cut it in place."

Without offering further explanation, Triss rummaged around her bag and produced a compact laser cutter. She activated the device and did a sample cut along the painting's bottom right edge next to the frame.

"Like butter," she said, and continued along the bottom.

"What should we do?" Alissa asked.

"Be quiet and let me concentrate."

The three members of the team followed Triss' instruction,

though Jack found himself growing increasingly more anxious the longer they stood still. It took seven minutes for Triss to complete her trimming of the large painting, and by the end, Jack was certain the guards would come looking for them any second.

"Give me a hand with this," Triss requested, breaking the silence.

The painting was only hanging within the frame by two narrow strips—one on either of the upper two corners. Triss motioned for Finn and Jack to each grab one side. When Jack was in place, she used the laser cutter to snip the final segment, and the painting's canvass went limp in Jack's hands.

Finn's end was soon freed, as well, and the two of them worked together to roll the painting lengthwise into a tidy bundle.

"And that's how it's done," Triss said with satisfaction.

"It's almost like you've done this before," Jack commented.

"Who says I haven't?" she replied.

Alissa crossed her arms. "You never talked about it, if you did."

"And you never told me until recently that you were the daughter of famous research scientists."

The group's captain sighed and picked up her bag. "Where's the next painting?"

"Upstairs," Triss responded.

The group walked further into the manor and took a different set of stairs up to the third floor. The second target painting was immediately to the left of the stairwell. Unlike the first, which was eye-gougingly graphic, the second painting was another matter entirely.

"It's a... square," Jack said, tilting his head as he stared at the painting. "A red square on a white background."

"Very observant," Triss replied with thick sarcasm.

"But *I* could paint that—and I haven't picked up a paintbrush since elementary school!" Jack exclaimed.

"I think you're missing the subtleties."

"*What* subtleties? It's a plain red square on a white background."

"Symbolizing the massacre of free thought perpetrated by the establishment," Triss shot back.

He stared at her, mouth agape behind his mask. "Seriously? You get that from this?"

Triss snorted. "Hell if I know. That's what the artist statement on the Net said."

"People actually believe that?" Finn questioned.

"Look at it this way: who wants to be the rich person to admit they don't 'get it'? No one. So instead, they keep outbidding each other to prove some sort of fictitious intellectual superiority."

Jack eyed her. "In other words, I could paint a black line, make up some profound meaning, and convince people to give me millions of dollars?"

"Only if you're 'discovered', though," Triss replied. "You must go from 'painter' to an 'artist'."

"And that happens by…?"

"Dumb luck." Triss shook her head. "But now Square #7 is ours." She activated her laser cutter.

Just before the beam touched the canvass, a clang sounded down the hall.

"Shit!" Alissa swore, pressing herself back against the wall.

Jack grabbed his bag and hid behind a potted plant. It offered no cover beyond his suit's capabilities, but at least he'd be out of the way if someone approached.

"Don't move," Alissa whispered to the team once everyone had found a place to hide out.

Another clang reverberated down the hall, followed by the indistinct voices of two men.

"I told you it was purple!" one said, accompanied by hurried footsteps approaching the *Little Princess II*'s crew.

"Well, the replacement we have is green," the other replied.

"So, our entire plan is shot!" The first man groaned.

The two men came into view. The one who'd just spoken was in his late-thirties and reasonably handsome in a rugged sort of way, while the other was slightly older and had the bent posture of an individual who was accustomed to being repeatedly humiliated.

"I'm sorry," the second man muttered.

The first glared at him. "Go get the rest of our kit. Maybe we can—"

The laser cutter dropped from Triss' hand.

"Who's there?!" the younger man demanded. He zeroed in on Triss' position, pointing to his eye. "I see that stealth suit. All four of you."

It was then that Jack noticed the iris of his right eye was

gleaming silver—a proper cybernetic eye, unlike the hack job Jack had in his own head.

“Do we fight him?” Finn asked.

“No,” Triss and Alissa replied simultaneously.

“I know him,” Triss continued. “This is Trent.”

CHAPTER SIX:
TENUOUS ALLIANCES

Jack stared at the strange man standing in the hall across from him. "The same Trent as ex-boyfriend Trent?" he asked into the comm within his stealth suit.

"The very one," Triss replied, then slipped the mask of her stealth suit from her face and touched the controls on her wrist. The rest of the suit's fabric returned to its shiny metallic finish.

"The hell...?" Trent inhaled sharply.

"Trust me, I'm as surprised to see you here," Triss said.

"Is that one of my stealth suits?"

"*Your* suits? I was the one who stole them!"

"On my orders."

Triss crossed her arms. "You weren't my boss then or ever. We were colleagues."

Trent scoffed. "And it's a wonder that partnership didn't work out."

"Shocking." Triss rolled her eyes. "At least I fared better than Kayla."

"You never stabbed me in the back—literally." He paused. "Actually, it was figuratively. Laser pistol, but she *did* shoot me in my back."

"I can see how that would cause a rift in your relationship."

"Slightly." Trent held his thumb and index finger half a centimeter apart.

Triss looked him over. "What are you doing here?"

Trent's eyes narrowed. "Stealing some jewelry."

"Oh. We're stealing the artwork," Triss revealed.

"Huh." He nodded. "I guess Vincent's going to have a bad day tomorrow."

"It would seem that way." Triss paused. "Why wouldn't you take the stealth suits for yourself, if you were breaking in here?"

"Wasn't a necessary part of the plan. Easier this way." He looked around the hall at the others. "Who's with you?"

Alissa removed her hood and gestured for Jack and Finn to do the same. "Hello, Trent," she said.

"Alissa? Didn't think I'd ever see you again."

"That makes two of us."

Triss took a slow breath. "This isn't a reunion. It sounds like we're both here for different things, so we should get back to it."

"Not sure I get the art angle," Trent said.

"You wouldn't," Triss said with a prim smile.

"How are you getting the art out with the stealth suits, though?" Trent asked.

"Stealth bags, of course. But we also have the cameras on a loop."

His face paled. "*We* already set up a loop."

Triss and Alissa exchanged glances. "What happens when two sets of nanobots try to do the same thing?"

"They'll fight each other," Trent replied. "It'll work at first, but eventually one will seek dominance and the system will glitch."

Triss checked the time on her wrist. "How long will that take?"

"Maybe twenty minutes?" Trent guessed. "I have no idea for sure."

"If that's the case, time's almost up."

"Shit!" He glanced back in the direction he'd come from. "Then the guards could be here at any moment. I guess a decoy gem doesn't really matter."

His companion looked slightly vindicated.

"No, that doesn't get you off the hook, Larry," Trent told him.

Larry scowled.

"We'd counted on at least an hour here," Alissa said. "Aren't there four more paintings?"

Triss nodded.

"I have another safe to crack, then one more stop. I'll never have time." Trent groaned.

Finn lit up. "Safe cracking, you say?"

Triss glanced between the two of them. "This may be a terrible idea, but should we team up? Finn can help you get the safe open in record time, Trent, and the four of us can break into two teams to get the remaining paintings."

Trent and Larry shrugged. "May as well," Trent agreed.

Alissa shot Triss a worried look but said nothing.

"Let's move." Triss motioned for Larry to follow her. "Alissa, you and Jack grab the two in the bedroom. We'll meet back here in ten minutes."

"Can we cut them out that fast?" Alissa asked.

"There's a higher setting. Won't be as neat, but it'll get the job done."

Alissa nodded. "See you back here." She restored the hood of her stealth suit.

Jack did the same. If the cameras might stop looping without warning, they needed to take all the precautions they could.

When they were away from the others, Jack switched his suit's comm to a private channel with just Alissa. "So, what's the deal with this Trent guy?"

"He's a jackass."

"Really?" Jack shook his head. "Word choice."

"Fine, and asshat."

"Better." He nodded. "Then why are we partnering with him?"

"Because if we pretend to play nice, at least we can delay him trying to double-cross us," Alissa explained.

"That means that Kayla..."

"Probably had a damn good reason for shooting him in the back."

"And we can expect him to turn on us?" Jack asked.

"Almost certainly."

Jack rubbed his hands together. "This is turning into some right proper drama!"

"You are way too excited about the prospect of someone trying to leave you on an acid planet to die."

"But look at us! Out doing things together, getting up to all kinds of shenanigans..."

Alissa sighed. "We really should have let you out of your room more."

"Let the record show you brought my reckless enthusiasm on yourself."

"I was getting that impression."

Jack halted when Alissa pointed up ahead. "I think this is the master bedroom."

The set of double doors opened into what certainly appeared to be a bedroom befitting of the manor's lord and lady. A four-poster bed stood against the back wall, complete with a fabric treatment cascading down either side of the bed. The right wall overlooked the manicured grounds, while the left had doors into the bathroom and spacious walk-in closet.

However, the greatest showpieces in the room were a pair of paintings on the same wall as the entry door, directly across from the bed. One was of a blue blob, and the other was a red blob. Granted, those with a particularly artistic eye would certainly find profound meaning in the forms and how the background faded at the edges. But to Jack, it appeared as though a child had broken out in a tantrum in the middle of finger painting.

"And what, pray tell, are these supposed to be?" he asked Alissa.

"The nature of feminine and masculine power in the interstellar era."

Jack raised an eyebrow. "This is all complete BS, right?"

"Oh, certainly." She switched on her laser cutter. "Come on, we're almost out of time."

Jack held the loose edges taut as Alissa worked her way around the perimeter of the first painting. When the final section of canvass came free, he began rolling the painting while Triss moved onto the second. He jumped in to brace the canvass for the final stretch. The fast cuts had caused some singes around the painting's edges, but it was nothing a new frame couldn't hide.

"There!" Alissa declared as the painting came free. "Now let's—"

"Is someone there?" a woman's voice interrupted her, speaking with a thick accent.

Jack froze. "She can't see us, right?"

"Our tools are visible, and someone is holding this painting," Alissa replied.

"What do we do?"

"I don't know! No one was supposed to be here."

Jack spun around to see a young, blonde-haired woman emerge from the bathroom. She wore a plush red robe and her hair was wet, as if freshly showered.

"I know you're there," the woman said, crossing her arms. "This isn't the meeting place."

Jack rolled up the bottom half of his face mask to expose his mouth. "Um, hi," he stammered

The woman's gaze passed from the rolled up canvass in Jack's hands to the empty frame on the wall to the laser cutter floating in Alissa's cloaked hand.

"This isn't what it looks like," Jack blurted, then snapped his mouth shut when Alissa slapped him on the arm.

"You're stealing our most valuable artwork," the robed woman stated.

"Well, maybe a little of what it looks like..." Jack admitted.

The woman scoffed. "Good riddance."

Alissa did a double-take, then rolled up the bottom portion of her own mask. "Wait, *what*?"

Merica fluffed her wet hair with her fingertips. "When I agreed to marry Vincent, I thought he actually cared about my interests. Turns out that he's only about acquiring objects—and people. You think I actually wanted to pay five million credits for a red square painted on a white background?" She scoffed. "The only painting I actually like in this whole house is a little mountain landscape by the servants' entrance downstairs."

"See?!" Jack glared at Alissa.

"We didn't say that we didn't like it, just that it had no market value," she replied.

Jack decided to drop the issue. "Anyway," he turned to the blonde woman, who was apparently Merica Ordello, "you're really okay with us taking these paintings?"

"Well, we'd agreed on just the jewels, but I don't see the harm in adding these," she said.

"Right, the deal..." Jack faded out.

"You know, to kidnap me and then help me fake my death," Merica supplied.

"Uh..." Jack looked to Alissa.

"And why do you want to do that, again?" his friend asked.

"Because Vincent is awful, and he'd never let me leave of my own accord. I arranged this jewelry theft so there'd be precedent for a kidnapping. Adding artwork into the mix is even better."

"Oh, you *hired* the thieves. Er, us," Alissa corrected. "Right."

"I know we were supposed to meet in the study, but I just wanted one final bath in this delightful marble tub before I departed. Let me get dressed and then we can go." Merica entered the walk-in closet and closed the door behind her.

"I knew Trent wasn't good enough to get in here on his own," Alissa whispered to Jack.

"Is she crazy? She hired someone to fake an abduction and murder?" he whispered back.

"People can do crazy things when pushed to their breaking point."

"But that's—"

"We need to get out of here, with or without Merica," Alissa interrupted. "Right now, with her seems like a lot easier option than her getting angry if we refuse and turning us in."

"Fine, but Trent is going to need a talking to after this."

"I'm sure Triss won't have any trouble taking the initiative."

A moment later, the closet door opened and Merica emerged wearing a sensible, fitted top and sleek, black pants. "Ready?" she asked.

"Yes." Alissa stowed the laser cutter and finished rolling up the painting she'd just cut down.

"You'll need to make it look official," Merica continued. "I have the ties and blindfold ready here." She walked over to the nightstand on the near side of the bed and produced a pair of pink fuzzy handcuffs and a sleep mask.

Merica twirled the handcuffs. "Who wants to tie me up?"

"Uh..." Jack faltered.

"Have at it, Jack." Alissa shoved him toward Merica.

"Um, right." He gave the strange woman an awkward smile.

"No reason to be shy," she said, placing her wrists together as the cuffs dangled from her right index finger.

"I'm not." Jack took the cuffs from her.

"Jack fancies himself quite the ladies man," Alissa explained to Merica. "Spoiler alter: he's not."

"He doesn't seem *that* bad." Merica looked him over while he secured the cuffs. "I mean, that eye is awful."

"She gave it to me." Jack nodded toward Alissa.

"Long story," his friend said.

Merica frowned. "Well, maybe anyone seems good after Vincent. I can't wait to get away. You've made all the arrangements, like we discussed?"

Alissa glanced at the door. "Uh, yeah. Our associate has it all squared away."

"Good. We should get out of here as soon as we can." Merica took half a step toward the door then hesitated. "Don't forget the mask."

"Right." Jack slipped it over her eyes.

"Lead me and I'll follow," Merica instructed.

"You're the boss." Alissa rolled her eyes.

Jack took Merica's elbow in preparation for leaving. Before he could move, an alarm broke the silence.

Alissa hoisted her carrying bag. "Well, that's just great."

CHAPTER SEVEN:
A DARING ESCAPE

"Something tells me that was *not* part of the plan," Jack stated the obvious.

"We need to find the others." Alissa took off at a fast jog into the hall, pulling her stealth suit over her head.

Jack followed her lead, guiding Merica as he ran.

The captive woman kept pace with him, but he could tell by the tenseness of her arm that she was uncomfortable. Not that she shouldn't be—handing her fate over to a bunch of strangers was a gutsy, or stupid, move, and an alarm was certainly a complicating factor. For someone who *wanted* to be abducted, having guards respond was pretty near a worst case scenario.

"We'll meet in the foyer on the first floor, like we planned," Alissa instructed. "Hopefully the others got their goods."

"I think the bounty is the least of our concerns right now," Jack shot back.

"Can't go home empty-handed."

"We have her," he said, indicating Merica. "I think we have our hands plenty full."

"She's Trent's problem."

"Oh, yeah, you really think we can just hand her over to Trent and everything will be just fine."

Alissa didn't respond at first. "No."

"Didn't think so."

"We'll deal with that once we're out of here," Alissa added. "For now, stay close."

Jack did as he was told, as silly as it felt to be running down the hall in a stealth suit while leading a handcuffed and blindfolded woman who would be plainly seen on any security camera. Add in the fact that she was the mistress of the house, it was clear that the afternoon was going awesomely.

As they approached the stairwell, Jack's suspicions of impending doom were confirmed by the sound of laser gunfire a story below.

"Of course." He sighed.

"Sounds like we'll have to shoot our way out." Alissa swung her bag forward so she could access the main pouch. A laser pistol seemingly floated in the air as she held it while in her stealth suit.

Jack retrieved his own handgun—a dainty weapon barely half the size of Alissa's. The others had insisted that they wouldn't get into trouble and the lighter firepower would be adequate, leaving room in his bag for the bounty. When he'd pointed out that *they* all had full-sized armaments, they had distracted him with a caramel lollipop, and he'd forgotten about the entire exchange until the moment he reached for his handgun.

Now, with a shootout imminent, he regretted caving to sweets so easily.

Alissa's gazed passed from the micro weapon to Jack's scowl. "Remember, it's not the size of the barrel, but how you use it."

He glared back at her. "I'm a great shot. Never had any complaints."

"Has there ever been someone *to* complain?"

"Oh, there were plenty before you started meddling," Jack told Alissa.

"What's going on now?" Merica asked.

Alissa smirked, rolling up the bottom of her mask. "Jack is feeling self-conscious about his tiny gun."

He rolled up his own mask. "Don't we have more important things to worry about right now, like the firefight going on downstairs?"

"As much as it pains me to utter these words," Alissa grimaced, "you're right."

Were the circumstances any different, Jack would have savored the moment. As it was, though, gunshots were the more pressing need. "Let's try the stairwell in the middle. We might be able to get behind the action," he suggested.

Alissa nodded. "Stay behind with Merica." She returned her mask to full stealth mode, then changed course to avoid the main stairwell. She continued along the corridor running the length of the second story.

Jack rolled down his mask and pressed forward. He fell farther behind Alissa than he'd indented due to Merica's cautious footsteps while blindfolded and cuffed.

"I won't let you run into anything," he whispered to her.

"She can't hear you through the stealth suit, Jack," Alissa reminded him.

"Stars, these masks are annoying! Would it have killed anyone to install an exterior comm option?"

"That was an upgrade. The guy they were stolen from was a total cheapskate."

"Next time, we're stealing from a splurger."

Jack was about to roll up the hood so he could speak with Merica, when Alissa suddenly held up her hand.

"Did you hear that?" she asked. "I think a new wave of guards just arrived."

"That would be our luck." Jack looked through the floor, cycling his cybernetic eye through its various settings. He saw a number of heat signatures advancing down the hall on the floor below. "I think they'll pass by—"

The helmeted head of a lone guard came into his peripheral view in the ancillary stairwell to his left.

"Alissa!" he warned, hiding his own weapon behind Merica's back.

Alissa's handgun was the only visible part of her, but it was enough to give away her position.

"What the…?" The guard leveled his weapon. "Drop the pistol! On your knees!"

Alissa balanced on one foot, raising her right knee to waist level. She set the weapon on it.

The guard frowned. "No, that's not—"

Jack took the opportunity to fire. He struck the guard in his right knee with a micro laser blast and squeezed off a second blast into the man's trigger hand.

The *pew* of the laser fire from the tiny handgun sounded like something straight out of a cheesy Earth cartoon from the archives, but it got the job done. The guard dropped to the ground with a cry of surprise and pain, giving Alissa the chance to grip her weapon and point it at the man's head.

She rolled up her hood to speak aloud. "I kneel for no man."

Jack placed his left hand on his hip. "Really? Snappy one-liners?"

"It sounded better in my head." Alissa shrugged.

Merica took step forward, bumping into Jack's hand containing the pistol. She jumped with surprise. "What's going on?"

Jack rolled up his mask. "Just a minor setback. It's fine."

"No, it's not fine!" she exclaimed. "You're kidnapping me!"

"Yeah, and take that..." Jack half-heartedly jangled her cuffs.

"We'll save you, ma'am!" the guard shouted.

"Ugh, here we go." Alissa clocked him in the temple with the butt of her pistol. "He won't be out for long, let's go."

"Good thinking," Jack whispered to Merica. "Keeping up appearances and all."

"Honestly, you're the worst kidnappers," she replied. "It's like you weren't even prepared for this part of the job."

"Yeah, weird..." Jack trailed off.

Ahead of him, Alissa began descending the staircase, her handgun trained ahead of her. "Cut the chatter," she said, her hood still rolled up to reveal her mouth. Her disembodied jaw set with determination, coupled with the laser pistol, made for an intimidating combo.

Jack stepped in front of Merica to simultaneously hide her from view and shield her from any stray fire they might encounter. The stealth suit wouldn't deflect much, but it was better than bare flesh.

At the bottom of the stairs, Alissa pressed herself against the side wall and peaked around the corner. She pulled back in and looked toward Jack.

"Looks like the rest of them continued inside. The one we encountered must have been a scout."

"Then that means they'll be expecting him to check in," Jack replied.

"I think they'll be too distracted to notice."

Before Jack could ask for clarification, Alissa peeked back around the corner and fired six shots in the direction of the guards.

A much deeper and more satisfying *pew pew* rang out in the halls, followed immediately by six grunts as the men collapsed.

"Come on." Alissa beckoned him forward.

She ran ahead while Jack awkwardly led Merica toward the sounds of an intense firefight waging in the distance.

"How did the guards know you were here?" Merica asked. "He wasn't supposed to know I was missing until we sent the demand letter."

"Well, plans change," Jack replied.

"*Nothing* has gone like we arranged."

"The, uh, guards had the wrong company name on file," Jack said to deflect. "They were onto us from the beginning."

"Ugh! It is *so* difficult to find good help."

"That's what we always say!"

"But you *are* the help."

Jack shrugged. "I didn't say we were any good, either."

Ten meters ahead, through the doors that had been closed when they first entered the manor, the corridor opened into a seating area. The room was presently bathed in laser fire, red pulses dancing across the white walls as the guards exchanged shots with the intruders.

Jack could just make out Triss' and Finn's locations, thanks to their stealth suits' interfaces with his own tech. Trent and Larry were hunkered down nearby behind a bizarre statue of a prone woman and a replica walrus skulls, respectively. These questionable décor choices were only overshadowed by the poor decision of using those two items for cover instead of an antique iron safe standing a mere meter away.

Eight guards were positioned between Jack and his friends, and at least half a dozen additional guards appeared to be on the far side, trapping them. What was curious is that no shots seemed to be connecting on either side.

"What's all the gunfire?" Merica questioned.

Jack tucked her into an alcove out of harm's way. "Wait here. I'll be right back."

He lowered his mask and then advanced with Alissa toward Triss' position, capitalizing on their suits' stealth tech and the distractions of the firefight to each get near a guard.

"Ready?" Alissa asked him.

He needed no explanation for what she meant. "Ready."

On her count, they each tackled a guard from behind and slammed their heads against the stone floor, dazing each.

The sounds of the assault were masked by the gunfire, so they took the opportunity to each tackle one more guard before darting to cover along the side walls to assess the situation.

Jack was now only separated from Triss' position by five meters and a lone guard behind a very charred potted plant.

He slinked along the wall behind the guard. Once close enough, he slammed the unfortunate individual's head against the stone chair rail.

The movement caught Triss' eye, and she ceased firing to look over. "You're late!" she hissed.

"Are we?" Jack checked the time on the HUD of his stealth suit. Sure enough, they were six minutes past the agreed upon rendezvous time. "Oh, sorry."

"What were you doing?!" she demanded while sneaking a peak at the battle scene.

"Uh, witty banter?" He shrugged.

"You're impossible!" Triss ducked back down behind the ornate storage chest where she was seeking refuge from the guards' laser fire.

"Well, at least now we have a hostage, too," Jack told her.

"What?! We didn't *want* a hostage!"

"Minor detail."

Triss groaned and squeezed off two shots, which hit just above a guard's head.

"What's going on? You're a better shot than that," Jack said.

"Trent told us we shouldn't hurt anyone."

"I know very little about the guy, but that doesn't sound like him."

"No, it doesn't," Triss agreed, "but that's why I listened."

A shot struck the wall mere centimeters from her left shoulder.

"And what about the guards? They trying not to hurt you, either?" Jack asked.

"Oh, no. They just have terrible aim."

To her word, the next shot struck a full meter above her head.

"Oh. Either way, we need to get out of here," Jack continued.

"Yes, we do," Finn chimed in on the comm's common band. "The thing with terrible aim is that eventually they'll hit."

"Gah!" Larry called out, almost as if on cue. He gripped his left leg, which had a fresh black and red streak across the top of his thigh.

"Want to rethink that whole 'not hurting the enemy' thing?" Jack asked.

"Arms and legs. No kill shots," Alissa instructed.

"Good enough for me." Triss took aim over the top of the storage chest. She made four shots in less than seven seconds, injuring the trigger arms of four guards.

Jack lined up his own victims and injured two more guards

in short order. The remaining enemies were quickly disabled by Finn's fire.

The guards would almost certainly call for backup if there was any available nearby. They'd likely be surrounded within minutes if they stayed put.

"What are you doing?!" Trent demanded as soon as he realized he was no longer under attack.

"Getting us out of here," Alissa replied after rolling up the bottom of her mask. She grabbed her bounty bag and ran over to Larry.

"Can you walk?" she asked him.

"Maybe with some help." His voice was strained. With a grunt, he staggered to his feet while Alissa supported half his weight.

Jack rolled up his mask and waved Trent over with the pistol in his hand. "What are you waiting for?"

"The job isn't complete," the other man responded.

"We have her, if that's what you mean," Jack told him.

"Merica? Where did you find her?"

"The master bathroom."

"She was supposed to be in the study."

"Apparently she wanted a bubble bath." Jack shrugged, though Trent couldn't see it.

Trent groaned. "Frickin' rich people."

CHAPTER EIGHT:
FRENEMIES?

Triss checked around the hall to make sure they had all the bounty bags. "We're good. Let's go."

Without hesitation, Jack ran back to where he'd left Merica.

She was still squatting in the alcove, a frown darkening her face beneath the sleep mask. "What happened to the guards?"

"They're just disabled, nothing serious," Jack assured her.

"That wasn't part of the deal."

"Well, plans change." He gripped her arm and pulled her to her feet. "Also, for supposedly being our captive, you're talking and making demands an awful lot."

"I thought I was hiring professionals who wouldn't *need* direction," Merica countered.

"Honesty time: we have no idea what we're doing." Jack held Merica's elbow and encouraged her to jog toward the door through which his group had entered.

"Our original egress plan is shot," Triss said as she jogged ahead of Jack.

Alissa nodded while she helped Larry along. "Provided there aren't guards waiting for us right outside the door, we should be able to make it to the crawler, at least."

"Not that it will do a lot of good. Can all of us even fit on it?" Triss asked.

"It can support the weight," Finn replied, "but it'll be slow and we'll be completely exposed."

Alissa frowned. "Is there any way to get the shuttle to us?"

"Not without disabling the shield," Finn told her.

Alissa looked to Trent. "How did you get down here?"

"Dropped off. We were supposed to steal one of the guards'

transport shuttles to get back to the ship."

"That's a terrible plan!" Alissa exclaimed.

Trent glared back. "It would have worked fine if you hadn't shown up!"

Merica scowled. "Wait, you're not together?"

"Long story," Alissa said with a groan.

"No time to argue! We need a way out of here," Finn urged. "I can program a pick-up flight path for our shuttle if someone can bring down the estate's shield."

"No way I'm letting him set foot on my ship." Triss glared at Trent.

He rolled his eyes. "What if we take your shuttle to my ship? If you can get it here."

"Fine," Alissa agreed. "Finn, do what you have to do. Jack and I will take care of the shield. We'll rendezvous at the crawler—the cloak will hide you until we get there."

Jack handed the blindfolded Merica over to Trent. "No funny business."

Trent scoffed. "You weren't even supposed to be part of the abduction."

"That's beside the point."

Alissa handed over Larry to Triss. "See you soon," Triss said.

The five of them headed for the exit door.

"Where's the shield generator?" Jack asked Alissa while they took off in the opposite direction from their friends.

"Probably in a fortified bunker somewhere."

"Then how are we supposed to take it out?!"

She gave a dismissive flip of her wrist. "No sense in trying to do it that way. We'll just destroy the base."

Jack's brow knit. "And how do we do *that*?"

"By just shooting it, of course."

"Right, of course..."

Alissa sighed. "Look, the field is meant to withstand an exterior assault. There's virtually no shielding on the interior of the field generators. All we have to do is fire a few well-aimed shots and the entire system will fail."

"Have you ever done this before?" Jack asked.

She shrugged. "First time for everything."

Jack breathed out between his teeth. "Nothing could possibly go wrong."

"Precisely."

Alissa ran the length of the mansion, passing through the

room filled with injured guards. When they reached the far side, they exited through a broad, sliding glass door that opened onto a covered patio with a gas-powered fire pit.

"Nice place," Jack commented.

"Oh, very nice indeed..." Alissa got a devious glint in her eyes. "Help me trace this gas line."

"Alissa..."

"I never dreamed they'd have such an antiquated fuel around here. This is the perfect way to take out the shield. They might even think it was just an accident."

Jack frowned. "If we blow this whole place, the guards..."

"You're right, no need to rack up a body count."

"You said we can just shoot it, no need to get overly fancy," Jack pointed out.

"Good point. Let's see what we're working with."

They ran into the garden, searching for the base of the wall surrounding the estate. A hundred meters from the manor, the stone wall rose from behind a row of bushes. At four meters tall, they had no line of sight or access to the top ledge, from which the shield extended.

"Okay, so that's an issue," Alissa admitted.

"If we can't shoot it, what if we overload one of the laser pistols to use as a makeshift bomb?" Jack suggested.

"*Now* who's the one getting overly complicated?"

"Do you have a better idea?"

Alissa shook her head. "Okay, that might be enough to buckle the system, if we find the right spot to stick it."

"What about in a tree?" Jack looked over at a nearby tree grove. Some of the spindly branches extended toward the wall.

"Yes, if we can loop a rifle around the end of a branch, it might be close enough to take out the base of the shield," Alissa assessed. "Only one way to find out for sure."

She removed her laser pistol from her stealth bag and began fiddling with the device.

"How do you even overload the weapon, anyway?" Jack asked her.

"Would you really like me to spend ten minutes getting into the technical specifications, or do you just want to watch it go 'boom'?"

"The second thing."

"Thought so." She got back to work.

Two minutes later, Alissa rose to her feet, holding the

weapon carefully at arm's length.

Jack eyed it warily. "That could kill us instantly, couldn't it?"

"Oh, most certainly." She walked over toward the tree closest to the wall. "Give me your belt."

"What for?"

"Just do it," she instructed.

Reluctantly, Jack reached inside his stealth suit to retrieve the belt holding up his pants underneath. "You better not make me run, because these pants are going to fall down inside, and—"

Jack cut off when he noticed that Alissa had secured one end of the belt around the tampered pistol and the other had been secured around a rock as a counterweight. She held the center of the belt and was twirling the handgun in a vertical circle. When she let go, the belt and its cargo sailed through the air, then wrapped around the end of the tree's branch.

She grinned. "Like a pro!"

The tampered weapon began emitting a high-pitched whine.

"Run!" Alissa shouted.

Jack grabbed the waistband of his pants through the outer layer of the stealth suit and took off toward the manor as quickly as he could, Alissa two strides ahead.

Behind them, the whine emanating from the weapon continued to intensify. After fifteen seconds, an explosion knocked Jack on his face.

His ears rang as he came to his senses on the ground. Gingerly, he pushed himself to his knees, spitting out a mouthful of grass. He looked behind him.

The top segment of the wall was gone, and the shield overhead flickered with dancing static.

"Come on..." Alissa wished under her breath.

The shield failed with a spectacular wave of electrical energy, making Jack's stealth suit light up with blue flecks.

"All right! We have to get to the crawler." Alissa grabbed his hand and led him across the garden.

Jack pulled his hand free of Alissa's to better hold up his pants. They found the pathway they'd used to access the manor and began tracing it back to the crawler's position.

"It should be right around here..." Jack murmured.

Rounding a bend, he spotted the faint outline of the cloaked dome. The discharge from the larger shield must have resulted in some interference with the tech, causing it to shimmer and emit occasional bright flashes.

Jack stepped through the field, and suddenly the crawler and the other members of their party came into view. "And here they are," he concluded.

"Shuttle is on its way," Finn reported.

"Yeah, I hear it," Triss said.

Jack pointed toward the sky. "That's not the shuttle you're hearing."

Coming straight for the manor was a seemingly solid pass of purple—hundreds of massive birds descending in one magnificent wave.

"Oh shit!" Alissa dropped to her knees and put her hands over her head.

"They can't see us," Finn reminded her. "As long as we stay under this cloak, they should leave us alone."

"I hate to break it to you, but the cloak isn't exactly working right now—it's flashing," Jack informed the others.

The birds drove straight for them.

"Finn, where's that shuttle?" Alissa demanded from the round.

Jack dropped to his knees to shield his head like Alissa had done. "This isn't how I want to die!"

A high-pitched whistle filled the air, and the birds broke from their dives, scattering in every direction.

Jack looked up to see Merica with two fingers in her mouth. She whistled again, and the birds flew farther away.

"Damn avian menace," she muttered. "Had to install the shield just to keep them out. They hate high frequencies."

"And love shiny things, apparently." Alissa rose to her feet and dusted off her knees.

"They'll be back," Merica warned.

"But we'll be gone." Finn's face lit up. "Shuttle should be coming into view... now!"

Sure enough, the craft arced over the top of the perimeter wall, coming to rest on top of a lone bush seven meters from the group. The back hatch opened.

Triss hopped into the crawler to drive it inside.

Jack ran into the cargo area with Finn, Larry, and Merica while Alissa and Trent took the controls in the cockpit. Once Triss was on board with the crawler, the door closed and they accelerated into the sky.

"I'll enter in the coordinates for my ship," Trent said, and he made entries on the touchpanel.

"Guess you don't need these anymore," Jack realized when he noticed Merica still had on the blindfold and fuzzy cuffs. He removed them from her.

"Thanks," Merica said. "That didn't go quite how I imagined. You kind of destroyed the place."

"What do you care?" Triss questioned. "Screw him."

"Yeah, you're right." Merica rubbed her wrists.

Jack checked the crawler and saw that all the bounty bags were secured in the back. "At least we got the goods."

"Yes, that we did," Finn agreed. "All thanks to my safe-cracking, I might add."

Triss rolled her eyes.

"None of this would have been possible without Triss," Jack said on her behalf.

She smiled. "Thank you."

The shuttle broke through the atmosphere and approached a ship approximately the same size as the *Little Princess II*, which Trent had identified as the *Thrasher*. Alissa piloted the shuttle inside, then opened the back hatch once they were docked.

"Let's divide up the bounty and be on our way," Alissa said, rising from the controls.

"Don't you want a tour?" Trent asked.

"Yeah, no thanks." Triss crinkled her nose.

"We can go through everything over here," Trent suggested, leading the group toward a stainless steel table near the shuttle's docking pad.

They hoisted the bounty bags on the table and unzipped them.

While Trent was inspecting the goods, Alissa and Triss exchanged a knowing glance. Alissa nodded.

Triss leveled a rifle on Trent. "Sorry to break up the party, but consider this a preemptive move against your inevitable double-cross."

Trent held up his hands, backing away from the table. "Hey now! I really had no intention of doing that."

"Really, just like Kayla was the one who wronged *you*?" Triss tilted her head.

"Leave the past alone, Triss." Trent began to lower his hands. "Let's just divvy up the bounty and part ways. We never have to see each other again."

She kept the weapon trained on him. "No, I know how you operate. You'll stab us in the back, even if it's not immediate."

Jack felt a cool cylinder press against his temple. "Uh, guys!"

"Surprise! Trent's not the one you had to worry about." Jack was shocked to hear Merica's voice coming from right behind him. Her arm looped around his throat while the other held the pistol to his head.

"What are you doing?" Disbelief laced Alissa's tone.

"You really think I'd let a bunch of lowly thieves take all my beautiful things? I hate Vincent, yes, but he was a means to an end. I could gather all the valuables I desired and use the proceeds to start a new life. All I needed were some pawns to get the goods away from the property," Merica explained. "Trent was just the patsy I needed."

"But you said you only liked the mountain landscape painting," Jack murmured.

"I heard how you talked about the art in the bedroom—you were clearly people with no taste. It was all a ruse to win you over." She tisked. "Honestly, you were too easy to manipulate."

"There's one critical part of this plan you didn't think through," Alissa said. "There are six of us and one of you."

"I'll kill him if you try to stop me!" Merica tightened her grip on Jack's neck.

"I think she's serious." He gulped.

"If you're looking for a hostage, you picked the wrong person on the crew to hold at gunpoint." Alissa placed her hands on her hips. "Jack often causes more trouble than he's worth."

"You don't mean that!" he exclaimed. "I'm a one hundred percent vital member of this crew."

"Are you, though?" She wrinkled her nose. "Really, Merica, you kinda backed yourself into a corner here."

Merica held her place. "You wouldn't sacrifice one of your own. You're just trying to distract me."

"Is it working?" Alissa asked.

"What? No, I—" Merica cut off with a yelp as a low-intensity laser blast struck her trigger hand.

"Guess it did." Triss lowered her weapon.

"You bitch!" Merica shouted, gripping her injured hand.

"She's really not the one worthy of name-calling here." Jack pinned Merica's good arm behind her back and held her in place. "And she's a really good shot."

"Well, *pretty* good," Triss corrected. "And I hadn't actually checked the sights on this rifle... I was, like, eighty percent sure I wouldn't hit you."

"That's... not very good." Jack frowned.

"Psh, you're fine!" Triss waved her hand.

He sighed. "What do we do with her?"

Merica squirmed in his grip. "Get your hands off me!"

"Gonna pass. First you held a gun to my head, and then you insulted my taste in art. Kinda lost any favor," he replied.

Trent stroked his chin. "What would you do with *me*?"

Triss raised an eyebrow. "You mean what we still might do with you? Drop you on the nearest habitable planet with provisions for a week and a transmitter to call for rescue—let you be someone else's problem."

"Sounds like as good a fate as any for her." Trent nodded. "The deal was to get her away from Vincent. That's fulfilling the contract."

Alissa smirked. "I have something else in mind."

CHAPTER NINE: Debts Paid

"How did you learn about this place, again?" Jack asked as the shuttle descended through the thick cloud cover of the remote planet.

"The school is one of the charities my parents donated to in an attempt to look less like monsters," Alissa replied. "However, it's all run through an intermediary. It'll be months before there's contact with anyone on the outside."

Jack smiled. "Perfect."

In the rear of the shuttle, a blindfolded Merica strained against her harness and shouted into her mouth gag. Her empty threats of killing them all had grown wearisome, necessitating the gag. Jack had felt a little bad about putting it on her at first, but when she'd asked about her fuzzy handcuffs as soon as she saw the gag, he suspected she didn't mind having it in all that much.

Alissa directed the shuttle to an open field adjacent to a small settlement nestled in the foothills of a jagged mountain range. The town consisted of five wooden lodges and a handful of huts.

"Wow, it's like stepping back in time," Jack commented, taking it in.

"That's precisely the point."

Once on the ground, Alissa powered down the engines and they unstrapped their flight harnesses.

"Time to see your new home," Alissa told Merica, removing the blindfold.

The other woman shouted objections into her gag when she glimpsed the planet through the open doorway.

"You wanted to start a new life. That's exactly what we're

giving you." Alissa grinned. "They were so thrilled to hear someone of your talents was looking to relocate."

Jack helped Merica from her seat and directed her through the hatch in the rear of the shuttle.

As they exited the craft, and elderly man and two women were approaching. They were followed by a herd of three dozen young children.

Alissa removed Merica's gag. "Welcome," she told her.

"Where is this backwater hell hole?" Merica demanded. "Take me to the nearest station immediately and I won't report you."

"Oh, nonsense!" Alissa laughed. "But you can make such a positive difference here."

"Hello!" one of the woman in the welcoming party called out. "We're so excited our new art teacher has arrived."

Merica's face paled. "Oh, stars, no!"

A group of children ran ahead toward Merica. Their fingers were covered in orange and blue paint.

"Are you our teacher?" a little boy asked.

"No, I am most certainly not!" Merica objected.

Alissa nudged the other woman with her elbow. "She's funny, isn't she? She can't *wait* to spend all day painting with you!"

"Yeah!" the children cheered in unison.

"We made you a picture," the little boy continued. He held out a piece of paper depicting a crude figure of a woman, and orange blob, and a single strip of blue across the top of the sheet. "This is you, and this is the sky, and this is a flower."

Merica's eyes widened with horror. "Kill me now."

Alissa clapped her on the back. "We knew you'd love it here!"

The old main in the welcome party beamed, revealing purple teeth. "I hope you like beets, because we have them with every meal!"

Jack and Alissa backed away as Merica's face turned an unnatural shade of red.

"Have fun now!" Alissa called out, and they made their retreat.

"She won't hurt them, will she?" Jack whispered to her.

"Nah, nothing to gain from it. I hope some time off the grid does her good."

They returned to the shuttle and locked the door, just in case Merica made a run for it.

"What if she reports us after she gets off here?" Jack asked once they were seated.

Alissa shrugged while she secured her flight harness. "She doesn't really know who we are, aside from some first names. And since she only ever communicated with Trent and saw his ship, it's doubtful she could trace anything back to us."

"Hmm, I guess that's true." Jack paused. "And what about Trent himself?"

"I guess we'll figure that our when we get back."

They ascended through the heavy cloud cover, and the sky slowly changed from blue to black. The *Little Princess II* and *Thrasher* were in geosynchronous orbit with an umbilical connecting the two vessels. Alissa headed for their own ship and docked in the hangar.

The rest of the crew and Trent were waiting for them.

"How'd she take it?" Triss asked on behalf of the group.

"Oh, positively thrilled." Alissa grinned.

"I guess this is where we part ways," Trent said, standing at the threshold of the umbilical.

Alissa nodded. "You have your jewels, we have our art. That was the agreement."

"Best of luck to you, then. I hope our paths never cross again," Trent said.

Triss crossed her arms. "The feeling is mutual."

He departed without further commentary, and they disconnected the umbilical. Once everyone was back on the living deck, finally allowed themselves a moment to celebrate in the living room.

"That was a hell of an op!" Finn exclaimed.

"I can't wait to unload this art." Triss smiled. "I'll reach out to that fence contact of yours, Finn."

Jack began mentally spending his share of the bounty, thinking about how he could order a pair of purple shoes to alternate with his gold light-up loafers. Perhaps he could even splurge and get the electric blue.

"Oh… that's not good," Triss said.

Alissa sighed. "What now."

"Um, that fence just told me the black market art scene has taken a downturn after a critic commented on Merica's vlog about Vincent's nude portrait, sparking a realization that, and I quote, 'most of it was meaningless shit and artists should go back to painting more mountain landscapes or something'."

"I told you so," Jack muttered under his breath.

"Even the painting of Vincent that everyone wanted to burn?" Alissa asked.

"Unfortunately, ironic art purchases are now among the worst offenders." Triss sighed and leaned against the wall.

Finn took a slow breath. "So, let me get this straight… we now have half a dozen worthless pieces of canvass, and we just let twelve million worth of jewels walk off our ship."

Triss nodded. "That sounds about right."

"Well, that royally sucks." He stormed off in the direction of his cabin.

The others wandered toward the living room.

"It was a good idea, Triss." Jack nestled into his typical place on the couch.

Alissa plopped down next to him. "At least it gave us something to do. We'll have other opportunities."

Jack looked at her. "Hey, you didn't mean what you said earlier, did you? About me being worthless?"

"I don't think I used that phrasing," Alissa replied.

"But that's what you meant."

She looked him in the eye. "No, I didn't. You're a goof, but you're our goof. I knew she wouldn't shoot you if she didn't think it would get her any leverage, so I had to break you down in her eyes."

"If you say so." Jack looked down.

Alissa reached over and tousled his hair. "You're one of us now, for better or worse."

"Thanks, Alissa." He smiled.

Finn barged back into the living room and collapsed on the couch adjacent to Jack's. "I take it this means we're not getting a new ship."

"The *Little Princess II* is just fine." Alissa patted the wall behind her. "If we treat her right, she'll serve us well."

"But what about all the layout issues?" Triss questioned.

"We'll get used it to. Considering the size of the original *Little Princess*, this is still huge," Alissa pointed out.

"Fine, we'll make it work *for now*," Finn agreed. "But the bigger issue: however will we pass the time?"

Jack leaned forward with his elbows on his knees. "You know, despite things going very badly, Merica did illustrate a need in the market."

"What's that?" Alissa prompted.

"Covert transportation of people."

"Uh… That sounds a little shady," Triss interjected.

Finn clapped his hands together with delight. "But oh so adventurous!"

Alissa massaged her eyes. "What do you have in mind?"

About the Author

Amy has always loved science fiction in all its forms, including books, movies, shows, and games. If it involves outer space, even better! As a full-time author based in Oregon, Amy primarily writes character-driven science fiction and science-fantasy with broad scope and cool tech. When she's not writing, she enjoys travel, wine tasting, binge-watching TV series, and playing epic strategy board games.

www.AmyDuBoff.com

Books by Amy DuBoff

Cadicle Space Opera Series
Vol. 1: Architects of Destiny
Vol. 2: Veil of Reality
Vol. 3: Bonds of Resolve
Vol. 4: Web of Truth
Vol. 5: Crossroads of Fate
Vol. 6: Path of Justice
Vol. 7: Scions of Change

Uprise Saga (with Craig Martelle and Michael Anderle)
Book 1: Covert Talents
Book 2: Endless Advance

INVASION OF THE KAVIIS

By C.C. Ekeke

When a young soldier's first military assignment looks like a career-killing dud, he is determined to turn that minus into an unorthodox opportunity for action, glory...and belly rubs.

Since childhood, Henar has trained to be a part of the Kavii Benevolency's grand military. On the day of his graduation from military academy, the young soldier's dream of being in the frontline of planetary conquest and rising up the Benevolency's military ranks was about to come true. But when Henar is deployed to the backwater world known as Earth, his expectations of adventure and glory are all but destroyed. Still, the young soldier is hell-bent on making the best of his first military conquest. When Henar actually arrives on Earth, what he finds there opens his eyes to a new and unorthodox chance at glory...and unlimited belly rubs.

CHAPTER 1

Henar never felt more proud. Dressed in a freshly pressed light grey military outfit made him feel taller. Stronger. Happier. Cooler. Even the fiery orange dawn spilling down from the twin suns orbiting the planet Kav felt brighter.

In fact, Henar felt any superlative ending with –er and –ier.

Only two days had passed since his graduation from Ka'Hoberk Military Academy, and Henar felt like he'd been a soldier of the Kaviian Benevolency Armed Forces for over two years.

"This one is a soldier!" he repeated to himself, wrinkling his nostrils in disbelief. He'd repeated that fourteen times now, and the title never lost its appeal.

The auburn-furred Kavii male, only twenty cycles in age, marched proudly across the quadrangle-shaped commons of the military base, awash with green grass and other Kavii soldiers milling about before the day started. Lofty buildings, off-white in color and shaped like half ovals, loomed everywhere. These buildings and this military base on Retakka 4 had been Henar's home for the last five years.

Like all young Kavii, Henar had attended a military academy since adolescence, then trained and learned for five planetary cycles, all so he could be on the frontlines when the Benevolency spread their way of life to another fortunate planet.

That was the dream of Henar and all young Kavii: serve the Kaviian Benevolency in any way possible.

And with an empire that spread across hundreds of worlds, Henar knew opportunities for him and his friends would be boundless.

He smiled, his long and webbed hind feet almost bouncing as he quickened his pace.

As great as graduation day had been for Henar and his friends, he knew today would be better. *Assignment day.*

Henar already knew he would be part of an invasion squadron. His test and performance scores had guaranteed that.

But to which planetary system? Henar prayed for one with planets that would be a challenge to the Benevolency. Where else could he show off his newly learnt martial prowess? "This one will be the best soldier the Benevolency has ever seen. No matter the planet!"

"Dreaming of conquest and glory again, Soldier?"

Henar jolted in surprise and whipped around. Behind him were three other Kavii, also dressed in light grey military uniforms like him. To uniformed species, he and his friends were identical in appearance. Thick and dark auburn coat covering their skin. Powerful hind legs with webbed feet. Paw-like front legs with opposable thumbs. Muzzle-shaped mouths and noses. Small, round eyes on either side of their heads, shiny and dark.

But after a closer glance, Osefa's coat was obviously shaggier than everyone else's. And Leakki's eyes were more a shade of midnight blue than straight black. And Nele liked to sway her haunches from side to side whenever she got excited and scurried over. A smile spread across Henar's face at the sight of his closest friends. "This one is dreaming of how best to serve the Benevolency, Soldier."

Nele snorted. "You're just excited to finally conquer some planets, Soldier."

Osefa threw his head back and guffawed, which sounded like a cawing noise. "That is correct, Soldier."

Henar wrinkled his nose at their mockery. "Go jump in a black hole...Soldier!"

That caused the whole group to burst out laughing. "This one will never, ever tire of our shiny new titles," Henar managed between chuckles. "Soldiers!"

"Now we get to travel the wide galaxy," Leakki agreed eagerly as the group began walking across the commons, "conquering in the name of the Kavii."

That was what Henar hoped for. He and his friends traversing the stars in the name of their great government. "Hopefully we all get assigned to the same battalion," he added, thoughts alight with possibilities. "We will stomp down those who would resist the Benevolency."

Nele turned to him with a disbelieving look. "Eeesh." The very thought made the female Kavii shiver from head to long, webbed toes. "Why any race would ever be so foolish to resist is beyond me."

"There have been historic exceptions," Osefa replied dryly. "More than a few."

"And those ones never lasted long," Henar added.

The group all shook their furry heads round and round in agreement. "Not at all." The Kavii Benevolency was kind to those species that followed the rules and integrated seamlessly into their régime. But those who dared to defy the Benevolency's kindness were met with fire and fury of terrifying magnitudes. Henar almost felt sorry for those who did. Almost.

"This one doubts there will be any glory for you and your lot," a condescending purr sounded from behind Henar.

And the jovial mood frosted over. Henar felt his features curling in disgust as he slowly turned to face his nemesis. Standing before him was a golden-furred Kavii more massive and muscular than normal. Atiga, a Kavii from the Black Mountains in northern Kav, where Kavii always grew like giants. A disdainful sneer was etched into his muzzle as if he was constantly sniffing someone's flatulence. Flanking him as usual were his loyal minions, Kamai and Akko, both equally mountain-sized and cruel.

Atiga and Henar had been enemies from day one in the Academy. Since then, a competitive rivalry between two ambitious students had festered into bitter hatred for five years. Henar was hoping to put that behind him and never see Atiga's punchable muzzle ever again. He almost clapped back. With Atiga, a response to his insults had become a reflex. But a glance at Leakki subtly shaking his head stopped him. With great difficulty, Henar sighed and turned away without a word. His three friends followed suit.

Atiga wasn't done. "That one thinks the glorious military will place someone as soft as Henar and his sucklings in active combat?" he threw back. That drew a roaring caw caw laughter from his beefy minions.

Henar stopped and whirled around. "Says the one who barely graduated!" His eyes narrowed. "Being the progeny of a commandant must be fortifying." Akko and Kamai stopped laughing. Atiga as well, his golden fur standing on edge in fury. "This one graduated without anyone's help, you piece of flotsam!"

That made Henar and his friends snicker. "Keep telling yourself that," he teased. "These ones all know your father called in favors, thanks to his progeny being as intelligent as an asteroid."

Atiga's dark red eyes nearly popped out of his head. "YOU—"

He lunged at Henar, who braced himself for the attack.

Akko and Kamai held Atiga back, just barely. The massive Kavii's retort quickly devolved into a string of curses. Filthy curses. This drew stares from many passersby.

"Let that one go," Henar dared, never flinching. Atiga may be larger, but his fighting skills were substandard. Just like everything else about him. Always relying on strength instead of skill, which was why Henar never lost to him in a fight.

A paw on Henar's shoulder drew him out of the battle haze—Osefa, who looked worried by all the attention this confrontation was drawing. "That one isn't worth the trouble. We should go. Mission assignments."

Henar took one look back at Atiga, still swearing up a thunderstorm as his friends dragged him away. The picture of class that one wasn't. Why get dragged down by a blowhard whose father could save him from any consequences? Henar had no backup of the sort.

Shrugging Osefa off, he turned and walked toward the half-ovular building nearest to them.

"This one would've enjoyed seeing you make Atiga wail like a newborn pup, again," Nele offered as they all fell in step with Henar.

That drew renewed laughter from the group.

The auditorium seating was arranged in a semicircle, with over two hundred Kavii graduates ready for combat. The ceiling above was an interstellar map of the entire Kaviian Benevolency, star to star.

Henar knew that map by heart. Every planet. Every star. Every moon. But gazing up while he took a seat was no less pleasing than when he'd first laid eyes on it cycles ago as a young pup. Ready...to serve the Benevolency. Noses and whiskers twitched in anticipation. A ripple of murmured conversations sounded as the graduates wondered what they would see.

"What planet will it be, my furries?" Osefa asked.

"This one hopes for a species that controls a planetary system." Leakki rubbed his paws together. "The greater the challenge, the more satisfying the win."

Henar smiled at his friends' enthusiasm. A planetary system would be nice, depending on the size. Hopefully not too big. As much as he wanted to serve the Benevolency, he'd heard about instances where young soldiers bit off too much on their first conquest assignment. However, he didn't want an easy win. Hard-fought victories made one a better soldier to the Benevolency.

The crowd quieted as an older Kavii took the stage below. He was a high-ranking military officer, shoots of white pockmarking his dark brown fur. The shapeless purple robe he wore billowed out around his hind legs with far too much dramatics for Henar's taste. But this military official was legend.

Ponoi, a one-time soldier without peer. Now he spoke to the soldiers of tomorrow and revealed their first assignment.

Weird purple robe or not, Henar's excitement bubbled through his veins like fire.

"The Kavii Benevolency!" Ponoi boomed, his voice filling the auditorium. "The premier power in this chaotic galaxy. A force for good! A pillar for justice! A bastion of power!"

The Kavii pontificated with such self-importance that Henar almost laughed. He swallowed his unintentional amusement as Ponoi continued with arms spread wide. "We spread our forces throughout the galaxy. Bestowing on many the wonders of our technology. The pleasure of our mercy. The gift...of our Benevolency!"

"That one loves his own voice," Leakki whispered.

Henar swallowed another laugh. "A speck," he whispered back.

Osefa and another Kavii sitting a row back shushed their soft mockery.

"Now this class," Ponoi continued in histrionic fashion on the auditorium stage, "is one of the best that the Benevolency has to offer." The older Kavii jabbed a finger at the map of the Benevolency above. "The brightest of stars in dark skies. The best soldiers to be produced from Benevolency military academies..."

Ponoi's monologuing on the star-shattering greatness of the

Kavii and their conquest continued to where even a diehard like Henar could no longer contain his temper.

Get. To. The Point, he mouthed.

"We have taken a considerable portion of this galaxy into our domain," Ponoi said, pacing now. His round eyes gleamed knowingly. "Many of the most advanced worlds bend to our unyielding might and martial skill.

"Now, with our ever increasing population, the Benevolency must turn its eyes to resource planets," he stated, wagging a pawed hand at the crowd. "While conquest of these kinds of planets might not be as...action-packed as other assignments, the Benevolency needs them in order to spread our interstellar seed across the cosmos."

"Sounds unclean..." Leakki teased quietly, poking at Nele's shoulder, "and intriguing."

She gnashed her teeth at him, eyes burning. "Shut that black hole of a mouth!" she whispered sharply.

Henar didn't laugh or even smile. As he continued listening to Ponoi's pontification, a sinking feeling began filling his stomach. Yet he could not figure out why.

"And now," the former soldier continued, gesturing with unnecessary theatrics. "You young soldiers will march forth into the black to conquer the next colony for the Kavii Benevolency. The next Dependency to further the Kavii's glory. Soldiers. Behold the Benevolency's next resource planet."

Ponoi stepped away from the center of the stage. Immediately, a 3D image of a planet floated in the space where he once stood. The audience leaned forward eagerly to behold this new world which would soon know the dominance of the Kavii. Henar shared none of the enthusiasm. The more he studied this planet, the larger the pit in his stomach grew. Smallish terrestrial world. Almost seventy percent of deep blue saltwater with large chunks of brown and green landmass covering part of the surface.

Confusion and growing disappointment spread through portions of this audience as they studied the holoimage closer. Henar's heart sank into his stomach. He didn't need Ponoi to reveal this world's name.

"Some call it Terra," the former soldier stated proudly. "Others call it Solara 3. But the inhabitants call it Earth."

And just like that, all traces of enthusiasm deflated out of the entire audience.

"Are you fooling this one?" one of their fellow soldiers complained, and not quietly.

Nele looked livid. "I can't believe our target is Earth, a backwater pisshole." She folded her arms indignantly.

"This one heard Earth does not even have a single world government," Leakki added unhelpfully.

"Which means the conquest will be easy." Henar shook his head, more downtrodden than before. "But this one wanted more of a challenge."

And the complaints continued growing in venom for a while.

Henar did want a smaller engagement on his first mission. But this would not even be a fight. The Military Command saw him and his class as bottom feeders who were only good to conquer pisswater worlds. *Guess this one has to prove myself to them yet again.*

Ponoi seemed either oblivious or willfully ignorant of the crowd's disapproval. "Learn every inch of its surface, its species, its defense, and its natural resources. In the next month, you will step onto Earth's primitive surface. Subjugate its backwater inhabitants and claim its resources."

Ponoi raised one curled paw into the air, black beady eyes gleaming. "In the Name of the Benevolency!"

Despite his disappointment in the future colony world they would be invading, Henar shot up to his feet before anyone else and began clapping.

"In the name of the Benevolency," Henar bellowed. Every other soldier in the auditorium quickly concurred.

But deep inside his core, Henar unleashed the same, filthy string of curses as Atiga had said earlier.

CHAPTER 2

The voyage to Earth took close to a month on a rotund Benevolency *Dominator*-class carrier. The whole time, Henar, his friends, and the five hundred other Kavii warriors chosen for this glorious mission were inundated with all things Earth. He stood in a learning chamber, bathed in a cascade of images and data fed directly into his brain.

Within a week, Henar was a master of basic Earth knowledge. The population, the different subspecies, the countries that were the wealthiest and posed the largest military threats. The musical types, all which Henar hoped would be outlawed once the Benevolency took over. Humans were terrible singers. Apparently Earth's ruling species, calling themselves humans, were bipedal with barely a hair on their bodies. They also dwarfed a full-grown Kavii in height and weight. As noted, no unified world government. No joint military. In fact, many of these human subspecies hated each other. The antiquated trinkets they touted as technology were laughable.

"Not only that," Nele said, unable to keep a straight face during one of their meals. "These humans apparently have never left their planetary system. *Ever!*"

"For serious?" Henar screwed up his face in disbelief. "By the Radiant Benevolency, this incursion will be over in less than half a moon's turn."

The soldiers also were tasked on studying much of Earth's climate and ecosystem. Who knew if the humans or Earth itself had any threats that could harm the Kavii?

This included the foods, the flora, and the fauna. Henar took severe umbrage with that last area after some in-depth study.

Oftimes, these humans subjugated certain types of lesser species as "pets." These pets, many which resembled the Kavii, were forced at times to perform asinine tricks for the humans' amusement. Earth's archaic communication networks had countless footage. Seeing just one caused hatred to scorch through Henar's bones. "This one cannot wait to make these unevolved sapiens kneel to our might."

"Agreed!" Leakki and others concurred, equally outraged.

"And stop their dreadful music!" Osefa added, pumping a curled paw in the air.

The one negative on this trip through the stars was that Atiga and his minions were also onboard. No thanks to his commandant father, of course.

Henar had made strides to avoid the trio. The priority was the mission to Earth. And since Henar had no family in the senior military command, he did not want to appear as a cause of disharmony.

But Atiga just couldn't help but get in his face, bragging and hurling insults.

"Think this is where you will make a name for yourself, you son of a bloody hairball?" the towering brute hissed one time. "You will gain no glory from this conquest. No stars on your record. Nothing!"

Naturally Henar shot back. "And you will probably get yourself killed, given that sterling intellect you barely possess." His hatred for Atiga was like a disease that knew no cure. Each and every time, Osefa and Nele had to pull him away, as Akko and Kamai did the same with a fuming Atiga.

After a particularly ugly quarrel where Henar punched Atiga in the loins, the commanding officers felt it best to move Henar to a different level of the ship. Away from his friends. That meant a different group to study Earth with. The only times he now saw Osefa, Nele, and Leakki were during meals.

Another conflict like that might get Henar thrown in the brig for maiming...or worse.

When the Kaviian Benevolency decided to bestow the gift of its rule on a fortunate planet, the incursion could happen in one of two ways that Henar knew of.

When not training in hand-to-hand and armed combat, or studying all aspects of Earth's history (and what a short one that world had), Henar dove deep into the Benevolency's Art of Conquest. It truly was an art refined over the near thousand years that the Kavii had dominated this galaxy.

Henar sat in his quarters crouched on all fours, the hum of the ship engines distant yet serene as he watched the holoscreen floating before him. In the peace and quiet, he digested as much knowledge as he could.

Some of these holovideos he had watched as a child. But Henar felt giddy and fired up watching them again.

The Benevolency all started when the Kavii colonized the planetary system of their homeworld Kav. Aside from a rudimentary defense force, the Kavii were a peaceful race focused on agriculture and mining. They had no ambitions of conquest or spreading their influence.

That was, until the Savage War happened.

This part always got Henar choked up. The carnage. The hopelessness. The malevolency!

Some bestial species called the Etamas trying to make their stamp on the galaxy surprised and attacked the Kavii.

Millions were slain. The Kavii Defense Force was overwhelmed. If the Etamas had been a more intelligent species, the wondrous Benevolency that Henar worshipped would have never formed.

Thankfully, the Etamas were the stupidest, most arrogant would-be conquerors to ever take space flight.

Several brave Kavii from what remained of their defense force hijacked a few of the Etamas' own warships and turned the tide of the war.

With true weapons of their own and a fury never seen before, the Kavii slaughtered the attacking Etamas. Every. Single. One.

The Kavii did not celebrate their victory. No. Not while fires still burned on their worlds. Not while millions of innocent Kavii lay dead. This victory had been sheer happenstance.

The Kavii had then realized what kind of savages existed out there in the black of space. Savages who could attack and lay waste to what the Kavii had built. Savages who had devastating weapons but lacked the intelligence to properly wield them.

"We must not only prepare ourselves for the worst that space has to offer," said Tolaath, the Kavii supreme leader from that ancient time. "But we must be a guiding force of benevolence in the darkness around us!" These words, repeated by another Kavii, still felt as if Tolaath himself had risen from the grave to utter them in Henar's very ears.

Electrifying! "We must show them the way. We must be the beacon that all in this chaotic universe look to in their time of need and madness!"

That day had marked the true birth of the Benevolency. The Kavii had buried their dead, rebuilt their fallen cities, and healed the wounds in their planetary system.

Beyond that, the Kavii reverse-engineered the Etamas' warships and devised their own. It took a number of years. But before long, the Kavii's new military forces had become a force to be reckoned with.

How amusing to Henar it was knowing the Kaviis' then intimidating force would have been 1/500 the size of The Benevolency's current armed forces.

"We all start somewhere," Henar murmured, eyes wide with wonder.

By the end of the history reel, Henar's fur stood on end. He was ready to fly to Earth by himself and take every single human down singlehandedly. "Puny, puny humans," he cackled, rubbing his paws together. "Wait till you get a load of Kavii!"

He was about to begin another video when a beep at his door gave him pause. "Come," Henar requested, furry brows knitting into a frown.

The door slid open with a hiss. In came a dark-brown-furred Kavii female, slender in frame and sleek in fur. "Henar, you busy?" Selotho and Henar had gotten friendly since his exile to this new ship level. She shared his passion for the Benevolency and making a name for oneself through conquest.

Henar felt his whole body warm at the sight of her. "Rewatching Benevolency history footage," he replied. "The Stages of Conquest. Not sure if you want to watch—"

"Are you kidding?" Selotho scurried into the room and plopped down by Henar's side. "This one has seen those holovids like five times since the trip started!"

Henar gaped at her as if she had a third eye growing on her throat. "Six times," he said in awe. "Twice yesterday."

Selotho's face split into a grin that displayed pearly, needle-like teeth. "Stop bragging and let's start watching."

The video started with the Eight star and blade logo of the Benevolency and a voiceover. Soon, there appeared footage of an unsuspecting bipedal species on their world as the announcer spoke about a species that posed no threat to the Benevolency.

"This scenario is approached with five steps. Observance, Infiltration, Invitation, Occupation, Assimilation." Henar eagerly rocked back and forth on his haunches, even though he already knew what came next.

"Observe the new species to learn everything about them, their defenses and their weaknesses," the voice said, showing Kaviis in camouflage watching the generic bipedal races. "Infiltrate their society and co-opt their points of authority." The visuals now displayed more Kaviis on the move, fast and silent, sneaking into the bipedal species' halls of power.

"Invite the species to join the Benevolency willingly." The footage now displayed Kavii military and diplomatic liaisons speaking with the bipeds, all who trembled before the shorter but more powerful Kavii.

"If they agreed, then the Kavii would occupy their planet and set in place institutions to properly assimilate the new species into the Benevolency way of life." The footage switched to showing the biped species living peacefully like before, except their previous buildings and architecture had been replaced by the familiar rounded and woven Kavii structures, with rotund and bulbous-shaped Kavii military ships soaring overhead.

Selotho grabbed Henar's shoulders, startling him. He turned to see her eyes alight with anticipation. "Ooooh, here comes my favorite part."

"If the species made the mistake of refusing the Benevolency's bountiful rule," the voice took a darker edge, "then we commence with the invasion." Immediately, the images of bipeds and Kavii at peace were washed away by chaos, fire, and explosions. Kavii warships dominated the skies, turbolasers raining down death from on high to shred through the biped species' towering metal and glass buildings. "And if the species has any useful resources on their world, we occupy and subjugate!"

Henar felt electric. A glance at Selotho on his right revealed a similar look. Her presence was a welcome surprise.

The voiceover went on to the scenario of a species that presented a possible threat to the Benevolency. A species who had a sizeable military and occupied a chunk of the galaxy. The visual was a sea of black dotted with a million twinkling stars, brigades of starships facing each other. Flashes of fire streaking back and forth between the opposing forces. Brief and bright explosions devouring a number of ships before the vacuum snuffed their lights away.

For species that presented legitimate threats to the Benevolency, the stages of conquest were more direct: Observance, Invasion, Occupation.

Hostile species only received the gift of assimilation after the Benevolency completely occupied their planet, subjugated their species, and installed institutions to properly incorporate the new species into the Benevolency way of life.

The presentation ended. The floating holoscreen in front of Henar and Selotho winked out of existence. The two young Kavii soldiers sat, wide-eyed. Henar's blood scorched as if just winning a battle. Every time he watched those videos felt like the first time. Exciting. Exquisite. To serve the Benevolency was an honor. "That was..." Henar couldn't find adequate words to explicate his love for the government he served.

Selotho tore her eyes away from where the holoscreen once hovered and gaped at him, whiskers stick-straight. "By the Benevolency! That was LEGENDARY!"

Henar nodded slowly, dazed. "This one knows. A shot of inspiration and bliss."

Selotho's beady red eyes crawled all over him in ways that made Henar's blood sing. "Is it just this one?" she began almost shyly. "Or do watching war propaganda make you...aroused?"

Henar jerked around to face her fully. *Who is this wondrous female?* "You as well? This one just gets an overwhelming..." Heat flooded his face, throat, and chest while he struggled to find the correct word. Then the answer slapped him on the face. "Warlust."

Selotho brightened at the apropos description. "So much fervor and no worlds to conquer yet." Her expression turned devious. "Wanna burn off that warlust together?"

"Absolutely!" Henar pounced on her. And Selotho pounced right back.

Burning off all the fervor took some time that evening, during which Henar howled "LEGENDARYYYY!" more than once!

A few days later, the Benevolency warship finally arrived at Earth. They floated just out of planetary orbit, sensory scramblers blocking the humans' paltry satellites. Henar, Osefa, and Leakki stared out of a wall-length, transparent viewport at the large blue sphere that they soon would be conquering.

Henar wrinkled his nose, unimpressed. "This one almost feels bad," he admitted. "The humans have no idea what they are up against."

Osefa shrugged. "Do not feel so bad for these unevolved creatures. A few years after assimilation, they will be thanking the Benevolency for taking over their planet and upgrading their laughable excuse for technology."

Henar snorted in agreement.

"So true," Leakki chimed in, cocking his head sideways. "This one can't believe the humans do not have global ground transport?"

That made all three shudder in disgust. "It's like they still live in the prehistoric ages!" Osefa remarked.

A chime sounded, demanding Henar and his friends' attention. A shipwide message. Henar hoped it meant assignments for Observation were to be announced.

"Attention, brave warriors of the Benevolency," a firm voice boomed on the ship's communication systems. "As the Observance of the planet Earth begins, you may now access which area of the humans' culture and infrastructure you have been assigned to."

Henar looked to Osefa and Leakki, who looked at each other and him. Without a word, squeak, or yowl, the trio dashed down the sterile corridor for the nearest elevator.

They weren't alone in their fervor, resulting in massive corridor and elevator congestion. Luckily, Henar, Osefa and Leakki had made sure to stay within spitting distance of an elevator at all times, grabbing the first available one they saw.

After getting off on his ship level, Henar raced into the safety of his room and plopped in front of his personal console. The overeager Kavii logged in and checked his personal transmissions. His breath caught.

A new transmission sat at the top of his inbox. **Observance Placement.**

For a long moment, Henar just stared at the screen to preserve this moment in time. To hold on to the excitement as long as Kaviianly possible. He had dreamed of this moment since he was but a naive pup whose only wish was to join the Benevolency Military.

Open it already, Henar scolded himself. He pressed a paw finger on the screen to access the transmission.

His 50" viewscreen popped up with the Benevolency stars

and blade insignia. Henar ignored that and read down the Observance Division he had been assigned to.

Henar gaped, reading it again. And then a third time. "That can't be right."

According to the transmission, Henar was not to be assigned to observe Earth's political systems. Or their military services. Or even their manufacturing and mining sectors.

Henar read the transmission a fourth time, and the Kavii's heart skipped several beats.

"I got placed in Domestic??" Even saying the words was a knife thrust to the chest.

Domestic. aka The Domestic Living and Culture Surveillance. That meant Henar, despite his high scores in all things active combat and field assignments, would be stuck watching the humans in their natural habitat.

Most soldiers placed in Domestic on their first conquest usually could not achieve enough escape velocity to leave this kind of surveillance on future conquests for the Benevolency.

"Which means," Henar realized through clenched teeth. "This one's career is already a laughingstock before it even begins!"

CHAPTER 3

"You too?" Henar exclaimed when Osefa, Nele, and Leakki all met him for dinner that evening in the fourth-level dining hall.

"Yep," Osefa admitted glumly.

"Affirmative," Leakki added.

Nele looked so volcanically angry she couldn't even speak.

Henar, sitting next to her, warily scooted away. Barely a day since placement and he already could see the shift in other Kaviis' perception of him. This morning, Setholo stopped by Henar's quarters. She'd gotten placed in Military Surveillance. And by the gleam in her beady eyes, she clearly wanted to partake in some "legendary" celebrating.

"Where did you get placed?" she inquired.

With great reluctance, Henar told her.

Setholo's expression instantly soured. "Best of luck, then, Henar," she replied stiffly, and scurried away so fast, she practically left clouds of dust in her wake. No more legendary copulation for Henar.

"Whatever," Leakki hissed bitterly. "You can find better sows than that superficial space for brains."

Osefa nodded in agreement. Nele just grunted and stared at her empty plate.

"How could this be?" Leakki wondered aloud, distractedly eating another pawful of stuffed greens from his plate. "All of us did so well in the academy and with training aboard the ship. Placement in Domestic for all four of us?"

That did strike Henar as odd. *Almost as if—*

Hoots of laughter burst out from behind him. Cruel, familiar laughter. Eyes narrowing, he turned.

Atiga sat two tables away, holding court with a large group

of lackeys including Kamai, Akko, and Setholo. All of them had been placed into Military Surveillance. Atiga pointed his paws at Henar with a smirk, saying something just out of earshot. The whole group glanced over and roared with amusement.

Henar felt his insides clench as recognition crashed into him. "Atiga did this to us," he murmured just loud enough for his three friends to hear.

Nele whipped her head around at Henar. "WHAT?" Her voice was like a swift slap.

Osefa's whiskers wilted. "That one made a call to his father," the shaggy-haired Kavii realized.

"Who then spoke with this mission's senior personnel," Leakki added.

Nele shot up from her seat. "This one will castrate Atiga with my teeth!"

She just might have if Henar hadn't caught her by the arm. "And what good will that do us?"

"It will make this one feel better," she threw back, struggling against his grip.

As more laughter washed over Henar and his friends, he had half a mind to let Nele go. Seeing her kick Atiga's behind would be a pleasure to witness. *And then what?* Another demotion no doubt. The realization curdled his taste for payback.

"Not happening...as amazing as that fight would be," Henar growled, and forced the enraged Kavii back down. "All we can do is make the best of a bad situation. Excel in Domestic Surveillance and achieve the escape velocity needed to switch to divisions with more prestige." Domestic placement would not be a death sentence for his career. Henar refused to surrender after all his hard work.

None of his friends shared the same drive. Even Nele, despite her previous fire, seemed deflated.

"You make that sound simple," Osefa snorted in bitterness.

Leakki was the one now quivering in rage. "Name one soldier placed in Domestic Surveillance that has risen high in the Benevolency's Armed Forces? One!"

Henar opened his lips to answer. "Of course there's..." He thought long and hard. He could think of no soldiers initially placed in Domestic who rose higher in their military careers.

A pang of hopelessness spasmed through his frame. Henar moved his plate away and slumped forward, his forehead smacking the table in front of him. "Our careers have been plutoed, haven't they?"

"Yes," Leakki, Nele, and Osefa all said at once, as more mocking laughter from Atiga and his crew collided into them.

Domestic Surveillance training was extensive, and soul-crushing. Surprisingly though, Henar felt the two weeks moved at lightspeed. Small mercies in a future that seemingly had so few. The kind of Kavii placed in Domestic were not ambitious...or physically fit. These Kavii all leaned more toward the doughy side, too laissez faire for Henar to handle them in anything beyond small doses.

Henar tried to keep an upbeat attitude, which wasn't easy. The planet Earth was his first conquest. Some Kavii never got to leave Benevolency Space, let alone their own planets.

"We're fortunate, my friends!" he urged his friends once at breakfast. His encouragement was met with sullen silence and a death glare from Nele. So Henar stopped...for fear of being castrated by his friend's teeth.

The day finally came to descend onto Earth. Henar felt a jolt through his spine. Osefa, Nele, and Leakki regained a modicum of enthusiasm knowing that they would be touching down on a brand-new, non-Benevolency world for the first time in their young lives.

The drop teams numbered 250 strong: fifty soldiers would observe Earth's many military services, fifty would observe the political systems of the most powerful nations, fifty to observe their manufacturing industries, fifty to observe their cultivation of natural resources, and fifty to observe their domestic living of Earth's citizens.

Each soldier received a single seed-shaped dropship, replete with food and liquids to last two weeks. They also received mission instructions and locations.

The fifty-strong team stood before two scrawny and short-haired Kavii, their commanding officers for Domestic Surveillance. Both Kaviis' overeagerness this early in the day seemed enhanced by narcotics, in Henar's honest opinion.

"You are a part of seeing how these humans live, what their habits are," the male known as Goab boomed, showing white and needle-like teeth.

"What their vices are," the female by his side added.

"What cultural mores bind them, and can break them!" The male curled his paws into fists, shaking them zealously. He cast a sweeping gaze over the assembly before him, eyes alight with mania. *Definitely narcotics*, Henar realized.

"Many may disregard your position. Consider you on the lower spectrum because you were placed on Domestic Surveillance," the female continued with similar fervor. "But consider this. After a planet is conquered, rebellions and seditions can spring forth in even the most modest homes of our unenlightened subjects. It has happened in many of these Earth countries we now seek to subvert. The data you will gather will help the Glorious Benevolency bend these pack of unevolved humans to the Kavii's will. Domestic. Is. No. JOKE!" she roared. Everyone jumped, even her fellow commanding officer.

"Is that one trying to convince us or herself?" Osefa muttered to Henar, who had to swallow a guffaw.

After they finished ranting some more, the fifty Benevolency soldiers headed to the flight bays.

"You know," Nele considered as each soldier readied to enter their dropship, "they have points. We will be the key to stabilizing Earth after the militaries and ruling governments are immobilized."

"She's right," Henar added. He caught a look at the Military Surveillance at the other end of this flight bay. Seeing their proud marches and boisterous shouts pained the young Kavii in his very bones. He tore his eyes away and focused on his three friends.

Leakki remained bitter and dubious. "But who will remember our glory? Who will remember our sacrifice? Those who ascend in the Benevolency Military are those who aid in toppling governments and armies. We are conquering *households*."

Henar was about to reply when his turn was up. He stepped into the launch chamber of his dropship. As the doors closed behind him, warm red light bathed the Kavii's fur. The confines were tight but large enough for him to move around and sit. Once seated and strapped in, the consoles across the chamber lit up. He saw the assignment before him. And the location.

"San Francisco, California State, United States of America," Henar repeated out loud. Spools of data to absorb scrawled next to the location, along with all kinds of images and audiovisual footage of this city.

"ENGAGE!" a voice boomed, startling him. A low hum in the background, the dropship engine, shuddered through the vessel.

A moment later, Henar felt weightless. The low hum became a steady, distant roar. The young Kavii's heart leaped into his throat as he realized what just happened. "This one's mission to help conquer Earth has just begun!"

Much later, Henar stepped out from his dropship into a whole new world.

The lush earth was covered in shrubbery and dark, loamy soil. He looked up. And kept looking up. And kept looking up.

Colossal sentinels covered in red bark towered over him, reaching up into the skies and possibly beyond. Their width alone was stunning. Henar never felt so diminutive in his life. He heard the sounds and calls of the local fauna from every corner of this "forest" around him.

"The humans can't be that bad if they grow flora such as this," Henar considered. "We will order them to grow more all over their planet!" He tapped a few buttons on a side console of his dull grey dropship and the vessel vanished. InvisiCloak technology would shroud his vessel from sight, smell, touch, and sound. Only Henar's wrist computer could locate the dropship when time came to return to the main Benevolency mothership.

"Now," he said with a grin that showed sharp teeth. "Time to start observing." From what his wrist console told him, he was in a forest known as Muir Woods Forest north of San Francisco. Not landing in the city assigned to him annoyed Henar for an instant. However, he would have missed this visual around him. Peaceful. Exquisite.

A length of time, or an hour in human temporal measurements, passed before Henar finally emerged from this forest of colossal trees. And sitting before him was a fine, pale swath of powdery rock. Henar remembered those were called beaches, heralds to one of Earth's water oceans. Waves lapped up against the edge of the powdery rock only to recede back, rush forward, and then recede back. A far-off roar emanated from the rippling oceans, soothing like the sound of a spaceship in flight.

The oceans beyond the beach went on and on. Earth's sun had already passed its zenith, sinking toward the ocean, casting an orange glow over the waves and the beach.

In the distance on either side, Henar spied far-flung silhouettes of civilization— lofty structures and bridges connecting nearby islands to the mainland. That was where Henar needed to be. Humans in their natural habitat was his mission. Something in that city would lift Henar out from the potential career-killer that was Domestic Surveillance. He could feel it from head to toe.

Henar reached for his wrist console to plot a teleportation course from his current location to San Francisco's city center. Then he froze.

The beach was not empty.

Two humans.

Tall, long-legged and hairless except for their heads. Henar still couldn't figure out how they didn't freeze to death.

The humans, an adult male and female, were obviously a couple. They lay horizontally and unmoving on the beach, swaddled in blankets and each other as they slept.

Henar's heart leaped. Finding a planet's native species and observing them in their natural habitat? He moved to step forward. Until his eyes landed on the dog.

Henar almost missed the enslaved canine altogether, lying on the other side of its human slavemasters. The poor beast, covered in shaggy golden fur, was facing the beach. Wearing a collar and leash.

Henar's joy soured. His loathing for Earth's residents returned with a vengeance. Right, this species enslaved those considered of lesser intelligence and economical value. "Don't fall too in love with this world," the Kavii reminded himself. Time for some quick reconnaissance. Henar tapped on his console again, skimming through a library of high-pitched noises only a domesticated canine could hear.

After selecting a high whistle of noise, Henar activated. The whine started like a distance, near inaudible call.

The canine's floppy ears immediately perked up.

Henar upped the intensity. The dog raised its head and turned in his direction.

The Kavii smiled. *Come here, canine, and get your freedom.* He upped the intensity again.

The dog jerked up to its feet and barked. Its human slave masters were jolted awake by the noise.

Henar swore. If the humans were roused, then this plan would go sideways. The Kavii kept making the noise more intense, higher in pitch.

And the dog rocketed in his direction, barking like crazy.

The humans, fully awakened, lurched up, calling out after the canine escaping their control.

Henar stood and waited as the canine pounded across the sand, leaving powdery clouds in its wake. The humans were running after their escaped slave, too far away to grab the leash trailing after the canine.

The dog made to pounce, teeth bared, paws raised. And Henar hurtled forward, burying a shoulder into the dog's midsection that drove the air from its belly in a surprised yelp. Just as quickly, he activated his personal invisiCloak.

By the time both he and the canine landed and rolled about the ground, they were invisible and inaudible to any other beings, including the human slavers.

The dog, eager and ferocious in mood, was three to four times heavier than Henar, But the Kavii, quicker, stronger, skilled in combat, and all in all smarter, easily flipped the brazen beast on its back.

The canine thrashed and howled, but Henar had it immobilized by twisting its front paws with his own feet. The human owners dashed past their former slave, yelling out whatever inane pet name they had for it. Their weak senses were unable to see through Henar's invisiCloak.

Good, he realized, typing into his utility belt to find a translator to understand and reply to this dog's barking language. It took little time.

"Stop. Fighting. Me!" Henar barked back in the dog's own barbaric yapping. "This one is trying to help you!"

The canine stopped, stared with dull brown eyes, and yapped louder. "Let me go, you crazy guinea pig. Or I will bite your head off. Master. MASTER!!!"

The humans would never hear him, even if the invisiCloak was off. They had already traveled far into the giant forest.

Henar shook his furry head, leaned down, and backhanded the shaggy ingrate across the muzzle. "This one is trying to free you from your imprisonment, you brainless brute." The Kavii got right in the canine's face. "You will no longer be a slave to the humans. All this one requires is information on their ways. Their habits. How they eat. How they sleep. How they defecate. How they contribute to the overall Earth society."

The canine stopped, stared with dull brown eyes, and let out rapid-fire howling that sounded like laughter.

Henar jumped off the canine and watched it roll back and

forth, explosively guffawing now. "This one isn't joking," the Kavii repeated. His patience had all but expired. *Better place an ultimatum.* That would sober this yowling cretin. "If you do not tell this one the requested data, then you will be sent back to those humans who—"

"You MORON," the canine barked, rising to a seated posture. He towered over Henar. "You think I'm enslaved to those two??" He nodded his muzzle in the direction his human owners ran. "Are you kidding??"

Henar blinked in confusion. "They have you on a leash and a collar. How else would you define being another's slave?"

The canine yowl-laughed again. "You furry little fool. I *own* those humans. They feed me almost anything I want, buy me toys, clean up my poop and piss, give me belly rubs, groom my fur. Plus, they take me on walks. They do everything and anything I need. Why would I want to ruin that?"

Henar was lost. "Wait...humans are enslaved to you canines?"

The golden-furred dog rocked on its hind haunches. "Some other dogs' situations aren't as good as mine, but the majority are as decent or better. You have to be from another planet not to know that."

The jab stung. Henar fumed and swiped a paw at his face. The dog howled in pain and staggered. "Why did you do that?"

"Because!" Just as quickly, the Kavii dropped the invisiCloak and then reactivated—without the dumb canine.

Early the next day, Henar received a group transmission from Osefa, Nele, and Leakki. Henar, who'd spent the rest of yesterday researching the canine's claims, remained silent while his friends all launched into grievance sessions over their respective Domestic Surveillance assignments.

The Kavii barely heard their many complaints about the mundane lives of humans in what was called 'suburbia." Nele was disappointed by the amount of women who stood by while their partners took all the glory and the financial earnings.

Leakki knew more about human cuisine than he cared to.

Osefa hated everyone. Domestic surveillance had killed his love for anything remotely engaging.

Henar barely paid attention. What he had learned swirled in his thoughts, coalescing from roiling shock into something potentially useful. Henar wasn't sure yet.

So caught up was the Kavii in his thoughts that Nele had to

call his name twice.

"Yes?" he asked distractedly.

"Talk about having your head in the stars," the female Kavii snarked. "How is your surveillance going?"

With his three closest friends in the galaxy staring back on the large holoscreen inside his dropship, Henar stiffened. He opened his maw to utter a feeble lie about watching humans walk their dogs all day.

In that instant, the shock and chaos in Henar's brain crashed together. As if Henar could see colors where only black and white once existed. His maw curled into a devious smile, to the surprise of his friends. "Fellow Kaviis," he announced, all his fears shedding like a cloak. "This one might have found something that will change our ill fortunes."

CHAPTER 4

"Surely you quip, Ensign," Johonek said. The older Kavii, one of the commanding officers for the Benevolency forces stationed around Earth, sat behind his half-circle. Johonek was a regal picture of sleek sable fur in his blood-red military regalia.

He was also the picture of confusion and anger. "You are asking the Benevolency to reconfigure its entire military strategy for Earth...because of your hunch?"

Henar's insides quivered in fear, despite him appearing unwavering on the outside. Currently the young Kavii officer stood in Commandant Johonek's ready room, small but comfortable and splashed in warm colors. The walls were covered in framed photos of his various conquests, along with souvenirs from each world he had assisted in conquering. "This one knows that the request sounds rather...unorthodox—"

"*Unorthodox* would be the mild description," Johonek cut in. He rose from his seat behind his half-circle-shaped desk. "Your request not only is impossible. It is the height of lunacy! Delay a Conquest...ha!" The commander actually chuckled, his large frame shaking with mirth.

Henar clenched his jaw, reminding himself to not blame Johonek whatsoever for his reaction. If the roles were reversed, how would he react to a lowly soldier questioning a conquest methodology unmatched for close to one thousand years?

But after a week of surveillance with Osefa, Leakki, and Nele, now Henar was more convinced than ever his vision would work. Also, if this helped elevate him and his friends from the purgatory that was Domestic Surveillance, all the better.

"If this one's request had no merit," Henar continued after

Johonek's mirth had subsided, "why would my two superior officers have felt strongly enough to get this one in the same room as you?" Actually, he had told his direct supervisor and then his supervisor's superior fragments of his plan. No way would he tell them everything and have those two steal his idea. That way, Johonek would have to hear the whole strategy from Henar himself. "Clearly they believe this one has a plan you would want to hear."

That gave Johonek pause, only for a moment. He stared back at Henar with narrowed and dismissive eyes. "You think you're the first brash, know-it-all officer that believes they know better than the will of the Benevolency?"

Henar shook his head. "This one never said that. This one lives to serve the Benevolency."

"As long as it serves you as well." Johonek scoffed and picked at his whiskers. He rounded his desk and stood face to face with Henar, noticeably taller. "This one read your file, and knows you had ambitions to join Military or Political Surveillance. Your motives are transparent, pup."

Henar felt a knee-jerk impulse to lie and plead he only wished to serve the Benevolency. But at this point, why bother? Johonek would probably see through that.

"This one will not lie, sir," the young Kavii began, shrugging. "Of course this one desired better placement than what was given. But this is different. This one sees an opportunity to conquer Earth with minimal bloodshed while retaining its main population in service to the Benevolency."

Johonek marched back to his desk. He looked unyielding still, opening his mouth to no doubt order Henar away.

"All that is required is a small portion of your time, sir. Please," Henar almost pleaded, but fought the urge to get on his haunches like some submissive from a pleasure house. "If you have no interest still, then at least you will have heard another strategy of conquest. One you will get all the credit for."

No way could Johonek refuse that offer. Sitting back down in his chair, the Kavii commandant steepled his front paws together. "Proceed," he ordered, stern and stone-faced.

Henar could barely contain his nerves as he whipped out a small, coppery holosphere as part of his presentation.

The small portion of time he requested lasted a while. Henar had included stacks upon stacks of footage from his exhaustive research of humans' pets, the love they received. How they were treated better than the humans who supposedly "owned" them. Henar showcased footage from the first dog he tried to "liberate" in Muir Woods, how the humans cried and hugged their pet with such effusive affection after finding him again. There was footage of parks in the rolling hills of San Francisco devoted just to humans and a plethora of dogs loping about the grass like grinning idiots.

More footage came from Osefa, Leakki, and Nele, all who included pet surveillance in their Domestic footage.

"Cats," Henar explained on feline creatures much smaller than a Kavii, "are as popular as dogs all around Earth." He pointed at the massive holo projected from his holosphere of a cat on his haunches, snow-white and shaggy-haired with probing and curious blue eyes. "Their circumstances allow them more freedom and autonomy than dogs. They can disappear for long periods of time. As long as they show up to get fed, receive the occasional snuggle from their humans. And that does not even begin to cover the other kinds of pets that humans debased themselves for—"

Johonek's stony expression began to show cracks. "By the stars above," he murmured.

Henar decided against any detailed explanations about any rodent-like pets, given that many spent the majority of their lives in cages or glass prisons. That would have killed Johonek's interest in his request. Instead, Henar focused on cats and dogs, particular images and footage of the powerful world leaders who "owned" them.

With a wave of his paws, all the images of the head of the English Monarchy with those ridiculously looking short-legged dogs vanished from sight. "Any questions?"

"This one assumes," Johonek said after Henar completed his presentation, "that all this has some relevance to military strategy."

Henar allowed himself a smile. "We install a Kavii soldier or political operative in as many households as possible, starting with Earth's most powerful leaders and its most powerful countries." Henar referred to his holosphere once more and conjured a world map of Earth. Seven countries were highlighted in red. "The United States, China, India, the UK, Germany, Japan, and Russia are seven of the world's wealthiest and most powerful nations. The United States' media reach alone dwarfs that of these six other nations combined." Henar faced this superior officer with all his trinkets of conquest. One day he would be in a similar position, and it all started here. "Have enough of Kavii live with American media influencers and the rest of the world will follow like the pawns they are. All the while, we still make to disable Earth's military and political systems while getting unfettered access to their leaders."

After that, Johonek stared at him in silence...

...and stared...

Henar grew nervous under such unyielding eyes. But the young Kavii soldier knew deep down this was the most important stare down of his entire existence. *If this one looks away, he will feel my cause is weak.* Despite the growing awkwardness, Henar kept staring.

"How do you know this will work?" Johonek finally asked.

"This one does not know one hundred percent for sure," Henar answered honestly. "But this one knows most humans love their pets, treat them exceedingly well and would do anything for them. Which is why this one asks to give me and three of my friends a week to infiltrate four humans' households in different parts of Earth." He waited again as the senior officer pondered the request. Never had Henar been more nervous, heart thudding so loud he swore Johonek could hear.

The older Kavii rose to his feet, spreading his paws out disarmingly. "You get a week and only one other Kavii soldier of my choosing. You will meet on Earth's surface in two days' time."

Henar almost protested the disregard of Osefa, Leakki, and Nele. Almost.

But the young, eager soldier caught himself just in time. No need to push his already plentiful luck. "Thank you, sir," he replied instead, nodding and then saluting. "This will be the right and best course. This one promises you."

Johonek frowned. "Do not promise anything, Soldier," he snapped in iron tones. "Deliver results."

The meeting concluded shortly after, and Henar exited the ready room as if floating on air.

Afterward, Nele and the others were ecstatic when he told them about the meeting, even though they had been excluded.

"When your plan succeeds," Leakki said, clapping his shoulders with both paws, "the whole Domestic Surveillance division will benefit."

"And our military careers might be saved!" Osefa added with a smile.

Nele's eyes narrowed. "Did he say whom you would be teamed with?"

Henar shook his head. "He said the soldier was already on Earth's surface and would be of his choosing." He was too shocked and happy to worry about the details.

Two days flew by far too quickly. But during that time, many Kavii aboard their vessel had grown impatient over the lack of movement after most divisions had completed their reconnaissance. Questions rippled through every level of the ship.

What was the holdup? Was the Benevolency still conquering Earth?

How soon until the Benevolency banned that hideous, mind-shattering pop music after the conquest?

Henar, while in favor of the last question, said nothing. A huge part of him ached to brag to those who had mocked his placement in Domestic Surveillance. Revenge like that would be sweeter than sex with Setholo had been.

"Success is the best kind of revenge," his parents had always told him. And sometimes, success meant silence before the strike. He repeated his mantra another five times. Then a sixth. He got halfway through the seventh repetition before feeling semi-satisfied. So Henar said nothing to anyone else up to the day of his departure.

The dropship had the landing coordinates near the locations of the soldier he would be teaming with: Moldof from Military Surveillance. The holo image of his profile revealed a wiry Kavii male with snow-white fur and a few black spots around his neck and belly. A normal-looking and physically fit Kavii.

As the red glow of entry through Earth's atmosphere lit up his dropship's viewports, Henar looked down at the blue and green sphere floating in the black with headshaking contempt. Earth's terrible satellite detectors missing countless Kavii dropships coming in and out of the planet felt galling to Henar. Much later, his dropship landed just outside of a row of domestic homes nestled between rolls of greenish land. The location was some offshoot city connected to the megapolis the humans called Portland, Oregon, United States of America. The small silhouettes of Portland's downtown skyline were tattooed against the warm morning skies even this far off.

Henar exited his dropship, invisiCloaked it, and took a long look at his new surroundings. The near identical houses sent a chill down his spine. Like whenever he watched a colonization astro-horror film. Shaking his head to focus, the young Kavii soldier tapped his wristcom, bringing up a small floating holo to pinpoint Moldof's location.

"Four point three Earth miles west," the wristcom announced.

Henar smiled and loped off on all fours toward the direction of his partner. The air was crisp and cool but tasted of moisture, like it was about to rain. Every Benevolency world had weather-control satellites. Henar wrinkled his nose and ran faster. "Earth has no control over its weather patterns?" he snorted. "The Benevolency will correct that."

He reached Moldof's location a little later, some sewer system outside of the small city. "Moldof?" the Kavii asked on his wristcom. "This one is at the spot. Please reply."

Static.

Henar frowned and tried contact again. No answer. "That's odd." Moldoff and him had spoken several times before he'd landed on Earth, the former always answering immediately.

Now Henar stood within the dank opening in a jut of rock leading into the sewer system. The location scan on his wristcom said Moldof was present half a mile into this tunnel. Henar now called out Moldof's name as he slinked into the shadows, stepping through puddles of grime.

Half an hour later, he reached Moldof's location. Correction, he reached the location of Moldof's wristcom...

...still attached to his severed forepaw. Henar's eyes bulged. "What the—"

The bright yellow flash lit up the tunnel from behind Henar.

Intense and immediate pain seared straight through his fur, then skin, knocking the Kavii clean off his feet.

Suddenly, Henar found himself face down in mucky water, the entire right side of his body on fire.

Against his better judgement, Henar had opted not to wear any armor besides the lightest of protection. The young Kavii had expected no attack, let alone any detection from Earth's so-called defenses. As pain scorched through him, he wanted to kick himself for such an oversight.

He spat out filthy sewage, brain trying to wrap around what just happened. His vision swam with wild, garish colors as he forced himself onto his back. *A posture of submission,* Henar realized in regret. But he had to face whoever had taken out Moldoff and attacked him.

His drooping eyes squinted in disbelief, then horror. "Y—you?"

"As fine a soldier as Moldof was," a familiar, sneering voice oozed from the darkness. "That one was such a braggart. And a brainless dolt. Especially when drunk. Talking about how you and he may have found a way to take over Earth without any overt military force."

Atiga stepped out of the shadows, a mountain of muscle dressed in Benevolency military fatigues. He pointed a silvery blaster gun in one paw at Henar. His expression was a study in cold malice. "This one will be draped in the glory of true conquest. This one will be my father's son in all the ways of our radiant Benevolency. And if that means you and Moldof are to be martyrs killed by the barbaric humans, then so be it."

Martyrs. Henar stared up at Atiga's triumphant gaze and the muzzle of the blaster in his hand. Dawning recognition was a cold knife thrust to his gut. "You killed Moldof." Now he planned to do the same to Henar.

Atiga shrugged. "This one did. Moldof screamed like a female pup in need of succor when this one vaporized him." He shook his shaggy head. "Correction...when the humans killed him."

Henar's right flank screamed in agony, so running away was not an option. And in his current condition, Atiga would make short work of him in a fight.

Meaning, Henar realized to his pained horror, *this one is finished.* "You hate me that much? That you would kill fellow Benevolency soldiers to get ahead? And lie about the cause of death?"

Atiga's smile never reached his eyes. "Killing you has nothing to do with that...and everything to do with you standing in this one's way." The muzzle of Atiga's blaster began glowing, about to discharge in Henar's face.

CHAPTER 5

"Goodbye, Henar," Atiga said. The smile playing across the Kavii's muzzle lit up his eyes as much as the golden burn from his blaster's business end. "Your and Moldof's deaths will ensure that Earth is conquered properly." His thumb started to squeeze the trigger. "Take pleasure in that before you—"

A loud clap of noise from outside startled both Atiga and Henar. The latter cringed, the sudden motion reigniting his wounds.

Atiga whirled around, eyes wide with panic, lighting up the darkness with a spray of blaster fire. "What in the five hells!"

Henar gaped as Atiga turned away. An opening. Brief, but welcome. Mind clouded by pain, he reached for his own blaster in his utility belt.

Atiga returned focus to Henar, who had taken aim with a shaky arm. The mistake landed on the other Kavii's face as he snapped his arm up to fire.

Despite his injuries, Henar shot faster.

Golden fire lit up the tunnel again. The blaster bolt missed Atiga's head, lancing instead through his neck with a grisly sizzle.

The traitorous Kavii sank to his knees, eyes wide in shock as both arms dropped to his sides limply. Atiga's blaster fell from dead fingers, splashing in the murky puddles around them. He faceplanted then into the same pool with a bigger splish-splash.

Henar pulled up to the side of the rounded tunnel, clenching his teeth the entire time. His right leg and side shrieked, causing tears to run down his cheeks. He stared at Atiga's body. He felt no remorse, no pity. Only sadness over his fellow officer's brainless and selfish betrayal. Atiga had him, could have killed him. But the fool with his three working brain cells had to parade his victory in Henar's face like it was a done deal.

"Shouldn't have monologued, Atiga," Henar said, his words laced with anguish. "Monologues are for the victors of battle, not pampered scions who've never won a battle without their father's help."

Two successive claps from outside shuddered through the tunnel, rumbling off into the distance. Henar jerked his head around in shock before recognizing the source. The rumble of thunder sounded from a distant, approaching storm.

"Saved by Earth's lack of weather control." The Kavii smiled at the irony, despite his pain. He gave brief thanks to this backward planet's shortcomings.

A thunderclap, however, could not heal Henar's nasty injuries. The Kavii could smell the stinking flesh and charred fur without even turning his head. He could have gone his whole life without ever looking at the extent of these injuries.

But Henar was a soldier of the Kavii Benevolency. He had been given a chance to leave a stamp in history, serve his government in ways most in his nascent career could not have even dreamed. One stinky injury from a traitorous soldier would not stop Henar in his tracks.

He looked to his right side. "Oh my stars and comets!" The Kavii's stomach twisted up in nausea. The fur from just under the armpit to above the hip had been scorched off, leaving blackened flesh pockmarked and knotted.

Henar turned away and vomited. Yep, he had been stopped in his tracks. "Unless I get medical attention…" He pushed up on hind legs, trying to shake off the dizziness.

First things first, vaporize Atiga's body. No dead Kavii body should ever be discovered on an unconquered planet. The results would be catastrophic.

Spots danced before his eyes as he pulled out a disintegrator cube, typed in a short radius, and tossed it at Atiga's corpse. One bright red flash later and the Kavii's body disappeared, vaporized into subatomic particles undetectable to human technology. Moldof's paw was thankfully caught in the blast radius, as Henar felt too wrecked to even bother dealing with that.

"Now…" Henar stated as he began moving forward. "The injuries…before this one passes out." Every step caused electric jolts of agony to shoot up and down his right thigh. He nearly collapsed right there. Only the slick sides of the tunnel kept him upright.

"Blaster salve," he grunted, pulling out yet another item from his utility belt. This item was a sizeable flexible tube of paste to begin healing wounds from blaster fire depending on the severity. Part of him wondered how so many items fit in this belt, but new shoots of pain shifted any attention back on his wounds. After slathering some of the neon orange paste up and down his right side and hip, the pain immediately dissipated into a dull ache. He breathed in several deep breaths as his vision began returning to normal and the dull ache lessened even more.

"Now...back to finishing the mission." Aborting this assignment had never crossed Henar's thoughts. Not once. He was a proud soldier of the Benevolency and would complete what had been assigned to him.

And most importantly...reporting back all the chaos that had consumed his mission before it had started would cause the Benevolency to end things straightaway. Even with proof of Atiga's attempt on his life and murder of Moldof, the Kavii knew the consensus would be to just go back to the original plan of conquest.

Meaning, no ascension beyond Domestic Surveillance. Henar winced. "This one would rather Atiga have killed me," he murmured.

But if help could not come from the Benevolency, then who else could Henar turn to? Unfortunately, Osefa, Leakki, and Nele were back on the ship. Henar knew they would give their lives for him. He also knew all private and military-related communications coming to and from the *Dominator*-class vessel would be monitored.

Henar was on his own. He cursed Atiga and his vile family from root to branch and pushed off the tunnel. The only sensible action right now was to head back to his dropship and mentally regroup while the blaster salve did its magic.

The determined Kavii then began limping back to the mouth of the sewer tunnel. Those few miles through hills back to the dropship felt like light-years away now.

Henar had just turned a corner when two voices stopped him cold. Two familiar, grunting Kavii voices.

Akko and Kamai. A peek around the winding corner confirmed what his ears heard. Yep, Henar would have recognized the silhouettes of those two hulking meat puppets anywhere. They paced back and forth at the head of the tunnel, sounding bored.

Henar bit down more curses and dove behind a rounded corner. Of course Atiga had brought these musclebound space-brains in on his assassin job.

"Why do these hairless humans call those noises thunderclaps?" Kamai asked, legitimately annoyed. "Sounds more like 'thunder rumbles' if you ask this one."

"Maybe there are creatures in the skies called 'thunders' that clap," Akko replied, as if he was an expert on the subject. "And their claps are so loud, they sound like rumbles."

Kamai didn't seem to be satisfied by that answer. "Then wouldn't a thunder have been catalogued in the database of Earth's fauna?"

"What if they haven't located one?" Akko asked with a gasp. "We could be the first beings to locate an actual thunder!"

"But..." Kamai interjected. "We have to wait until Atiga has completed whatever his scouting survey with Moldof and Henar was. Until then, you and this one are to guard this tunnel's mouth."

Surprise crackled up Henar's spine. *They don't know what Atiga did to Moldof,* he realized. No doubt they were clueless as to what Atiga had planned for Henar.

A booming clap of thunder interrupted, causing Akko and Kamai to jump.

"Another one!" Akko yelped.

"After the Benevolency conquers Earth," Kamai gushed, breathless and eager like a pup, "we hunt for thunders!"

While Akko and Kamai continued their epic intellectual debate, Henar squatted in the sewer muck, running down the ways to engage this new obstacle.

A straight-up fight was out of the question. Even at full strength, Henar knew he could not match these two behemoths whose ungodly strength more than compensated for their combined black hole of wits.

A sneak attack where he blasted Akko and Kamai to oblivion would do best. Then Henar's mind flashed back to Atiga; the energy bolt shredding through his neck, the wound's charred stink, the life fleeing from Atiga's face as he slumped to the ground. Henar's first military kill... Then there was poor Moldof, an innocent soldier whose dedication to the

Benevolency was as strong as Henar's. His only mistake was becoming another victim of Atiga's toxic entitlement. Had he known terror in the moments before Atiga murdered him? Had he fought with every fiber in his furry body with his life on the line? Or had that entitled (and now dead) coward Atiga sneak-attacked him too? Probably the latter.

Henar suddenly felt nauseous. Horrible as Atiga was, he had been a fellow Kavii in service to the Benevolency.

Correction...in service to himself, Henar amended. Regardless, killing another Kavii that he should be standing shoulder to shoulder with felt wrong.

"No more killing other Kavii," he told himself. Besides, Henar had used his only disintegrator bomb on Atiga's traitorous corpse.

The solution struck him then: sneak past with invisiCloak. He scolded himself for forgetting such a simple counter. Tapping on his wristcom, Henar could feel the cloaking energy field envelop his entire being. A couple flickers rippled through the field before it stabilized.

Then Henar emerged from his hiding spot and snuck forward. Akko and Kamai's eyes were locked on the overcast skies beyond the tunnel. By the stars, these Kavii had no right to be so HUGE, furry mountains of muscle. Henar sucked down another gulp of breath and kept creeping forward. A limp still hindered his movements as he moved, but the pain was barely noticeable thanks to the salve.

Henar now stood right behind Kamai and Akko, close enough to reach out and touch.

His heart thundered against his chest, loud enough to echo off the sewer tunnels. Henar felt relief.

Almost there. He moved past his two fellow Kavii soldiers.

A popping fizzle startled Henar, but not enough to stop his movement through the tunnel exit.

Kamai turned and looked directly at Henar. His eyes widened. "What the—!"

That grabbed Akko's attention. He jumped back in surprise. "Henar!"

Henar froze. *They can see this one?* Which meant his invisiCloak had been damaged.

The three Kavii stared at each other in silence. Henar's heart leaped into his throat, unsure whether to run or grab his blaster.

Akko and Kamai decided for him, clawing for their weapons.

Henar bolted off for the nearest thick clump of grass. Knives of pain shot up his right side. But staying still meant death. He pushed off his left leg, diving behind the thick brush. Bright flashes of blaster fire shredded up loamy earth he had just stood on.

Drawing his own weapon, he set it to stun and rolled about to the next bush of grass.

"HEY!" Henar called from behind his hiding place, streaks of blaster fire scorching past the grass stalks. "Why are you shooting?"

"Why did you run?" Akko bellowed back with a hailstorm of blaster fire.

"Because!" Henar popped up from his hiding spot, blaster cocked, spraying a volley at Akko and Kamai. "This one thought you'd try to shoot on sight!"

Both behemoths wisely dove for cover within the sewer tunnel.

Kamai answered first with a return salvo that would have scorched Henar's head off had he not ducked. "Our blasters are set to stun!" he hollered, as if that statement rationalized their aggression.

"We thought you found out that Atiga had captured Moldof," Akko added. His attacks burned like comets out of the dark, shredding Henar's meager hiding spot apart. "That one told us to stop anyone from finding out!"

So Akko and Kamai weren't trying to kill him. Henar found that sparsely reassuring as he scrambled from his destroyed cover on all fours. "Did he also tell you about killing Moldof?" He squeezed off a trio of shots as he dashed behind another thick clump of grass and shrubbery.

"What?!" Kamai sounded surprised amid the blaster fire scorching back and forth. "No!"

"We captured him," Akko added, peeking out of the tunnel, only to duck from a stray blast from Henar, "so Atiga could talk some sense into him about your dumb conquest plan for Earth."

The dig on his plan boiled through Henar.

He popped up. "First off, my conquest plan is NOT dumb," he cried, a blaster shot punctuating each word. Henar ducked as Akko and Kamai retaliated with a flurry of shots. "Secondly...Atiga killed Moldof...and tried to kill this one!"

That caused Kamai on the left side to stop shooting. "You're lying!" he snapped.

Henar popped upright, juking left to evade return fire, and squeezed off half a dozen blazing rounds of his own. "Have you ever known this one to lie? About anything?" The Kavii ducked back down and waited.

"No!" Akko fired back, with his anger and his blaster.

More shots sheered through more shrubbery in Henar's hideout, leaving another tattered ruin of flora.

The sight chilled him, realizing how exposed they were. Even worse, Atiga's awfulness was turning Kavii against Kavii. The epiphany cratered his stomach enough to stop shooting. "Wait. Let's stop shooting at each other and talk like rational Kavii! If a human came across this..."

That finally stopped the stream of blaster fire from the sewer tunnel.

Henar holstered his blaster and stepped out into the open, paws held high in the air. Surrounding him were rings of burnt and destroyed plant life. Foreign beauty ruined by Kavii violence. *Who are the savages now?*

After a short while, Akko and Kamai stepped out of the sewer tunnels. Even from a distance, they towered over Henar.

Akko wrinkled his nose, clearly distrusting. Despite his sleek and blood-red fur, he was not a handsome Kavii. "Fine. No more shooting."

Kamai stepped forward, his dark green eyes like cold daggers. "Where is Atiga now?"

Henar's breath caught. *Right. That issue.* He was almost afraid to reveal the fate of the traitorous Kavii. But to gain Akko and Kamai's trust, they had to know the truth. "Atiga is dead," Henar admitted with a heavy voice. Suddenly, guilt he never knew was there bubbled up his throat. "This one killed him."

Akko and Kamai grabbed for their blasters again.

Not good! Henar raised both paws and nearly stumbled backward. "WHOA. If this one hadn't, he would have killed me. Just like he killed Moldof!" His words hit a fever pitch as his heartbeat skyrocketed yet again. "This one saw his severed paw!"

The twin Kavii lowered their arms, but not their guard. Henar felt brief relief but knew these ones required further convincing.

Kamai's eyes burned with hatred. "You killed a fellow officer!"

"In self-defense," Henar amended, paws still raised in peace. "He would have killed me if not."

Akko paced back and forth like a caged savage, shaking his head in disagreement. "You do not know that."

"Want proof?" Henar reached for his body armor where Atiga's blast hadn't damaged. A few pressed buttons activated the desired function. "Our armor, even the light attire, have video recording to track our missions. Here. Watch!" He brought up a floating screen showcasing the entire encounter with Atiga. That included the confession to murdering Moldof.

Just like that, all the distrust and anger bled from Akko and Kamai's faces.

"By the Benevolency!" Kamai cried out after the video ended with Henar shooting Atiga through the throat.

Akko looked close to tears. "Why?" he cried out in anguish. "Why would Atiga do that to one of his own? A fellow Kavii!"

Henar was glad these two mountains weren't trying to shoot him anymore. But his true sympathy went to Moldof, the real innocent in this mess. He walked up to the two Kavii so they stood face-to-face. "Because Atiga is...*was* selfish. And spoiled. And greedy for power at anyone else's expense."

Without Atiga there to guide them, the duo looked like lost pups in need of their parents. "What...what now?" Akko asked forlornly, looking to Henar for instructions.

Henar did some quick thinking...and the actions were not favorable to anyone. "Atiga's actions will be reported. As will mine. Self-defense or not, this one killed a fellow officer." Whatever lay ahead, he would face it like a true soldier of the Benevolency. But only after he completed his assignment. "But first, the mission Moldof and this one were assigned must be completed. And...this one needs both your help to do so."

Akko and Kamai exchanged a look. Henar's heart was ready to sink, already knowing how these two morons would reply.

The duo turned back to him. "What do you need us to do?" Kamai asked.

Henar was so flabbergasted by their acceptance he couldn't find his voice for a few moments beyond sputtering gibberish. "It's simple," he finally managed to say. "We—"

A bladelike hiss cut through the air. Then another...

Then came a choked gurgle from Akko. Henar's jaw fell open as Akko and Kamai both went rigid, eyes bulging cartoonishly, limbs twitching. Both had silvery dart-like flechettes sticking form their necks.

The humans found us, Henar realized. Of course they did with all the noise their blaster fight had caused. The two large Kavii then toppled over simultaneously and went into full-on spasms.

Henar tensed to grab again for his blaster.

A third dart hissed forward before he could take one step.

Pain lanced his neck. He grabbed at the long projectile sticking out of him, staggered by the agony. "OWW! That stung...kind of..." The pain faded quickly, replaced by waves upon waves of drowsiness. "...feeling kinda...numb..." Everything spun around and around. "Feeling kinda..."

The ground reached up to swallow Henar whole. Then he felt and saw nothing.

Chapter 6

Smears of light swirled slowly back into Henar's vision. Warm colors edged by a dark tunnel. A chill rippled over the Kavii, causing his fur to stand on end. And he felt as if he wore nothing save some kind of sticky covering on his right side.

"Whaa?" Henar attempted to say. But the words came out in some kind of unrecognizable slur. Memories of his previous moments began leaking through the mental fog.

Humans had found him, Akko and Kamai, drugging them. Now they were in some kind of prison. Consciousness cleared a little more, revealing him to in fact be naked, except for a pinkish body wrap around his lower extremities and his military bracelet. Where the rest of his gear was, Henar had no clue.

"Where? How!" The Kavii patted his furry frame down in panic. Then again.

He was a prisoner of war. A prisoner of the humans. That reality terrified him.

His surroundings were a set of rectangular metal walls, save the gaping mesh sitting before him where harsh yet warm light blazed in from outside. To Henar's right-hand side, Akko and Kamai dozed peacefully, two bulky balls of fur.

Whatever kind of cell the humans had thrown them into, Henar could tell it was at the bottom level of the prison he was in.

And coming from outside the cell, Henar could hear all kinds of other fauna barking, yowling, whining, and purring. No doubt they were in cells similar to this one containing Henar. More prisoners of the humans.

"Have to escape..." Henar attempted to stand and figure out

an escape plan. Except the world began swimming again. Before Henar knew it, he was stumbling to the left and colliding into an unyielding wall with a loud clang. That sent Henar's raucous cellmates nearby into an uproar. Dazed, the Kavii landed hard on his belly again.

A loud series of squawking sounded from outside.

Henar frowned in recognition. *Humans!*

Desperate, he tapped onto his wristband to see if it retained any function despite being separated from the rest of his gear.

At first, Henar received nothing but a sputtering reaction.

The squawking grew closer, quicker. Henar tapped more furiously on his wristband.

Finally, the language translator popped up before his eyes.

Thankful to the point of tears, Henar ordered the wristband to focus on the human dialect nearby.

Henar heard nothing but squawking still. For a moment, his heart sank.

"I will check on our new rodent friends down below," a high and clear human voice spoke from outside the cell, clear as day for him to understand. The light from outside was blocked as a silhouetted human crouched before the pen.

She was not a large human, skinny in build with pale and bare skin except for the strawberry blonde hair piled atop her head. But for Henar, all humans were quite massive. Her eyes were large and green and probing.

"Hey there, sleepyhead!" she stated, bright as a clear sunrise. Her curiosity and uncertainty were on display, along with a gentle warmth Henar did not understand.

He scurried back to the furthest corner of the cell and tensed to defend himself.

If the human had discovered Henar and his allies in less hostile fashion, then Henar wouldn't have felt so threatened by this human's warmth. Yet the three Kavii had been taken down by darts—discovered wearing military gear. Despite how unevolved humans were, this individual must have more than a few questions about what Henar had been wearing.

"Hey," he hissed at Akko and Kamai. "Wake up! We're trapped and need to escape. WAKE! UP!"

Henar might as well have been speaking to pillows. Perfect.

"Awww! It's okay sweetie." The human pulled the door to the cell open and reached her massive hands toward Henar, blocking out all light. "I won't hurt you. Just wanna check your injuries."

Henar cringed and scrambled as far away from those hairless hands with their hairless fingers. But the cell was small and cramped. Soon those fingers clutched his body like vises.

Henar shrieked and scrambled, but the human's power was unyielding and the Kavii was not at full strength.

His last cry finally jolted Akko and Kamai out of their apparent comas. But by the time they fully came to, the human closed the cell again and had lifted Henar high off the ground.

The human cradled Henar in her arms like a human would a child of their own. Henar could barely think straight. Around him were concrete walls and flooring, with other animals of all sizes in similar caged cells like his. Canines barked and whined. Felines meowed or hissed. Even some avian species with their chirps. And in the cells nearby, was that a Kavii-like creature with floppy ears?

Henar could hear Akko and Kamai frantically slamming their bodies against the mesh cage of their cell, so far below now. They called out in anger, desperate to escape and rescue Henar. But to no avail. Looking into the deceptively gentle eyes of his human captor, Henar's mind jumped to what would happen to him next.

Would she start with bribes for information? Or would she go straight to threats? Would be it be an interrogation followed by beatings? Or would the beatings and torture be part of the interrogation?

"Okay, sweetie," the human cooed and smiled, revealing big white teeth made for chomping. "I know you're scared. I just want to take a look at your injuries." Her face darkened for one brief, scary moment. "I better not find whoever burned you," she seethed. "Or else I'd do the same to them."

Henar froze. *Too bad Atiga was already dead,* he mused. Or else watching humans dispense justice on him might be entertaining. Like watching Kavii pups learn how to walk.

The human's ultra-bright smile returned as she placed him on a cold metal table. Looking around at the cages and the tools on the surrounding countertops, Henar recognized the place as a medical facility. *Or is this some kind of torture labs for alien invaders?* So far, no sign of interrogations or violence. Except for the massive pair of scissors the female human just whipped out.

Henar popped up and made to run. To where, he had no clue. Maybe that open door across the room. To get help so he could rescue Akko and Kamai. Henar had no ego admitting his plan was a mistake. Time to go back and do this conquest the old-fashioned way.

The human pushed the Kavii down on his side with surprising force. "Relax, little one," she said, never losing her warmth at all. "I need to take off your bandage and check the wounds." But Henar was in a panic, fear of those scissors puncturing his exposed fur-covered flesh.

"Jesus, you're stronger than you look." The human looked up. "Jenny, get in here. Need a little help!"

Another human female scurried into the room, shorter and squatter and darker in complexion than the one holding Henar down. Her attire mirrored her pale human counterpart's: light blue drab V-neck short with baggy drab light blue pants. She clamped her cold hands over Henar's head and hindquarters, effectively pinning him to the hard metal table.

"Thanks," the pale human said gratefully. "He's a strong little fucker."

"No problem, Pam," the human called Jenny replied.

"Almost slipped outta my hands," Pam commented, directing the pointy ends of her scissors toward Henar's exposed midsection. "Now let me cut this bandage off..."

Henar squeezed his eyes shut, helpless and fearing the worst...

And suddenly his legs were unfettered by bandages. He wriggled them and felt absolutely no pain. Not even an ache. That salve from earlier worked better than expected.

"Wow," Pam gaped down at him. "There is no sign of any burns. And the fur covering this area of his body...completely grown back."

Jenny took a long look of her own. "Yeah, you're right!" Her small brown eyes widened in awe. "Good work, Pammy!"

Henar watched and listened to these clueless humans continue congratulating each other with such relish. *As if their paltry medicines had anything to do with this one's recovery.* He struggled not to laugh aloud.

Then the one called Pam began stroking his head with long, doting fingers. "So, do we know what he and his friends are?"

Doubt it! Henar mused. Despite his better judgement, he relaxed further.

Jenny, who had relaxed her grip on the Kavii, shook her head. "Other than him looking like a giant rabbit but without the floppy ears? No idea. Blood samples say he's from the rodent family. But can't positively ID any of them." Her face contorted in confusion. "That doesn't explain all the weird armored shit those three were wearing. Or these bracelets that won't come off."

Pam eyed her friend with similar bafflement. It amused Henar how expressive these humans were. "I know, right? This guy and his buddies even had miniguns. Whoever used to own them must've been into some kinky Star Wars shit or something. I tossed most of that stuff into the trash after we pried it all off."

Henar's eyes bulged. *My armor is nearby.* He popped up on all fours. Also, these humans had no clue that he, Akko, and Kamai were aliens. A few positives after a string of setbacks. Henar had to make a dash and find one of these "trashcans" holding his armor and weapons.

"Easy, not-so-little guy." Pam hugged her arms around Henar to keep him in place. "We're still checking you out. But you must be hungry!" Pam nodded at Jenny, who then scurried out from the room.

"Who put you in that silly armor?" she asked in a weird baby doll voice when they were alone. "Don't worry. I'll make sure you never see them again!"

Henar certainly hoped that wasn't the case. But Henar didn't mind the stroking atop his head. Or his belly. Pam's affection seemed genuine, especially when she nuzzled her bare cheek against Henar's head. Yea, that felt nice. Henar closed his eyes and purred despite himself.

Jenny soon re-entered the room carrying a small bowl filled with green plants and small yellow bulbs. "Lunch!" she announced with a smile, and placed the bowl in front of Henar.

The Kavii, his wits dulled by Pam's cuddling, stared blankly at the bowl. *What do they expect this one to do here?*

"You have to feed him, silly," Pam scolded her friend. The human scooped up a palm full of the mixture and held it directly under Henar's nose.

She's feeding this one?? He leaned down and sniffed what was in her hand. The smell wasn't terrible, and the Kavii was starving. So he took huge bites of the food, devouring it quickly. Okay, not bad.

"Someone's hungry!" Jenny exclaimed.

"Have some more!" Pam scooped up more of the food, and

Henar scarfed down the rest. And in that moment, being stroked and fed by these two simple yet lovely humans, Henar's brain lit up with possibilities. After finishing his meal that these humans took turns handfeeding to him, Henar looked up at Jenny and Pam with the largest doe eyes possible and nuzzled his face on Pam's hand.

She all but melted into a puddle.

"Aww," both humans cried affectionately. As both held him tight, Henar barely swallowed a guffaw. *Thank you, Atiga,* he mused to himself.

Thanks to an arch nemesis trying to kill Henar and his plan, Moldof would not die in vain. And Henar's plan for Earth's conquest had just been proven. Humans loved furry creatures. They loved catering to them hand and foot.

"I know we shouldn't take these guys home or anything. But who knows what would happen if we report him and his buddies to animal services?" Jenny admitted, her dark features contorting with concern.

"But we have no clue what these guys are. What kind of diseases they might have. If they are some kind of guinea pig or giant rat or…" Pam's eyes widened. "A whole new species!"

Henar made a face. *Nononono!* He shook his head. If Henar and his friends were carted off to a lab, then the humans would surely discover these were not some typical rodents from Earth. Not good.

Jenny sighed heavily. "What if they are taken away, poked and prodded like lab rats?" She placed a hand on the shoulder of her doubting friend. "What if we take them home, just as a trial run, and see how that works."

Yesyesyesyesyes! To further emphasize his approval, Henar scurried over to Pam and nuzzled his face against her chest.

The chorus of "Awwwwwwwww" and "how cute!" variants that followed were elementary.

"Okay!" Pam finally caved. "We'll take them home tonight. Temporarily…"

Henar smirked. *Nailed it.*

Later, after, some more belly rubs, Henar was returned to his cage. Akko and Kamai were waiting, teeth bared and ready to pounce at Pam.

Henar's eyes widened. "NO." He threw his whole body in their path just as the twin behemoths launched themselves forward.

"What are you doing, Henar?" Akko snarled.

"We are without armor or weapons. That was our chance at escaping!" Kamai agreed, struggling to get past as the door shut.

"We cannot," Henar declared, standing between the two large Kavii and the closed door. Both Pam and Jenny expressed concern over the commotion they just heard before leaving the room. "We can feed the other two when they calm down," Jenny stated.

"Let's hope so!" Pam said. "I don't want any drama between these three and my fur babies at home."

Soon they left the room, leaving only the discordant symphony of other animals in their cages.

"We're not escaping!" Henar ordered. "Nor are we attacking these humans."

Akko and Kamai gaped at him as if all his body fur had fallen off. "Why not? We're prisoners—"

"Not exactly!" Henar cut him off. "If you had bothered to turn on your language translators, you'd have heard what the humans were talking about."

Akko sank onto his haunches, still fuming but more open to listening. "Which is what?" The top of his head nearly touched the ceiling of this cage.

"They are taking us into their home, willingly!" Henar replied, smiling. "That was the plan all along. Gain these humans' trust, infiltrate their homes as a test case on how to invade Earth without firing a shot. That way, these humans will feed us, bathe us, and take care of us. Basically be at our beck and call." Henar walked up to his fellow soldiers and clapped their shoulders. "We rule them without them even knowing it. Until the Benevolency is ready to announce itself to its newest colony. Then at the end of the week, we present the plan to our military commanders."

Akko and Kamai looked at each other, visibly gobsmacked by the brilliance of Henar's plan. Of course they were. "But…but what if the humans catch wind of our invasion beforehand and retaliate?"

"And what if they retaliate after we have already occupied their world?" Kamai added.

Henar had thought of that possibility, and had a perfectly logical response. "We will already be in their homes, compromised their defense systems and military, as well as their food supplies…should the humans be foolish enough to fight back."

Now Akko and Kamai perked up.

Henar smiled. These two seemed almost civil now that they were away from Atiga. "Do not be aggressive. Do not snarl or bare your teeth in hostility." That caused Kamai to close his mouth with a snap. "Give them the happy face defense with the doe eyes like we were taught in academy." Henar mimicked the exact, sweet and cuddle-worthy facial expression to highlight his point. "Cuddle up with the humans. Tolerate their petting. Let them feed you like newborn pups and you'll never have another care in the world."

When Pam and Jenny came back, Akko and Kamai grudgingly put on their happiest faces, even wriggling their butts in false joy.

Soon they were scooped out of the cage by both humans, who fed and petted both Kaviis. After some time, Henar didn't bother hiding a guffaw at the sounds of Akko and Kamai's blissed-out purrs.

The true victory came when Pam said, "Alright already…let's take all three of them home. The house should have extra space."

Later that day, they rode in some roofed, four-wheeled vehicle that might have been used for ground transport some 700 years ago on Kav. Yet this relic was considered modern by these humans.

Henar sat perched in the "car's" rear seats with Akko and Kamai while the two humans sat in the front. He exchanged mute, bemused looks with the two larger Kaviis. *How much these humans have to learn*, they tacitly agreed.

Pam and Jenny lived in quite the rustic abode, red-roofed with orange walls, near other homes ringed with green shrubbery and trees.

"You three will love it here," Pam gushed as she approached her front entrance. "There's enough space for everyone. Jenny cradled Kamai as she walked behind Pam. The beefy Kavii had the biggest grin of bliss on his face. He and Jenny had taken a real liking to each other. Akko and Henar trotted after them, each on all fours.

"This one doesn't know about this," Akko murmured. He moved rigidly, tensed and nervous.

Henar nodded. "Neither does this one," he admitted. "But look at what we are about to accomplish? This will cement our names in history. You and Kamai. We can do this."

That calmed Akko down significantly as the door to Pam's abode swung open. The insides were expansive and seemingly crafted of polished wood. With more fluffy pillows everywhere.

A string of excited barks outside grabbed Henar's attention. Two canines.

Pam then scurried deeper into the house. "I'll deal with Beans and Billy. You get those guys settled in, Jenn?"

The shorter woman nodded and placed Kamai on a fluffy divan contraption as Pam disappeared into a darkened corridor.

Night had fallen completely on the outside by the time Henar, Akko, and Kamai had been fed again and then given a fort of pillows in the common room. The humans had gone to the house's second floor to get some sleep after hours upon hours of playing and cuddling with their Kavii guests. As they had departed to their separate rooms, Pam and Jenny were quarreling over what to name their new "pets." Henar found none of their choices appealing.

He and the other two Kavii lay on their backs, stuffed and content. Their bed had been constructed from a wreath of seven bulbous and square-shaped pillows from living couches.

"This...is...the life," Kamai admitted, and then burped. "This one does not want to leave."

Henar, nearly in a food coma, nodded in agreement. Akko was already passed out and snoring.

Henar's eyes began drooping, until realizing he had probably missed his check-in.

With considerable effort, he pushed up to all fours and scurried into another room. Henar remembered not to run too fast, as the glossy wooden floor was slick enough to slide across. Finding what appeared to be a human lavatory room, he slowly eased the door closed to not make so much noise.

Henar should have contacted his commanding officer first. But with all the craziness going on, the Kavii longed for a friendly face. Tapping onto his wristcom, he opened up a floating holoscreen to contact Osefa first.

The response was not what Henar expected. Osefa appeared disbelieving and stunned. Plus, he was dressed in his military combat uniform. Odd, unless they were running training drills. "Henar? Why...how...?"

Henar gave his friend an odd look. "Great seeing you too."

Osefa shook his head to clear it, then gazed upon Henar as if never seeing anyone else like him. "Nono...this one is overjoyed to see you. It's just..." Osefa placed a paw on his forehead, barely able to communicate. "HOW are you still alive? And why are you naked?"

Now Henar gaped at his longtime friend in shock. "Alive? Osefa, this one never died. We saw each other over four days ago."

Osefa shook his head again. "Commandant Johonek declared you and Moldoff had been killed in action."

"Killed?" Henar repeated with a bark, then looked around and cringed. The last thing he needed was to wake up his human hosts. The Kavii turned back to the holoscreen. "How?"

"Killed by our human enemies..." Osefa's voice trailed off as he gaped again at his friend.

"But this one still has at least three days left to complete my mission," Henar detailed more to himself than a gobsmacked Osefa. His head was spinning, questions upon questions piling up. Only one rose to the top.

"Why would Johonek announce a boldface lie unless...?" The answer struck Henar hard. Unless the commandant wanted this mission to fail and use the excuse to openly attack Earth. *He never believed in this one.* Did that also mean Atiga didn't try to kill Henar on a jealous whim? The order to have both Moldof and him killed might have come directly from Johonek.

The realization was a piston-like kick to Henar's gut. The Kavii looked again to his old friend from military academy on Kav. Through the heavy fog of disbelief, he took note of Osefa's attire again. "Why are you dressed for battle?"

Osefa straightened in posture, adjusted his fatigues, and frowned. "Come tomorrow," he announced as joylessly as possible, "the Benevolency attacks the planet Earth, with extreme prejudice."

CHAPTER 7

For several long moments, Henar gaped back at Osefa. The shock was too blunt for the young Kavii to form coherent thoughts. His brain matter seemed to have melted out through his tiny round ears, rendering him mute and dumbstruck.

Hearing that the Benevolency would finally lay siege on Earth should have thrilled Henar. This was what he had trained for since adolescence.

During the weeks of space travel to Earth, the young Kavii had been beyond excited to be part of his first planetary conquest, eager to prove his worth and cement his status as part of the Benevolency Military.

Except, Henar was not to take part. He was supposed to be dead. A martyr for the Benevolency's cause.

The first-strike impetus of the Earth conquest had been built on an egregious lie. The lie that these humans had killed Henar and another Kavii in a declaration of war.

"Henar?" Osefa's worried voice brought the dumbfounded Kavii out from the abyss of shock. He turned to his friend and straightened, cold anger washing over him.

Henar's oddball plan to pose as a human pet had initially been a means to liberate him and his friends out of a dead-end division.

Now, that oddball plan was proof of his existence. A mark of his survival. "This one has to speak to Johonek," he demanded flatly. "Now."

Osefa jerked back. "Why? What is happening?"

Henar shook his head. "A whole lot of treachery." Then he revealed everything that occurred over the last few days, Moldof's death, Atiga's attempt on his life, being brought to Pam and Jenny's house. The only thing he did not reveal was his suspicions of Johonek attempting to have him killed.

By the time he had finished, Osefa was the one who looked like his brain had melted out of his ears. "By the stars above..."

"That is why this one needs to speak with Johonek," Henar pleaded now. "As ranking officer over this entire conquest, this one must tell him about Atiga and Moldof."

Osefa shook his head side to side as if to clear the cobwebs. "It will be hard, as he and the other commandants are making final preparations before tomorrow's first strike. But..." On the holoscreen, the other Kavii's face twisted with hesitation before he spoke next. "Given what happened, is it wise speaking with someone with Johonek's influence over a private communications channel? Especially when you do not know why he falsely declared you dead?"

Henar grimaced. His friend was right. "Then what is this one supposed to do?" he hissed, pacing back and forth in frustration. "This one has been stripped of armor, utilities, and weapons. This one is miles away from my dropship. And there is no way this one would reach Johonek's flagship in time. Not before tomorrow's battle begins."

Osefa scratched his chin, calm amid Henar's tantrum. He always could keep a level head during extreme stress. "This one might know a way to get you an audience with Johonek."

Henar stopped and wheeled around. "How would you do that?"

Osefa's mouth pulled into a devious and toothy smile, meaning a good idea had come to mind. "All this one needs is remote access to your wristcom," he said. "And for you to not answer any other communications until Johonek himself contacts you."

Henar frowned. This plan made no sense. "But why—?"

Osefa held up a paw to silence him. "Trust this one. Oh, and when Johonek calls, make no mention that you are not at your dropship."

Henar sighed and granted his friend remote access to his wristcom. "Understood."

"Exquisite," Osefa beamed. "This one will be in touch. Stay still and wait for Johonek to make contact." After exchanging farewells, the transmission winked out, plunging the bathroom into darkness once again.

An hour of Earth time passed before Henar's wristcom lit up

with incoming transmissions. Not one. Not two. Not even half a dozen. Hundreds. All of them fellow soldiers, some he'd barely exchanged more than a few words with.

The Kavii was strangely touched watching the cascade of caller IDs scrolling down his wristcom monitor. "What did you just do, Osefa?"

Before long, a blocked caller ID finally appeared.

Henar's insides clenched up again.

He didn't need to guess who that might be. The Kavii drank in a deep, steadying breath before answering.

The Kavii commandant appeared on Henar's floating holoscreen, his furry face a stony mask that gave away nothing. "Henar. It appears rumors of your death have been greatly exaggerated. And you made sure the whole fleet knew it."

Henar swallowed a laugh. *Oh, this one sees what you did, Osefa.*

The Kavii's friend must have sent out some beacon fleet-wide telling them Henar was alive, but using Henar's wristcom. "It had been a few days and this one is far—" The Kavii almost revealed he wasn't near his dropship, but remembered Osefa's warning to keep that quiet.

"This one has been away from my fellow soldiers far too long," Henar corrected himself in time. "Looking forward to rejoining them." He watched the commandant's face carefully, looking for any crack in his composure.

Johonek was pure ice. "And you will rejoin them soon." He nodded stiffly, slamming a curled paw down on his table. "Your presence will boost morale after what the humans did to Moldof, and what they nearly did to you."

Now for the moment of truth. Henar straightened. "The humans did nothing to me and Moldof." He shook his head. "Atiga killed Moldof. He tried to kill this one, but failed."

Johonek's beady eyes narrowed, his whiskers twitching. "No," he stated in iron tones. "The humans discovered you, Atiga and Moldof, tried to kill all three of you. Only you survived to tell the tale of the humans' xenophobia and hatred for our kind."

Henar leaned away from the floating holoscreen. He didn't want his suspicions to be accurate. But this bald denial of the truth brought all the facts home like a meteorite strike. "That is not what happened. Atiga tried to kill this one. Now you are attempting to cover that up. Why?"

Johonek barely flinched in the face of Henar's defiance. "Because this one had expected Atiga to do his job and kill you, pup." His voice never raised, never showed any anger. The commandant spoke so coldly and businesslike, Henar shuddered in revulsion.

"You..." He tried to find words, but the nausea washing through him nearly choked off his voice. "Is that why you...approved my mission? All so you could get rid of this one?"

Johonek shook with laughter and rose to his feet. "Do not be so self-absorbed, pup. This one had received scant resources for this conquest. But if an opposing force murdered a few soldiers on a peaceful surveillance, then High Command becomes far more generous with what military resources a conquest receives. You with all your youthful naiveté presented this one with an opportunity to bring fire and fury from the stars down on these bare-skinned cretins. You and Moldof represented martyrs to the Benevolency cause. If not you, then someone other would have sufficed."

Henar stumbled back, almost falling over. For the first time in memory, he felt ashamed to call himself a member of the Benevolency. He meant less than nothing to them and their war machine. "So this one was just a disposable pawn to you?"

"Martyr," Johonek corrected, leaning over his desk. "You, Moldof, and now Atiga would have been martyrs. But alive...you can be a symbol. Your career can still soar to heights undreamt of." The older Kavii smiled at Henar, almost resembling someone's favorite relative. "All you have to do is state that the humans were the perpetrators of Moldof and Atiga's deaths."

Henar looked up at the commandant, seeing only cold probing green eyes waiting for an answer.

At a surface level, this seemed like an easy choice.

Go along with the lie and get everything he'd ever dreamed of from the Benevolency military.

Go along with the lie, and become a war hero.

Go along with the lie, and lose your soul.

Henar knew what his answer would be then and there. "This one is a soldier of the Benevolency. This one will not lie."

Johonek jerked back, fur bristling, eyes hardening. "A very foolish mistake you just made, pup. If you will not be a beacon, then you will most definitely become a martyr."

The two of them stared at each other a long moment. Henar

looked at him sideways. "You'll have to come get me yourself then, commandant," Henar spat in defiance.

Johonek looked hard at him. "Why...how are you still living?"

"Because he is not at his dropship," Osefa's voice announced out of nowhere, startling the daylights out of Henar.

Johonek's fur stood on end as his head darted back and forth. "What in the—" he gasped in surprise. "Who is there?"

"Oh, just this one..." Osefa continued wryly. "And nearly one thousand Kavii soldiers of varying ranks. All listening in on your enlightening conversation."

Now Johonek was the being who looked ill. "Do you understand how many laws you have broken, insolent pup?" he fumed, regaining his color. "How dare you—?"

"NO," Henar cut him off. "How *dare* you call yourself an officer of the Benevolency? Ordering the deaths of innocent soldiers under your command. All to justify an early first strike on these humans. How many laws would that be?"

"Several," Osefa commented, "and then attempting to murder Henar when he refused to go along with your treachery?"

Johonek suddenly disappeared, replaced by familiar rolling hills doused in nightfall. Henar looked closely as an oval-shaped vessel appeared. "My dropship," Henar exclaimed.

"Formerly your dropship," Osefa corrected.

The reference made no sense, until Henar saw the dropship erupt in a plume of orange and gold fire, then vanish into quickly cooling embers.

"Guess redirecting Henar's location signature was a smart idea, huh?" Osefa bragged.

Henar fell to his knees. Johonek, his commanding officer, just tried to kill him again. But Osefa had saved him.

The visual disappeared, replaced by Johonek. The commandant had slumped back behind his ready room's desk in horror. He'd been exposed and knew it.

"And now..." Henar said, somehow fighting through the shock and the disgust bleeding through his fur and skin. "Everyone has seen your crimes. You are not fit to hold any position within the Benevolency military."

Johonek looked to Henar as if just realizing he was there for the first time. "You will regret the day you ever took your oath, you bottom-feeding scum. This one will make your life—"

A commotion off-screen interrupted Johonek's rant.

Suddenly, half a dozen burly Kavii security guards burst onto the screen, tackling Johonek out of his seat. Henar watched in wide-eyed shock as a scuffle ensued until they finally pinned the traitorous commandant to the ground.

And just like that, the shouting and thrashing Johonek was carted off-screen and out of his own ready room by military security.

Another stern-looking commandant appeared onscreen, dark red fur and a stern look. Kailopha. He turned to the screen. "This one's apologies, Soldier. Johonek will pay for his crimes. An escort will come acquire you—"

"Actually sir," Henar held up a paw. "This one's original mission, despite the many setbacks, has been successful. If you had some time, this one would love to discuss with you tomorrow."

Commandant Kailopha nodded. "Acceptable. This one will pick you up at your current location...wherever that actually is. The attack on Earth will be postponed until after our discussion."

Henar saluted and smiled. "Will do, sir." The transmission ended. After which, Henar immediately called Osefa. "There are no words this one can use to thank you enough."

His friend shrugged. "Loyalty is what the Benevolency is truly about. You and this one are more family than blood relatives."

Henar's head was spinning with joy, surprise, and triumph. He opened his mouth to speak. Footfalls, muted and approaching from the other side of the bathroom door.

Henar swore, almost forgetting about the humans who lived in this house. "This one must go. Thank you and see you soon." He shut down the floating holoscreen and dropped to all fours right as the bathroom door swung open. The lights switched on, chasing away all shadows. Pam stood in the door way, her eyes puffy from sleep, wearing a baggy shirt that reached down to her knees.

"Hey baby," she said in a drowsy voice. "Thought I heard someone down here. Why aren't you with your buddies in the living room?"

Oh, if you only knew, Henar mused. Instead, he provided a distraction. Scurrying over to Pam's bare feet, the Kavii sniffed at her leg before crouching and leaping into her arms.

"Oh. My GAWD," Pam giggled, cradling Henar properly in her

arms. "Someone is happy to see me." She snuggled her face against the Kavii's soft fur.

"You have no idea," Henar said aloud. But to Pam's simple human ears, he had made some pleased yowling noise.

"That's it!" Pam gaped at him. "I'll call you *Happy*."

Henar glared at her.

She stopped smiling, clearly sensing his displeasure. "Not a fan? Okay. We'll keep looking."

CHAPTER 8

The next few weeks flew by quickly. Johonek had been prosecuted for a string of criminal charges, including treason, first-degree murder, among others. He was stripped of all ranks and titles, sentenced to life in prison with no chance of parole.

Still, Henar never felt more fear in his life when he, Akko, and Kamai returned to the fleet orbiting around Earth. As great as it felt to wear actual clothes again, the creature comfort was ephemeral at best. Bittersweet at worst.

Killing Atiga still hung over him like a dark cloud. Given that Atiga was the son of a powerful military leader back on Kav, Henar expected to receive the same brutal sentence as Johonek. The day that Benevolency task force had picked him, Akko, and Kamai up in the dead of night had been terrifying to stomach.

However, Henar thankfully never got charged with even a misdemeanor. His armor had been found by Benevolency scavengers who replayed the footage to see Atiga's attack and attempt to kill him. Plus, there had been his efforts in exposing Johonek's crimes against fellow Kaviis.

Akko and Kamai also weren't charged as accomplices since they had no clue of the murder. And Henar vouched for the two.

"Now," Commandant Kailopha spoke to Henar after he had been cleared of any wrongdoing. He stood in the commandant's ready room, with a wall-length window displaying a backdrop of star-sprinkled black. Osefa, Leakki, Nele, Akko, and Kamai stood at Henar's side. He refused to meet Kailopha without witnesses after the Johonek episode.

"You had a potential plan to limit the use of military force now that we have successfully infiltrated Earth's military defenses, yes?" the commandant inquired. "A plan that would call for Kaviis to infiltrate the homes of humans posing as pets while the Benevolency forces weaken Earth's political and military forces?"

"Yes, sir." Henar nodded his head. Everything felt light and fuzzy after the past few days, so he tried limiting how much came out of his mouth. No need to embarrass himself.

Kailopha walked up to him, considerably taller, lean and fit in his military uniform. "How about we employ that plan with a few modifications?"

Henar wasn't entirely surprised. The Benevolency military would be giving him special treatment for a long time now. "Are you only listening to this one's plans because of what happened with Johonek?"

"That's part of the reason," Kailopha admitted without hesitation. "However, you also presented a solid plan. But this one has a more effective way of helping it spread more quickly." Kailopha then turned to Nele and Leakki.

Henar turned as well, baffled.

Nele smiled at him before beginning. "Being on Domestic Surveillance taught this one much about human nature. Especially how they consume data and who they listen to."

She activated her wristband, producing a floating holoscreen. At first the images seemed random and chaotic. But as Henar and his friends focused more closely on the visuals, they saw a montage of what looked like entertainment and news broadcasts.

"Humans *love* their media," Nele began, her smile broadening. "Whether it entertains or informs or inspires, they are junkies. Media guides their decisions and their purchasing habits, especially on their worldwide web network." She then shut off her holoscreen. "And the humans who appear on these media outlets are the primary influencers. Especially the entertainment ones. They post about some new chicken bone and their followers will all want to buy said chicken bone."

Henar let his gaze linger on his longtime friend, still lost. "So what are you saying?"

Kailopha chimed in. "What if we could have some of our soldiers gain access to these influencers, posing as cute and furry pets. We Kaviis can pose as a brand-new species discovered somewhere in Earth's many forests. But with those influencers showcasing our 'cuteness' to the world, everyone will want a Kavii of their own."

Henar's eyes bulged. "Meaning that the humans will be helping us take over their own world. And not even realize it."

"And by the time they do realize what we've done," Kailopha finished for him. His eyes twinkled. "The Benevolency will move in and take over." The Kavii commandant held out a paw. "So...you and your friends want to help this one take over Earth, one Kavii pet at a time?"

Henar felt warm and giddy all over, as the eyes of all his friends were on him. This was what he had been waiting for ever since joining military academy. The moment was dizzying, exhilarating, and frightening.

"Count this one in, sir." Henar accepted Kailopha's paw, his heart bursting with pride.

The rest of Henar's friends grinned as they all barked in unison, "Yes, sir!"

About the Author

C.C. Ekeke is the author of the Star Brigade space opera series. C.C. spent much of his childhood on a steady diet of science fiction movies, television shows and superhero comic books. He discovered his desire to write books in college when studying for a degree in advertising. His love of domestic and international travel provides further inspiration for the aliens and worlds seen in his writing.

When not writing or building new worlds, you'll find him reading and watching the latest films and globetrotting to parts mostly known.

www.CCEkeke.com

Books by C.C. Ekeke

Star Brigade Series
Book 1: Resurgent
Book 2: Maelstrom
Book 3: Supremacy
Book 4: Ascendant
Traitor: A Star Brigade Strikefile
Star Brigade: Odysseys – A Short Story Collection

A VISIT FROM MY CYBORG NANA

by Zen DiPietro

A redshirt confronting cyborg overlords is madness.
Except for when it isn't.

Charlie Kenny didn't expect to live past the age of twenty, much less become a space-traveling adventurer. A redshirt like him mostly just cowers in a dark, quiet place that doesn't have sharp corners or choking hazards. That was his plan, too, until he met Greta and Pinky, who have changed his life completely.

Although reluctant to return to Earth, where most of his personal misfortunes have occurred (like that time his dad got structurally rearranged by a yeti-gator), Charlie can no longer avoid it. His dear, sweet cyborg nana needs help. Her overlords are refusing her proper maintenance, which is downright bogus. Why go around assimilating hapless nanas if they aren't going to take decent care of them?

Charlie and his erstwhile friends Greta and Pinky are going to teach those cyborg overlords a lesson they'll never forget.

CHAPTER 1

As I watch Greta Saltz, the love of my life (though she does not yet know this), I'm struck by her golden glow, her good humor, and her appalling manner of eating.

I've tried to get used to the way she decimates a hapless muffin into a pile of crumbs before eating it, but I can't. It's weird. To take a perfectly delicious-looking muffin and reduce it to hamster bedding is a crime against perfectly good food.

That muffin did nothing to deserve this kind of treatment.

But then Greta looks at me from the corner of her eye and smiles, and I know I'd forgive her anything. She could eat crackers in bed, and as long as I was there next to her, getting crackers in my crack, I'd make it work.

Even if it was the salted kind.

Not that I've even seen her bed. Or the inside of her cabin, for that matter. I've been on the *Second Chance* for months now, staring death in the face and screaming...ahem...I mean *overcoming.* Overcoming like a badass.

Yeah, that's right.

By this point, I've figured out what's what when it comes to living on an interstellar ship. How to properly use the water closet, how to get by Gus the Head Porter's scathing condescension for sectarian rubes, and even how to mix a good cocktail.

I make a fantastic Indefinite Tailpipe Twister, and my Oblivious Flashers are every bit as good as Pinky's.

I've always known that a redshirt like me can't get a girl like Greta Saltz. She's cute, fun, smart, and gosh-darn-it, people just like her. Part of it is her luck—a preternatural cosmic black hole of good fortune that comes her way. But part of it is also just

Greta. She's a Garbdorian goddess, as far as I'm concerned.

Yes, I'm a dipshit for refusing to acknowledge that she's out of my league. But you know what? Screw leagues. This isn't baseball. This is my life, and for a redshirt—a guy who should have already died from a papercut or a yeti-gator or some shit—I am *the man.* Charlie Kenny: a rock star among my people.

It's all relative.

As I watch Greta eat her disgustingly pre-pulverized breakfast, I'm not looking at her with rose-colored glasses, or beer goggles, or any other eyewear that's catastrophic to my life choices. I'm looking at her as a man looks at a woman who is flawed and imperfect and more beautiful to him than anything else in the universe.

That's true love, right?

"Want another Backdoor Special?" Pinky asks from behind the bar.

It's become my breakfast drink of choice, from the very first time she served me one on the very first day we met. I don't have them every morning. Only on the mornings we do fork training to help me work through that particular phobia.

Pinky is the other great love of my life. Not in the way that Greta is, though. I'm not nearly man enough to think about even being adjacent to a bed with Pinky anywhere near my relative vicinity. I'm not sure anyone is.

Actually, I really, really want to see the guy who can go toe-to-toe (literally) with Pinky and live to tell the tale. He'd have to be something amazing. Seven feet of pink Mebdarian mutant is enough to give any guy serious feelings of inadequacy.

And I know guys are her thing, so don't think I'm assuming, like some sectarian rube.

I think this is a good time to let you in on a little secret. Remember that whole affair with me and my fishwife? Being a married man and then a divorced man, and then just kind of a confused man, helped me get my priorities straight.

At least marriage is good for something.

I realized that I have a lot more life to live. Not the scuttling-under-a-rock-like-a-frightened-crab kind of a life. I mean the big picture. What I want out of life. What I want to experience before I die.

That's what made me realize how precious Greta is, and that I must cherish every day I get to spend in her presence. Ideally,

I'd like that to be in the I-get-to-see-her-naked kind of way, but even if it means nothing more than being friends, I'm good with that too.

That's how much I love her. It's not about what I can put claim to. It's about what I'm lucky to receive.

Back to the secret. I meant to tell you about that, then I got distracted with Greta. It happens a lot.

Anyway, I bought a red shirt.

I know. I *know.* Don't look at me like that. I bought it, but I haven't worn it yet. Even having it folded in my tiny little storage compartment feels like I'm sitting on top of a bundle of warmth designed only for attracting a heat-seeking missile.

So don't give me a lecture about how a redshirt owning red shirt is just begging for trouble. If anyone knows that, it's me. Seriously. I fucking *know,* okay?

But think about it from my perspective. I'm sitting across the bar from Pinky, the baddest person who has ever been born on any plant, ever, and sitting next to Greta, the love of my life.

Can you blame me for wanting to be more than the sum of my parts? For wanting to look death in the face and laugh? Okay, to be honest, I don't laugh. I just hide behind Pinky. But still. I'm right there, facing death, all the same, and surviving. That's a long way from the guy who intended to live out his days on a Mebdarian retirement planet.

The way I figure it, my phobia about forks, and the one about being strangled by my pants and—well, okay, all my phobias—it all comes down to me being a redshirt, right? So if I actually put that thing on, and I wear it, and I don't die...doesn't that mean I've won?

Not that today's the day. I feel like tomorrow's not the day, either. But the shirt is there, where I could even touch it if I wanted to. And my intent is in place. So one of these days...yeah. One of these days, I will face the redshirt apocalypse, and wear that red shirt, and I will survive, and it will be glorious.

Just not today. Or tomorrow. Next week doesn't look good, either.

I mean, I'm not stupid.

"I miss Waldorf," Greta sighs. "He was so sweet."

"Not like his bastard of a brother," Pinky notes. "I'm glad to get that paranoid nut off my ship. If I'd known he was disembarking, I'd have attended, just so I could kick his ass on his way off."

Greta and I pause to look at Pinky. It's a certain solidarity between us, our mutual appreciation for Pinky's take-no-shit attitude and the social discomfort that sometimes comes along with her blunt views.

I've said it before and I'll say it again: if I hadn't fallen for Greta first, I'd have fallen for Pinky.

Pinky turns away and begins her violent ballet of drink making.

I'm a little sad about our recently departed Waldorf. He and his brother have left us for Mebdar IV. Ironically, it's the retirement colony I was planning to inhabit when I first arrived on the *Second Chance.* But Waldorf will quickly become popular, I'm sure, and his brother Statler will hopefully find the right elements to keep him content in his own cranky milieu.

"Our next big port is Summadonna," Greta says between bites. "I'm trying to think of a nice boarding gift for the new guests."

As the brand ambassador of the Garbdorian Fleet, Greta has a duty to the guests of the *Second Chance.* Recently, she handed out flower necklaces as newcomers boarded, which I'd described to her as leis. That resulted in much confusion and hilarity, and she's switched to welcoming guests with more benignly named goods.

"Should we visit Summadonna?" I ask. "I've never been there."

Greta looks thoughtful. "Most of the planet is basic suburbia. Pleasant enough, but nothing special. The port, though, has a great laundromat. That's why so many people board from there."

"Really?" I can't imagine what makes a laundromat such a popular destination, but it must be pretty good. "Laundromats are really dull where I'm from. Let's check it out."

"Cool," Greta says. "It'll be fun. Pinky loves the laundromat."

"What's so great about it?" I ask Pinky.

She shrugs. "It's a chance to get out of the rut and do something different."

Maybe this is a cultural thing that humans have been doing all wrong. For us, it's a mundane necessity at best.

"I'm looking forward to it, then."

Greta looks pleased. "I didn't think you'd want to go. This will be fun." She notices the time. "Oh, I'd better run! I have a teleconference on the lightstream in five minutes." She stands, stuffing the last of her muffin crumbs into her mouth as she does.

"New job offer?" I ask. She gets them all the time. Most of them, she turns down. She only chooses the ones that sound interesting or fun.

She nods and, since her mouth is full, she strikes a bodybuilder pose, with her arms hanging in front of her, bent at the elbows, hands in fists.

"Exercise equipment?" I guess.

She shakes her head.

"Nutritional supplements," Pinky says.

Greta nods, waves, and hurries out of the bar.

"She won't take it," Pinky predicts. "She doesn't like that kind of thing. Too much of an individual-results-may-vary thing."

"Yeah. She doesn't want to rep anything that disappoints people."

"She's a peach that way." Pinky clears Greta's plate and wipes the bar.

"I like that about her, too." I finish the last sip of my drink, which is only aperitif-sized because I have work of my own to do today. "Well, I'd better get to work. Those statistics won't analyze themselves."

Pinky shrugs. She has no interest in my work.

"I'll come back to help with the dinner rush," I add. Pinky always gets inundated with drink orders from the dining room and room service that time of day.

"Sure. See you then." She doesn't turn to look at me.

I don't take it personally. I walk the long way around the corridor to my cabin, stretching my legs a bit before I sit down for hours of analytical work via the lightstream.

I crunch numbers, do regressions, and interpret results for the next eight hours. Finally, when I'm ready to join Pinky to work the dinner hour, I check my messages. My boss has been known to deliver end-of-day work that absolutely must be done immediately. He's kind of a jerk that way.

There's nothing from work, but I have received a letter from my nana.

Dear Charlie,
Received your message. The news that you are not dead is very satisfactory. I had assumed your

death to be a foregone conclusion. Your accomplishments show an adequacy previously unknown to our family.

Nana used to be like other grandmothers. She patted my head and praised even the most basic of efforts, and always had baked goods to share. Ever since the cyborgs assimilated her, she's been underwhelmingly...well, underwhelming. I realize that's repetitive, but it's the best description of her. You'll see.

She's sort of like my nana, in that she remembers her experiences and still likes baking. However, she's not the nana I once knew due to her marked lack of warmth or personality of any kind. She's just so robotic, and for good reason.

Nana's crazy strong now, though, and has much greater perception than us mere biological beings. I guess that's some sort of trade-off for the other things.

Anyway, back to the letter.

Given your recent improbable success, maybe you could provide me with assistance. The cyborg union has denied me a replacement for my acoustic interlink, as well as repairs on my right shoulder. These things are problematic. I either can't hear what I should, or I hear things that don't exist. My shoulder prevents normal movement. If you get back to Earth, maybe you could help me find replacements? I also wouldn't hate seeing you for a visit. I'll make you some raisin bread.

Love,
Nana

She only uses that last bit because she knows she's supposed to. I don't think she's capable of feeling love as we know it. She needs help, though, and she's still my nana. Why the cyborg union goes around assimilating hapless grannies and then not giving them proper maintenance, I don't know.

If I'm lucky, she'll forget her promise of raisin bread. Nana used to be a first-rate cook, but everything she makes now comes out tasting like robot ass. I prefer not to think about why.

I pull up the current itinerary of the *Second Chance*. We're already on a course back to Earth, so visiting Nana is a no-brainer. First we've got the stop at Summadonna, then on to Mars. From there we'll be full-on to Earth.

A certain ambivalence comes over me. Earth is home, and home is always a good thing. On the other hand, my entire life on Earth was one of anxiety and bad luck. If it weren't for Nana needing help, I don't think I'd even leave the ship during that stopover.

But what kind of guy doesn't help his ailing nana, even if she is a cyborg? I don't really have a choice here.

That means after the laundromat and Mars, Charlie Kenny will be making his triumphant return to Earth.

CHAPTER 2

"Going back home, huh?" Pinky jiggles the hell out of a silver cocktail shaker, looking more like she's murdering the thing than mixing a drink.

"Yeah." I've explained to her my nana's plight, and am hoping she'll offer to help. I'll need her and Greta both if I'm going to make this work.

"I've never visited Earth," Pinky muses as she pours a Cheerful Seagull into a glass and garnishes it with an orange slice. "I guess I could check it out with you. You can show me some sights after we help out your grandma."

If sightseeing is the price I must pay for Pinky's help, then that's what I'll do. "Sure. We can get some funnel cake."

"Funnel what?" Pinky's looking at me like I've suggested we lick filth off the floor.

"Cake. It's a fried dough. They put sugar on it. It's good."

"Oh, fried dough. Mebdarians invented that. I like it."

Pinky thinks her people invented a lot of things. I just agree with her because it's easier.

I'm mixing a Mendacious Moocow, and I can't remember the proportions. "Is it one part rum and two parts coconut milk, or the other way around?"

"Trick question. It can be either. It just depends on how it was ordered."

I squint at the drink order. "It just says Mendacious Moocow."

"Two parts coconut milk. But if it's a Mad Mendacious Moocow, then you flip the proportions, and add four drops of cayenne sauce."

I shudder at the thought of what that must taste like.

"Have you heard from Greta?" I ask. "She usually shows up

around now."

"She said she's ordering room service in tonight. She has some emergency voiceover work to do."

As I mix the Moocow, I wonder at what would constitute an emergency for voiceover work. I come up with nothing, except maybe the person who was supposed to do the job fell through and they were on a deadline or something.

Regardless, if the job went to Greta, it must be a lucky break. That's the only kind of break she gets.

I was looking forward to seeing her, but I decide I'll take room service in my cabin, too. It's been a couple weeks since I watched movies and went to bed early. I'm due for some robot western fun. I'd invite Pinky to watch with me since she's also a fan of the genre, but she'll be tending bar most of the night.

Besides, it will give me a chance to write Nana back and let her know that soon, her grandson will be coming for a visit.

***

We've arrived at Summadonna. The *Second Chance* has connected to the elevator down to the planet, and I'm going to meet Pinky and Greta to check out this amazing laundromat.

I'm left with a dilemma. I only have a few outfits, and I send out my clothes every two days to the cleaning service on the ship. I don't have much to wash. But who shows up at a laundromat without stuff to launder? With a feeling of desperation, I put my one dirty outfit into my duffle bag, then add all my clean ones, too. Even the swimsuit I bought for the time we went to Mar de la Mar.

On second thought, I remove all of my underwear from the bag. I don't want Greta looking at them. It's weird.

But wait. If I don't *have* underwear, wouldn't that be weird? She might think I don't wear them or something. So which is more gross? Her seeing my underwear and presuming they're dirty, or her thinking I'm a freeballing, take-my-chances kind of guy?

This is complicated.

I stuff the underwear at the bottom of the bag, then put the other clothes on top. This way, I can delay the final decision until we get there. Maybe there will be some clue to help me decide.

My hand grazes the red shirt and I eye it, like a robot cowboy sizing up the enemy during a duel.

Nope. Today is not the day. I close the door to my storage

compartment.

You win this one, red shirt. But there will come a day when we do battle and I win.

Pinky and Greta are at the elevator when I arrive. I feel the situation begin to go sideways when I see how they're dressed.

Greta's wearing glittery bright-pink shorts and a neon-green halter top that's so vivid I feel my pupils dilating. Her pale-green hair is up in two ponytails, and she's tied pink and green ribbons into them. Her makeup is strangely sparkly, and, combined with the natural gentle luminescence of her skin, she's so shiny that I keep blinking.

She's also wearing the green swirled-glass necklace I bought her. Aw.

Pinky's wearing turquoise pants with a thick black stripe down the outside of each leg. She's also sporting a tank top that shows off her bulging biceps and her womanly assets in a way that makes me cover my eyes altogether.

"Are you okay, Charlie?"

I peek through my fingers to see Greta peering at me with concern. "I, uh, got something in my eye. Ow."

I put on a show of rubbing my eyes, then blinking rapidly. "I think I got it."

They're both carrying smallish bags. I guess I overpacked on the laundry front.

Pinky asks, "Where are your clothes for the laundromat?"

I pat my duffel bag. "In here."

She nods. "Gotcha."

I feel a little better. They must be wearing weird clothes because it's laundry day and everything else is being washed. Maybe those bags of theirs are bigger on the inside.

My anxiety ebbs. Until I hear a familiar, unwelcome, automated voice.

Welcome to the Chance 3000: A new experience in elevators.

Greta and I groan.

"I thought they fixed this," I complain.

"Shh! It'll hear you!" Her eyes widen with panic.

We've developed the Chance 3000 to better serve you, our guests. We elevate you because you elevate us. Please enjoy your elevator experience.

We remain silent.

State your desired destination.

"Down," Greta says.

You said, "Down." Now going down.

Greta and I exchange a look of relief. The Chance 3000 has given us troubles in the past, but maybe Gus got all of that sorted out.

Stopping for a moment of contemplation.

"Who's contemplating?" Greta whispers to me. "It or us?"

"I don't know," I murmur, helpless. "Let's just quietly contemplate something and see if that does the trick."

"What do we contemplate?" she whispers.

I don't know. I look at Pinky and say the first word that comes to mind. "Flamingoes."

Pinky gives me a thumbs-up. She likes flamingoes.

Concluding contemplation. Continuing to down.

I hold my breath. Hopefully we can continue unmolested from this point.

Stopping for dance party.

"What?" Greta's face is a study of confusion that reminds me of the first time I tried to use the water closet in space.

Commence dancing.

A fast bass beat fills the elevator with an *oonf oonf oonf oonf* sound. And now there are strobe lights. I throw a perplexed look to Greta and Pinky.

Pinky is not one to panic. She shrugs and begins stepping from side to side, pumping her fists in the air.

She's surprisingly good.

Greta drops low and starts doing some sort of movement that makes her behind bounce around like a bowling ball in a paint shaker.

I didn't know a booty could do that.

The space-time continuum seems to shatter around me. Everything goes white.

Then Pinky's heavy hand on my shoulder reminds me that I'm supposed to be dancing. I shuffle awkwardly to the left, then to the right, and raise my hands, willing them to do something cool. Something manly that says, *Hey, ladies, I'm a man of the universe.*

They flap like dead chicken feet.

Fuck. I don't know how to dance.

But the Chance 3000 seems to be satisfied. The music shuts off and the lights stop.

Nice moves. Proceeding to destination.

I hold my breath until we get to the bottom.

Arrived at down. Please depart.

Usually, I ascribe to the idea of ladies first, but I get my ass off that elevator faster than I even knew I could move.

Since the elevator is a direct link to our destination, I immediately get a good look at it.

This place doesn't look like any laundromat I've ever seen. We seem to be in a large atrium, like the ones at huge concert halls where people mill about when waiting for the big event to open up. Visitors stream in and out of a huge pair of double-story doors.

Everyone's dressed in bright colors like Greta and Pinky. I see glitter, fringe, and—in one case—a guy wearing chaps.

Popular misconception: there's no such thing as assless chaps. All chaps are, by design, assless. Chaps with an ass in them would be regular old pants. But it's entirely accurate to say that the fellow wearing them did not have pants on under his chaps, and my day was turning out to feature a lot more ass than I'd anticipated.

This couldn't be coincidence. All these people couldn't be so bizarrely dressed because all their other clothes were dirty.

I ask, "What is this place?"

Greta looks at me, puzzled. "The laundromat."

"I don't think it is."

"It is," she assures me. "This is the best laundromat in the galaxy."

"Okay, so define 'laundromat.'"

A little frown forms between her eyebrows. "You know, a place where people dress up, and dance, and there's lots of nakedness and drugs and stuff. A regular laundromat."

"That's not what a laundromat is on Earth."

"Oh." Greta looks all cute and serious. "So what is it on your planet?"

"It's a place where you go to wash dirty clothes. And get them clean. And dry. You know. Laundry."

"Ohhhhhhhh." Greta now understands my confusion. "No, this is different than that."

"Right." Here I am, at a nightclub with the woman I love, carrying a bag full of my supposedly dirty underwear.

Pinky's eyes fall on my duffel bag. "So that means that's not an awesome outfit. It must be..."

"My laundry," I admit.

Pinky takes it from me. "Don't worry, Charlie. I'll put it in a locker for you. Go on in, and I'll catch up."

I notice she's also wearing the necklace I bought for her, and it makes me feel better. If Pinky values something I gave her, I must not be a completely useless sectarian rube. "Okay."

"We'll have fun." Pinky pats my shoulder and disappears.

She is ridiculously stealthy.

Greta grabs my hand and pulls me through the giant doors. I don't know what to expect, but I'm pretty sure whatever happens won't be good.

It's not that I'm a negative person. That's just statistical probability.

I follow her in, though. Both because it's Greta and because her luck bends statistical probability the other way. That makes this endeavor a total crapshoot.

The place is as big as a warehouse and full of loud music, gyrating bodies, and a weird smell I decide not to think about too hard.

As I'm looking around, a guy walks up. He's a tall, good-looking Garbdorian and only has eyes for Greta. "Want to dance?"

She hooks her arm around mine, resting her other hand on the inside of my elbow. "Thanks, but I'm with someone."

I know she means as a friend, but that doesn't stop me from feeling a rush of pleasure.

My warm fuzzies dissipate when the guy asks, "Who?"

Like she isn't standing there with her hands on me. As if I'm invisible.

Greta only smiles. "The best." With a little tug, she leads me away. Once we get some distance, she asks, "Want to dance?"

I'm about to say no when the fast song playing segues into a slow song. Normally, I'd say no to dancing because, as you already know from my sad performance in the elevator, I can't dance. But slow dancing is nothing more than standing across from someone with your hands on them and swaying a little.

Even I can do that.

"Sure," I agree.

She beams at me and leads me into the middle of the crowd. I can't count how many couples we pass. I don't care. They're just scenery to me.

She picks her spot and puts her hands on my shoulders. I put my hands on her waist. Then we sway.

It's nice.

"I'm glad we came here," Greta says.

"Me too."

"Life has been so much more interesting since I met you."

"I can say, without reservation, that the past several months have been the best in my life." There's no comparison. The times I've had with Pinky and Greta have been amazing.

We stop talking and enjoying the swaying for a while, but then we have a lot of eye contact and the silence starts to feel awkward. I need to say something.

"How has your work been going?"

"Good. Actually, I just landed a small part in a movie. It'll only take me a day to do, and I'll be able to get it out of the way when we drop by Mars on the way to Earth."

"That sounds exciting." I've never seen a movie set.

"Yeah. I've always wanted to do a movie. Just for the experience of it. You should come and watch the filming."

"Think that'd be okay?"

She nods and her hair ribbons flutter. "Yes, I already asked."

"Great."

All too soon, the music ends, changing again to a fast, driving beat. I step back, my arms falling to my sides.

She looks uncertain. "You don't want to dance anymore?"

I look down at my feet. "Well, I just don't know how to dance to music like this."

The guy from before butts in, putting his hand on Greta's arm. "Looks like your friend wants to sit this one out. How about you dance with me?"

I'm not happy about this, and I can tell that Greta isn't, either. She hesitates. This is where I should step in on her behalf, but I'm just not the kind of guy who steps up and makes a scene.

Fortunately, Pinky is. She appears and her arm slides around the fool. Since I never got his name, I'm going to just call him Guy.

Anyway, she hugs him in tight to her side. "I am dying to dance! Thank goodness someone else here is, too!"

"I never knew you liked dancing so much," I say.

Pinky lifts her chin. "Oh, yeah. I'm the best. Galaxy class."

Guy looks frightened. Good.

Pinky takes him by the hand and clears a wide swath. Apparently, her dancing requires a lot of room.

Then she breaks out the moves, and I realize she wasn't kidding. She's incredible. She's got her hips swaying and footwork going, and her posture is fantastic. She spins Guy out, pulls him back in, and strikes a dramatic pose with one finger pointing straight up. Then she pulls Guy back in and propels him around the entire space she's cleared.

Most people have stopped to watch at this point. Some are just staring in amazement, others clap to the beat and call out encouragement.

Guy doesn't look like he's having fun. He should be. Pinky's making him look like a total dance pro. She picks him up for a fancy lift move, then swings him back down to his feet. And on they go with more footwork, working the dance floor.

When the song finally ends, the crowd erupts in applause and whistles.

Everyone else is looking at Pinky, so I'm the only one who sees Guy running for his life.

The music starts back up, and people drift away to do their own dancing or mingling or whatever.

"That was awesome, Pinky. You're a very dynamic dancer."

She seems pleased. "Thanks. Want me to teach you some moves?"

Do I?

I peek at Greta, who nods.

"I guess? Just something basic I can do in a situation like this. Nothing fancy. I'm not very coordinated."

"Nonsense," Pinky argues. "Anyone can dance. It's just a matter of doing a little practice so you don't look stupid."

Encouraging but blunt. I never have to wonder what Pinky really thinks.

She leads me through a sidestep thing, showing me what to do with my arms so they don't look like dead chicken feet or pinwheels or something. Then she shows me how to step forward and back.

"If you just do that, changing the pattern, no one will notice you can't really dance. They'll just see you moving. And after you've done this a while and gotten comfortable with it, you can add in some more things." She moves so easily, she makes even these basic steps look really good.

"Thanks, Pinky. For the dancing and for making that Garbdorian guy buzz off."

"Buzz off?" She starts looking around. "Did he go? Damn. He was a good dance partner. Limber. I like that."

"Kind of a jerk, though," Greta points out.

"Well, there's that," Pinky admits. "But if he was nice, I'd have felt bad about swinging him so hard. So it worked out."

"I guess it did." Greta seems pleased even though Pinky looks disappointed to have lost her partner.

We shuffle through a few songs. Well, I shuffle. My friends look great. They're the best dancers in the place, in my opinion.

"Should we get some punch?" I ask. "Or some food? I saw a refreshment table over there."

Greta's eyes widen. "Oh, no. You never eat or drink at a place like this, unless you want to go flying so high you won't come down for a week. Literally, a whole week."

"Oh. Well, let's not do that."

"Don't put on any stickers, either," Pinky warns.

"Okay." I was unlikely to do that anyway, but it's good to know.

"Oh, and don't accept any chewing gum."

"Right." I think I've got this place figured out. "Don't put anything in my mouth or let anything touch my skin."

Pinky looks thoughtful. "Yeah, that should pretty much cover it."

After a shuffling through a few more songs, I feel thirsty. "So what am I supposed to drink down here? I could use something cold."

"There's a bar next door." Pinky stands up straight. "Want to go?"

"I was thinking about just a water or something, but yeah, if that's where we need to go."

"I could use something, too." Greta somehow looks as fresh as she did when we first arrived.

After an hour of close confines in a warm space, I feel kind of sweaty and smelly. Walking back out through the big double doors is some relief, as the temperature immediately drops a few degrees.

We follow a walkway, then enter a bar. It's not like other bars I've been to.

Pinky's place, for example, has barstools, plus some tables and chairs. Mostly, it has drinks. It's a nice enough watering hole, but Pinky hasn't gone out of her way to give it a decorative ambience. That's what I think of as a bar.

But the place we've entered is different. It's bright white, with orange, red, and yellow décor. The feeling of the place is super cheerful. I see what looks like a milkshake mixer and some other odd equipment I've never seen in a typical bar. Actually, this looks more like a sundae shop.

"What kind of place is this?" I ask.

"It's an ice cream bar." Pinky gives me a weird look, like I should know that ice cream bars are always adjacent to laundromats that are actually discotheques.

I'll just roll with this one. "Right! Great."

I hope I can still get some water.

Pinky orders an actual ice cream bar, size extra large. I've never seen frozen novelties come in a variety of sizes, so I'm curious to see this. The bartender comes out carrying Pinky's dessert with both arms. He's lifting with his knees, but his back is rounded and his shoulders are hunched forward.

That is one big ice cream bar.

With an immense look of happiness, Pinky sits at a high table near the door and begins chomping.

Greta orders a sundae with just about every topping they have. Which is a lot. When the cup comes out, I can't even see any ice cream under there. I see gobs of candy covered with oozing toppings.

I love her, but her eating habits are gross.

I choose chocolate ice cream with cherry boba. If you've never seen boba, they're little candy bubbles that break when you bite them and release some liquid candy. They're yummy.

As if it has only just occurred to me, before I turn away with my ice cream, I ask, "Oh, you don't happen to have water, do you?"

The bartender serves me a large cup of water.

I totally nailed that.

Pleased with my success, I sit down with Pinky and Greta and begin eating my ice cream. After a couple of bites, I notice how big Pinky's bites are. I mean, they're huge. If I ate that much ice cream that fast, I'd get a—

"Ooh," Pinky says, clapping her palm to her forehead.

"Brain freeze?" I ask sympathetically.

"Yeah." Her face is scrunched up for several seconds before she opens her eyes and gives her head a shake. "Awesome."

She resumes her rapid ice cream consumption. I guess she likes brain freezes.

Greta is the last to finish her treat. She scoops up the last bite, then sits back and sighs. "That was yummy. Now what?"

"Why don't you two go back to dancing? This has been fun,

but I think I'm going to go back to my cabin."

Greta brightens. "I didn't want to say anything, but I'm tired. I'll come back with you."

We look at Pinky.

"I'm not leaving. I have a lot of dancing to do. I'll see you two tomorrow." With that, she chucks her napkin in the recycling vac and boogies out of the shop. Literally. She's dancing as she goes.

I admire her confidence so damn much.

As we walk back to the elevator, Greta hooks her arm around mine, like she did before. It's nice. Fewer people are moving through the atrium, so either the party is as hot as it gets, or people have gone somewhere to sleep. Or whatever they do after visiting the laundromat.

"What do you think the Chance 3000 will have in store for us this time?" I ask.

"I'm not sure how it could top the dance party."

"What do you think all that elevator nonsense is about?"

"I haven't wanted to say anything, but..." she glances around quickly, as if worried someone might overhear. "I think Pinky did it. It has her sense of humor all over it."

"Really? Can she do something that complex?" I wouldn't have expected programming to be in her wheelhouse.

"I've found that there is very little Pinky isn't capable of. And she loves punking people. I'd have to say she's the most interesting person I've ever met." Greta smiles.

"I'd say you and she are tied, for me. You're both pretty amazing. I'm lucky to have found such good company."

She gives my arm a jiggle. "Don't sell yourself short. You're the second most interesting person I've met."

"Me? That can't be true. You've met tons of people. I'm just a statistician with statistically unlikely bad luck."

We've arrived at the elevator. It opens and we step on. I hold my breath.

Welcome to the Chance 3000: A new experience in elevators. State your desired destination.

"Up," I say.

You said, "Up." Now going up.

I let out the breath I was holding, and Greta goes the same.

She turns to face me. "Really, Charlie. You're a great guy. The bravest person I know. You'll try anything, and you're kind to people. It would be really easy for you to be bitter about what life has handed you, but you're so nice. You even help Pinky out at the bar. It's inspiring."

Wow. I consider myself kind of a sad sack, but she makes me sound really great. And she means it.

Her gaze burns bright with sincerity, and she's grasped my hands with hers. We're looking into each others' eyes and *oh my god, we're having a moment.* Not just awkwardness, but an actual *moment.* I feel like I should confess how fantastic she is, but she moves a little closer and I wait to see what she's going to do, hoping it's what I think she's going to do.

Activating night vision mode.

What? No!

We've plunged into darkness, except everything's gone green. Instead of just having pale green hair, Greta's now all green. Except for her eyes, which are little black holes in her face.

"Charlie?" Greta's voice sounds anxious and her hands grasp more tightly to mine.

"It's okay. Just stand still." I put one hand on her waist to help steady her.

"Right. Thanks."

We're silent until the elevator stops.

Arrived at up. Enjoy your stay on the Second Chance.

If I could punch an elevator in the face, I would.

The doors open and Greta and I gratefully step onto the ship. I've lost her hands in the process, and grabbing them again now would be weird.

The moment is lost. But it happened. You saw it.

I walk her to her cabin. She stifles a yawn behind her hand. "Wow, I'm really tired."

At her door, we pause, and rather than our usual easy camaraderie, there's a definite awkwardness.

Is that good? Does that mean there's some chemistry going on here? Or does it mean things have gotten screwed up? I have no frame of reference for these things.

She smiles and says, "Do you want to come to my cabin for dinner tomorrow? We said we'd watch a movie together sometime."

I restrain myself from expressing the rabid enthusiasm that fills me. "Yeah, that would be great."

Smooth. So freakin' smooth.

"Good! I'll see you tomorrow." She disappears into her cabin and I'm left standing in the corridor, staring at the door, like a dingus.

I don't care, because I'm a dingus who has a date with Greta Saltz.

***

I'm going to level with you. You've been with me since I left Earth, expecting to quietly live out my days on a Mebdarian retirement planet. So I feel like I owe you some honesty for sticking with me for so long.

I've never been on a date.

Yes, there was that one time I hung out while girls were present, but mostly they were having fun with my classmates while I went home early to avoid being pulled into their youthful hijinks.

Hijinks and redshirts do not go to together, let me assure you.

So dating is new to me, and I just don't have the experience I'd like to have in this regard. I need advice. Some wise guidance from someone who's blunt as hell and will tell me what I really need to know.

Pinky is the only possible choice.

When I arrive at the bar that morning, she takes one look at me, comes around the bar, and then closes the place. It's like she knows.

She sits in a chair in the middle of her sanctum and makes an I'm-gonna-make-you-an-offer-you-can't-refuse gesture, directing me to the chair next to her. She sprawls comfortably, with one arm on the chair back and the other resting on the table.

"Tell me about it," she says.

I have a very weird sensation, like if I do this right, I'll be a made man, and if I do it wrong, I'll wake up with a horse head in my bed. Those are some pretty wide extremes, so naturally, I clam up.

My palms sweat. My heart races. I can't figure out how to start.

Pinky's seen me at my worst. That time when I almost choked to death on a tater tot comes to mind. She knows who I am and where I'm from. This shouldn't be so hard.

She makes a small wave of the hand, a gesture that says she's got this covered. "Okay. I'll start, then."

A tsunami of relief crashes over me. Pinky gets me.

"This may sound strange," she begins, "but it's all completely normal."

Oh, good. Whew. Normal. I like normal. Right smack-dab in the center of a normal distribution, with no outliers, no need for even thinking about standard deviations because here we are, smack-dab in the middle of *completely normal.*

Pinky nods, wearing a look of sympathy. "When two people are attracted to each other, biological forces come into play."

That's a weird way to start, but dating has a lot to do with a person's natural makeup of attraction and interest, so I'm prepared to ride this out with Pinky. See where she's going with it. Surely there's some wisdom once she gets to the point.

"The details depend, of course, on the anatomy of the two people. Or maybe more than two, if you're Gvertflorians or some of the other species who..."

Her voice becomes an odd sort of buzzing. I think my brain has shorted out. I'm pretty sure this conversation has gone a very wrong way, and I'm afraid to tune back in. But a date with Greta hangs in the balance, so I focus on tuning out the static and listening to Pinky.

"...penis."

Oh, no, good galaxies, no. I just...I can't. I can't listen to the birds and the bees, with Pinky's very blunt and galactically cosmopolitan twist.

This isn't what I signed up for.

"...might seem a little weird..."

I'm on my feet, and I don't remember standing up. "I..uh..." My brain searches wildly for some excuse. Any reason to leave the room. All of the cells in my body are telling me that escape is the only option at this point.

"Combustion!" I yell. I'm not sure where that came from. "Freakin' bats!" Don't know where that came from either. I think my brain has reverted to some Neolithic sort of self-preservation.

I run away. There is absolutely zero thought process involved. This is not a conscious choice, so don't judge me. It's like when you shield your eyes from bright light. This is pure, inborn instinct.

When I'm capable of processing my surroundings again, I realize I'm in the water closet near my cabin. Why here? I don't need to pee.

Oh, hell. I run my hands over the front of my pants.

No. No, I'm good.

I lean against the cool wall by the sink and try to make sense of it all. I'm like a person post-blackout-drunk, trying to remember what happened the night before. Trying to pinpoint the moment where it all went wrong.

"Charlie? You okay?" Pinky's voice echoes off the hard surfaces of the water closet.

"Yeah. Good. Fine." I try to make my voice sound deep. I don't really know why.

"Are you sick?"

"No. I just...uh..."

Pinky comes into view, big and strong as ever, but with a soft look of concern. It's the concern that undoes me.

"I freaked out a little," I admit. "I wasn't looking for a sex talk. I just wanted some advice on how to make a date nice. For Greta."

Pinky frowns. "Well, when I go on a date, I always like—"

I sense this going into a bad territory again, so I cut her off. "Just a date. Like, first date. Innocent. Nice. No penises involved."

Oh my god, did I actually say that?

But Pinky brightens. "Ohhh, I get it. Right. Sorry about that. I misunderstood."

My whole body sags with relief.

"You sure you aren't sick?" she asks.

"No. I'm just, uhm, you know."

"Lame," she concludes sympathetically.

"Yeah." Fine. I'm lame. Pinky gets it. I'm good with that.

"I think I went at this the wrong way," she says.

This makes me feel better. "Yeah?"

She nods. "Yeah. Let's get out of the toilet and go talk in your cabin."

As far as I'm concerned, those are some pretty golden words. "Yeah. Okay. It's this way." I lead her out and to 25J, the place I call home.

It's only when we're both standing there that I consider Pinky's mass versus the maximum capacity of my tiny cabin.

Whatever. Physics be damned.

I go in and fold down a pair of chairs from the multipurpose furniture assembly that's so cleverly built into the wall.

I sit and gesture to the other chair, which Pinky eyes warily.

"I haven't sat in something like that since the blagrook incident of '94," she says. Then she shrugs. "Whatever. Go with the flow, right?"

"I've been trying to," I agree. "Ever since I came aboard here."

"Right." She looks like she's thinking deep thoughts. "Right."

I feel like she's going to come to some kind of point or logic or conclusion or something, so I just sit and wait.

"So here's the thing," she says. "Dates are nothing. Not even a thing."

"How's that possible?" I ask. "Human culture is practically engineered around the concept of dating."

"Well that's stupid," Pinky says, dismissing my species' entire way of life. "Dating means people hanging out together, spending time. That's it. You and I do that all the time."

"Yeah, but it's different."

"Not really," she argues. "We hang out together because we like it, right?"

"Yeah," I admit.

"And you're nice to me and I'm nice to you, because we like each other, right?"

"Yeah, but—"

"But balls," she says.

I feel like that must be a phrase where she comes from because she says it so authoritatively.

"That's all dating is," Pinky insists. "Two people who like each other, hanging out, and not being assholes to each other. What's hard about that?"

"When you put it that way, it sounds easy," I admit. "But when it's you and me, there's no wondering if there's going to be, you know, something more."

"Like pressing squishy bits together?"

I don't know if she means kissing or other stuff, but either way, I do not want to pursue the thought further. "Sort of. Just intimacy in general, you know? How do you know if someone's interested?"

"Ahhh." Pinky nods in an I-understand-everything-now kind of way. "You don't know when you should up the ante."

"Exactly." Finally, she understands.

"For a guy like you, it's easy. Just wait. Let her up the ante."

It can't be that simple. "Don't women like a guy who takes charge?"

"Sometimes. Sometimes not. That's a highly complex concept,

and, frankly, you're not up to it. So, for you, the best approach is to wait for her."

"I don't want to be passive," I say. "I have feelings. Strong ones. I don't want her to think I'm just…"

"Lame?"

I didn't mind when she said it the first time, but now she's kind of rubbing me the wrong way. "I don't want her to think I lack interest or passion. I want her to know that my feelings are strong, and that I want to face whatever the galaxy brings, with her."

Pinky squints at me and purses her mouth, nodding slowly. I wish I knew what this means.

"I get you," she says. "I get where you're coming from. Pay close attention to her. Let her make the first move, but when she does, you move in and close the deal. The last thing you want to do with Greta is leave her hanging. Got it?"

"I think so?" I understand what she's said, but I'm not sure how to connect this to a real-life situation. "How do I recognize a move?"

Pinky presses her lips together and makes a deep "Hmmm," sound. She seems to be taking the question seriously. "That might be tricky. Greta is by nature an open, honest, and happy person. There have been times that people assumed an interest when she was only being friendly."

"Am I doing that?" I ask. "Is she only being friendly?"

"I don't think so." Pinky frowns. "She's different with you. She's been different since meeting you, too. I think you're something new and different to her. I think she's actually interested."

I blink at her several times. I suspected that my date with Greta was a real date, but to have it confirmed by someone as realistic as Pinky is something else altogether.

"Wow," is all I can say.

"Yeah." Pinky's tone is all agreement. "So don't screw this up, pal, or you'll regret it forever."

Well, that's quite a pep talk. Instead of feeling invigorated, I feel the spectre of the grim reaper on my shoulder.

She slaps my knee lightly. "Don't look so serious. Just be yourself. Natural. Have fun with her. If you two are right, it'll happen."

I feel better about that. "Thanks, Pinky."

"You got it, pal."

We sit in companionable silence for a moment. It's just long enough for me to notice how ridiculously outsized Pinky is for my teeny little cabin. She looks like a basketball player sitting on a preschooler's chair. If she were to yawn and stretch, she'd probably punch out my lightstream.

"What are your quarters like?" I ask.

"Bigger," she says. "Pinker. And way cooler. Although," she looks thoughtful for a moment, "your Renard paintings are awesome."

I look to my pair of robot-western paintings, and I'm proud of them. Not just because Pinky thinks they're cool, but because I thought they were and I bought them from the artist himself. To me, they are a symbol of my entire adventure in space.

"I'd better go reopen the bar. People get pissy when they want a drink and can't get one."

"I'll come help," I say.

Pinky holds up a staying hand. "Nah. You hang out. Think about your plan for the evening. Think about just having a good time, and going with whatever happens. Get yourself in the right headspace."

"Right. Thanks."

She gives me a gentle pound on the shoulder as she unfolds herself from the chair. "No problem. Just remember to name your first kid after me, if you ever have one."

Truth be told, I think about that for a long time before I switch to getting myself into a go-with-the-flow headspace.

Chapter 3

When I get to Greta's cabin, she's wearing a pale-green dress that stops just above her knee. It's cute and sexy and modest all at the same time, and is just so very Greta, because she's all good things at once, too.

She's ordered pizza for us, both Earth-style and Garbdorian-style, and we both have some of each while chatting about this and that. Then we watch a movie—some Garbdorian romance, which is a little far-fetched but has enough humor to keep me interested.

We chat. We eat. Briefly, during the movie, she shifts and her shoulder is against mine. It's nice.

I'd like to be able to describe some epic scene where we declare our love and one thing leads to another and suddenly there are fireworks and rockets and other thinly veiled imagery. But it's just a very nice evening, and I'm not sorry. A mere pleasant evening with the woman I love is more than I ever hoped to get out of life.

Our fingers don't brush one another, and I we don't get into some big tickle fight that becomes a whole romantic interlude. But I'm in her cabin, which is about twice the size of mine and decorated in sunny yellows and oranges, and I feel like she's really let me into her life for the first time.

It's a beginning, and that's an amazing thing.

Afterward, she sees me off at the door, and we have a moment of awkwardness after saying goodnight.

"I'll see you tomorrow, then," I say, ducking my head to hide my uncertainty.

"Okay. We can have breakfast at Pinky's." Her eyes are big and beautiful, and I feel like she's kind of inviting me to kiss her, but I heed Pinky's warning.

I wait.

Greta's smile suddenly brightens into a grin and she steps closer, then kisses my cheek. "Goodnight, Charlie." She looks at me from under her lashes, looking so happy, and I know this is not a chaste sort of kiss. It is an opening salvo kind of kiss.

"Goodnight," I say as the door closes.

I owe Pinky one. She was right. Any other guy would have kissed Greta first. But not me. I'm the one guy who wouldn't, and that means I'm the one who tempted Greta to kiss him first.

I am *the man.*

And Pinky's a genius.

***

In the morning, I wake, dress, and feel like this is a new beginning for me. I pass right by the dining room, forks and all, and don't even hurry my step. When I get to Pinky's, Greta's already inside, eating a waffle sandwich.

It's a Greta thing. It's two waffles with eggs and sausages and chocolate chips inside, and all the innards have been coated with candied sweet potatoes. The kitchen makes them special for her, and good thing, because I think the mere sweetness factor would choke most people.

"Yep. I have a real appetite this morning." She takes a big bite, which smears her cheeks with orange.

Pinky shoots a look at me but I do a it-wasn't-me shrug. Pinky squints at me hard before returning my shrug.

"Maybe it's this upcoming movie role," Greta muses after a sip of her juice.

"What are you playing?" Pinky asks as she mixes a drink.

"Oh, it's nothing." Greta looks embarrassed. "It's just a little walk-on role. The lead of the movie has just broken up with his girlfriend and as he walks off into the crowd, he bumps into me. He says, 'Excuse me,' and I say 'Don't worry about it,' and then the movie ends."

"Shouldn't take too long then, I guess," Pinky says. She sets a plate of eggs and potatoes in front of me. Apparently, that's what I'm having for breakfast today.

I've found it's easier to just let Pinky give me what she thinks I want. She's usually right.

Greta chuckles. "No, it'll just be a few hours of shooting. It's nothing. I just think it would be fun to be on a movie set."

I eat quickly and excuse myself to get to work. I'd taken the previous day off to mentally prepare myself for my date with Greta, so I'll have a lot to keep me busy.

After slaving the day away with statistical analyses, I order my dinner to my cabin and plan to watch a movie. Or part of one, anyway. Just enough of the beginning to help me fall asleep. I've always found it pleasant to drift off with the sound of robot cowboys defending their territory in the background.

To my surprise, Gus himself delivers my dinner. Gus is the head of service on the *Second Chance* and not just some porter. He doesn't handle food. When I see him outside my door holding a tray, though, I immediately suspect something is amiss.

"Here's your dinner, Mr. Kenny. I hope you'll find it satisfactory."

"I always do, Gus," I assure him. "Your kitchen staff is stellar."

He gives me a tight little bow and looks to one side, then the other, with a furtive look. Something is definitely going on here.

"Is there something I can help you with?" I ask.

He hesitates. "I hate to ask, but I'm in a desperate situation. Can I come in for a moment?"

For ultra-formal Gus to ask to come in, there must be something serious going on.

"Of course." I take the tray from him and step back, leaving space for him to enter my cabin.

Putting the tray on my table, I ask, "What's going on?"

Still he hesitates. He pulls his fancy hat off and holds it in his hand, worrying the brim of it with nervous fingers. "The thing is..." he clears his throat. "What I mean is, you're friends with Pinky, aren't you?"

"Yes."

"I think I made her angry a few weeks ago. I didn't intend to."

"What happened?" I'm aware that Pinky has never been fond of what she considers Gus's superior attitude.

"I said the wrong thing. A porter asked me to get him a drink, and I was on my way to make a report to the captain and, in my distraction, I asked him if I looked like a bartender. I didn't realize Pinky was nearby."

Oh boy. Yeah, implying that a bartender is somehow a lowly figure would definitely piss Pinky off. "I see."

Gus rushes on, "I didn't intend it as a slight. People choose to travel on this ship just for the drinks she mixes. She's a legend in the Chance Fleet. I just wasn't thinking, that's all. I have a lot of pressure on me."

He hangs his head, looking down at his hat.

"Okay," I say slowly, trying to put this together with his need to talk to me. "So what did she do?"

"I think she highjacked the elevator. I can't prove it, but all that Chance 3000 nonsense happened right after I made that comment, and hasn't gone away since. I've spent more hours than I can count soothing agitated guests and trying to get technical support to repair the elevator. Somehow, every diagnostic comes up just fine. No tech can ever replicate the problem."

I stifle a laugh. The idea of programmer after programmer checking out the elevator and finding it perfectly operational when it's actually stopping for dance parties and moments of contemplation strikes me as funny.

Poor Gus.

"I was thinking, since you're friends and all," Gus ventures, "maybe you could talk to her for me. Help me get the elevator back to normal."

This is tricky. I'm in between two important figures who run this ship. "I promise to talk to her about it. I can't guarantee it will make any difference, though. Maybe it isn't even her."

"Maybe," Gus allows, though I can tell he doesn't believe it's a possibility. "But if you'd talk to her about it, I'd be grateful."

"Of course," I say. "I'll see what I can find out."

He bows enthusiastically. "Thank you, Mr. Kenny! You have my undying gratitude."

"Then, do you think you could call me Charlie?" I'd rather he address me informally.

But Gus looks horrified. "Like a sectarian rube? I'm sorry, sir, I simply cannot."

He stalks out of my room, chin high. He is a proud, proud man, that Gus. That's probably the attitude that got himself saddled with a dance-party elevator.

***

The week leading up to our stop on Mars is pleasantly uneventful. I get a lot of work done, watch some movies, and Pinky teaches me a couple more drink recipes.

I don't see much of Greta, though, and that's a real downside. She's occupied with her own work, and preparing for her movie role. I don't know how many ways there are to say, "Don't worry about it," but it must be a lot.

On the big day, she tells us to come to the set at noon. She's arranged passes for us and everything. She leaves a few hours before, saying they do photography and stuff beforehand, for promotional reasons.

The time crawls. I'm more eager than I expected to see the movie set. Or maybe it's just that Greta will be in the movie. I do some work, but I'm not as focused as I should be so I put it aside. I tidy my cabin, but that only takes about a minute.

I can't even go help Pinky in the bar. She's taking a day off. I might as well take a walk. The exercise is good for me.

It's rare for me to have a chance to be bored. I usually keep quite busy. I do an entire circuit around the ship, and then take a second, slower lap. Along the way, I scrutinize the ship in a way I haven't before. I admire the neat rows of identical doors, the immaculately clean deck plates, the evenness of the rivets on the bulkheads.

This is a good ship. Well-designed, pleasing to the eye, and completely comfortable. It feels like a real home to me.

Noon finally rolls around and I meet Pinky at the elevator. As we get in, I consider what Gus asked me and whether I should broach the subject now.

I wait for the Chance 3000 to start some weird crap, but it takes us down to Mars without making a sound. It's a little eerie.

We descend beneath the planet's surface and I feel a little claustrophobic. Finally, the doors open and, again, the elevator makes no sound.

"That was odd," I say as we step onto a moving sidewalk.

"It didn't do anything," Pinky answers. "How's that odd?"

"That elevator has been so strange lately. It's established a habit of it, to the point that I've come to expect it. So when it doesn't do something, that seems odd."

Pinky grunts, looking uninterested.

"You don't know anything about the elevator, do you?" I venture.

"What do you mean?"

"Well, I thought maybe it was like the poorly translated signs you have up around the ship. You know, something you'd find funny." I don't think I'm doing a good job of tackling this subject.

Pinky stares at me. "You think I could do all that to an elevator?"

"I think you can do whatever you decide to do," I answer in all honestly.

She frowns at me, but then her expression morphs into a smirk. "Good. I like that."

The moving sidewalk ends and we need to switch to another one. I move toward the one with the blue stripe along its length, according to Greta's directions.

"You sure it's not the yellow line?" Pinky points in the other direction.

"Positive. Blue line, all the way down. Then there's supposed to be someone to greet us and take us the rest of the way."

She shrugs. "All right, if you say so."

"It's definitely blue," I insist.

"I said okay. Jeez." She steps onto the blue line with the look of someone who has been nagged most heinously.

I also notice that she has sidestepped the issue of the elevator, which is suspicious. But I decide to let it drop. For now.

One line leads to another and then a young human guy meets us, as Greta promised. He ushers us to a room with lots of cameras, an overabundance of people, and a strange, charged atmosphere.

A sign is lit up with *Live Set*. A stream of people cross what looks like a street intersection on Earth. Except, of course, we're a mile below the surface on Mars.

Hooray for movie magic.

I spot Greta. She's walking along, wearing an expensive-looking suit and looking important. A tall guy bumps into her and says, "Excuse me."

Wow, we arrived at the perfect time to hear Greta deliver her line.

She looks up at the guy with a cursory smile and says, "Don't worry about it." She barely breaks her stride.

"Wait..." The guy seems stunned. "Elizabeth?" He touches her shoulder.

Greta turns, and her smile has slipped. She pulls her sunglasses down to peer over them. "Can I help you?"

"Elizabeth?" he says again.

"Do we know each other?" Greta asks.

He nods. "Yes, I'm Rob! Remember?"

She frowns, then a light of recognition dawns in her eyes. "Rob? Oh my gosh! I didn't recognize you!"

She flings herself into his arms and there they are, hugging and laughing while the crowd streams around them.

"And cut!" A tall, skinny man shouts. "Fantastic, you two! Greta, you're a natural."

The entire space erupts into a flurry of activity. I can't even see Greta because there are so many people and so much equipment moving to and fro.

Greta appears, hugging Pinky then me. "You made it! Did you see?"

"We saw," I confirm. "You were great. Like a real movie star."

"Looks like they expanded your part." Pinky observes.

Greta beams at us. "Yes! They liked the chemistry between me and the lead actor, and decided to tie me into his backstory. His long-lost love from high school. How fun is that?"

"Very cool," I say.

Pinky shrugs noncommittally.

"Want to meet him? Glen's a real pro, and a nice guy, too."

"Glen?" I ask.

"Glen Gresham, the actor I was just working with. Don't tell me you didn't recognize him."

I shrug. If he's not in robot westerns, I'm not likely to know him.

Greta makes a sound of exasperation. "He's been in lots of movies lately. He's the it-guy for romantic dramas."

"I don't watch many of those," I say carefully.

Pinky is less tactful. "Bunch of stupid kissy junk. If stuff doesn't blow up and no one gets shot, it's not a movie worth watching."

Greta deflates a little. "Oh. Well, okay. Let's just go then. Do you want to do some looking around before we go back to the ship?"

"We just got here," Pinky says. I guess that means she'd rather stay for a while.

"Actually, I feel claustrophobic down here," I say. "Why don't you two have some fun, and I'll go back on my own."

It could be risky, me traveling on my own, but I'm reluctant to make them go right back to the *Second Chance* just because I don't care for being underground.

I mean, it doesn't even make sense. Being underground is no more perilous than being on a space ship. In fact, it's far less so. But I just don't like it down here, and there's no rationalizing with the kind of fear that makes you feel like your bones are trying to get outside your skin."

"That's okay," Greta says. "I've been down here lots of times. I'll go back with you."

Pinky frowns at us. "It won't be as much fun without you two. But I'll do my best anyway."

Before we can get off the set, I hear a voice behind us. *"Who is that?"*

Must be some big star or something. We keep walking.

"You there! The tall one! Please wait!"

We pause, exchanging looks. Do they mean Pinky? We turn around to see the director hurrying our way. His eyes are glued to Pinky.

"Who's your agent?" she asks.

Pinky gives her the look that Pinky reserves for people who aren't very smart. "I don't need an agent in my line of work."

The director, a fairly nondescript human with messy brown hair, blinks in puzzlement. "You're not a stunt actor?"

Pinky smirks at her. "I'm a stunt liver." Then she frowns. "Not, as in, like gizzards and stuff. I meant I live my life that way. That came out differently when I said it than it sounded in my head."

The director laughs. "Welcome to my line of work! Look, you'd be perfect for a movie I have coming up later this year. I'm trying to get Greta in on it, too. Would you be interested?"

Pinky shrugs. "I guess it depends on the details. Like everything else in life. I already have a job, but it could be fun. Have your people call my people."

She reaches into her back pocket, fishes out a business card, and hands it to the director. Then turns and walks away, like a total badass.

I scurry after her while Greta giggles.

On the way back to the ship, I chat with Greta about who she met and how she likes the experience of being in a movie. Pinky parts ways with us to go get some Martian food about midway.

"Was it fun?" I ask.

"At times," Greta says. "It was neat to see all these people working at creating something we only see as a finished product. I liked that part. I don't know that I'm cut out to be an actress, though. It was a lot of waiting around, and I bore easily."

"You were great, though," I say.

"Thanks. I did like the acting part. Especially when they gave me more lines."

"Be careful," I tease her as we arrive at the elevator. "If you get too famous, you might be mobbed by people everywhere we go."

She laughs. "I doubt that will happen from just a few lines at the end. But you're right, I'd hate the life of a major celebrity. So I guess I can check this experience off my list and keep looking forward to what's next."

"Like our visit to Earth?" After the glamor of all this movie stuff, my hometown might be a downer.

But she says, "Yes! I'm looking forward to seeing the places you think are worth visiting, and meeting your nana, too."

"She's not like she used to be. It's sad."

"None of us is what we used to be," she points out. "It's just life. And we keep living it until we can't anymore."

"You're right." The elevator's taking a long time. It must have been at the top when we arrived. "I'll keep that in mind. At least Nana's still around. At her age, that's something, for our family."

"Yeah!" She swats my arm in a way that, where I'm from, means, *You asshole!* But for Greta, it's just playful agreement.

I wonder if there are mental adjustments she's had to make to interact with people from Earth. Surely there are things we do that would normally mean something else to her.

I'm about to ask when the elevator doors open and a group of six *Second Chance* travelers shuffle off wordlessly, looking stunned.

Greta giggles as we board. "What do you think happened to them?"

"I don't know. I'm just hoping this thing has had its fun and will leave us alone."

I brace myself.

Going up.

Without even asking? Greta and I exchange a look, but don't dare to speak aloud. The Chance 3000 might take it as a hostile act and retaliate.

A hundred and fifty thousand people die on Mars every day.

Is that a threat? It kind of feels like one.

Greta is not wearing a look of confidence either. She mouths *What now?* at me, but all I can do is shrug.

The average person on Mars spends six years of their life waiting in lines.

Is it...is it trying to depress us? Is this what happened to the people who were on here before us?

One in every three thousand Martian babies is stillborn. No reason has been found.

Greta's mouth drops open.

Arrived at up. Have a nice day.

"Nice day, my ass!" Greta says. She's carefully waited until we've exited the elevator before speaking. She turns and kicks the door. "Wasted lives and dead babies! You're a dickweed, Chance 3000!"

We turn back around only to see a nice family of four staring at us in shock.

Greta's eyes widen and she bolts. I bolt after her.

When we're out of earshot, she hisses, "I'm probably going to get complained about for that!"

I'm sympathetic. I really am. I'd hate for something like that to happen to me where I work. But for it to happen to Greta, who's surely never had to endure something so embarrassing, is kind of funny.

I snort.

She looks at me in surprise as we reach her cabin door. "Are you laughing at me?"

"No." I try to smother a snicker but fail, and not only laugh, but cough painfully on top of it.

I clamp my lips together and hold my hands over my stomach, trying to contain my mirth, but it doesn't work. I'm shaking, laughing, and gasping for breath.

After a moment of looking outraged, Greta giggles. She holds her hand over her mouth as she laughs. "Oh, I shouldn't be laughing...stop it!"

She swats my arm.

"You stop it." I swat her arm right back.

We laugh there in the corridor for two of the best minutes of my life. Then she swipes her hands over her eyes. "Ugh. I need to get to the showers and wash off all this movie makeup. It's not like the regular kind. This stuff seems like it's made from tar or glue or something."

I'm disappointed to part ways, but following her to the showers is a total creepo-pervert move, and I don't care that for some water-conserving species it's normal.

Since I don't want my disappointment to show, I say, "I guess I'll check in with work, make sure nothing important came up. Want to meet for dinner?"

"Sure. That'd be nice. At the bar?"

I was kind of hoping she'd offer her cabin, but I act like I totally meant the bar. "Yep. Just give me a call when you're hungry."

"Will do." She gives me a funny little salute. "Thanks for coming down to the set today. Sorry you didn't get to be there longer."

"I'm not," I admit. "It was interesting, but I don't think Mars is my kind of place."

She nods sympathetically. "Okay. See you later, then!"

She disappears into her cabin.

I linger for a moment, just in case she remembers something and pops right back out. She doesn't, though, so I scoot on down to my own cabin. In my book, it would also be a creepo-pervert move to stand outside her room, waiting to see her shuffling down the hall with a change of clothes and her loofah.

***

We have dinner that night, and it's entirely ordinary. Regular food, regular conversation. Since Pinky is still on Mars, we don't even have her unique perspective to mix things up.

But ordinary is good. Normal is really, really nice. Between the two of us, sometimes our luck skews her way, and sometimes it leans mine. But the equilibrium we have for this dinner, in all its average glory, is pretty special to me.

Afterward, she walks me back to my cabin. "This was nice. We don't even have to be doing anything special, and I still have a good time."

"I had a good time, too," I say.

We proceed to have a perfectly normal, run-of-the-mill awkward moment. I'm so flush with our ordinariness that I lean forward and give her a kiss on the cheek.

She smiles and I bask in the moment, until Gus comes hustling around the corner. When he sees us, he slows his roll and tries to be all proper.

"Is something wrong?" Greta asks.

"It's the elevator, miss. It has deeply insulted some Gvertflorians by implying that they appear to be octopi."

I grimace. I'm glad dealing with that situation is Gus's job and not mine. Gvertflorians do not have any sense of humor at all. They are dreadfully serious.

"Poor Gus," Greta says when he's out of sight. "I'm sure that won't be fun to deal with."

Funny. For once, someone is having worse luck than I am.

After Greta's gone and I'm tucked up in my cabin, I take some time to appreciate my change in fate.

CHAPTER 4

The next three days are pleasantly mundane. Whatever happened on Mars seems to have energized Pinky. She's been particularly cheerful lately. The three of us fall back into our regular routines of fork training every other morning, breakfast together, and working during the day.

I could easily spend forty or fifty years this way.

Then we arrive at Earth, and my feet are suddenly made of lead. Earth is part of my old life, when I was never happy and I was due to die any day. I just don't have good associations with the place and I feel like going there will be begging bad redshirt luck to come find me again.

It's like a joke. Why did the redshirt return to his doom? To help his cyborg nana.

Fine. I didn't say it was a good joke. Quit judging. I'm worried for my life, here. Hahas are scarce when you're fearing a grisly death.

Maybe I should be making more progress with my phobias, but I've only had six months of this kind of life, compared to twenty-plus years living under the spectre of doom.

These things take time.

I'm using all of my self-calming techniques as I descend to the planet of my birth. I breathe deeply. I visualize my health and well-being. I calculate the odds of various possibilities. Most of all, I stick close to Pinky and Greta. They are the only way I'll make it out of this alive.

The elevator doesn't give us any shit, and for that I'm grateful. I have enough occupying my headspace right now.

Greta's been trying to teach me to look on the bright side. So, on the bright side, at least my cyborg nana is less likely to disapprove of me hanging out with a Garbdorian and a Mebdarian mutant. I think she'd have been fine with Greta even before she got assimilated, but I could see her finding Pinky unnerving. Nana lived a fairly sheltered existence as a redshirt. Until the cyborgs showed up, anyway.

We reach the bottom and the doors open. Here we are. On Earth. My old stomping grounds. The place of my birth.

The place I hadn't intended to return to.

Nana still lives in the same little house. You'd think her daily life would change a lot more after assimilation, but it isn't like that with the cyborgs. They're not raising an army or anything. They're slowly building a consensus, which will eventually become a majority. Then they'll be able to control things on a political level. It's smart, in a slow-moving, grass-roots kind of way. Since people who are assimilated are still citizens of their respective planets, they can't be deported.

All Nana really has to do, outside of her knitting and her crappy baking, is report to the cyborg union every week. She says the meetings aren't so bad, either. Cyborgs aren't much for waxing poetic or playing to the crowd. They just announce basic information and that's that.

Plus, Nana gets a monthly stipend from the cyborg union. So it's not all bad. I like knowing she has plenty of pocket money to play canasta. Even after her big change, she's a wicked canasta player. Her implants actually make her better at it, to the dismay of her card buddies. So the change hadn't been all bad for her.

I hate the idea of her suffering equipment failures, though.

We walk up the neat little stone path that leads up to her door. She used to be a good gardener, but not so much these days. Though she weeds and waters regularly, she has no eye for landscape design. She mashes plants together in one space, then leaves adjacent swathes entirely barren. And she tends to make everything way too geometric.

Not everything needs to be a sphere or a cube, Nana. These are shapes that just don't occur very often with plants.

I step up, ring Nana's doorbell, and wait.

Nothing.

I ring again. I can hear the bell inside the house, so I know it isn't broken. She said something about her acoustic processor not being right, so maybe she can't hear?

I try the door, but it's locked.

"Charlie?" A voice comes from behind me.

I turn and see Nana's neighbor. "Hello, Mrs. Dubstep. Nana's expecting me, but not answering the door."

"Yes, she left a message with me. There was an emergency canasta session, and she'd gone to it. She said to tell you she'll be back in four hours."

"An emergency card game session?" I'm unsure what would constitute such a circumstance.

Mrs. Dubstep nods.

"And it will last four hours?"

She nods again.

"Ah, okay, I guess." What else can I say? "We'll come back later."

"It's good you've come to visit. You're such a good boy." Mrs. Dubstep smiles at me. "Her hand keeps falling off, and it's driving her crazy."

My nana's hand keeps falling off, but she's off on an emergency four-hour canasta bender. Sure. That makes sense.

Mrs. Dubstep disappears back into her house, which is a mirror of Nana's cute little cottage.

I look to Greta and Pinky. "I guess that leaves us some time for sightseeing."

"Yay!" Greta hops up and down. "I want to buy a funny hat."

Is that a thing where she's from? "I'm not sure if there will be hats," I say. "I mean, maybe. Mostly we have t-shirts and water globes as souvenirs. But we can look for hats."

As soon as I say it, I feel like a putz, because if Greta wants to find a hat, she will. But she just beams at me, full of apparent excitement.

"Okay. Should we start with the Statue of Liberty? We'll need to take a train, then a ferry."

Greta hops some more. "Let's do it!"

Pinky nods, so I lead them down the lane and we catch a taxi to take us to the train.

Pinky frowns at me. "A taxi, to get to a train, so we can get on a ferry? This is inefficient."

"I know. This part of New France is like that."

"New France?" Greta looks puzzled. "I thought the Statue of Liberty was on some island near New York. I had to memorize a lot of sightseeing facts when I started with the Chance Fleet, and I'm sure I remember it."

"You're right," I assure her as we get out of the taxi and

purchase train tickets at the automated kiosk. "Historically, this part of Earth was known as New York. It's part of a region that was known as the United States until recently. About fifty years ago, we struck a trade alliance with France. One stipulation of the deal was renaming the state *New France*."

"Those are the wine and cheese people, right?" Greta's face scrunches up as if pulling these facts from her brain is painful.

"Yeah, no one saw that change coming. And between you and me, behind closed doors, we just keep on using the regular names. The renaming is just a commercial thing. It'll change back in a few years anyway, when the naming rights expire."

"Wow." Greta seems stuck between being impressed and being confused. I frequently feel the same way about it.

We walk across the train terminal to the boarding platform.

"We wait here until we get the signal for boarding to begin," I explain.

Pinky's looking at the train the way a five-year-old might. All big eyes and enthusiasm. "Think they'll let me shovel coal?"

I hate to disappoint her. "No, they haven't used coal for a few hundred years. Too messy and inefficient."

Her expression falls. "Is there anything I can shovel? I've always wanted to do some manual labor aboard mass transit."

It's a strange dream, but who am I to judge?

"I don't think so," I say gently. "But maybe you can meet the driver." Usually this privilege is limited to children, but I think in Pinky's case they'll make an exception.

"I guess it'll do," Pinky says sourly, crossing her arms over her chest.

People hustle by, carrying bags and suitcases. I'm glad we're not at the station during a peak time. I hate crowds. Already, this place has more activity than I'd prefer.

A man in a dapper hat yells in a resounding voice, "Allll aboard!"

I start forward, but Pinky and Greta keep standing there. "That's the signal to board," I say.

"What, that bellow?" Greta blinks at me.

"Yes. It's nostalgic. From the days before electronic messaging."

"Oh. Cool. I guess." Greta shrugs and follows me.

Pinky looks unimpressed. I think she's still mad about not getting to shovel coal.

"Do you think I could get a hat like the one the guy who

yelled has?"

What's with her and hats today? But I don't say anything about it. "That's the one you want?"

"Yeah. I like it. It's so...stripey." Greta nods.

"I'm sure we can find one somewhere."

"One for me, too," Pinky says. "Stripey is cool."

We board and find our seats. Greta and I sit side by side facing front, while Pinky has the opposite pair of seats to herself. She faces us, frowning. Scowling, actually. The people across the aisle have noticed and are getting nervous.

A car attendant hurries over. "Is everything okay over here?" Waves of worry seem to roll off her.

I defer to Greta so she can work her magic.

She gives the attendant a big smile and, is it just me or does she seem a little extra luminescent for just a few seconds there?

"Hi," Greta says warmly. "We were wondering if we could visit the engine car and meet the engineer at some point. It's our first trip on an Earth train." She says this last in a confiding way, which comes across as delightfully endearing.

The attendant glances from Greta to Pinky and back. I don't think I even exist at the moment, as far as she's concerned. "I'm sure that could be arranged. Welcome aboard. Is there anything else we can do to make your ride enjoyable?"

Pinky's scowl eases into a mere frown. "Do you have that drink stuff Earth is famous for?"

The attendant looks puzzled, but keeps smiling. "We might! Do you know the name of it?"

"I've heard it's yellow and sour like battery acid." Pinky looks hopeful.

The attendant has no response to that. She just keeps smiling bravely.

"Pinky, do you mean lemonade?" I ask.

"That's the one!" Pinky nods.

How is a bartender unfamiliar with lemonade? If it were anyone else, I might suspect some sectarian rube-ishness at play.

The attendant nods. "Of course! Shall I bring three lemonades while I send word to the engineer?"

"That'd be sporting of you," Pinky says approvingly.

The poor woman looks so relieved that I feel sorry for her, and she hurries off to score some lemonade.

I peek at the people across the aisle. They keep giving us

furtive looks, but don't seem as anxious as before.

Twenty minutes later we're sipping lemonade, watching the landscape fly by the window, and waiting for the engineer to call us up. I don't really want to visit the engine. I don't hate trains or anything, I just don't need to visit the place where the driving happens.

When the attendant returns to let us know we can go back to the engine, I opt to remain. "You two go have a look. I'll stay here."

"You sure?" Greta asks. "I could stay here if you'd rather."

"No, go ahead." Pinky's already on her way, so I whisper, "Just keep Pinky out of trouble."

She giggles and nods before hurrying off after our tall friend.

They remain absent for the rest of the ride. I don't mind. With the gentle rocking of the train, I could almost fall asleep. But I won't. Because falling asleep in public is a great way for a guy like me to get robbed, beaten, or wake up in a tub of ice in Hoboken with both my kidneys missing.

Not today, organ pirates!

The train has stopped and the other passengers have disembarked by the time Pinky and Greta finally return. Improbably, they're both wearing train conductor hats and looking quite pleased about it.

I say nothing.

I continue to say nothing on the ferry ride, and by the time we finally step out and get a good view of the Statue of Liberty, I've kind of forgotten about the hats.

We stand looking at the big green metal majesty of the statue. Pinky nods slowly. "I like it. She looks like someone I could be friends with. Do you think I could get a pointy hat like hers?"

A big, metal crown with huge spikes? I doubt it. But I say, "Hm, I don't know. Might be tough."

"A shame. Everyone should have one of those. Maybe I'll get one custom-made. I know a guy."

I feel a strange sense of synchronicity. Somehow, Pinky fits in Old New York/New France better than I ever did. She does it without even trying, too.

We wander around, eat some funnel cake, and just kind of waste time until we can get back to Nana's house. It's nice. It makes me think of how I would have misspent my youth if I'd had the chance.

Better late than never.

The trip back to Nana's is easier going. My friends are already champs at taking the ferry and the train, and though Pinky complains again about the taxi, we return to Nana's in good spirits.

I ring the doorbell and almost immediately the door opens. Nana steps out of the house.

Back in her day, Nana was a bonafide beauty. She's pretty even now, with the left side of her face covered in cybernetics. She always said her left eye was a little lower than her right anyway. Now it doesn't matter. She has a carefully coiffed puff of thick white hair, done up in an old-world style of wavy glamor. Most of her body below her chin is hardware. It's good that it cured her arthritis, but bad that she can't get repairs when she needs them. She wears a feminine dress in some old-lady style, with lacy stuff around the edges.

"Charlie. Come give your nana a hug." Her voice has a metallic ring, but it mostly sounds like her.

I give her a hug, careful not to dislodge any hoses or scrape myself on metal.

"I'm so glad you came. Who are these people?"

"Greta and Pinky." I point to them in turn. "The best friends in the universe."

"I didn't think I'd live to see the day," Nana says. "But then, I didn't think I'd have an exhaust hose instead of a rectum, so there you go."

Greta laughs in surprise, but Pinky nods approvingly. "I like her."

Nana didn't used to be so blunt, but now that I see Pinky digging it, it occurs to me that the two of them have things in common. Huh. I wonder if that has something to do with my nearly instant liking of Pinky.

"You've done well." Nana's looking at my friends. "You should marry her. You'd have cute babies."

Even cyborg nanas worry about marrying off their grandkids.

"Which one?" I ask, wondering if she can pick up on my love for Greta.

"Either. They're both good. I can tell." Nana tilts her head to one side. "Though, I doubt you could handle the big one. Sexually speaking."

"You got that right," Pinky agrees.

You probably think I'm dying a thousand deaths of embarrassment, but actually I'm not. Sure, my nana and my friend are talking about my sexual prowess, and right in front of the woman I love, too, but I long ago gave up the idea that I even had any sexual prowess. So nope. I have no feelings to hurt in that regard.

Besides, I agree with them.

"Come in, I'm making tea." Nana doesn't wait for an answer. She just goes into the house and leaves us to follow.

As we enter, she greets Greta and Pinky likes guests going through a receiving line at a wedding. She clasps their hands and thanks them for coming. "You can call me Rose. Or Nana, like Charlie does."

"You got it, Nana Rose." Pinky points at Nana and makes a loud click sound with her tongue.

We sit at Nana's little table in the kitchen and she fusses with cups and saucers and pouring tea. When I take a sip, I'm relieved to find that it's not bad tea. It's thoroughly tolerable.

Then she breaks out the cookies. "I almost forgot these," she says as she arranges them daintily on a plate. "They're Charlie's favorite."

I try to warn my friends with my eyes, but it's tough to convey panic and destruction without Nana also seeing it.

Greta takes a polite nibble, smiles, and sets the cookie down under the guise of sipping her tea. She's clever like that.

Pinky's chewing thoughtfully after tossing a whole cookie into her mouth. "Minty. I like it."

Oatmeal cookies are not supposed to be minty. But, because I love Nana, I take a bite and chew, smiling as if hell demons of doom are not dancing on my taste buds.

What is that other flavor? It's kind of...grassy. And then there's the weird taste that is both metallic and oily, and seems to be the signature flavor of all her baking.

"I added some green tea leaves, to make them fancy," Nana adds.

This is not what fancy tastes like. But I smile at Nana all the same, while formulating a plan to dispose of the cookie when she's not looking.

If I talk, I can't eat. "So, Nana. What's the problem you're having with unrepaired parts?"

"My joints all need to be realigned and tightened. My hearing is not right. And my shoulder has a tendency to hitch at the most inopportune times." Nana rubs her right shoulder.

"Mrs. Dubstep said your hand keeps falling off," I say.

"Oh, that busybody. I wasn't going to mention that. Don't want to seem like a complainer." Nana pouts.

"Nobody thinks that," Greta assures her. "You deserve to get the maintenance you need. We'll make sure you do."

"It won't be easy," Nana warns. "The cyborg union is notoriously chintzy when it comes to repairs. You pretty much have to have an entire system failure for them to do anything."

"Not cool," Pinky says after swallowing another cookie. I think she actually likes them, and that makes me question things about her. "Greta's right. We'll make sure you get what you need."

"Hot damn, I'll be swimming in oil tonight!" Nana rubs her hands together.

Nana always liked the phrase "hot damn" but the idea of swimming around in oil only became an appealing one to her after being assimilated.

She takes off her apron, hangs it on a peg, and smooths her dress. Then she stands by the door. "Well?"

Oh. She wants to leave *now.*

We jump up and follow Nana.

"You got it, Nana Rose," Pinky says on the way to Nana's car. "Let's go make those bastards fix your hand, and the rest of you, too."

"Damn straight." Nana holds up her metal fist and Pinky fist bumps it.

What's happening here? Greta and I exchange a look of uncertainty.

Pinky has apparently won front-seat privileges, because Nana tells me to sit in the back with Greta. Or maybe she's still working the marriage angle. It's hard to tell with her.

Nana was an iffy driver back in the day when she was entirely biological. Now, she's a downright terrifying one. She calculates things so precisely that she can drive in a way that, for anyone else, would be insanely reckless.

It doesn't help that every time our bodies get crushed down with g-force thanks to a sharp turn, Pinky raises her hands and yells, "Whooo, that's it, Nana Rose! Metal to the pedal!"

The first time this happens, Greta says, "Isn't it pedal to the metal?"

"Nah," Pinky says, pointing at Nana. "Cyborg."

I laugh. Greta laughs. Then Nana takes another sharp turn and I feel like I might lose my tea.

In no time at all, we pull up to the cyborg union office. It occurs to me at this point that we haven't come up with any specific plan. We're showing up with nothing but the desire to help Nana.

Well, we also have Greta's luck. And everything that Pinky brings to the table.

So, yeah. We're good. We got this.

We get out of that car gangsta-style. I wish I could film it, because it's like a movie. Nana and Pinky lead, with Greta and me flanking them. We walk side by side right up to the door like a group of highly intimidating vigilantes. I imagine what we would look like in slow-mo.

Nana opens the door and the moment is ruined because we have to line up single file to enter, and that's just too orderly to be cool anymore.

But we're in now, and those cyborgs are going to get an earful. Well, if they have ears. Okay, let's just say they're going to have their asses handed to them. Wait. Same problem.

Damn, why do so many phrases for throwing down involve body parts?

Whatever. We strut right up and...take a number. Because there's no one here but a number-ticket machine. Apparently this place is entirely automated.

Of course. Because cyborgs.

We are so screwed once cyborgs compose the majority of the population.

We sit down on the hard, uncomfortable chairs and wait. Even Pinky cannot make sitting in a waiting room look cool.

Even though no one else is in the room, it takes a good fifteen minutes for the sign on the door to change to *Now serving number twenty-eight*. A latch mechanism in the door pops.

Pinky stands up.

"We're twenty-nine, dear," Nana says, waving her ticket.

"Well, today, we're twenty-eight." Pinky opens the door.

Yeah, she's got her cool back. I don't know if it comes across to you while you're reading this, but it's the way she said it that matters. She sounded like Zorbo Blergbot in the movie *Laserfight in the DNS Corral*. All tough and gritty and stuff, like she eats steel beams and spits them out.

On second thought, maybe she does.

We follow Pinky's lead and enter a room with cyborgs sitting at teller windows. One window is labeled *Employment*. That's not the one. The second has a sign that says *Referrals* and I don't want to think too hard about what that means. The third says *Maintenance*, which seems like the place for us.

There's only one chair opposite the teller, so we encourage Nana to sit. She's probably tougher than any of us, but it seems like the right thing to do for an old lady.

"Can I help you?" the teller asks.

"I've sent a dozen requisition forms, but I haven't been able to get repairs. I need joint maintenance. Especially for my hand." Nana holds out the faulty extremity, palm up.

"You look functional," the teller says, scrutinizing Nana.

"Well I'm not falling over or unable to activate my circuits, but is that what it takes to get service?" Nana asks.

"If we give everyone free tweaks that they don't really need, how will we have time to service the people who really need it?" the teller reasons.

"I don't know, maybe you let the people who are struggling decide if they really need it? Aren't they the best judge of that?"

"No." The teller sits straighter, and I can tell she's about to refuse to help Nana.

"Look," I say. Everyone looks at me. Uh oh. I didn't have a good speech planned or anything. I'm just going off the cuff. This doesn't bode well. "You cyborgs go around assimilating people and then not living up to your obligations. Nana didn't ask to be assimilated. You did that. If you don't start stepping up and helping people who ask for it, I'll..." My mind races for a threat. I mean, what can I really do about it? What can anyone do? If cyborgs were easy to thwart, we'd have found a way to keep them from assimilating poor old nanas in their own kitchens.

My gaze goes to Greta. Greta of the golden glow and the woman I love, who has all the luck. How far can I push that luck?

Let's see.

"I'll call the Gvertflorian prime minister and ask his people to rid Earth of cyborgs once and for all."

Everyone knows that Gvertflorians have a blood feud with cyborgs. Dang, there's the body-part issue coming up again. Can you have a blood feud with cyborgs? They don't have much blood. Maybe they have an oil feud or a coolant feud or something.

Urg.

Anyway, Gvertflorians hate cyborgs and would be delighted to come rain hell upon them. That'll never happen because the fallout would be tremendous and Earthlings aren't about to sign up for that.

The teller clearly doesn't believe me. She shouldn't either. It's a ridiculous claim. Here's where I back up my claim with some fake proof. I hope.

I hand my telcoder to Greta. "Call the prime minister's office and tell them we may need to call in that favor."

Greta gives me a look of panic, but she takes the telcoder and begins punching in numbers. A lot of numbers. Like, fifty of them. Intergalactic calling is a nightmare.

She turns her head, so only Pinky and I can see her look of surprise. "Oh! Yes, please hold one moment."

She hands the telcoder to me.

I hand it to the teller. "Here. This is the prime minister's private secretary. Heed my warning: you will be thinking about whatever happens next for the rest of your life. Don't make it something you'll regret."

The teller looks unsure. She takes the telcoder. "Hello?"

The servo on her neck makes a popping sound. She thrusts the telcoder at me. "Take it!" she hisses.

I say into it, "Please stand by," as if there is something to stand by for. Then I fix the cyborg with a look.

She backs away. "I'll arrange Rose's repairs immediately. I will also call an emergency union meeting with all representatives. We wish to avoid a Gvertflorian conflict."

"Yeah, ya do," Pinky drawls. "Get your robot ass moving. Nana Rose needs fixing."

When the teller leaves through the back, I want to sag into a chair, but there isn't one. I will my bones to remain solid for at least a little while longer. I lean against the wall and let out a long breath.

Oh no, the telcoder. I put it to my ear, and the line is still open. Crap. "Apologies," I say. "We'll call back later."

Pinky, Greta, Nana, and I are trying to contain ourselves. We're well aware that there are probably listening devices, and maybe video monitoring, too. Though I have a strong desire to cheer and celebrate our success, I hold it all in.

A cyborg man wearing a white coat enters. "Hello, Mrs. White. I hear you're having joint issues? If you'll come with me, we'll get those fixed right now."

He leads Nana away, and the teller returns.

Pinky leans toward her. "If we have to come here again, I'm not going to be nearly so nice. And I'll be looking for you, personally. Got it?"

The teller's neck servo makes another popping sound. "I assure you, the issue has already been handled. This won't happen again."

"Make sure it doesn't. I like punching stuff."

She walks back toward the waiting room.

"She really does," Greta says before following.

I feel like I should leave some last, parting words. Something really cool like Zorbo Blergbot would say.

Nothing comes to me. It seems I've used up all of my cleverness for the day. I just point at her menacingly, then follow my friends.

We go right past the waiting room and outside the building. Once in the outdoors, I feel like I can breathe again. That building was downright oppressive.

Greta, Pinky, and I cheer, hug one another, do some funky victory dance moves, and generally make people either stare or turn around and walk the other direction.

We're so hyped up on our success that I send Nana a message that we're going to do some window shopping while we wait. I don't know how long cyborg maintenance takes, but I'm guessing she's going to get the extra-uber deluxe treatment, so I figure we have time to kill.

The first shop is a jewelry store, and while I'd like to do the cute shopping-for-a-ring thing with Greta, that experience is way off in the distant future. Maybe. I hope.

We skip the jewelry store. We also have no need for the beef jerky store. Why is there a whole store for that? It defies explanation.

The third store is a winner. It's a monument and sculpture store, but Pinky spots something and strides right in.

With surprisingly little resistance, although with a hearty helping of puzzlement, the man inside removes a metal crown from a sculpture.

"But what are you..." he begins as he hands it to Pinky.

She puts the Statue of Liberty crown on her head. I must admit, it looks rather regal on her.

She looks to me for an opinion.

"Majestic," I say.

"Magnificent," Greta adds.

Pinky looks to the man, who looks taken aback.

"Uh...dignified?" he offers.

Pinky nods approvingly. "I'll take it. How much?"

The man says, "It's really not meant to be an individual..." he sighs and shakes his head. "How's two hundred?"

"Sold," Pinky declares as if he'd been plying her with his wares.

He rings up the sale. Being the professional he is, he asks, "Would you like a box for it?"

"No thanks, mate. I'll wear it out."

We do some more window shopping before going back to meet Nana. We find nothing else of interest, but it doesn't matter. Nothing could have topped Pinky's find.

***

We arrive back at Nana's house in a wave of triumph and satisfaction. We troop into her little cottage and she embarrassingly regales us with stories of my childhood.

Even cyborg nanas are biologically required to engage in this rite of passage.

Pinky wears her glorious crown the whole time. Instead of objecting to her wearing a hat in the house, Nana wholeheartedly approves. She and Pinky have so much in common, it's spooky.

Meanwhile, Greta hugs my arm while she laughs about the time I narrowly avoided a kidnapping by a man who turned out to be a serial killer.

Yeah, I know. It sounds dark. But the way Nana tells it, it's a hoot. She's got a knack for storytelling and a certain comedic timing. I hadn't previously realized this about her.

But Greta's hugging my arm and laughing and I can feel her heartbeat and some other, softer things against my elbow, and I don't give a damn about anything else. So I laugh, too.

All too soon, it's time to leave. The *Second Chance* will be moving on, and we must move on with it. I'm sad. I feel like I'm just getting to know this version of my grandmother. But my new home is in space, and a starship waits for no man, woman, unspecified, or Nana.

It is a rule of the universe.

Nana seems sad, too. "What's your next port?" she asks.

"First, Earth's international space station, and then on for a tour of the Alpha Centauri system," Greta says.

She always knows what's ahead. She's a good brand ambassador.

"Do you think there are any tickets left?" Nana asks as she removes her apron. She's served us another round of tea and horrible cookies. At least this time, I'm able to shunt all my cookies Pinky's way, and she wolfs them down like a starving Labrador.

The Labrador species of people, not the Earth variety of dog. I'd never compare Pinky to a dog. She's far too majestic with that crown of hers.

Hell, she's too majestic even without it.

"I'd have to check to be sure, but I believe so. It's rare that we're booked solid." Greta answers.

"Could you get a ticket for me, dear? Just around the Alpha Centauri system, then back to Earth again. I'd like a chance to do some traveling while I'm in good working order, and to spend time with Charlie and his friends." Nana hangs her apron on its peg and smooths it.

Greta's eyes cut to me, frantically asking if this is okay.

"It would be great to have you aboard, Nana," I say. "Greta and Pinky are the best galactic tour guides in all the solar systems."

Greta beams. Both from her happy smile and a slight increase in luminescence. It's always easy to see when Greta's happy. "Absolutely! I'll do it right now."

Greta pulls out her telcoder and, after several long moments, she announces, "Done. And, as luck would have it, I was able to get you a free room. I get comps through my employer on voyages that aren't sold out."

Nana leans forward and gently pinches her cheek. "You, my dear, are a peach." She turns to me. "You be nice to this girl, or I'll never forgive you."

Pinky saves me from having to respond to this. "Greta's not a peach. *I'm* a peach. I'll show you things in Alpha Centauri that will make your servos short out."

"Well," I say, "not actually short out. Right?"

Pinky snorts. "Not literally. But almost."

I feel like we've gotten into a weird territory. To distract, I say, "Do you need help packing, Nana?"

Nana doesn't answer. She leaves the room and comes back a

moment later with a suitcase. "Nope. All cyborgs are required to be ready to evacuate at any moment. Union rules."

Right. Okay. This should be interesting.

CHAPTER 5

Back aboard the *Second Chance*, I've gotten Nana settled into her cabin. It's across the ship from my cabin, but maybe that's okay. Gus will be looking out for her, and I can get over there in just a few minutes if I hurry. Plus, it leaves me some room for romantic freedom.

You know, just in case I need it.

Cyborg or not, Nana still goes to bed at eight o'clock in the evening. With her comfortably dozing, I join Greta and Pinky in the bar for a drink.

I arrive and, as is our custom, wait for Pinky to tell me what I'll be drinking. She likes to choose for people, and she's usually bang on.

"Cheerful Seagull," she announces, pointing at me with an accusing finger that, in other circumstances, would vex me greatly.

"Isn't that a morning drink?" Last I knew, she was only serving them as a breakfast aperitif. But Pinky makes her own rules and changes them often, so there's no telling.

"Most of the time. It's what you need right now." She spins away to perform her violent ballet of drink making, then sets a glass in front of me.

Greta's already sipping a Thunderstorm, which is an old favorite of hers. It's what she had the first day we met, now that I think about it.

I sip my Cheerful Seagull with appreciation. Pinky's perfected the recipe, and it does, indeed, suit my mood. It has just the right mix of carbonated effervescence and acidic juice.

"Are you really okay with Nana Rose being aboard?" Pinky asks. "I'd feel weird about having my grandma along."

"Yeah. It's nice, actually. I've changed, she's changed, and it's good that we have a chance to get to know each other again."

"That's so nice." Greta looks so happy, I try extra hard to ignore the carnage of her lushfruit muffin.

Someday, I'll ask her about it. Just like someday, I'll wear that red shirt and show it who's boss.

But not today.

Today, I'm just glad to be here with my friends and my nana, looking forward to some new adventures.

I lift my glass. "To the future."

Just to be clear, this is not a normal toast for my people.

Greta clicks her glass to mine, and Pinky grabs a tall, skinny cylinder so she can join in. The glass is empty, but her sentiment is not.

"To the future," Pinky and Greta repeat, in unison.

To the future, I say again to myself. *May it be full of adventure and happiness.* I look at Greta's honest, open face, and add another private thought. *And love.*

About the Author

Zen DiPietro is a lifelong bookworm, dreamer, 3D maker, and writer. Perhaps most importantly, a Browncoat Trekkie Whovian. Also red-haired, left-handed, and a vegetarian geek. Absolutely terrible at conforming. A recovering gamer, but we won't talk about that. Particular loves include badass heroines, British accents, and the smell of Band-Aids.

www.zendipietro.com

Books by Zen DiPietro

Dragonfire Station
Book 1: Translucid
Book 2: Fragments
Book 3: Coalescence
Intersections: Dragonfire Station Short Stories

Mercenary Warfare
Book 1: Selling Out
Book 2: Blood Money
Book 3: Hell to Pay

THE HORRIBLE HABITS OF HUMANS

by S.E. Anderson

One mission away from retirement, and Strax just had to be assigned babysitting duty of a new race – the humans had better be worth it.

Commander Strax is the best the Order has to offer, but he's ready to settle down now. Just his luck that his superior officer has assigned him to take the Human race out for a test drive, and see if these fleshy beings are a good fit to join the Order.

But when a simple dimplomatic mission goes sideways, it's up to Strax to save the universe, with the Human in tow. And the human has some grand ideas of his own…

CHAPTER 1

The thing before him stood pink, fleshy; altogether disgusting.

And it was baring its fangs.

They were short, white fangs; not as pointed as some of the creatures Strax had encountered planetside, but still, oddly grim to see, and somewhat threatening from this repugnant creature. Strax made it a point not to let the stranger hear the small, sharp intake of air that he used to cleanse his nostrils of the fowl odor.

"Commander Strax, is it?" The stranger asked, baring its teeth even more, revealing pink gums. Everything about this creature was in shades of pink, except for the eyes, which were a bright, chlorophyll green. They reminded Strax of the mold that grew in the ship's containment system, purifying their water and air.

But there was nothing pure about this... thing.

"It's an honor to meet you." The fleshy creature bowed at its midriff. At least it knew how to show respect. Strax did not bow back. "I'm hoping this mission is as fruitful as our two nations anticipate."

This time, Strax did not hide the cleansing breath. The creature seemed startled. How primitive.

"As do I," Strax responded, internally sneering. One of the perks of having an exoskeleton was the ability to write inside one's own shell, unnoticed. "You must be the human."

"Well, one of them," the stranger swiped his digits through the odd ruffled tuff above its head. Strax didn't have time to learn the terminology: the human wouldn't be here long. "Michaels, Patel and Juarez are assigned to other parts of the ship. But it seems Admiral Ma'kurajaa-" he said this with great difficulty, while still showing its teeth, "wants me to shadow you. And, in that manner, for you to observe me, as I prove to you my species is a good fit for the Order."

Good fit? Strax didn't see this puny human lasting even a day on his ship. From the little he could tell of the species, they were physically weak, and yet insanely confrontational, territorial to the point of killing millions over small patches of land. Thank goodness the Order was civilizing these primates.

"Very well," Strax said curtly, "I expected you to follow my commands to the letter. I cannot have you stepping out of line. The second you do, the offer from the Order is rescinded, do you understand me?"

"Loud and clear, commander."

"I see your translator is working well?"

"I wasn't fitted with one," said the human, "I learned all 57 languages of the Order so that I might get picked for this mission. It is my top priority."

Fiery furnace, what a weird race. The human didn't need to know all 57 languages, it only needed to know *one*. Negotiators coupled with translators would handle the rest. It wasn't as if they were going to let this human into diplomatic meetings.

"Then let us commence. Follow me, if you will."

Strax turned his back on the human, and strode down the hall, giving the thing no other option than to follow. Its steps echoed through the pristine chambers of the massive ship.

Strax was proud to be assigned command of the *Ascendant*, one of the most remarkable ships of the fleet. The human wasn't even dignified to grace its many halls. Why was the creature continually showing its teeth? The commander kept his eyes riveted on the hallway beyond: he would not give the human the benefit of being seen. That would only go to its head.

He realized then that he had no name to call the human. Even *it* knew how rude it was to simply call a subordinate by its race alone, and Strax knew he had to play nice with Ma'kurajaa if he wanted to be relived of this babysitting duty.

Then again, if he did an awful job, they would never assign a new inferior being to his ship, and the prospect of that kind of freedom filled the commander with glee.

If you could call it glee. It was maybe an odd, bubbling excitement, one that rose through his chest and made him simmer in his shell. Once he got an idea like this in his head, it was impossible to get it out.

But in the meantime, he had to know what to call the human, who was now trotting beside him, fleshy lips drawing a pink line on a pale pink face.

"You may address me as Commander," said Strax, delicately prodding the human to introduce itself, "or Commander Strax. Never simply Strax."

"Understood, Commander," the human replied, right where Strax wanted him. Strax prided himself on how he could get anything he wanted without even asking. He understood other races more than anyone else could. "My true name is *Stevenson*, but as the *son* sound is difficult to pronounce without human teeth, I usually go by *Steve*. Though you may call me lieutenant if it makes it easier for you."

Lieutenant? Strax hid his surprise behind his facial antennae. When other races were assimilated into the Order, their military hierarchy was thoroughly studied for a generation in order to see how they would fit into the Order's grades. If this creature was already being referred to as a lieutenant – despite the planet only having been discovered less than a decade ago – meant he had some serious claws.

"Lieutenant *Steve*," he said aloud, though in his mind he was scoffing loudly, "In my language, Steve means shitface."

"As I am well aware," the human shifted shades of pink, but did not flinch. Did they have a camouflage trait that the Order didn't know about? The color was making him stand out more, not less. The Calistrians could turn almost invisible when called to hide, but this human was changing color and emanating heat as a response to threat.

Which, of course, was exactly what Strax wanted to see. If the Order needed to know how the humans reacted under pressure, then he would put the pressure on, and he had no intention of letting up.

The human was silent. Good. Strax felt a small thrill inside of him again – the feeling that could almost be glee. He had hated the idea of having humans on board, but now, the thought of being able to make them writhe with such visible discomfort was giving him more energy than he could ever had expected.

He would enjoy making Human-Steve, or lieutenant shitface, writhe.

"Have you been given the tour of the *Ascendant* yet?" he asked, trying to make himself sound pleasant. No excuse for the Admiral to accuse him of being unnecessarily cruel.

"Not a real one, no," said the lieutenant, "I have seen digital, holographic renderings, so I know my way around, but this is my first time on board, and I have not visited the ship yet."

"Well, you should know we went to a lot of trouble to make you and your fellow humans feel comfortable."

This was not exactly true: he himself had just signed the papers, without really reading them. The four humans would be sharing one room, with bunks, as was the human way. The bunks needed sheets of foam, which Strax found incredibly odd, but if that is how humans rested, then he was obligated to provide.

Other than that, no changes had been made. That morning, the earth military had given the *Ascendant* a few crates of what they called "shelf stable" meals, which meant the cafeteria didn't need to alter their already extensive menu. They were told to provide water to the humans at all times of the day – like they were plants, or something – and that they needed 8 hours of sleep per night. None of this impacted the rest of the crew in the slightest.

If the humans wanted to be part of the Order, they would have to fit in on their own. They would not be given exemptions.

In a few days, this human would be scrambling for his approval. It was amusing, to have such power over an inferior being.

It might almost be fun.

CHAPTER 2

"Have you seen how odd their food is?" Myla's mandibles quivered in amusement. "The colors! How outrageous!"

"I heard one complain to another that what they were eating wasn't pleasant because its molecules were not vibrating at the right frequency. Fiery furnace, how ridiculous!"

Strax enjoyed his evening meals. The trough before him was full of wriggling, freshly caught squalupins, which he stabbed with his pincers, bringing them to his eager mouth. With him were his officers, sharing in the feast, finally away from the stress of the massive ship.

Three days, the humans had been with them. Three days, and no one could talk about anything else. They were a noisy bunch, frequently modulating their words when they were together to create wails and moans that filled the ship with soulful sound. Sometimes, Strax through they sounded like dying squalupins, just like the ones he has just impaled with his right claw, while at others, they were more like a crashing pile of rocks. He found the sounds altogether unpleasant, though some of the other races on the ship had taken quite a shine to what the humans called *song*.

The crew was enamored with them, though Strax could not for the life of him comprehend why. They were loud and clumsy, like the animals in the wild back on his home planet of Hydraxia. Why anyone in their right mind wanted to put wild animals on the *Ascendant*, and consider them for a seat in the Order, was entirely beyond him.

But he had much bigger problems. Much, much bigger. The Ascendant carried over 2,000 soldiers and engineers, and despite the humans on board, the missions still had to go on.

The last squalupin stabbed and scoffed down, it was time to speak of more important matters.

"We have a diplomatic meeting on the books for tomorrow, do we not?" he asked, leaning back in his chair as the waiters placed the tabletop back over the feeding trough.

"We do," Myla conjured the computer interface into existence, letting it hover before her face. It was pleasantly symmetrical, and Strax wondered why he had never proposed copulation to her.

But he was getting distracted. Maybe it was managing the humans, the exhaustion of practically babysitting them, but today he truly felt old. He hadn't considered retirement, but maybe it was time to start thinking about it. Get out of the army while still ahead, bring glory to the Order by birthing a healthy brood. Myla was practically his age, though she looked much younger. It would certainly be a pairing his elders would approve of.

"Commander?" she said – no, repeated. He had gotten lost in his thoughts, another sign of his oncoming age. He clicked his mandibles pleasantly.

"Yes, continue," he said, trying to catch her eye, but she was too focused on the holograms that drifted in the air before her to notice him.

"We have a meeting with the emperor of Sybillia tomorrow, set for 1400," she recited. "A formality. Contact was established over a century ago – by the Sybillians – but they have never made a request to join the Order. Admiral Ma'kurajaa has requested this time slot for you, with him."

"A simple meet and greet, then," Strax agreed. Not an exciting mission with life or death consequences, just a simple hello and goodbye, the once-a-decade check in to make sure these outsiders weren't up to no good.

"Admiral Ma'kurajaa has requested you bring the human."

"Shit."

The entire table turned to stare at him, and Strax realized he had said that aloud. Ouch. What an embarrassment. The humans were having a terrible effect on his usually calm state of mind.

"Apologies, officers," he said, letting out a cleansing breath. "I simply do not think bringing the human-lieutenant along is a good idea. What is supposed to be a simple meet-and-greet will turn into a disaster."

There was a sound from across the table, like that of a deflating balloon. Strax wasn't surprised to see such obvious disdain from the head of sciences.

"Have something to add, Master Statstic?"

"Your disregard for the humans under our employ comes off as an insult to Admiral Ma'kurajaa himself, commander," said the engineer. Strax's mandibles bristled. Statstic had been a pain in his claw since day one, and got away with it, too, seeing as how he was a contractor, and not an actual subordinate.

"I mean no disrespect to the Admiral," he replied, "but it is unwise for us to bring an untrained, and dare I say untested species to greet our neighbors?"

"The humans on this ship might seem strange," said Statstic, "but they are trying their hardest."

"You make it sound as if they are children."

"They might as well be. Their race has just discovered the stars, and they are making every effort to please the Order. What makes you think they will disrespect it now?"

Strax was steaming under his shell. He wanted to bring his pincers to the engineers' neck, and snap it clean off.

"If Admiral Ma'kurajaa had ordered it, then it is how we shall proceed," Strax conceded, "but if this goes poorly, the blame shall not be on me."

"Noted," Myla interjected, sending him a look which said – what did it say? Strax was confused. Females had different facial antennae, and he never knew how to read them properly. Which eye of hers was a phantom eye evaded him, since every female had it in a different place. He blew air in her direction: that at least was a clear expression of thanks.

"We shan't need a full away team," he said, "simply the human and I should suffice. We need the gift basket for the Sybillian emperor will be in order as well. The entire process should take less than an hour. If we are gone for over five, send an intercept team, and retreat to a safe distance."

Easy. Just a hello, a few questions, and then off again.

It was being trapped, alone, in a shuttle with the Human-Steve that made him uncomfortable.

The thought of retiring popped back into his head, and he let it linger. After this mission, he'd have a good talk with Admiral Ma'kurajaa. He simply did not have the patience for babysitting anymore.

CHAPTER 3

The Human seemed excited to be in the shuttle, despite the fact it was probably older than he was.

"May I pilot?" it asked, excitedly. Why anyone would want extra work was beyond Strax: flying was tedious, and not to be taken lightly.

"No."

The human's mouth pulled into a hill shape, but it said nothing. Not a complaint or a word of anger. Strax was impressed and confused, all at once.

Strax initiated the takeoff sequence, leaned back, and they lifted off the dock with grace. The human looked out the window like he was discovering flight for the very first time.

"Is this your first time in a shuttle?" Strax asked, realizing how odd it was that he was asking the human an unprompted question. Why was he suddenly making conversation? In that same wavelength, what a poor question was that? Of course the human had been in a shuttle before: it's how it boarded the Ascendant in the first place.

But the human did not shame him. Quite the opposite: it turned towards him, with the eagerness of a newborn child, eager to see the world.

"No," he said, showing its white fangs again. "I was a pilot in the Air Force back on Earth. But flying is so incredible, isn't it? Every flight is an entirely new experience."

Strax silenced himself – he would not laugh. The human had this innocent trait to him, something so similar to a child. An eagerness. So obnoxious. The lieutenant had to take this seriously. He knew already how his report to Admiral

Ma'kurajaa would go.

The Humans are not ready for the serious nature of the Order, he wrote mentally, as he urged the little shuttle out of the hangar bay and into the vastness of space. *They need a few centuries to grow up, mature, and return with more focus.*

He was dreading presenting this man-thing to the emperor of the planet below. While Human-Steve leaned forward and stared at the glowing orb before them, Strax calculated trajectories, and quietly planned a way to speed up the human's demise.

Such fragile creatures, humans, all flesh and meat. Just about anything would kill them. It would be so easy to open the airlock and let him writhe in the vacuum of space. Of course, it would be an accident. He would mourn the loss along with the rest of the crew, and then, move on. Never having to add humans to the Order, never having to listen to their awful group-moaning again.

As a matter of fact, the human was doing so now. It was vibrating its mouth-flaps to different pitches as they neared the planet, quietly, maybe to avoid Strax hearing him do so.

Hum.

Hum.

Hum!

Hum Hum!

All the while, the corners of those pink mouth flaps turned upwards.

Neither creature said anything for the remainder of the trip.

Strax landed in front of the Sybillian palace, setting the shuttle down in a field of yellow grass, near some trees. They swayed in the breeze, and Strax grimaced at the thought of stepping out into a place where the air current was not controlled.

He snapped his suit shut all the way around his neck. This should at least block the worst of it.

The human, however, wasn't wearing a suit at all. It wore the order's uniform, but hadn't brought a breathing mask, face filter, air containment system, or even a pressure suit.

"You have come willfully unprepared, Lieutenant." Strax thought of all the ways the human could die now. Maybe he wouldn't have to intervene at all: just let nature take its course.

"No sir, the climate here is fine for me," Human-Steve bared its fangs, "as is the air. I am told it resembles my home world's country of Texas."

Ah, humans and their global divisions. Strax had almost forgotten the lines that separated them on their home planet – not that he cared. He did hide his disappointment at not having such an easy way to dispose of the creature.

"I read in your file you were from a country called *United States,*" Strax pointed out. Why he remembered this odd factoid, he did not know. Perhaps it was the irony of naming a place "united" when it was so impossibly divided.

"From the state of Virginia, actually," the human seemed surprised; too, that Strax had retrained that fact. The mouth flaps were fluttering now as it spoke. "But I'm a farm boy, I can handle the heat."

"I thought you said you were with the Air Force?"

"I was born and raised on a farm, enlisted when I left high school," he explained, "don't worry, not all humans have this awful accent!"

Was the human trying to be humorous? What was it trying to do? Was it trying to earn his pity? Strax had to stop thinking about this odd creature, or he would never leave the ship and accomplish his mission. He clicked his mandibles to demand attention.

"Right, lieutenant. As you do not have a translator, I do not expect you to talk during this encounter. You shall stand behind me, representing the welcoming nature of the Order. You shall defend me if it comes to that. And stay here as collateral if this emperor requires negotiation of any kind."

"All part of a day's work," the human bobbed its head up and down. "Sir, yes sir. And do not worry about the translator: I have learned to speak Sybillian from the ship's computer. All three dialects on file."

"You have?" Strax could not contain his surprise, "but the mission was only announced yesterday."

"Learning languages is a bit of a hobby of mine," the human said, pumping its chest out. Was that vanity? The human pride he had heard so much about?

"A hobby?"

"A pass-time."

Why would anyone need to pass time, when there was so little of it to be had in a lifetime? Strax had no need for distraction in his life, his work took every waking moment of it. These humans had an odd way of living, one without focus. It must have been an existential hell.

"In any case, do not speak a word while we are in the palace," Strax ordered, "is that clear?"

"Sir, yes sir."

"Good. Now we come in peace, so leave all weapons at the door of the shuttle."

"Understood."

The human unholstered his laser pistol, placing it under his jump seat. Strax was glad to see the human was good at obeying orders.

But now was the true test of the human's metal – and Strax's as well. If all went well, this would be Strax's last diplomatic mission.

Though if things went poorly it would be his last, as well, though for majorly different reasons. Namely, that he wouldn't be alive anymore.

He tried not to think about that possibility, as it was no possibility at all. This would be easy. He'd be home before dinnertime.

The palace before them was grand, made of massive blocks of stone, so large in fact it appeared the entire place has been carved out of a single mountain. This was perhaps the case, as there were veins of emerald and ruby running through the front wall.

The human let out a long, high-pitched sound. Strax glared at him.

"What are you doing?"

"Whistling," the human lifted its shoulders, than dropped them again. "I'm impressed. Sorry. I'll shut up now."

Strax didn't reply. He didn't need to. He was impressed too. This whole "walking up to the stranger's gates unarmed" was a tried and true tradition of the Order, showing the local ruler that they were peaceful and meant no harm. The massive ship in the sky was kept neatly out of view.

"What does the Order want with the Sybillians?" the human asked, taking Strax by surprise.

"That is none of your concern, lieutenant."

"It is my concern, commander," the human insisted, "Admiral Ma'kurajaa was adamant that this exercise was not only to see if I was a good fit for the Order, but for the Order to prove its value to planet Earth. I need to know what we're getting into."

Strax took a deep breath to cleanse his soul. The human sure was a mouthy one.

"I don't see any ships, or high technology here," it continued, "and there was no talk of mining installations. Sybillia doesn't have much to offer the Order."

"That is a correct assessment," Strax agreed, "it is the placement that matters most to us. Sybillia is the only planet around this star with sentient life, and thus by Order law they control the system. We need to gain that control if we want to stand a chance against the Travan Empire. Sybillia is a key strategic figure at play: it's the only thing in between the Travan and the Order."

"That's one thing I never understood about space alliances and federations," the human continued, "why not just go over, below, or simply around the Sybillian star?"

Ah, humans, and their primitive technology. They truly knew nothing about interstellar affairs.

"It is simple, really, lieutenant," he explained, "if the Travan empire were to take control of this star system, it would be able to place a resonance ring in orbit around its star, and thus create a hyperdrive path straight to the Order's front door."

"Ah, and if the Sybillians were to enter the Order, we would be the ones to control the highway right into Travan territory."

"Precisely."

"And with Travan activity being spotted in the Dorian system, we need to act fast in order to secure this area for ourselves."

Strax was taken aback by the human's thinking. "Yes, that is also correct."

"Then let's make this count."

As the duo approached, a sentry let out a loud call, and slowly, a crack began to form in the wall. The crack opened, revealing a door larger than the hangar bay on the Ascendant.

If Strax could make that sound the human had made, he would have. It was damn impressive. But alas, his mouth wasn't so creepily dexterous.

As the massive door lowered, a procession began to appear. Men with spears and shields poured from the gates, leading a chariot drawn by eight beasts, each one bigger than the shuttle they had just left. The human balked, glancing first at his commanding officer then back at the beasts.

"Fucking dragons," the creature intoned. Neither of the words meant anything to Strax, who put them down as exclamations at the grandeur of the procession.

The chariot that the scaled beasts were pulling carried only one thing: a man in a throne. Eight creatures were definitely not necessary, and Strax knew they were only a show of strength. He did not care. His ship in orbit could destroy the entire procession, and palace too, with a single shot if need be. They were no threat to him.

As they drew closer, the armored men spread out, building a large circle around the little envoy. All the noise and weapons were making Strax nervous, but he held his ground. His finger tightened over the communicator ring that would call for reinforcements if things went sour.

Finally the chariot arrived, and the beasts ran a complete circle around Strax and the Human before coming to a stop. The man - if indeed it was a man, it was always hard to tell with other races - who sat on the throne made a sweeping motion and stood, gazing down upon them like he was about to pass judgment.

Strax hated being in such a lowly position, but he said nothing. It was all part of the job description. Once again, something tugged on him inside, telling him this was yet another good reason to end this nonsense and focus efforts instead on breeding the next generation of commanders and generals.

The emperor he'd been assigned to meet was a stout creature, but whatever height he had given up for width he had reclaimed with the oversized chariot. Like the winged creatures that drove him, he was scaly and green; akin to the reptilians Strax was fond of working with.

"Greetings!" he said, waving a thick green arm to the heavens. "I see you found the place alright."

"Greetings, mighty emperor of the Sybillians!" Strax bowed a polite bow, as was customary. "It is an honor to finally meet you, and to represent the Order here today."

"So, I see they sent you to try and add our humble planet to the Order's impressive collection," the emperor made a grimace. "I have always said no in the past, but you know I love hearing your offers. I love seeing you grovel. Now come on, then, the banquet is going to get cold!"

"Banquet?" now it was Strax's turn to balk. He hated having

to eat on other planets, the food always messed with his digestive system. No one seemed to appreciate good, fresh, still squirming food.

"Yes, yes, in your honor!" the emperor did a show of bowing, "the great commander Strax, it is truly a pleasure to have you."

Before Strax could wonder how the emperor had gotten hold of his name, the man had taken his seat on the chariot again, and waited, as if expecting Strax and Human-Steve to follow. Strax took the initiative and climbed up behind him, urging his human to do just as much.

The human said nothing as it climbed onto the chariot, but it was doing that thing where its camouflage was failing. Instead of fading into the background noise of the procession, the human was glowing.

Strax would have preferred to have him walk with the rest of the footmen and soldiers, but the Order still needed to be represented here, and the human would be respected as a member of his crew. Anything less was an offense to him, personally.

The emperor made a flourish with his hand, and all at once the procession was off again, this time heading for the castle. The human crossed its hands behind its back and stood erect, the perfect soldier.

Strax was glad of that. He was already dreading the banquet, but at least he wouldn't have the human to worry about.

"So, tell me," the emperor said, not turning back to look at his passengers, "how is the great Admiral Ma'kurajaa doing these days?"

"He is the pride of the Order, your excellency."

"That is so nice to hear. I knew him back when he was just a commander like you, you see. He came to try and convince my father to join the Order. We always had a lot of respect for the man."

"He continues to be worthy of that respect."

"Good."

The team of massive steeds pulled the carriage effortlessly behind them, and Strax struggled to stay standing and balanced. The emperor hadn't given him a place to sit, an obvious power play. But the man wouldn't see him struggle.

They rode through the doors to the city, and all at once they were surrounded by overcrowded homes and an excited mob. People flocked to their windows to watch the procession, and

Strax avoided eye contact, as their customs were not known.

Up the small inkling they went, then through a smaller gate, this time into the palace itself. The city fell away at this second wall, leaving only luxurious gardens, and soldiers at the place of the mob. The beasts brought them right up to the double doors, and stopped, allowing the emperor to rise.

"We shall discuss all these matters first, and then we shall feast," the latter said plainly. Strax inclined his head in understanding.

He looked back at his human, who was no longer glowing. Good. He needed to be calm, to blend in. But once again, the creature's mh seemed to be in a reverse parabola. For some reason, it made Strax uneasy.

"Come along," the emperor intoned.

"Thank you, for your gracious hospitality," said Strax, shaking his human protégé out of his thoughts. The emperor waved him off as if it was nothing.

Inside, the palace's walls were overwhelmingly tall, dwarfing Strax quite a few times over. The human nodded to itself, as if he too saw the building as overkill, overcompensation. The emperor's likeness was on every wall, carved in a radiant green stone.

The room they were led too was very small by comparison. A table sat in the middle, surrounded by short stools. Strax took a seat before the emperor, leaving Human-Steve to stand behind him, against the wall. He didn't want to have to think about him during these proceedings.

Or at all.

"Have you considered the generous offer the Order has sent ahead of me?"

"Right to the point," the emperor made a waving motion with his clawed hand. "I like that. Sin'ha, can you get me and our guest here something to drink? Nothing too strong so as to obscure our negotiations, but strong enough to make them enjoyable. What do you say, commander?"

Strax bristled. "Only water for me, thank you. I am on duty."

"One drink cannot hurt, surely."

"I would rather be on my best behavior, emperor."

The emperor let out a brief noise, showing humor, perhaps. Strax kept his composure, adjusting himself on the hard emerald stool. He hoped this would not take long. He was growing more and more uncomfortable by the minute, and his seat had nothing to do with it. The emperor was putting him on edge.

"To answer your query: yes, I did receive your envoy from the Order," the emperor did the waving motion again – did that convey agreement? Strax slapped himself mentally for not having a photographic memory of the mission packet. "And I am willing to make a deal with you, though the agreement as it currently stands does not please me in its entirety."

"Which is why I am here."

"To please me?"

"In a way," Strax felt his nerves tingle. He didn't like being spoken to in such a manner. "To come to a pleasant agreement which will benefit both our peoples greatly."

The servant named Sin'ha returned then, placing green goblets before the two negotiators. The color made it near impossible for Strax to determine its contents, so he ignored it. That was, until, the emperor drew attention to it.

"Join me," he said, and it sounded like an order. Strax wanted to refuse, but there were diplomatic notions to uphold. He lifted his glass, reaching to tap it against the emperors', sloshing the two liquids so they mixed. Strax noted his own drink was transparent, but that could mean anything.

The emperor downed his glass, and Strax took but a sip of his. Didn't taste unusual, but it was definitely not water. Though anything on this planet had more flavor than the filtered liquid he drank back on the *Ascendant*. He put it back down.

"Ah, ah, ah!" the emperor chided, "on Sybillia, it is rude to not drink the entire contents of a glass."

Strax scowled internally, slipping his tongue to the side to open up a gap into his shell. He poured the liquid down his mouth, letting it flow through the little hole. It was always awkward having water – or whatever this was – sloshing in between his belly and shell, but it was worth it if meant not getting doused with something foreign.

He planned how he would 'eat' the feast later, but it wasn't going to be pleasant. It was why he always ate a good meal before leaving.

"What do you think of Sybillian Ale?" asked the emperor, obviously proud.

"It has a distinct taste," the commander replied, having actually tasted it before it went down his side-gullet, "a truly floral bouquet with a minty finish. Very delicate. I shall be buying some from your stores to share with Order high-command."

The emperor seemed pleased. He put down his glass for good, making and maintaining eye contact with Strax

"So, let us talk about this... offer."

"Commander."

Strax felt a fleshy hand on his shoulder. He would have screamed in shock if he hadn't been in front of the emperor: then again, it would not have been such an affront if it hadn't been in the majesty's presence.

"Lieutenant, please, we shall speak later," He said, as politely as he could muster.

"I feel unwell."

"Then go outside."

"I feel... very unwell. I need you to return me to the ship."

"We're in the middle of something."

"Oh, this could get disgusting!"

What was this puny earthling thinking? Making a fool of itself, in front of the emperor, before negotiations could even begin? Strax looked up at the human – who looked as disgustingly fleshy as always, no different – and gave him the most furious glare he could muster. But the human was unperturbed.

Except that it blinked with only one eye.

"If you are going to make a scene, please do it without being connected to me," he snapped, then turned to the emperor. "I apologize. This human is new to the Order, we are testing his ability to comply with our way of life. As you can see, we only accept the best, and we test and train relentlessly. If your world joins the Order, you would receive the highest of care, access to defense no other planet in this quadrant has ever seen."

"I'm gonna blow!"

But the emperor was unmoved by this tirade. In fact, he looked furious. Strax wanted nothing more than to slap the human across its fleshy face (part of him did want to see how wiggly it would be) and show the emperor just how dedicated his was to the cause.

But the human was gently tugging at his uniform now. It must seriously be ill. How embarrassing.

"You didn't drink," the emperor chided.

"I did, and it was very good," Strax was distracted now, and was losing his edge. He wanted nothing more for the human to spontaneously combust, which is a thing he heard they did from time to time.

"You did not. Finish. Your glass."

"Commander, You are going to hate me for this, but I have no other choice."

Before he could reprimand the human, it had already pulled two small pistols from gods-know where, taking aim at the emperor and incapacitating him in the arm in one swift motion. Strax flew to his feet.

"HUMAN STEVE!"

"Run, Commander!" the human shoved a pistol into the commander's hand, the heat of it firing up his senses. "It's a trap!"

Chapter 4

Strax wanted to shout at the human, to reprimand him for being such a *fucking* idiot, but the lieutenant was too fast. He grabbed a stool in one swift motion, using it to shield both himself and his commander, taking aim at anything that moved in the room.

To the commander's shock, every single servant was armed. They flocked to their emperor and drew their own weapons, firing a steady stream of plasma at the tiny diplomatic crew, which Steve deflected with the brandished stool.

"Take point!" Steve ordered.

"I am the commander here!" Strax threw out one of his stumpy legs, stabbing one of the attackers with a well-sharpened pincer. The reptilian screamed as life left his body, crumbling to the floor. "Human-Steve, what the hell are you doing?"

"We were betrayed! Run, I'll explain later! The ship's in danger!"

Anyone could threaten Strax's life, but the *Ascendant* being in danger was out of the question. He slipped the safety off the pistol and fired rapidly into the crowd of armed servants. Before a single one could reach its target, he felt his arm explode.

"FIERY FURNACE!"

The pain was unbearable, like nothing he had felt in years. The burning rose up his arm, making his pincer feel as if it has been ripped clean off. He screamed, dropping the plasma gun.

"Just run!"

The pain was altering his perception of time. He turned, dashing out of the room, taking orders from a human, a human that was covering his every move, shooting anything that was trying to get close to him.

He hated to admit it, and maybe it was the pain talking, but the human was a damn good shot.

"Take this!"

The human shoved something into his hands, and Strax grabbed it like his life was depending on it. It seemed to be one of the emerald carved murals of the emperor, and it was heavy to boot, but it made the perfect shield. With adrenaline coursing through his body, and possibly poisoned drink sloshing through his outer shell, the commander rammed towards the exit, trampling anyone who lay in his path.

"Tell my wife – oof!" the sentence was cut short as Strax stepped on the soldier's stomach, winding him.

The human covered the rear, but it seemed as though he had deflected any of the servants behind them. But soldiers stood on ahead: They were ready, prepared. Strax realized with a start that they had been expecting his escape.

Human-Steve was right: this had all been a trap.

And he had tried to get them out by feigning illness – bless.

The human was breathing heavily, leaning past the emerald shield to shoot down the soldiers ahead before Strax could plow through them. With a resonating crash, Strax slammed into something – possibly someone – hard, throwing him into the air, tumbling overhead.

"Good one!" the human complimented.

"Do not speak to me! You are not-"

"If you have nothing nice to say, don't say it at all, Jeez Louise!"

"Who is this Jeez Louise? Why do you call me that name? It is not my name!"

"For the love of god, shut up, commander!

Bright light burned against his eyes as they burst into the courtyard. Strax lowered the shield just enough to see over it, and promptly dropped it. The gates were closed, and what appeared to be an entire army was standing before them, blocking their escape into the city.

"Very good try, lieutenant," he said, "but it seems we are outmatched."

He hissed as his arm reminded him of his injury, masking the movement by snarling at the enemy. They stood at the ready, the front row holding primitive spears as the back row carried pistols.

Pistols… plasma pistols. By all accounts, the planet should not have that kind of technology. They were still too rudimentary, too primitive, too uncivilized to carry them.

The drink sloshed in between Strax's shell and body, making his discomfort even worse. He knew this was the end. They had him, and he would never crumble for the Order. He prepared himself mentally for the torture, for the thought that the last thought he would ever have in life would be filled with pain.

No retirement. No companionship. No brood, no descendants. Just him, standing strong against the enemy. Maybe he would be commended – posthumously, of course.

"Where are you going, oh great commander?" a voice chided from behind him – the emperor. Human-Steve had not killed him, after all. "The party's over here!"

He turned to glare at the creature, looking uglier now than he had when he had first met him. Strax despised the man, this creature that had been so quick to betray him and his kind.

"You're never getting away with this!" Strax shouted, but it felt anticlimactic, as he had nothing to back that up with. Ah, yes – his ship, in orbit. It would work just fine without him, and they would save the day.

He lifted his hands in the air, reaching for the sky. The injured arm screamed as he stretched it, but he was ready. He gently turned on his com with the tip of his antenna.

"Statstic! Now!" He called, and laughed. "Did you really think we would let you get away with this? The Order? Not hardly. Prepare to be…"

"We actually *have* your ship, Strax. You should give up now. Your entire crew is under my control. Or, I should say – under Travan control."

The arms dropped. Well, he was not excepting that.

"I should have known! What did he offer you, that the Order couldn't give you?"

"The only thing the Order would never accept: to leave me alone," the emperor gave a curt nod to his men, who started edging forward, closer, and closer. "he's taking the liberty of holding back your crew. You're going to have to stay with us for a while."

Strax lowered his head. This was it, it was over. All was lost. He dropped his head to look at his human protégé: oh, how he wished for someone, anyone else to be at his side in his last moments.

"You did well in there, lieutenant," he said, "I am sorry your tenure with the Order will be so brief."

"The Order!" the human practically shouted. "Order of the Phoenix! Harry Potter! Deathly Hallows - All is not lost, Commander, I know what to do! We're going to Gringotts this bitch!"

"What?"

"With me! Now!"

Once again, Strax was shaken by this human taking liberties with the chain of command, but if it knew the way out of here, hell, he'd follow the thing anywhere. And the somewhere in this case seemed to be right to the massive chariot, where the winged beasts were still being removed from their ornate reigns.

"Come on! Faster!"

Strax sped up, struggling to keep up the pace behind the human, who was blasting wildly in the general direction of the beasts. The creatures were rearing, screaming in fear, their trunk sized legs rising and smashing back down. The handlers dropped the reigns and went running from the scene, all except one who was clinging to the leg of a creature for dear life.

"Creating a distraction! Good thought, Human-Steve! Great initiative! I can't wait to tell high command about this!"

"You might not like this next part!"

"Next part?"

Without a second thought, the human ran up to one of the massive, rearing beasts, and leapt onto its leg, his hands barely grabbing the harness around the creature's neck. It tried to buck him off, but the human held tight, and with incredible dexterity hoisted itself up on its back, climbing in between two of the ridge spikes and wedging himself in there.

Strax froze. No way: any torture, any day, but not this.

"No, not this!" he shouted.

"Fine, I can leave you here," said Steve, sternly, "but I don't think you'll be very happy, you know."

"Find us another way out! Or leave without me!"

"Commander," he snapped, leaning over the side of the spikes. The creature didn't like having him on his back, and reared, screeching. "As a potential member of the Order, I have to abide by everything it stands for. And leaving you here would not be in the Order's best interests. So, are you climbing up on this dragon, or am I going to have to make you?"

CHAPTER 5

Strax hissed, and threw himself at the dragon. He caught the halter with both arms, a ripping pain running through his injured one. He clasped his pincers tighter, begging not to be thrown off.

The human reached down, grabbing him by his uniform and hosting him, panting, onto the beast's back.

"Now hold on," said Human-Steve, "If this is anything like in Harry Potter, it's going to be a bumpy ride!"

He leaned forward, digging his heels deep into the dragon's neck. The beast reared, lifting its massive legs forwards, clawing at the air. The wings beat the air, creating small tornados, knocking down the oncoming wave of soldiers.

And definitely not flying.

"Get it to move!"

"Hold on," said Steve, "I have no idea how to fly this thing."

"Well, do something!"

"Why are you yelling at me? Shoot at them!"

Strax turned to see that the harness was still attached. He reached low with his good arm, using his large pincer to sever through the leather straps that kept the beast tied.

"Haha! We're moving!" the human laughed.

The dragon stomped forward, sending Sybillians flying with a sweep of its massive tail. But still, it beat its wings without getting any air.

"How do we get it to fly?" Strax stammered.

"It needs incentive!" Steve shouted back.

Strax took a deep, cleansing breath, turned back, and stabbed his good claw as deep as he could into the dragon's flank. A blast of pure flame was vomited from the beast's mouth, right onto the three soldiers before him – toast, before they even knew what hit them.

Despite the thrashing and stomping, the dragon was surrounded on all sides now, the soldiers keeping a safe distance, but close enough to chuck a spear or two at the two men on the dragon's back. The Emperor was screaming something in the back, clasping his head in terror.

They were trapped, on the back of a monster straight out of a fairy tale for children. And Strax was trapped sharing his last moments with a meaningless human.

This day was getting worse and worse.

"I have an idea!" Human-Steve shouted.

"Another one?"

"Always!"

"A good one, this time?"

"I don't see you dying right now! Do you?"

"My arm is hanging by a tendon!"

"That's your fault for not listening to me!" he scoffed, "now, scream!"

And with that, the lieutenant ripped off his shirt and started making loud whooping noises to the sky, kicking the dragon with swinging legs and punches. To top it off, he shot the plasma pistol in any and all directions in the air, making a complete and utter fool of himself.

"Fire!" yelled the emperor, "but don't you hurt Muffins!"

Before they could even get a shot in edgewise, the dragon pushed off the ground, roaring, belching fire on the soldiers. Terrified, it took to the skies, beating the air with its leathery wings in an attempt to get away from the many guns.

"Yeehaw!" the human shouted. "Fly, Muffins, fly!"

The dragon flipped in the air, almost knocking the duo off, but Strax clutched a spike tightly with his free hand, holding his breath as the drink that have been in his shell came spilling out his mouth. The poisoned drink rained down upon the soldiers, who shot up at the dragon as the emperor shouted in terror.

"Good boy, Muffins!" said Steve, the pitch of his voice rising. "Keep going! That's a good boy! Or girl! You're a sweetie, aren't you?"

The dragon huffed smoke, turned right side up, and kept pumping forward. Now that the world was right side up, Strax was beginning to get his bearings, but vertigo was setting in mighty fast. He clasped the ridge spike before him tightly with his claw, his injured arm hanging limply, uselessly, by his side.

"I'm not quite sure what you mean by *sweetie*, Human-Steve."

"Just Steve, thanks," the human grumbled.

"Just-Steve, why are you calling this massive creature sweet, when in fact it wants the two of us dead?"

"Aw, shucks, maybe so it might like us? I don't know, Commander, it's worth trying!"

"Good girl, sweetie, good girl," he cooed, flopping his limp arm against the dragon's hide in a poor imitation of a gentle caress.

Now in the sky, the dragon seemed more contented with being freed than angered against the duo for hitching a ride on his back. The swoops and whirls became that of joy, no longer trying to buck them off. The harness fell away as they gained altitude, which only seemed to make the beast even more delighted – if you could call it that.

"Now, Just-Steve, land Dragon-Muffin so we can take back my ship!"

"I'm not flying her, commander," said the human, bashfully, "she's making her own path. I'm a soldier, not a dragon tamer!"

The vertigo seemed to double now.

"So we have no way down?"

"She'll land when she wants to. Right, Muffins?" The human gave the beast a gentle pat on her shoulder. She seemed rather contented, now. Her wings beat a swift, gentle rhythm as the three of them rode through the clouds. Little droplets of moisture clung to Strax's uniform, but the cold wasn't what was bothering him.

Now that the fight was over, and the castle was shrinking to a pinprick in the distance, he was beginning to feel the true pain coursing through his arm. He couldn't release the claw that was clamped to the dragon's spike, as it was the only thing keeping him balanced. The adrenaline stopped making its way through his body, and in turn, the blood began to sputter and pour from his wound.

He was bleeding out.

"Human-Just-Steve," he said, weakly, "I need medical attention."

"Shit," he said, "sorry! I should have a better grasp of my language in times like this. I'm sorry commander, I have no way to land this beast."

"What about those soldiers? The ones who fought at your battle of Gringotts?"

"It's from a book. In it, they just let the dragon tire itself out."

"Ah."

"How long can you hang on, back there?"

"Well, seeing the rate at which my artery is spewing blood, and the current wind speed and the... *chopsticks*..."

"Hang in there, commander! I'll make her land!"

Strax could barely hear him. He could barely see him, either – or anything else, really. When his body turned to soldier mode, the adrenalin thickened his blood so it would stay inside his veins. But as relief washed in, so did blood thinners, and now everything was running out of his wounds like it was being power washed before a committee show.

Everything was very green. And loud.

He heard the blast of a plasma gun, then nothing more.

CHAPTER 6

Strax awoke to blue skies, green nature, and the smell of roasting flesh.

He scrambled to his feet, a move he regretted instantly. He needed to think, to focus, not to let instinct take him over like an animal. He should have scouted the area quietly before making a move. He didn't need his captors knowing he was awake.

The events of that day came rushing back to him in an instant: the betrayal, the escape. The Travan Empire taking over his beloved Ascendant! He steamed inside his shell at the very thought.

"Ah, good, you're finally awake!"

Just-Steve appeared out of the corner of his eye, a stack of firewood in his hands. He dropped the wood on the ground, crouching beside the small pile and making as if to start a fire. He glanced occasionally at his commander, his fleshy face distorted in some odd way Strax could not understand.

"How long have I been unconscious?" asked Strax, relieved not to be in enemy hands. He still kicked himself mentally for forgetting his training.

"Not very long. About two hours? You were in and out there. I kept your chest hydrated with some water I found in a nearby creek: from what I hear about your species, it's the easiest way to be sure you don't have any complications."

"Complications?"

The human brandished a twig in his direction, pointing it at his arm. "Complications. I cleaned the wound best I could, cauterized it with my pistol. Washed away as much of the blood as I could. The arm should be salvageable: as soon as we get back to the shuttle, we've got the medical kit that can stitch it right up."

"You shouldn't even have a pistol. You were meant to leave that in the ship."

"Well, if I hadn't brought them, we would still be in that palace, possibly as little piles of ash."

Strax has nothing he could really say to that: the human was right, gods dammit. He had been so focused on making a good example of himself for the Order that he had walked right into a trap.

"How did you know?" He asked, as the human finished his primitive little fire, lighting it with his pistol.

"How did I know what? How to clean your wound? Easy, I read it on file. Or do you mean, how did I know to bring a pistol? You can never know when you're going to need one. So, I brought two."

"Do not be facetious. I meant, how did you know we were standing in a trap?"

"Easy. I overheard the servants speaking as they went to fetch the drinks. They had to be sure which one was poisoned, so as not to give it to the wrong dignitary. Not that it mattered: the emperor has built up an immunity to the very poison he was trying to kill you with. Very *Princess Bride*."

"There was nothing of a princess about him," Strax scoffed, "and even less of a bride."

"It's a reference to a... a tale in my culture. A cautionary tale. Yes, that's it."

Strax wanted to strangle the small man. Why were humans so annoyingly obsessed with tales and stories? *Princess Bride.* Whatever this *Gringotts* thing was. Although, the commander had to admit that that last one had saved their lives. The human was a quick thinker, and maybe full of inspired ideas because of the references he so loved, not despite them.

"But the servants were right behind me. I would have heard them."

"You did, I'm sure of it," Steve rose, wiping the dirt from his hands. "But your translator is attuned only to the upper language of Sybillia. Not the common tongue."

"And you're telling me you speak their common tongue?"

"Yes," the human bobbed his head enthusiastically, "I mean, no, not conversationally. I just recognized enough of their words to tell what was going on."

"But..." Strax sputtered, then realized suddenly it was the first time in his career that he was at an actual loss for words. "But how? We do not have their language on record!"

"You do, but high command didn't think it necessary to hire a voice-guy for the translators," he said, "not while they were so unwilling to sign over to the Order. It costs money to program those things. I read a book on the common language here, memorized most of what I could. It was worth not getting any sleep last night, totally saved our skins."

"And ruined diplomatic relationships between Sybillia and the Order for the rest of eternity."

"Commander," the human froze, "please excuse my language here, but I think that relationship was tarnished the moment Sybillia decided to *fucking kill you*!"

"Fair point."

"In any case, the coms are down," the human said, now calm. The use of offensive words had an oddly calming effect on the creature. "I think the emperor was not making an empty threat when he said he was going to take over your ship."

"So, he has the Ascendant."

"We can assume as much, yes."

Strax rose to his feet. His damaged arm was stiff, somewhat numb, but it was no longer causing him pain. The human had done everything properly to clean his wound. As much as he hated to admit it, Human-Steve was upholding every value the Order stood for.

Well, except for sneaking those pistols in. They had saved his life, but still.

"We need to regain control of my ship," he said, his entire focus on keeping his composure. "We need to let the Order know that the Travan are in control now, not us."

"Agreed," the human said, "but night is falling. It would be unwise to attempt anything in such foreign terrain, when darkness shields our senses."

"I would agree," said Strax, "but any moment we waste waiting means the ship moving further away from our clutches."

"The ship cannot fly without you on board," Human-Just-Steve reminded him, "not unless your first mate marks you as prisoner of war, or deceased. Either status would determine Sybillia to be in need of re-enforcements, so the Travan would not want that."

"So… what are they planning? To wait in orbit for my return?"

"I would assume as much," said the human, "they probably meant to drug you and bring you on board, so they could leave with you on the ship and skip over loss protocols. They didn't account for your escape."

Strax liked how the human downplayed his own involvement with the matter – as if it hadn't been he who had not only noticed the betrayal first, and planned their escape.

"Whatever happened to the dragon?" he asked, confused, "Muffins, was it?"

"I begged her to land when you started falling off her back. She understood well enough, and owed us one, after all. She flew off towards the east."

"We're going to have to walk."

"At least until we reach the shuttle."

"Unless they've found the shuttle already."

"Fair point."

The human sat down by his fire, extending his pink palms towards the flame. He was calm, poised. He did not relax by the heat.

"Step one, assess access to the shuttle," Strax said grimly, taking a seat across from the human, letting the fire warm him as the day around them slowly ended. "Step two, take back my ship. Step three…"

"I'm pretty sure those steps won't be that easy, commander."

"I never said they would be."

"They need sub-steps."

"Most definitely."

"We have nothing but two plasma pistols and a bit of fire," Human-Steve said to the flame, "and only three working arms between us."

"Once we get the shuttle back, we'll have much more."

"Perhaps. But it is a far cry from a specialized team, capable of doing anything to get the ship back."

Strax was impressed: it was the wisest thing the human had said all day. Almost as if he was aware of his own incompetence.

"I'm going to sleep," the human said, suddenly. "It's been a long day. I need to recharge my batteries."

Strax did a double take. "I didn't think humans had batteries. I assumed you were…"

"It's a figure of speech, commander."

"A what?"

"An expression," he explained. "Something you say when you mean to say something else, to create... I don't know, a more relatable image."

"How is recharging batteries relatable? Do you assume I am a mechanical being?"

"No, but the image is accurate, is it not? Like a robot, I am tired. I sleep, and when I awake, I have energy. My batteries has recharged."

"But a robot, or any mechanical being, needs to be plugged in to charge."

"And sleeping is like plugging in. Do you get the metaphor?"

"Metaphor?"

"The comparison."

"I do not."

"Then I guess I'll stop using it."

"Why do you guess? Why not simply do?"

"Good night, Commander," the human said, sharper than he expected. "I hope you see the daggers in my eyes and the sparks that fly off my tongue."

"I do not see any..."

"It's *figurative*!"

With a sudden burst of anger, the human turned away from him, curling into a ball on the soft ground by the fire. And that was the end of that.

Strax leaned back against a tree and let out a cleansing breath. But it did nothing to alleviate the anxiety he felt. He thought of his crew, in orbit so high above them, fighting an alien threat so much bigger than themselves. The Travan were a mighty warrior race, and having their full force focused on the Ascendant meant that he did not have much chance of getting it back.

But who knows. The human seemed resourceful, after all. Maybe he had a story that could get them out of this mess.

And maybe, just maybe, save the world.

CHAPTER 7

Strax slept poorly that night. It probably had something to do with the cold, the foreign air, and the arm hanging limply by his side, but that was beside the point.

The commander had always prided himself on being able to fall asleep anywhere – hell, in his younger days, he had managed to sleep through the boarding of the *Golden Truncheon* by pirates. He had even managed to fall asleep hanging from his legs, when he had been taken prisoner by the Travan. The first time he had encountered them, actually. He was one of the few to have ever returned from their grips alive.

And, surprisingly, without the aversion to poetry that most POWs came back with. He counted himself lucky.

But tonight, sleep eluded him. Which was good, because it kept him awake enough to witness his second betrayal of the day: The human was a spy.

Just as expected.

Sometime during the night, Human-Steve had quietly risen to his feet – or, at least, had attempted to rise quietly. Strax, being awake, heard every shuffle of his fleshy feet on the soft ground.

The human stirred the fire gently, sending sparks rising in the air. Then, still thinking himself to be perfectly silent, he walked away from the little encampment.

At first, Strax thought the human was relieving himself. He knew next to nothing about the human digestive system, and did not want to know. But when the minutes drew too long, he decided something was amiss, and rose to follow him.

The human was easy to trail: his body gave off so much heat, it left a path as clear as day through the underbrush. Strax poised himself on the points of his spear-like feet, tiptoeing to Human-Steve's side.

And, much to Strax's surprise, Human-Steve was on a com.

"And they haven't hurt you?" he said, his voice tense. Strax crouched behind a bush, keeping his breathing as still as possible. He closed his eyes, having read somewhere that humans were sensitive to stares.

"No, no, but they haven't exactly found us yet," said a voice on the other end of the line – female? One of the other humans on the ship, perhaps.

A ship they were not meant to have any communication with. Strax would kick himself later for putting his trust entirely on this untested, untrustworthy being.

"But the rest of the crew?"

"They've been sent to their quarters," continued the voice through the com, cracking slightly. The connection must have been poor. *"The upper brass is contained on the bridge, though what's going on there, we don't know. I think they're waiting for your commander, seeing as the leaving protocols are still in place."*

"It's what we've assumed as well," Human-Steve said sternly. Then, in an instant, all calm demeanor was gone. In its place came the voice of a child. Strax forced his eyes open, and in the dim light of the human's communication device, it seemed as though Steve was leaking through his eyes.

For a second, the commander thought to approach him, to see if he could fix the human's malfunction. But he was curious to know where this was going.

"God, Paige, I'm so scared," he admitted, his voice wavering. "Are you safe up there?"

"I'm hidden," she replied, *"I'm as safe as I can be. They found Michaels – he's back in the dorm, confined to quarters - but Patel and I have managed to evade capture for now. Patel hacked the ship's directory and deleted our presence from the logs, so they're not looking for us."*

"Good, that's really good," said Steve, "Look, Strax and I are going to try to get back there."

"Don't! The second he boards the ship, they'll be able to leave the solar system. They'll fly the ship right into Order HQ, and the Travans will have access to earth."

"We need a plan," he said, "what about protocol beta?"

"We need Michaels for that."

"Think you can break into his dorm, get him out?"

"Patel could, I think. I'll keep you updated."

"Call me with a signal," said Steve; "I don't want Strax to know I have someone on the ship. He will want to take command, and there's no way he can work with us."

"Agreed," the human female replied, *"The Order is not in the habit of making bold decisions, and if Strax knew about us, he'd overthink everything. See what you can do about pulling that stick out from his ass."*

A stick? Strax reached for his posterior, confused. He had nothing up his rectum, he was certain of that. The humans had no idea what they were talking about, and they were going to ruin this entire operation! Not that it was much of an operation – yet.

What did they mean, he'd overthink everything? These rash, primitive humans never took the time to think their options through. What they were doing now, actually hacking into the Ascendant's logs… that was dangerous, and not to mention illegal on so many levels.

He should have burst through the bushes right there, demanded the human hand over his com, and solve this issue once and for all. But the consequences of that action could be relentless. He stayed in waiting, quiet as the bush that hid him.

"If you want my opinion," said the female, *"we're perfectly capable of handling this entire rescue mission on our own. We're basically Earth's A-team. I didn't spend eight years training as a Navy SEAL, flying jets, and studying astrophysics just to deliver fish juice on an alien's ship."*

"Look, we're the first generation of Astronauts to ever get this far," said Human-Steve, "we do need to make a good impression. We still need Strax to think he's in charge."

"He will never listen to you."

"Hey, I just pulled a Hermione over here and saved both our asses," he insisted, "And did I mention the dragon?"

"You did mention the dragon. Three times. Four, now."

"He owes me his life, a few times over. I think I can at least gently push him in the right direction."

"And we will receive no credit whatsoever for saving the entire Order from their worst enemy?"

"Probably not."

There was a pause. Was that a cleansing breath from the female?

"I think we're in agreement," she said, *"we go SEAL team 6 on the Travan's asses."*

"If we have to," said Human-Steve, "see if you can find where the Travan leader is hiding out. Is he on the ship, or on the planet? That will determine our course of action."

"Rambo the place out, if you have to."

"That's probably what I'll end up doing. We'll have to coordinate our strikes, so neither can ask for reinforcements. Divide and Conquer."

"I'll set everything up for a swift and easy takeover, Captain."

"Thanks, Paige. Oh, and just a reminder... I love you, sweetheart. Stay safe up there."

"I love you too, Hunter. Now go kick some Travan ass!"

"If you kill more than I do, I owe you dinner."

"You still owe me for last time, sweetie. Now go! Let me handle things up here."

"Love you."

"I know it."

Strax realized suddenly that the conversation was over: and that meant Human-Steve going back to the campfire, with Strax missing. But the human did not move: he stared at the coms device, his eyes still leaking like a faulty tap.

Strax turned to return to the campfire, leaving the human to cleanse in silence. He could have confronted him: he probably should have. But that certainty... the human truly thought him, and the other three humans, could take down the entire Travan threat by themselves. How naïve! He should call off this charade.

Or, better yet, watch them and see how this played out. Knowing what he did now, he would not let himself be tricked.

But still, he wanted to know where this was going.

CHAPTER 8

Strax made a great effort the next morning to pretend he had slept all night.

"What a sleep!" he said, pounding his chest in a morning ritual. "I feel revitalized!"

He hopped on his feet, flipped forward onto his pincers, and proceeded to do pushups, while chanting his early morning waking rhyme.

"Sleep is the enemy! I banish you! I banish you!"

The human didn't seem to have a morning ritual. He just got up, kicked some dirt over the fire, and pretended not to stare at his magnificent commander, this finest specimen of his species.

Well, that's how Strax saw it. And with the vigor that came with knowing more than the human thought he knew, of secretly one-upping the opponent, came a self confidence that could shatter a mirror.

"Did your batteries recharge, Human-Just-Steve?" asked the commander, chortling. He wished his fellow commanders could see his impressive humor today.

"Enough for what lies ahead. And please, it's Just Human-Steve. I mean Steve. Dammit."

"Good, because we have a ship to reclaim, Just-Human-Steve," said Strax.

"It's Steve. As I am well aware. What is the first step here, commander?"

"I was hoping you could tell me."

The human seemed taken aback: he probably did not except for Strax to fall into his manipulation so easily. Strax was eager to hear, though, how a rag tag team of primitive humans could ever hope to accomplish the takeover of his infiltrated ship.

"Well, the clear thing would be to reclaim the shuttle," he said, "which would enable us to contact the ship in orbit. However, that might be difficult, seeing as how we're in the middle of nowhere."

"I have a tracker."

"You what?"

"Did you not hear properly? Would you like me to repeat?"

"I heard fine. I just can't believe my ears. Why didn't you tell me this last night?"

"We don't park the shuttles without a way of retrieving them, we do have a way to track them."

"And does that tracker have a homing device?"

"Please explain what you mean by that," asked Strax.

"You know, a way to call the shuttle to you."

"Now, that would be work of fiction, Human-Steve."

"Jeez, it's worth asking," the human scoffed, "what else aren't you telling me?"

That I know your secret, Strax thought, and a thrill traveled up his spine at the idea of being so far ahead of this small creature. He did as the humans did, and bared his mouth. He did not have fangs, only bristles and bone, but it had the intended effect, and the human looked uneasy.

"I hide nothing from you, lieutenant, just as you hide nothing from me. Now, come along: we're going to find my shuttle, and assess the status of the Ascendant from there. Now come along!"

The human did not appear to be pleased at being called like some kind of house animal, but he thankfully did as he was told. He ran his flashy appendages through the odd coif on top of his head - were those feathers? Strax still could not tell - before placing a hand on the pistol on his hip.

"How far?" he asked.

Strax opened up the finder on his pocket computer. Five bounds: not too far off. He relayed the information to the human, who only bobbed his head up and down, grunting like some kind of dust hog.

"Let's get moving," he said, "we need to reach the shuttle before the Travan fleet does."

"I do not think they know it exists, Human-Steve."

"Well, we wasted all this time, sleeping, I think we need to make up for that lost time."

"I think you're having trouble speaking, Human-Steve.

Perhaps the sleep was not as fitful as you claim."

That made the human go silent, very fast.

They began the arduous walk towards the shuttle. Strax let his pocket computer guide them, but the terrain was foreign and traitorous. Every so often, they had to stop, thinking they heard one of the massive dragons storming through the woods, but not once did they see one in person.

They emerged from the woods soon after, but the tall grasses proved to be much worse to hike through. For one, they offered no cover from above: but it did not seem that the enemy was using dragons, or ships to fly low overhead. Strax proceeded with caution, but it seemed as though no one was trying to find them.

Having had nothing to eat that morning, Strax was beginning to feel hunger gnawing at his stomachs. He could imagine a creek running not too far ahead of them, or a coast, with live fish swimming down them, easy to stab to death and shred to a million pieces with his powerful jaw. His mouth salted at the thought. He coughed, little grains of sodium spilling onto the earth, and instantly killing the grass there.

Human-Steve said nothing to this, even when Strax brushed the grains off his uniform in silence.

Soon, they reached the road: the only road for miles, it would seem. The long dirt expanse stretched to the city in one direction, and back to the ship in the other. Strax was eager to get to the rations, but more importantly, to get back to his beloved ship.

He fucking loved that ship. Why had he even considered retirement? He belonged there! The Ascendant needed him! He could practically hear it calling from orbit: *Help me, Strax! Bad men are trying to take me!*

"I'm coming, my sand dollar," he said.

"What's that?"

Strax snapped his head in the direction of the voice, but it was only the human. He said nothing. The human gazed forward once again.

"Wasn't this where we parked?" he asked, pointing a pink finger straight ahead.

"If it was, then the ship would be there."

"Check your locator: I'm pretty sure someone's taken our ship!"

Our? Strax wanted to smack the human across its face. To

watch that skin flop, without an exoskeleton to protect it.

Strax zoomed in on the little beacon on his computer's screen. They were close, but Human-Steve was right, the shuttle wouldn't be anywhere near the main road where they had actually left it.

"Gods," Strax refrained from crushing the palm computer in his claw, "they have taken our shuttle! And our ship! When will it end?"

Human-Steve didn't answer. Instead he crouched on the ground in the space the shuttle should have laid, touching the grass with his hand outstretched.

"The ground is colder here than over there," he said, "and the grass is folded over. Which means the shuttle was here, and moved rather recently. The sun hasn't had time to warm the space under it since it's been displaced."

Strax was taken aback: so, the human was moderately intelligent. His deductive reasoning sure was impressive.

"And which way did they take it?" asked the commander.

"Your claw."

"My what?"

"Your claw... palm?... thingy."

Strax writhed beneath his shell, pulling out his computer. The human was right, after all – he was the only one able to track it. But he wasn't going to admit that, boost the human's ego even more.

"It's been taken in that direction," he said, pointing down the road – away from the castle.

"It might be safe to assume it wasn't the king's men who took it," Human-Steve bobbed his head, "hopefully it is not in Travan hands."

"I share your enthusiasm," Strax said, seething.

They followed the locator away from the fortifications, keeping out of sight in the trees along the road. Then beacon took them further away from any settlements, seemingly to the middle of nowhere. But the shuttle was stationary, if the beacon was accurate.

The forest was denser here than it had been near the encampment, and it was difficult to navigate. Deeper and deeper they went, pushing through the underbrush. The human's arms and legs were soon covered in small red lines, and Strax took pleasure in knowing his exoskeleton truly was superior in every way.

He didn't realize he was clutching his limp arm, though.

"It should be right up ahead," said Strax, pocketing the computer. He crouched low in the underbrush, noting how they were now near a clearing. The Human followed.

"A dwelling of some kind?" the Human said – asking a question with a very evident answer. Before them, through the underbrush, stood a stone hut, round and tall, with an opening at the top letting out dense smoke. Human-Steve brushed the leaves aside to get a better look, before retreating.

"I see the shuttle," he said, jutting his chin forward. Strax looked in that general direction, squinting slightly, and saw the front end of the ship, cleverly dissimulated in a brush pile.

"If they're hiding it so, I would like to bet they're just scavengers, not connected to the fight in any way."

"I would like to agree with you, Human-Steve, but we must still proceed with caution."

"I never said otherwise," he stepped back from the leaves. "What's our plan here?"

Strax had no clue. There wasn't anything in the Order's handbook about dealing with locals.

"What do you think?" he asked, "I'm in charge of vetting you. Give me your honest opinion; call it part of your assessment."

The human gave Strax a look, the hair above his eye knotting together. Strax was beginning to understand the human's many looks, and this one seemed to say that he knew exactly what Strax was up to. But he said nothing.

"I see two options," he said, "we have the keys to the shuttle, so we could just walk up and take it. However, the brush covering it could take a while to clear, and we do not know the extent of the damage the ship has received being dragged here. Or if that dwelling is inhabited – which I assume it is, if there's a fire going."

"So what is your second option?"

"We befriend the locals," he said, the corners of his lips pulling upwards, "we tell them we're travellers from the stars, give them something good worth trading, and take the ship. They'll be more likely to be silent that way, and everyone is happy."

"I dislike the second option," said Strax, "we are not cleared to make negotiations on behalf of the order."

"So? Isn't it our job?"

"No."

"Look, commander," the human crossed his arms in front of his chest. "We need this ship. Doesn't the Order have some kind of... emergency protocol? We should be able to do whatever we have to. In order to save our people."

"This is why the human race is not ready," Strax replied, "you're too rash. Stubborn headed. In the Order, we believe in weighing all of our options, taking our time to make the right decision."

"If we wait any longer, we lose our ship, Commander." Strax disliked the way Stave called the Ascendant "ours" again, as if he had any claim to it. "We need this shuttle."

"Then we go with option 1, Human-Steve," Strax strode forward, "we reclaim our ship in the name of the Order, and anyone who interferes will be restrained."

"Shouldn't we..." but Strax, not able to take another minute of the human's wretched mewling, strode powerfully forward towards his shuttle. Yes, his, and no one else's. The human was nothing but a passenger, a deck hand at best, and would just have to do as he was ordered if he wanted any part in the rescue mission.

CHAPTER 9

The second he took a step into the clearing, the ground exploded at his feet. He flew into the earth; gravel covering his back, pelting his shell like bullets from the sky.

"What the trees are you doing on my land?" screamed a voice, "get away, you filthy spaceman!

"I am commander Strax, of the Universal Order," the commander shouted, pushing himself to his feet, attempting to stand tall. "And I am here for my…"

"I do not care where you're from, or what you want! Get off my land or I will blow your head clear off!"

"As a commander, I order you to…"

"Everyone stay calm!"

Strax blinked the dust from his eyes to look in the direction of the new voice, shocked to see Human-Steve, standing bold, his hands in the air. As he watched, the human placed his pistol on the dirt before him, keeping a neutral expression.

"Hi, I'm Steve!" he said, "and I fell from the sky. Sorry. Who are you, good sir?"

The Sybillian man who stood before them was clutching what looked incredibly like hand grenades in his talons. The other hand held a slingshot: apparently, combined with the little egg shaped explosives, it was enough to send Strax to the ground. His shame grew inside his stomach.

"Yaris," said the Sybillian, "and I want the two of you to go, right now."

"That's actually something you can help us with, Yaris," said Steve, "you see, we need our ship to get home. And you happen to have found it."

"You mean that mobile home's a vehicle?"

"It's what brought us to this planet, and we need it to get home. And we're willing to trade for it."

"A trade?" the man lowered his slingshot. "What do you have to trade?"

"How about your life, small reptile man?" Strax scowled, "we come from the Order, what part of that do you not understand?"

"I'm sorry about my buddy here," Steve interrupted, shooting a glare in Strax's direction. It was like being stabbed between the eyes. "He just really needs to take a dump. And he doesn't like doing that in the forest, he'd much rather use the one in the ship."

Strax wanted to strangle him. But he was managing to de-escalate the situation.

"Dad? What's going on?"

At the stoop of the dwelling stood a young Sybillian woman, a reptile in a loose flowing dress. She could have been called beautiful, if you were into that sort of thing.

"Go back in side, sweet fang," said Yaris, "Daddy's conducting business."

"Who are they?" she asked, "Are these spacemen?"

"They are, I guess, they're from some place called the Order," he said, "but don't worry about them."

Then Yaris abruptly did a double take. Before the woman could turn around, he grabbed her by her arm and brought her into the clearing.

"Folks, meet my daughter Yana," he said, "and if you can find her a suitable husband, you can have my ship."

"Hi Yana," said the human, "I'm Steve!"

"Hi Steve," said Yana, "do you mind holding on for one second? I need to murder my father."

"Now Yana, be reasonable..."

"Are you so desperate, dad?" she snapped, "You need me to marry so much, that you're going to put my future in the hands of these... space freaks? No offense, space freaks."

"None taken, stranger," said Steve. Strax wanted to shoot these two down on the spot for showing such disrespect to an agent of the Order, and could not tell what was stopping him from doing so. So, he did what any officer would do: he pulled out his sidearm and fired.

Of course, with his arm off, he missed.

Part of the house exploded, the wall flying out in small chunks and covering the ground with more gravel. Three pairs of eyes turned to Strax in anger.

"Give us what we came for, and no one will get hurt!"

"Why you-"

Yaris reached for his slingshot, and Strax reacted instinctively: he shot out a warning blast, and missed.

Yaris fell dead at his daughter's feet.

"DADDY!" she cried, falling to his corpse and letting out a wail of pain.

"And the humans are the rash ones?" Steve shouted, dashing to her side.

"I was defending myself!"

Steve said nothing. He crouched beside the girl, tentatively reaching an arm for her shoulders, but before he could touch her, she dropped her face and began to nibble on her father's arm.

And then, she really tucked in.

The two men watched as the sobbing reptilian woman completely devoured her father, blood spilling across her face, hungrily eating him down to the bone. Strax felt horror inside his shell, a cold sensation like ice in between his layers.

When she finished, she stood up, wiped an arm over her mouth, and let out a belch loud enough to wake the entire Ascendant in time for morning rotation. It was only after the gas had fully cleared her mouth that she lunged at Strax.

"You killed my father!" she screamed, her hands outstretched, ready to strangle him. Which was useless, considering he never really had a neck. He evaded her easily, sidestepping away.

"And you ate him!" he said, clasping her hands easily in one of his claws and twisting them back so that she could no longer make an attempt on his life, "and stole my ship, I might add."

"Stress eating! And it was honorable!" she snapped, "I was supposed to kill him! Me! It was my duty as daughter to kill and eat his remains when his line was passed on! And now I can never murder him with my own hands!"

"You hear that, commander?" The human said gingerly, "you robbed her of the chance to kill her father."

"I heard quite clearly, Lieutenant," he replied. He wasn't so pleased having everyone come up against him. "Now, Yana, was it? We're taking our ship."

"The hell you are! You robbed me of my father, you will not rob me of my ship!"

"She has a point, commander," said the human.

"She robbed us first!" said Strax.

"Look, Yana," Steve turned to her, "we're sorry about all this. You have a little blood, there, by the way. Anyway just tell me what you want for the ship. We'll be gone before you know it."

"Hell no, I'm keeping the ship," she snapped, "with my father dead, I no longer have anything to barter for marriage. The ship is mine. Not get off my land!"

"You forget who has the upper hand, girl," said Strax.

A second later, she kicked him in the shin, sending a splintering of pain up his leg. He howled, and in the process let go of the woman, who dashed off, grabbing the grenades before he could say another word.

"Get back!" she said, clutching one of the small bombs above her head, "get off my land! I'm warning you!"

"Come, commander," said Human-Steve, "we'll leave her in peace. So sorry, Yana, you've been through so much today."

"Lieutenant, we cannot leave."

The Lieutenant met his gaze, and then, very slowly and deliberately, closed one of the eyes. It was exactly like the look he had thrown Strax in the negotiation room. Perhaps the human had a plan this time as well.

"Fine, we leave. You will be compensated for your father's death, girl."

"Whatever, just get off my gravel, I need to have it properly raked now."

She burped again, and the duo left the property, walking back into the forest with their hands empty.

"I assume you have an idea, Human-Steve?" said the commander, the second they were out of hearing range.

"Yeah, you stay here, and don't show your face to that poor girl ever again. Understood?"

"Lieutenant, I..."

"I have a plan," he continued, cutting him off. The Nerve. "I'm going to seduce her. I know, it's a base thing to do, what with her having just lost her father, but it's the easiest way for us to get the ship. I distract her with some simple comfort and you get the brush off the shuttle. Then I'll sneak out and we can leave the planet together."

Strax balked.

"Ok, let's do this, then," said the human, taking his commander's silence as grounds to begin his stupid plan.

"Human-Steve!"

"I know, but it'll work, I know it will."

"Seduce the reptile? You?" Strax blew air out heavily from his nose. "Not hardly. I should be the one to try, she would appreciate me far more."

"The man who just murdered her father."

"A commander of the Universal Order!"

"She doesn't know what that is! And might I remind you, you killed her father?"

"But you are pink! Fleshy! She would fine my shell lustrous and appealing."

"So what is this, now? Do I need to pull down my pants and grab a ruler?"

"Only if that helps you feel better about having a lesser chance with the lady Yana, sure."

"I don't believe you," said Human-Steve, practically snarling. "First you accuse my race of being brash and stubborn. Then you storm this stranger's house, shoot her father dead, and expect her to find you attractive? No, even me trying to seduce her will be a long shot. But with you..."

"And you," the commander scowled down at this insubordinate human, "you disgust me. You try and bargain with these lesser beings. You strut around like you - you! - know better than me. And now you will betray your mate and lie with a..."

"My mate?" Human-Steve changed colors again, this time turning bight red, almost purple. "Who are you..."

"Human-Juarez, I believe their name is."

"How did you know Juarez and I are a couple?" he took a step back from the commander, eyes wide with shock. "The only way you could... you heard, didn't you? You overheard me talking to her last night!"

Strax blew out a cleansing breath. He had underestimated the human's intelligence. This creature was becoming more and more of a nuisance with every passing moment.

What did he even need the human for? He could finish this mission alone! The pesky creature was constantly getting in his way, thinking he could take him over without a second thought... well, he had a lot of nerve!

"I did," said Strax, proudly. "I heard every word. I heard you speak as if you and the other humans could do what thousands of the Order cannot... So yes, I do think humans are brash! And vain, and egotistical and..."

"Can we just stop? We have a mission here," said the human, "I have tried to keep it professional, but you have no faith in me. I have trained my entire life to be on missions like this one, and have already proved more than my worth to you. So are you going to trust me, at least until this mission is done, or am I going to have to take matters in my own hands?"

With his good hand, Strax retrieved his pistol from his holster, holding it up to the human's eyes.

"Lieutenant Human-Steve," he said, "you are hereby relieved of your duty."

"You've got to be kidding me, after everything I've done? I saved your life!"

"Please relinquish your weapon and..."

"We're the only two people not under Travan control!"

"Don't make this any harder, human."

"You know what?" Steve tossed his weapon to the ground, glaring. "You realize this isn't just for the Order to test out humans, right? It's also for us humans to see if we want to be in the Order. And right now, you're not making the Order seem like such a great place."

"It looks like you just wasted your opportunity."

"And it looks like you just wasted yours," the human left out a very long breath, "but I care too much about this universe to let it go without a fight."

With that, the human punched Strax squarely between the eyes, knocking him out cold.

CHAPTER 10

"Did you kill him?"

Strax woke up surrounded by women, which was a very odd sensation. Especially when he couldn't feel any of his extremities.

"Human!" He shouted. There was no point in pretending he was unconscious, when so many had seen him awake. "Show yourself, Human-Steve!"

As his vision began to clear, he saw that what he thought had been a crowd of women was, in fact, only three people. Two human females, and Yana, the reptile woman from before. And she was wearing an Order Uniform.

"Ah Strax, thanks for joining us."

The human women stepped back as Steve emerged, cleaned up and looking smart in a freshly laundered uniform. Without the blood, dirt, and ash on his face, the human looked quite remarkably like he belonged in the grey and blue of the Order.

But that was probably the chemicals in his brain talking. The endorphins that swam in his green matter, telling him he was alive. And, for some reason, that Steve was wearing his uniform in a handsome way.

Fuck those endorphins.

"You rendered me unconscious!" he shouted.

"Well, you were holding me back," Steve replied, pinching the bridge of his nose. "Look. Since you've been out, my team here has recaptured the *Ascendant.* It's in Order control. Good, right?"

"How the... what?"

Strax didn't know what to reply. Recaptured the Ascendant? But how? There were only four humans, and their leader had been here, planetside, with him. How they could have defeated an entire Travan legion was beyond him.

"It was easy," said one of the human females, looking smug. "The thing you and the Travan have in common is that you wait a fucking long time before taking action. This plan has been in place for most of a decade, believe it or not. And the one variable they hadn't taken into account were us humans."

Strax was beginning to feel a sensation he hadn't felt in a long time. Not since he was in basic training, all those years ago. Was it... fear? He struggled to keep himself centered, the urge to reprimand these creatures becoming overwhelming.

"So you took the *Ascendant* back – the three of you?" he asked, disbelieving.

"I have to admit, the Travan's plan was excellent and effortless. They had the ship surrounded before the Order could react – well, they could have reacted, if they weren't waiting for orders and following protocol. Since they understood the Order's strategy of waiting for sure outcome before acting, the Travan overwhelmed the ship in just a few minutes."

"So how did you take it back?"

"Simple: we pulled a Leroy Jenkins," said the small one – Human-Patel, was it?

"And what is a Leroy Jenkins?"

"We knew the Travan were also counting on orders and control in order to keep the ship," she explained, "so once their commander was out of reach, we ran in, guns a 'blazing. It was simple, really. They never knew what hit them."

"You... let me get this straight. You just..."

"Burst through doors, took them all by surprise, and gunned down everyone inside. Grabbed all the weapons in the armory, and reclaimed the ship, room by room," she said, baring her white fangs, "Distributed weapons to our own, and kept going until the ship was all ours again. Your people took a while to understand how to act in such a situation, but once they were firing, they really got into it."

"We have over fifty high ranking Travan officers in the brig," the other human female said. This one was the one Human-Steve was coupled with, Human-Juarez. Or Human-Paige? It was hard to understand human names. They had too many of them. "Our man Mike is with them now. We came down to the surface to help you and the Lieutenant take down the Travan overlord."

"He's here?" Strax sat up straight, though his head was still groggy. The human had really done a number on him. He would have reprimanded him, but he was too much in awe of the news he had just been told to do anything about it.

They had saved his ship.

By storming into rooms and shooting up the invaders.

Genius.

Terrifying.

"The Travan overlord is convening with the Sybillian emperor as we speak," said Human-Steve, "and we're going to kill them both."

"Come now," said Strax, "there must be a diplomatic..."

"You hate the Travan empire!" he scoffed, "you've been at war with them for over a thousand years! And now that you have the chance to take them down, you're going to pass it up for diplomacy?"

"There's always a..."

"Fuck no," the human spat, "we live in this universe too. We might not be in the Order – yet – but we don't want the Travan playing us for the fools the way they've been dealing with the Order since before humans even conceived the concept of aliens. If you're not going to kill him – we are. It's our duty to the universe."

"But..."

"Listen," Human-Steve moved in close, glowering. Strax could feel the creature's warm breath on his cheek, the smell of earth strong on his breath. "We're not in the Order. Whatever we do, we do in the name of Earth, and you don't have to be attached to it. So, if you want to sit this one out, fine by me: this mission will go forward whether you're on board or not. But if you want a chance to actually take down the biggest villain this galaxy has ever known, you're invited. Not as my commander, but as a commander, my brother in arms. What do you say?"

"Wait, you're inviting this freak?" Yana snapped at Steve, "He killed my father! I thought you said I could rough him up a bit before we went?"

"Just take out your frustration on the emperor who's been making your family live in exile all these years," he said.

"This... creature is coming with us?" Strax couldn't understand why the human would even want this dead weight to come along. She was a farm girl who had just eaten her father, not a trainer war hero like himself. Being put on the same level as her was demeaning.

Discovering that three soldiers from a primitive planet like Earth could do what his entire crew could not was demeaning as well, but let's not go there.

"I told Yana here she can come with us when we're done," the lieutenant said to Strax, "she doesn't have to be involved with the Order, but we're giving her a ride in exchange for her help."

"We don't need her," Strax scoffed, "and who are you, doling out rewards for non-Order..."

"As I already said, you don't need to be a part of this mission," the lieutenant looked stern, but somehow calm. "You can take the shuttle, reach the Ascendant, take your crew and warn the Order about what happened here today – or almost happened. We'll take it from here."

"No," he said.

He found himself standing now, pushing himself to his feet, giving the human an appraising look. Even if he was shorter than the commander, he somehow had the air of someone much more imposing. Strax had to admit – he was impressed.

Even more so at himself, and what he would say next.

"I want to do this." He couldn't stop the words once they started flowing. "As much as I hate to say this – your methods work. And I am not going back to my ship with the Travan threat still so close. And you are correct: even if we were to return to the Order with this information, they would take months to decide on their next course of action: in which time the Travan would advance even further. It is time to fight. Just show me the way."

"Wow, this is beautiful," said human-Patel, "I never thought I would see one of the Order's own commanders embrace the way of the fuck-all attitude so quickly."

"Don't push your luck."

"No sir," she replied, but she was showing her teeth very much now. It was rather unsettling. But, in an attempt to gain her trust, Strax feebly did the same. He lifted his upper lip flap, turned the corner of his mouth upwards, and made eye contact.

Now all the humans were doing the same. Only the Sybillian remained with an expression that looked, if Strax was reading it right, rather peeved.

"Might I remind you – he killed my father?"

"You were going to do the same."

"It's not the same! He's a monster!" she spat, "The patrimonial killing is a coming of age in our culture. Without having a father to kill..."

"The emperor will do nicely, though, won't he?" said Human-Steve, "think of all the gourmet meals he's been eating while the rest of you have been starving... he'll be quite delectable."

The woman licked her lips. "I do like the sound of that."

"Then it's settled," Human Steve said with a wide show of teeth, "you don't have to like each other. You just have to not shoot at each other when we storm the castle."

"And how exactly are we doing to do that?" asked the commander.

"You leave that to my team," said Steve, "the three of us will lead the way. Now, here's how we do it on Earth: you take a rifle, right..."

"And you shoot at the enemy," Human-Patel explained, "shoot at anything but us. We call it the Rambo method. We're going to strap each of you with as much ammo as you can carry, and you're going to take down anything that gets in our way, all the way up to the Emperor – and the Travan overlord."

"This method sounds idiotic."

"With all due respect, this method reclaimed your ship, commander," the human female said gleefully.

"Then, I shall defer to your judgment."

"You'll be happy you did. Get ready to kick some ass!"

Strax found his mind buzzing at the prospect. What was this odd feeling in his chest, somewhere between panic and exhilaration? Was it excitement?

Or was it the foreknowledge that he was about to do something incredibly stupid that would most certainly result in his death?

Oddly enough, even knowing he might die today, Strax was sure this was the best plan he had ever heard. And for some reason, he didn't mind dying if it meant going down like this. Whoever this Rambo and this Leroy Jenkins fellows were, he must have been one hell of a human hero.

CHAPTER 11

Which is how, an hour later, Strax, Steve, and the rest of their small crew found themselves at the gates of the Sybillian fortress, armed to the proverbial teeth. Strax had two belts of ammo crossing his chest, a rifle in each claw – including the arm that was working poorly, but it was going to put in its best effort – and two slung across his back. Along with pistols at his hips.

The humans, with their meager stature, carried far less, but they were far more at ease with the bulk of their weapons. They wore black gear, sleek and shiny, fitted to each of their bodies like they have been molded of the same material. Now in their own shells, Strax found the humans more intimidating than he had first assumed.

"Ready?" asked Steve, his grip tightening and listening around his pistols. They glistened with sweat.

"I will never be readier, Human-Steve," Strax found himself replying, with no small degree of admiration, "Is there any kind of ritual you humans entail before heading into battle?"

"None specifically," he said, "Why? Do you?"

"We usually thank our limbs for carrying us this far, and hope to see them after the fight."

"I like that," Steve said, "we do have an old, holy saying on our planet... it goes, Yippy Kayay, Motherfuckers!"

"If you find yourself screaming at any point, let it happen, ok?" said Patel. "Let it out. It's going to be a lot."

"I'll take that into consideration."

"Can we go now?" asked Yana. "I'm itching to do some killing."

"Fine - Yippy Kayay, Motherfuckers!"

And Steve... there was no other way of saying this, he

pounced.

Like an animal, he ran at the massive stone gate, holstering his weapons and dashing up the stone face like it was a flight of stairs. He disappeared from view, but a few minutes later, the gate began to slide open, crashing to the ground in a massive cloud of dust.

As the cloud settled, Steve appeared in the middle of the newly cleared road, facing up the tiny streets as if they were the only important thing in the universe.

"So? You guys coming?" he asked, before running forward once again.

Strax extended his weapons, finger poised on the trigger. But it was no use: the streets were cleared. It was as if they knew the humans were coming.

"Damn," said Patel, "they were expecting us. Who tipped them off?"

"I would assume the fact we reclaimed the ship might have done the trick," said human-Juarez.

"Stay close. Be on high alert." Human-Steve nodded slowly. "And if anything moves, don't hesitate, take the shot."

Strax wasn't sure what to make of this foolhardy approach, but, armed to the teeth, he felt better about the outcome. If he didn't like what happened, he could shoot it until it led to a better result. Easy. Great philosophy. Humans.

They marched in a loose, automatic formation up the hill, following the winding streets he had seen from the chariot just one day ago. It was odd, following an untrained, untested human into battle, but even stranger so was how safe Strax felt in the human's presence. Like they would stop at nothing to reach their goal.

Something to report to the Order. Maybe these humans did have something to teach them.

But the true test would come when they reached the actual army. Which, until now, they had not.

It was only when they reached the top of the hill, and stood facing the walls of the imperial city, that they started to see any signs of life.

"This is the place," said Sybillian-Yana, "the place we lived before the emperor wanted us dead. The place we were banished from."

"Are you going to be able to do this, Yana?" asked Human-Steve.

"Anything that moves is the enemy," she said, "I'm ready to shoot some scum! Yippe Cayenne Mother frosties!"

Before anyone could say a word, Yana dashed at the gate. It was as if the world had been a video on pause until that very moment: the instant she broke past the city's walls, the world burst into action. From all directions, soldiers came flooding in, bringing with them their Travan firepower and ornate formations.

The crew of five stared at the troops, Travan and Sybillian forces united in a single place square. But they didn't stare long.

Yana opened fire, and the world fast forwarded. Everything was moving in fast motion: the bright light, the explosions, the sounds that destroyed Strax's ears. And here he was, wielding lightning from his hands, aiming his weapons straight into the enemy lines, releasing a torrent of bullets so rapidly he could no longer feel his arms.

He was doing it!

He felt a power surge inside of him, so massive, that it burst through his mouth through the form of a shout. He screamed, his own voice masked by a wall of gunfire, but he was screaming, laughing, his hands tingling.

He felt alive!

But the feeling had opposition. Before long he too felt the wind of bullets sailing past his ears, and he realized that his crew was gone. Where was his line? Where were his men, his crew? They were five to come into this battle, but alone to fight it. Strax had to think fast, which was not his forte.

He watched as Human-Steve flung himself over two men manning a grenade launcher, smashing their two heads together, taking the weapon for himself and taking aim at the front door of the palace. The wall burst into a million flaming pieces, crumbling to the ground, forcing the backup lines of the Sybillian force out into the elements.

Despite no longer having any ammunition for his launcher, the lieutenant was still using the launcher as a weapon. He spun it in his arms, using it to take down a hoard of Sybillians who were running his way. His body armor was dented with the repeated hit of bullets, but he still stood strong.

"This is for my father, Strax!" said Yana, shooting a man straight through the chest, then devouring his still beating heart in one swift move.

"For... me?" Strax didn't know if it was a thought or

something he had actually said, his voice drowned out by the thunder around him.

"Take that, Strax!" she shouted, before dismembering another one. Strax had the chilling realization that, as she killed, she was plastering his face over the faces of her targets. However, after being initially repulsed, he found that the thought filled him with an even stranger feeling, one he couldn't quite put his finger on.

It might have been akin to admiration.

Before he could ponder this any further, a massive roar brought the gunfire to a sudden and terrifying stop. The crash of wings beat above him, a shadow obscuring the sky.

"Muffins!" Steve's cry could be heard throughout the courtyard. "You came back!"

The dragon flew over the army, blowing his fire upon a handful of its ranks. But it was only a diversion: he swooped low to the other side of the courtyard, breathing fire on the massive door that held his brethren back. The entire team of dragons burst from within, roaring and rearing, trying to rip the chains from their legs.

"Help me!" Human-Patel ordered, and while Strax's first instinct was to shout at her for pure insubordination, he instead dashed off behind her, slipping through the ranks of the angered beasts, using his plasma pistol to sever the chains that kept the magnificent beats bound.

One by one, they were freed. They flew up to join Muffins, and together they burned the hoards of soldiers in the yard, taking turns sending jets of fire down below.

"This way!" cried Human-Patel, grabbing his claw. Strax didn't even realize the touch was a touch, he simply ran along behind her, dashing for cover in the palace's grand hall.

They were not the only ones. The enemy forces were also seeking refuge, and ran like madmen to reach the hall. In their rush, they didn't take notice of a few flashy strangers, and Patel and Strax used this to get inside unnoticed. It was only then that they encountered a problem.

"Where to next?" asked Patel, in urgent whispers, as they tried to keep to the walls to avoid being detected.

"I do not know the layout, human."

"Fuck."

"Is this when we shoot again?"

"Have some tact. We're in cramped quarters with a few

hundred well-armed enemies. This isn't when we shoot, this is when we regroup, and avoid detection."

"Your human logic astounds me," said Strax, "one minute, it's "shoot everything with impunity" the next it's "have some tact." I simply cannot follow."

"And that is why," the human said, "we'll always have the upper hand."

It was then that a torrent of bullets came bursting through the front doors. Yana appeared, riffles in both hands, screaming into the mass of soldiers as she plowed them all down.

"STRAAAAX!" she screamed, rushing forward through the mass of corpses she was creating, "take that Strax! And you, Strax! And you, stupid fucking commander! Die, alien scum!"

By the time she reached Strax and Patel, she was out of breath, but looking exhilarated. Strax didn't know if he should stay, or if he was next. Thankfully, before he could ask, Patel and Juarez appeared, the latter missing a leg.

"What the hell, Juarez?" Patel intoned, "I thought the commander told you to keep all your limbs!"

"I must have dropped it somewhere," she laughed.

"But your limb!" Strax stammered, "it's..."

"Tis but a scratch! I always wanted to say that!"

"Keep moving, team!" Steve said, gathering them with his words, "we're close now! Yana, which way?"

"Do I have to do everything around here?" she scoffed. "it's down the overly ornate hall covered with portraits of the guy. A little hard to miss."

Strax wanted to ask why they even brought her along, but he was beginning to feel more than just a twinge of fear about this woman, so he let it slide. She was as fearsome as a fireball, and twice as deadly. Now he knew what humans meant by imagery.

Now that the army had been burnt to a crisp, it was easy to take down the few remaining stragglers between the five of them and their outstanding firepower. Strax found himself easing into the quiet comfort of the massacre. There wasn't any thought, there wasn't any planning: the only idea was to kill the enemy, and he felt good doing it.

Every soldier dead was a victory for the Order, and fifty pages of paperwork. But he would have someone else do that. Today, he could enjoy claiming a piece of territory no one in the Order had claimed in over a century.

"Through there," said Yana, pointing at yet another ornate green door. Steve gave a low, solemn nod.

"Let's end this."

With a blast of his plasma pistol, the doors flew open. Strax's heart fell. Before him stood two stout alien men, one reptilian, one insectoid, both cowering in fear. Their bodyguards rushed at the crew, but they were no match for the humans. In seconds, all that was left was the leader of the Order's worst enemy, and some random Sybillian with too much power.

They scrambled back from the door.

"This is it?"

Strax only realized he had been the ones to say the words after they had come from his mouth. He marched forward, angry and exasperated.

"Commander..." Human-Steve reached for his arm, but Strax pulled away, making towards the emperors.

"This is what we've been so afraid of?" he let out a laugh. He never laughed. Today was a day to try new things. "we've been at war with the Order for thousands of years. And their leader is a..."

He looked like he was about to be sick on Strax's shoes. A small, round insect like being, with a thick blue shell on his back and a mopey eyed expression. He looked like a poster for some seasonal disease back on Strax's homeworld.

"Finish him off, commander, and end this war," said Human-Steve.

"No, I cannot," Strax spat on the Travan overlord, and the creature only squealed.

"Don't hurt me! Please! I have a family! Five thousand larvae! I have mouths to feed!"

"If you can't, I will," said Yana. The Sybillian emperors' head exploded. "That's for my father, scum."

"Are you good?" asked Strax. "Should I be worried?"

"Yeah, we're good," she said, "I think I've gotten it out of my system. Well, I will."

She crouched down and began to eat the emperor's copse, sobbing through every bite. This only made the Travan overlord more scared, and he squirmed deeper into his chair.

"I will not kill him," said Strax, "I have something better planned for him."

THREE MONTHS LATER

Strax pinned the insignia upon Steve's chest with pride.

"We embrace the Human race as one of our own, and welcome Planet Earth into the Order. Long live the order! Long live our unity!"

The hall erupted with cheering, screaming, whooping and pleasant moans. Human Steve bowed low, doing that human thing where he glowed (he now knew the anti-camouflage was referred to as "blushing" or "beaming" depending on the resulting color, and was completely out of the humans' control, which he realized fit the description of the word "cute" he had also learned) as he took in the acclaim.

Strax bowed to him, as was customary, and found himself not resenting the action. He had grown fond of Human-Steve, of his team, his race, his horrible little habits. He enjoyed watching him in battle, though he would never say it to his face.

"It is an honor, and a privilege, to be here today," the human said. "I never thought I would see it come to pass. The Order and us Terrans have many differences... but one thing we certainly have in common is our need for justice. Our need to see things through. To make things right. And I am proud that Earth will be joining in the Order's fight to bring justice to our shared universe."

Strax was certainly proud of this small creature. Proud to have testified to have him join the Order. Proud to know – though Human-Steve did not yet – that he would be the next commander of the Ascendant, now that Strax was going to settle down.

His retirement might have come as a surprise to high command, especially to Admiral Ma'kurajaa, who wanted to promote him for his capture of the Travan Overlord, but Strax knew he was doing the right thing. He had found the perfect place to retire: a little planet on the edge of the Order, though the Order was reclaiming much of what had once been Travan, so it wouldn't be the edge much longer.

Sybillia was a much happier place without their dragon-imprisoning tyrant. Muffins was enjoying her freedom – for it was a her – and the two species were slowly learning to coexist again. Muffins had formed a powerfully matriarchal draconic society, and hosted weekend barbecues with the locals. It was becoming quite a nice place to live.

Especially when the current queen of the planet had discovered that maybe the feelings she felt when looking at Strax weren't rage and anger, but some odd excitement he shared too. After a single night in bed with her, Strax had decided retirement was definitely necessary, and contacted Admiral Ma'kurajaa from bed to tell him he wasn't leaving Sybillia.

Well. Except to invite Steve into the Order.

As for the former Travan Overlord? Well, in some cases, the Order's consistency with process and procedure were worth worshiping. In the three months since he had dropped the overlord into high command's hands, he was still sitting in "incoming prisoner" handling. It would be many years before he would reach a trial, and until then, it was a lot of waiting, paperwork, going back for more paperwork, and waiting again. It was, quite literally, hell.

"Congratulations, Steve," said Strax, patting the small fleshy thing on the back, "the Order is better for having you."

"Thank you, commander," he said, "I've been meaning to tell you something, you know."

"Oh? Tell away! You know how eager I am to hear your stories," Strax did the thing humans liked, smiling, "but I am no longer your commander. Call me Strax."

"Well, it's something I've been meaning to tell you… Strax," he snickered. "You see, since day one, I've been holding onto this nugget. Waiting until this very moment to tell you."

"Tell me, Steve, tell me!"

"Well, on my planet?" he grinned, "Strax is pronounced shithead as well."

About the Author

S.E. Anderson can't ever tell you where she's from. Not because she doesn't want to, but because it inevitably leads to a confusing conversation where she goes over where she was born (England) where she grew up (France) and where her family is from (USA) and it tends to make things very complicated.

She's lived pretty much her entire life in the South of France, except for a brief stint where she moved to Washington DC, or the eighty years she spent as a queen of Narnia before coming back home five minutes after she had left. Currently, she goes to university in Marseille, where she's studying Physics and aiming for a career in Astrophysics.

When she's not writing, or trying to science, she's either reading, designing, crafting, or attempting to speak with various woodland creatures in an attempt to get them to do household chores for her. She could also be gaming, or pretending she's not watching anything on Netflix.

www.SEAndersonAuthor.com

Books by S.E. Anderson

Starstruck
Alienation

THE LONE RANGER RETURNS

By Michael Anderle

You can't outrun a legacy.

Her Grandfather is gone, his legacy remains. It takes a while for this granddaughter to realize you can't outrun the Grimes legacy.

Chapter One

Far Outer Torcellan Quadrant, Space Station Yu'mfred 60699

There had been seven of us at the beginning of this game, but now we were four. Hopefully there would only be three after this poker hand.

And I would be one of the three. At least, I sure hoped so.

It wasn't really poker, but it's the closest way I can explain the game, and it is how I think of it.

I desperately wanted to get off this infested fucking space station and back out where I could do something decent with my damned life.

"You..." the rat-faced cyborg across the table from me laid down her cards—three aces high, and a pair of black fours, "can all suck my ass."

The Torcellan next to her made a face and folded his cards, pushing his metal cash into the pile. "I'm out, and it's 'kiss my ass,' you cybernetic cretin. Get a damned dictionary."

"Fucking hell." James closed his cards and tossed them onto the pile.

I looked at Rat-face McAssSuck and grinned. "Bite my shiny metal..."

PEW PEW!

"The fuck?" John yelled as the large mirror behind the bar exploded into shards, two pieces implanting themselves into Bob the bar guy. "Take it like a man!" someone told poor Bob as blood erupted from his mouth.

I didn't think he was going to shake that one off.

PEW!

I hit the fucking deck and everyone else scrambled when the laser blasts started flying. Thinking clearly for the first time since last...uh... *Shit.*

Day before last month?

Whatever. I reached up over the table to grab my money and pulled it back down to me, stuffing it into my jacket on my second try. These fucking tits of mine are too damned big.

Teach my sexy-ass to get a body-mod when I was floating high as a wind skiff.

I looked around to see what was going on, and that was when I saw that James wouldn't be doing anymore kissing—or sucking— ass, mine or others. Not with that hole through his skull.

That kind of bit the long cylindrical vegetable. He was good in bed on Tuesdays—or was that Thursdays? Well, dammit.

Had James been any good at all?

I had to stop thinking about these existential questions when I was in a bar that was being shot up to hell and gone.

Rat-face McAssSuck was grinning at me from the floor on the other side of the table, daring me with her eyes as her arm reached over the table to grab more of the pot. I had to give it to her—she had balls.

No, really! I could tell now that I was on the floor that Rat-face McAssSuck was actually a male. "Shiny balls you got there!" I yelled over the screaming and explosions rocking the place. I looked over my shoulder at the three Indie mercenaries who had pulled up a table and were using it to try and hold off four of the local merc military police by the front door.

Shit.

Rat-face McAssSuck screamed, and I turned back—his arm was on fire. He was flinging it about, then spotted the toilet rooms and started running in that direction. One stray beam went toward him before he made it inside, and I grimaced.

I could only imagine the decision he had to make, having his arm burning and looking at that toilet, thinking he had to shove it into that disgusting filth.

I turned back to the Skaine merc-military police, knowing that if I had to choose between my arm burning or sticking it in one of those toilets? Fucking hell, I wasn't going to stick my arm in that stank sludge. I'd rather eat plasmium bolts and be done with it.

One of the errant blasts came streaking in, and my leg jerked. I scrambled to the side and looked down to see the damage to my feet.

"YOU FUCKING SONSABITCHES!" I screamed. The shot had taken off the bottom two inches of my favorite three-inch heels.

"I got these in Larkatia!" I reached down and unbuckled the screwed-up pump and rolled over to throw it toward the front door. "I hope one of you chokes on it," I groused to myself as I unbuckled the second shoe. "Anybody have a damned clue how hard it is to get a passport to shop in Larkatia?" I bitched as I flung it after the first one.

The next bolt hit another mirror on the wall a few feet away, showering me with glass.

This bar fight was burning off all the drugs I had spent a shit-ton of money to purchase and drink, eat, and shoot up, trying my best to forget the last job I had been on.

These military motherfuckers had just wasted my high. Worse than that, they had caused me to remember.

My love was dead.

Chapter Two

Welcome to the life and times of Meredith Nicole Grimes. You could call me 'Merry' if you had known me back in the Etheric Federation, 'Nickie' if you were my friend, or 'Scary-ass Bitch' if you pissed me off and my neck was stinging from the mirror shards raining down on me.

I had *officially* been pissed off.

Now, I like a good fight as much as anyone else. Hell, I was raised on fighting—or 'practicing,' if you wanted to call it that. I called it 'slave labor' and my Grandfather John just smiled at me like he knew what kind of person I was going to turn out to be.

Well, joke's on him. He's in some other god-forsaken galaxy helping aliens or kissing their stank-butt or whatever, and I'm right here getting shot at because I wanted to go out, see the worlds.

And get my ass handed to me.

Fuck my Grandfather and his incessant need to be right all the time. If I'd had a way back home I might have taken it, but his friend the Etheric Empress had given me seven years-to-life to go figure out what kind of future I wanted.

I'm in Year Six, and if I don't pull my head out my ass soon I might as well French-kiss it goodbye, since my head is already so close.

I hated it when Bethany Anne was right.

I reached under my jacket and engaged all the advanced tech that ran through my body. This was some shit I hadn't done in all six years of my so-called—or more accurately, forced—vacation from the Etheric Federation.

Systems came online that I had hated to use in my youth. I could have used them earlier, but if I had, those that wondered where I might be would absolutely know.

Sometimes you don't want family to pull your ass out of the fire.

The nanites kicked into gear and what little buzz I had left vanished faster than Kurtherians around Bethany Anne. My hand ignored the normal pistol everyone saw and wrapped itself around the special one. The one my grandmother had made for me.

The pistol whose onboard computer checked me out as the sweet feeling of a lover's curve graced my palm and I yanked it out of my backup holster.

Time slowed down as the enhancements kicked in. I looked around one last time and noticed another patron hiding under his poker table and staring at the pistol in my hand.

These fuckers are *rare*.

You don't want to be around one in use, and for God's sake you don't want to try to use one that isn't safety-locked to you personally. Just use your own pistol—eat the barrel and pull the trigger. It would be less painful.

That patron's eyes locked on me and then he started crab-crawling toward the bathroom. There are rumors about people like me. People who have a Jean Dukes special.

I wondered if he would find a dead McAssSuck or a smelly one?

Giving up that line of questioning, I rolled over and started having fun.

***

My name is Grim'zee P. Bonesticker ('Grim' or 'Z' to my friends). I grimaced when the table I was hiding behind received a fresh laser hole just three inches from where my Yollin mother's favorite son was hiding his head.

I shuffled my two-legged exoskeleton=covered ass down a little lower. "You got any extra packs?" I called to the next table to my left. Two of my shipmates were stuck behind that table now; they'd had to ditch the last one when the merc-cops busted into the place.

"Skaine-loving pissants," was all the poor Torcellan Kremlich got out before those same Skaine-loving pissants drilled him through the chest, making the question of needing *any* of his packs a moot point. Fortunately, his partner Shara, a human, bit down her scream of surprise and kicked his gun over to me.

I grabbed the gun, checked the safety and the charges remaining, and looked to my right.

And that was when *she* stood up, eyes blazing red, and I knew the Skaine Merc-Police behind me were dead.

I just didn't know if my mother's favorite son was about to die as well.

***

"I'm telling you," the main merc-cop ground out as he shot for the fifth time into the table; the hole he had drilled finally exploded and he was satisfied to hear the grunt of someone dying on the other side as blood splattered the wall beyond, "that the Skaine captain wants the human for a slave, so don't waste her!"

"What about the Yollin?" Quarter-three asked.

"Cred a dozen," Prime Quarter answered, and started shooting into the table the Yollin was hiding behind. "I don't have a Yollin skull yet, so try not to mess it up too much."

***

There is 'enhanced,' there is 'merc-enhanced,' and then there are the scary sonsabitches from the Etheric Empire. That group had been from Earth, once upon a time.

(Yes, there are a shit-ton of history books on that story. I don't have time to tell you about Auntie Bethany Anne and Grandfather John Grimes (may someone kick his ass sometime soon), my grandmother Jean Dukes (who I love to death), and the rest. If you are interested, go look it up–I'm sure it is just *riveting* reading.)

Anyway, I'm here to tell you about those scary sonsabitches and me. I'm one of the offspring. I've got shit inside me that still hasn't been turned on, and I know my ass will explode if someone tries to get to it.

Which explains the asteroid-sized chip on my shoulder.

There was talk about how those at the sharp end of the stick in the Etheric Empire were protected to the best of their abilities, and their kids… And for a select few, their kids' kids.

I had just wanted to be a wild child, and so I was.

But these Skaine motherfuckers had pissed off a Grimes.

The first merc barely registered that I had stood up (It was part of my upgrades, the ability to move much faster than a normal human.) Two of their party were already dead, their bodies and blood blown back through the open doors while the HUD I could see in my eyes tracked to the next two targets.

I heard this asshole's last comment. "I don't have a Yollin skull, so try not to mess it up too much." I shot him through the ear, blowing the right side of his skull completely out.

"Fucking racists!" I yelled. Wait, were they racist or alienist or what? I never get that right.

I hate those who hate other aliens, and Skaines. Especially Skaines, so I hated that one twice as much as the next one I shot.

Then it was my turn to twist to my left and dodge as rounds whizzed past where I had just been. On my third twist I nailed the sonofabitch.

I stopped turning and looked around, making sure no one was about to shoot me in the back. I stepped carefully across the floor, fucking glad I hadn't gotten any glass in my feet while I had dodged the fire.

A Yollin and a human woman stuck their heads up over the table. In the background I heard a lamp crash to the floor and a grunt, and I turned to see a patron laid out with the lamp covering his head.

Fucker never saw that *coming.*

I looked around the place. "Ah! Just what I need." I found a woman, her shoulder and abdomen punctured and blood around her on the floor. I bent down, unbuckled her boots, and pulled them off. "Sorry, but you won't need these anymore and they *are* Robotens, so they shouldn't go to waste."

It took me a half-minute to pull out a few pieces of glass I hadn't noticed in my feet and put them on. By that time the human and the Yollin were standing up. "You guys got names, or shall I call you 'Slave Bait' and 'Cad?'"

"'Cad?'" the Yollin asked.

I pointed to one of the Skaines. "Cred a dozen," I told him. "He didn't think you were worth saving, and they wanted *you*," I pointed to the woman, "for a slave."

The female, I'll give her credit. She walked around the table and spit on the dead Skaine. "*Putoh*!"

"Well, I'm getting out of here," I told the two, and walked to the door, stepping over two of the dead Skaines, then bending down to rifle their pockets. "Ah, good." I slipped their money and whatever else I figured was valuable into my pockets."

"You're robbing them?" she asked me.

"They are paying me back for my shoes," I told her, going through the Prime Quarter's pockets. "They haven't nearly paid me enough for my fucked-up outfit or the new monkey on my back." I grabbed another couple items I would need soon.

"You know," the Yollin commented, "the Skaines are going to come after you."

I pulled a pistol and turned it sideways to check its charge, then flipped the safety on and stuck it behind my back. "I doubt it."

"Why not?" the female asked.

I stood up and looked at her. "Because they will be dead. I'm not done with those assholes."

"Who the hell *are* you?" the Yollin asked, his voice somber.

"I'm mad as hell, in need of a ship, and someone who recognizes that leaving pissed-off Skaines behind me with a ship that I need would be a bad idea."

"Right." He moved over to me and tried again, sticking out his hand in human fashion. "Grim'zee P. Bonesticker. 'Grim' or 'Z' to my friends."

I shook it. "Meredith Nicole Grimes, 'Merry' or 'Nickie' to my friends."

"Don't rate that yet, but I'll work on it," he replied.

I liked him. "You do that."

"Want backup going after the ship?" he asked me.

I looked at him, and held my hand back out. "Call me Nickie."

***

Two sets of boots clomped down the hallway as the human and the Yollin took a right.

They both heard the *clomp clomp clomp* of booted feet coming in their direction from the space docks. When the Skaine contingent came around the corner, we both took a step to the side to allow them to *clomp clomp clomp* right between us.

The eight of them ignored us, since we seemed to be appropriately cowed.

I stepped back out from my little nook in the wall and turned toward their retreating backs, pulling my pistol. I had shot four of them down when I heard Grim'zee's pistol firing next to me.

I nailed the leader next, then worked my way back as Grimmie took another one out.

The eight Skaine bodies littered the hallway.

"Cleanup, hallway…" Grimmie looked around, "P3K-3R."

I smirked. "Grimmie, you are such a dick."

"Thank you," he told me as we resumed our walk toward the docks. "I don't remember offering that as one of my names."

"It fits, so shut up."

"Ok, Mickie," he replied.

I considered my comment as we turned the last corner—probably thirty more steps to the last door. "Yeah, ok. I'll go with 'Grim,' and if you call me 'Mickie' one more time I'll shove your foot up your own armored ass."

"Grimes and Grim," he said as we walked up to the door. "It has a ring to it."

I smiled. "It kind of does."

"Any idea how we are going to get on the ship?"

"Yes," I told him, digging around in my pocket. I pulled out a ship's security card. "The main man back in the bar thought we should have this."

I pushed the button to open the door. "Well, if we fail, it's been nice knowing you."

He chuckled and I looked at him. "What's so funny?"

He was shaking his head when he looked at me. "You really don't know who you are, do you, Nickie?"

The door had opened as the two of us stood there having a damned argument. I pointed toward the docks. "Get the fuck in there."

He chuckled and started into the space docks. "Any idea which of these berths is theirs?"

"Yes. The one with the new set of Skaines coming out of the doors leading into the space station." I nodded to a ship two berths down.

Sure enough, this time we had four Skaines in battle armor coming at us. We kept walking and talking, and I slapped Grim as if to get his attention. "Take a look! Someone is going out partying!" I lifted my voice. "Guys, that's not the type of protection you need for prostitutes!"

The four Skaine marines double-timed past us, but one lifted their hand in a galactically understood version of fuck-you.

I middle-finger-waved back.

"Do you usually push everyone's buttons like this?" Grim asked me.

"Only when I plan on doing the impossible."

"Which is?"

"Every *Gott Verdammt* day." I smiled at the marine before he turned back around and they went through the lock.

"What now?"

I looked at him, my eyes probably turning a bit red. "I'm still pissed about my shoes."

I walked toward the exit door, pulling out my security key. "Ding-dong, the Bitch is here."

"The *what*?" Grim asked.

I just chuckled. Inside my head, I heard a voice.

ENHANCEMENTS UNLOCKED.

***

The first shot took out the dock guy's arm. I slugged him with the butt of my pistol and walked into the entryway. "Let's get in there, Grim," I told him, and shoved my security card into the slot. I looked over the instructions and my eyes went back and forth before hitting two buttons, then spreading my fingers and hitting two more simultaneously.

"The problem with Skaines," I told him as the door shut behind us, "is they don't believe anyone is superior, no matter how many times my grandfather and aunt have taught them differently."

"What about those marines?" he asked me, jerking a thumb behind him.

"Locked out," I told him.

A female voice spoke in my head. ***Welcome to the fold, Meredith Nicole Grimes.***

"This wasn't exactly what I wanted to be doing today," I said out loud.

"Me either, but for what it's worth, I'm happy to have met you." Grim said as my fingers danced over the screen.

"Sorry, Grim, wasn't speaking to you," I told him and tapped my head, "I've got a partner."

"They talking to you over a communication device?" he asked me. "And are they coming to help?"

"Not that kind of partner," I told him. "This one doesn't have a body." That kept him quiet for a moment as I looked at the controls. "Ok." I pulled my Jean Dukes out of their holsters and turned the power down so they wouldn't puncture the outer skin. "Let's take this ship."

***

They have figured out you are on the ship.

Got that, Meredith. Any chance you can get into the system and help?

Little girl, I'm already in the system. But, you are not taking charge. It's time to own your destiny.

I've been fighting my destiny for six fucking years, Meredith.

I know. It's been quiet.

Yeah, sorry about that. I was told by my inner EI I have a bit of a hard head.

You're a Grimes—it's genetic.

I snickered. *Yeah, Grandpa is a hard-headed motherfucker, that's for sure.*

Such language, young lady!

I'm fucking twenty-four!

Still a baby.

Hey! I have it on good authority your ass was created for me.

I am a copy of a copy of a... Well, I'm old myself.

Yeah, but you were only brought online when I was born, so don't give me this age shit.

I've been lonely, just watching.

Way to pull a guilt trip in the middle of a battle to take a ship.

There would have to be a battle for that to be true. We are just walking down a hallway to the end where they are setting up an ambush.

I stopped. "What the fuck do you mean, an ambush?" I squeaked.

"I didn't say ambush," Grim said from behind me.

I looked over my shoulder. "Sorry, talking to Meredith."

"That's got to be weird," he allowed. "One of the fabled versions of ADAM?"

"How do you know that?" I asked him.

"I know the Empire: I come from Yollin. My history is now your history."

"I didn't pay attention in history classes," I admitted. "*Now,*

Meredith, what about that ambush?"

A view came up on my HUD and I looked at a top-down view of the ship's schematics and, a bright yellow-lit area with two red dots indicating Grim and myself. Then she brought in a video feed from the ship to show me how the Skaines were arranged.

"Four tangos up ahead," I hissed to Grim.

"Four who's?" he asked. "I thought we were fighting Skaines."

I rolled my eyes. "Four enemy agents," I told him. "What the hell is your occupation?"

"I'm a cook," he told me.

I actually almost broke situational awareness. "You are a COOK?"

"Yeah, but I've got mad skills."

"You're a cook who has mad skills," I repeated, rolling my eyes. "Great, I'm going to get a cook killed."

"Nah," he told me. "I'm just here to make sure no one gets in a cheap shot. You got this."

I had to admit, it felt good to hear him say that. I think my ego grew three sizes at that very moment. "All right, I own this." I breathed out.

Behind her, Grim nodded.

I saw the tip of the gun so I swung around and caught Grim's arm, pulling him toward me. Then I pushed with my legs and both of us slammed into a door, knocking it open as we fell backward. The hallway beyond lit up from laser fire.

"*OOF!*" My lungs exploded when Grim's full weight hit me. I'm pretty sure I now had a cracked a rib. I pushed him off and stood up, ramping up my maximum speed and timing the laser fire.

Meredith?

You have only to ask.

Why are you making me ask? I bitched. *We used to work this so much better.*

That was when you cared.

I watched the fire pass me; it looked like it was slow motion with my increased speed. I bolted forward, racing across the hallway and jumping. Landing on my left leg, I pushed up again and rocketed toward the ceiling. The hallways inside a Skaine ship aren't that wide, and they have exposed pipes along the ceilings. I jammed one foot against one wall and the other against a pipe and started firing, blowing guns apart, or hands if I got a chance.

The laser fire started to dwindle.

These were the best they had left. Unfortunately for the captain, he had probably sent his actual best off the ship already. That last group of four might have been wearing the ship's whole armor inventory, and if that was true, I had been lucky.

One left, Meredith informed me.

I released my legs and dropped toward the floor. Running down the hall, I asked, *Left or right?*

Right.

Good to know.

When I had about ten feet to go I threw myself into a slide through the middle of the hallway and shot up at the last Skaine as I approached, blowing his brains into the ceiling behind him.

His body fell as I finished my slide.

Standing up, I winced. "Fucking slide-burn." I peeled my pants aside and grimaced. "That's going to leave a mark."

No it won't. My onboard-all-the-damned-time-but-hadn't-spoken-to-me-in-ages-EI replied.

It's a saying. When someone does something rather stupid, they say 'It's going to leave a mark.'

Ok, then that is going to leave a mark.

Now you are criticizing my work?

You just said that yourself.

I looked at the dead bodies. One was only halfway to dead, but was speeding there as blood kept draining out of his arm.

I walked across the hall and slammed my fist into a first aid cabinet's glass door. It took me a second to find what I wanted. While I was futzing around in the first aid cabinet, Grim arrived. "Make sure we don't get surprised," I told him.

I yanked open the packages of gauze and a needle for painkiller with anti-infection support.

Once I had finished with the almost-dead one, I checked the others. "Sorry," I closed the eyes of one of the Skaines, "but you guys started this."

"Girl," Grim said.

I stood up and looked at him. "Huh?"

"She's a girl." He nodded to the one whose eyes I closed.

"Yeah, I know. It's just a saying. Means 'you people.'" He shrugged as I looked around. "Ok, ready for the boss battle?" I asked him.

"I haven't done much so far," he replied, "so, sure."

I grinned. "You are a crazy sonofabitch, you know that? You are keeping up with me, and you aren't crying and blubbering."

He smiled and told me, "You are one strange human female." He looked around, seeing if he could find any threats. "I thought we would have to fight more of them."

"Well," I started, and nodded down the hallway, "we killed five in the bar and eight in the hallway."

"That felt like we were cheating," he said.

"'You ain't trying if you ain't cheating,' is what I was always told." I applied some painkiller to a cut on my cheek. "I've checked with Meredith—she shut down the station video so no one in this ship had any way to know what was going on, and she's locked non-essential personnel into their berths or their workrooms now."

"You are going to have to tell me more about Meredith sometime." Both of us heard metal boots *clomp clomp*ing down a hallway somewhere ahead of us. His eyes grew a bit bigger. "But not right now."

He tries a door on the right. "Locked." He turned to his left, stepped across the hallway, and tried a second door. "Locked." He pulled up his pistol and shot three times at the lock, then tried the door again. "Still locked." He lifted his pistol and shot twice more.

I grinned.

He twisted the knob, looked at me, and smiled. "See? One dead door, no need to pull me into a room." He pushed open the door, then stopped once inside, his voice coming from behind the door. "Oh, and one freshly dead Skaine, body still twitching." His voice trailed off.

"Be safe in there, Grim," I yelled and headed toward my adversary.

***

"If you want to do it right," came a mutter from the general vicinity of the *clomp clomp clomp*ing, "you have to do it yourself."

Moments later, a Skaine wearing an advanced SKPP-09 combat suit came around the corner.

He stopped. I gawked.

"What the hell is an SKPP-09 doing in a fucking Skaine slave ship?" Sometimes my mouth gets ahead of my need to keep my ass safe. Seriously, it's not like I've not had my ass handed to me multiple times for speaking before moving.

Fortunately, he was just as surprised to see me as I was to see him. We both hesitated.

All my abilities came online. This time Meredith wasn't fucking around.

You move now or I jolt your ass with ten-thousand volts!

I moved.

Half a tic later the SKPP-09 let loose at me with a nasty set of laser bolts. I had been running down the hallway toward my adversary, but he had been able to move his arm faster than I could run. I ducked and slid on my ass as the laser bolts burnt nice holes into the wall above my head and in front of me. I twisted, kicking off the wall to switch sides as his cybernetically-enhanced reactions tracked the laser pistol to where I had been a second ago.

Move it! Meredith could be calm and yet yell at the same time. I had no idea how someone could calmly yell, but she had the trick down. I levered myself up to jump toward the top of the opposing wall and angled off, dialing my pistol up to eleven.

Level ten is a bitch. Level eleven is when you are up Shit Creek and no antigrav support is going to get you out of it. I snap-fired toward the laser, hoping to annoy the shit out of him, and if real lucky, take it out.

I was lucky...sort of.

The kickback from the Jean Dukes was a bitch. (The pistols used a form of antigravity rail-gun technology—another class I didn't work too hard to pass. I already knew the basics from Grandma Jean herself, so why study?)

I should have studied harder so I would have remembered that rail-gun technology works best when your acrobatic ass isn't up in the air. The recoil caused me to turn violently toward my right, throwing off my planned landing. Instead of my left arm stopping my momentum, the back of my head did it for me.

Searing, horrible pain exploded as my skull intruded on the immoveable wall. Then the rest of me slammed into the wall and dropped unceremoniously toward the floor.

I had enough focus left to look over at my adversary and notice he wasn't doing too well himself.

SKPP-09 armor was badass, no doubt about that. But that armor design was ten years old at a minimum, and not much could handle a Jean Dukes dialed up to eleven.

If I'd had the right rounds in my pistol I could have shot right through his armor, but those rounds were saved for those doing good deeds and fighting the good fight.

I had been running from the good fights, so I didn't get the good stuff.

I rolled across the floor, hoping my advanced healing would give me a bit of a boost, but all it accomplished to take my split-open head wound down to merely the pain level of a migraine.

Lucky me!

I could hear his servos working against the joint in his leg I must have screwed up.

I didn't trust myself to cross the twenty-five meters between us before he could blow my kidneys all over the wall, so I forced myself up and started running for the nearest intersection of hallways.

I looked behind me in time to see him aim a weapon in my general direction.

I jumped into the air, arms outstretched, and saw a laser bolt pass underneath me. While going head-first toward the floor from my dive, I rather hoped he couldn't keep unleashing those damned bolts of destruction.

I executed a rather beautifully done tuck-and-roll, then stumbled back up and followed that impressive move with a dodge-the-hell-around-the-corner maneuver.

I landed in the blood of my enemies.

Blood I had caused, but still… "*Gross*!" I spit on my hand, wiping my palm against the clothes of the nearest Skaine.

"I shall take you out, you annoying human!" he yelled at me. I busied myself by finishing my cleanup.

Because, *priorities.*

I stuck my head out around the corner; he was walking toward my area. He couldn't run, so that was something. My body was healing—another benefit of my enhancements, and one I appreciated at the moment. It was right up there with the ability for Meredith to shut down a lot of my pain receptors. I backed up seven steps and then raced forward, hitting the floor in a slide to go through the intersection of the passageways at the lowest angle I could to Sir Lots-of-Metal. As I flew through the intersection, I pelted the servomotors on his shoulders with both pistols firing as fast as they could.

An attachment rose over his shoulder…

"Ohhhh!" My eyes grew large as I saw the ATK-0N3 Organic Fire-and-Forget Rocket lock into place and his helmet pivot to watch me. "Fuck meeeee!" I yelled, and twisted around so I was sliding backward. I kicked over my head and somersaulted upright, turning to run for my fucking life.

I heard two noises at the same time.

One was the eruption of the chemical ignitor on his rocket, and the other, right after, was a massive electrical explosion.

The second was a curiosity, but the first was a problem. *My* problem.

Meredith put up the overlay of the hallway in my HUD as she tracked the rocket coming around the corner. I was running as fast as my mostly healed body would go. There was no fucking way I would heal if one of those missiles nailed me.

"Gimme some good ideas really fucking fast, Meredith!" I yelled, grasping at straws.

"Door opening, two down on the right," she replied into my ear receptors. Sometimes hearing is better than mental communication, and now was one of those times. My body was amped-up, running on Etheric energy and desperation.

The door was only halfway open when I stiff-armed it, reached in to grab a surprised Skaine in a white onesuit and yanked him out of the room while I simultaneously threw myself inside.

It worked, mostly.

The Skaine was hit by the rocket, but I was only four or five feet away and the door was only partially closed. The blast not only splattered my outfit, but the concussion knocked me violently into the room. I slammed into a set of cabinets about ten feet inside, which knocked me a bit loopy. That was before something stabbed my leg, and I screamed, as much in surprise and shock as pain.

I had been impaled by a damned kitchen knife. I looked up to see a complete variety of knifes and what looked like hatchets above me, all shaking from the collision.

"FUUUUUCCCCK!" I reached down and yanked out the knife, then started rolling away from those sharp bastards above me. Three more dropped, but I was clear.

Shutting down pain receptors in your right leg. Administering Energy Pack 003.

"Wait," I mumbled, "what happened to 01 and 02?" Hopefully I was tracking what she was saying correctly.

One was used to get you back together on your last mission before your emotional bender, and Two was used to flush your system of the drugs and amp you up to start this argument with the Skaines.

"For the record," I groused as I dragged my body over to my first pistol, "I didn't start the argument. They did."

Noted.

***

My mind was speeding through options as I realized two things: I had pulled the chef into the hallway to his speedy death, and I was probably going to die in a Skaine mess hall.

This was no way for a Grimes to die.

I grabbed my second pistol and made sure both were turned to eleven. The fuckers would hurt like a sonofabitch again, but better my hands than my leg, or ass, or anything getting shot by another one of those rockets. Which reminded me—I smelled of Skaine guts. "*Gross!*"

I needed to stop thinking about my predicament.

I listened but heard nothing *clomp clomp clomp*ing down the hallway, so I grabbed the edge of the counter and pulled myself up. As I moved toward the door I heard some moaning, but that was it.

I pulled the door all the way open, ignored the last decorative effort of the chef, and looked down the hall.

I saw a Yollin lying in the middle of the crossing of the halls, and a metal head. The rest of the armored body was hidden behind the wall.

"Grim?"

The Yollin's head turned, his mandibles clicking together slowly, "You Grimeses are hell to follow," he moaned. I started down the hall, looking over my shoulder to make sure I didn't have some engineering weenie about to shoot me in the back.

"What did you do?" I asked as I got closer and saw that the armored suit was dead, face-down and immoveable. "Is he alive?"

"She, I think," Grim mumbled and turned over to look up at me.

"You shouldn't lie down during attacks." I looked around the four hallways, but the only bodies were the ones we had killed. "It doesn't look good."

"Says you," he grumped, but rolled over again and pushed up to a stand. I kicked the suit, "What the hell?" I asked and looked at him.

"Always know the suits of armor that are active, and their weaknesses," he told me. "It was something your grandfather always told us."

The blood drained from my face, "No fucking way..." I whispered.

He looked at me and nodded. "Yes fucking way," he replied, and glanced around. As I stepped back toward the wall I noticed a black case that had fallen to the edge of the floor, which he reached down to pick up. He looked at me. "One day your..."

I put up my hand. "Don't say it. Let me believe for one goddamned minute that the person who saved me wasn't in some form or fashion helped in his past by my bastard of a grandfather."

While I was bitching, Grim stepped over to the suit of armor and knelt, taking out another tool. "I fucked up the first tool shorting the two connections. He was too focused on blowing you to bits to realize he had someone on his six."

"His six?" I asked.

He turned to look up at me. "You don't know what a person's six is?"

"Of course I fucking know what a person's six is." I exhaled. "I'm a Grimes—it was in the Grimes baby book."

Grim looked at me a moment, his large mandibles opening, then closing, then opening again. "I can't tell if you are joking or not."

Incoming, Meredith sent.

I checked my HUD, twisted to the right, and fired two shots. Both Skaines who had come around the corner were blasted in their shoulders. Pistols dropped and both went to the floor, trying to hold their blood in.

"Guess the family talk can wait," Grim agreed.

"Agreed." I nodded back the way the armored statue had come from. "Let's get the bridge taken care of and pull this baby out of here."

We both ran down the hall, my body finally patched up decently enough that Meredith was letting me feel the pain again.

Don't suppose you would keep the pain dialed down for a while? I asked as I checked my HUD again. I took a left at the next hallway, Grim behind me a few steps.

Before the turn that would take us to the last hallway and the bridge of the ship, I reached into my bag and pulled out a small triangular rod. I halted and unclipped one of my belt pouches, opening it and looking at the six silver balls inside.

Grim stopped behind me. "What are those?"

I took the two on the far right. "Some of my aunt's favorite toys," I replied and tossed them into the air. They zipped around the corner, hovering five feet above the deck and. I watched the video input on my HUD.

"Who the hell is your aunt? You are too damned crazy to believe."

"You haven't seen anything yet," I replied. "Crazy comes calling when I get my hands on grenades or when I say, 'Hey Grim, watch this shit!'"

Surprisingly, the hallway was clear. I sent the video drones into the bridge. "*There* you are," I murmured as I found two Skaines hiding behind the doors holding high-level blasters.

I considered the shielding they were behind. "Can't shoot them from here."

Grim stepped around me, his body causing me to take a step back so he could look around the corner of the wall. "I don't see anyone."

"That's what they want," I told him. "They are camped out on the other side of the door.

"You can't shoot through the shielding around the entry to the bridge."

"Who are you teaching basic Skaine boarding techniques to here, Tweedle-dee?" I asked. "Geez, you act like I'm a wet-behind-the-ears grunt Guardian Marine or something."

He looked at me. "You aren't?"

"Hell no," I told him, and threw my next two little silver spheres into the air. They too zipped down the hallway. Although it should have been damn near impossible, they both jerked into ninety-degree turns as I watched the video take. Both the Skaines' heads exploded in gore, drenching the areas behind them as their bodies dropped to the floor.

"Gah!" I bitched as I hit Grim on the chest and started running toward the bridge. "Someone is going to have to clean that up."

"Clean what up?" he asked. I stayed quiet as I ran past the opening.

Seconds later, he called from behind me, "Oh… Shit, woman! Warn a guy next time!"

"I did," I answered as I sat down in the captain's chair and started punching buttons. "Find a seat," I told him as I hit the tab to take me to communications. "Hey, that guy in the armor you drop-punched was the captain."

"Wasn't drop-punching anything. I knew the deficiencies of powered armor. As for the captain," while he spoke I could hear the clinks as he messed with the seat's restraining devices, "didn't you think of that already?"

"Sure, but it's nice to know," I told him, connecting the captain's communication link to the space station. I checked the ship's accounts. "Wow, we are loaded," I murmured.

"What?" Grim answered as he fumbled some more with the restraint harness for his chair. He quit trying to figure it out, disgusted. "Don't crash," he told me. "Otherwise we went through all those impossible battles while I was still healthy, wealthy, and wise only to have me become a splat on the inside viewing screen."

***

The ship had apparently come back from a trading mission in slaves and contraband. The amount of credits in the ship's accounts was impressive.

"This is Skaine Ship DD-76-PyK3r," I told the Stationmaster. I looked over at Grim, who had grabbed a ship's tablet. He looked up. "Meredith still has everyone locked in their rooms, so nobody can mess with the engines, gravity, or environmental."

"Good to know," I told him.

The station replied, "Ship DD-76-PyK3r, what is your request?"

"I need to leave, have my ship registry changed, and…" I flicked through the screens on the captain's display, "be topped off with fuel." I realized what I had just said and added, "Not necessarily in that order."

"Request for fuel purchase has been sent. I have your approval to pull from ships funds with a maximum limit of two thousand credits. We have you in the queue for fifteen minutes for fuel, and we also have a request to speak with a Captain Mong'leck relating to a bunch of his people who are now dead or severely wounded. Your marine detachment is making a bunch of people very annoyed."

Well, crap. I had forgotten about those guys. "Define very annoyed," I requested, checking the locks on the ship.

"They are shooting at each other. We made multiple calls to your ship, but they have been ignored."

Was that you, Meredith? I asked my internal EI.

Yes. It seemed like a secondary issue when we were dodging organic homing missiles.

Too true.

"I understand, Stationmaster. I will send detailed instructions for them to stand down, but I can let you know they are not out there with instructions shoot up your station. We were trying to bring back a human female when your bar customers started shooting our people."

"Your away team was destroying the bar. What did you expect?" he asked.

While he was talking, I confirmed the amount of fuel we would need to safely get to the next logical station which wouldn't know about an issue here.

Don't worry, Meredith sent. ***I'm in their computers, and set a flag to re-route any messages about this ship. Further, I'm finished. We have a new download re-flagging this ship as Torcellan.***

How the hell? I asked.

Don't ask, don't tell, Meredith replied. ***It's something we have been able to do since Ranger Two intercepted and stopped a horrible act of piracy centuries ago.***

How many little cheats do you have?

As of yesterday?

Well, sure.

Twelve thousand four hundred and thirty-five.

I have confirmed we have more than enough fuel for three of the five locations I'd like to go to.

That's ...incredible, I finished. *Stop fueling, and I assume, based on your abilities, you can unhook us?*

Yes.

Make it happen.

Will do.

I watched the screens to confirm the fuel wasn't flowing and the locks were disengaged before I replied to the Stationmaster.

"I expected…" I ground out in the Skaine language. I rather hated Skaine, to be fair—the language was too guttural for my preference. "For you to allow the Skaine Mercenary Police to do their job and help us, not make me send in multiple groups for support." I hit the buttons informing those few still on the ship that we were leaving. The silent running lights flashed while the red light of movement came on in every location on the ship. "However," I finished, "I now expect those who are on your station to submit to your authority or die."

That last I said in the language of the Etheric Federation. It took my station contact just two seconds to realize he had been had. I saw the locks try to extend, then shut down again.

Meredith was on the job.

"WHO IS THIS?" he yelled at me.

"Why is everyone so bossy?" I asked no one in particular as my fingers raced over the controls of the ship.

"Meredith!" I called. Grim was surprised when she answered me through the speakers on the bridge.

"Yes?"

Grim's mandibles stayed open in surprise.

I turned to my left, yanking down another video screen and pulling up the arsenal. I hit two commands and locked the missiles down until I gave an override. "We ready to kick this pig?"

"Yes."

"Pull us out," I commanded, my future falling invisibly over me like a blanket. I could feel everything I had fought for so long hugging me like a long-lost lover. This time I didn't fight it.

Rather, I embraced it right back.

"I said," his voice was loud and annoying as he screeched, "WHO IS THIS!"

I turned off my communications with him for a moment and turned on the ship-wide speakers.

"Hello." I spoke common Skaine, although I was pretty sure that they all would understand me in Federation. "This is the new captain of this ship, temporarily redesignated the *Penitent Granddaughter*. Since you are now employees of this ship, not slaves, we need to get a few things understood."

I kicked in the push-off jets. *Take us toward Syberius 7755.*

Where are we going from there?

It's a short hop, but it will throw off our followers, who will want this ship back.

"First, I am not here to listen to your bitching. If you want to make a complaint about your new management, please write it on a paper form and then step outside the ship to deliver to the nearest station or spaceport. Since we will be in space, that might take you a while to find. If you choose to try and mess with this ship, you will be stopped and we will kick you out the airlock in the general direction of the nearest planet. Should we be close to a planet, we will watch your body burn up in the atmosphere." I looked at the time. "We will have a meeting with the engineering, janitorial, and what is left of the security group at the top of the hour."

I left the all-ship radio on as I turned back to the space station and clicked the communication connection.

"WE WILL BE SENDING OUT SHIPS!" My favorite Stationmaster was yelling through our connection. I wondered if his voice was getting hoarse. "YOU WILL TURN AROUND AND ALLOW THESE..."

I cut him off. "Motherfucker!" I yelled back as the ship turned and the rear engines kicked in. "This is Meredith Nicole Grimes. The granddaughter of John Grimes, the Empress' Bitch. While others can call me 'Nickie'...'

I felt the final activation of my upgrades turn on as Meredith read my intentions and my conviction.

"You may call me 'Ranger Number Two.'"

The sputtering on the other side of the line stopped. I reached up and wiped away a tear before I unlocked a small belt pouch. From inside, I pulled out a chain that wasn't new.

In fact, in was well over a hundred years old. It had been around the neck of one of my best friends as I grew up. She had been everything to me, and I had believed my grandfather was responsible for her going away.

At least, he had been the one who told me the news.

I had never told Auntie Tabitha how much I loved her. How much her reading me stories or telling me of her adventures with those Tontos of hers excited me.

How I worshipped the ground she walked on.

How much Ranger Number Two setting down her badge to follow the Empress into Space to rarely come back had hurt.

I unwrapped the chain that supported a pendant bearing a number in the circle. I lifted it up and over my head, and pulled my hair back to rest the chain against my neck. I made sure the symbol could be easily seen on my chest.

"That's preposterous!" the station's commander finally replied. "The Federation doesn't use the Rangers anymore. They were disbanded!"

I leaned forward to punch the button to activate video, then leaned back, a hard smile on my face. I watched as he looked at the emblem and realized that for me to call myself a Ranger would immediately be my death warrant if I were lying.

"She's gone," was all he said.

"*The Lone Ranger is back,*" I replied. "I suggest everyone realize law can't be killed."

I disconnected.

You realize that you just told everyone on the ship you are the boogeyman? Ranger Tabitha doesn't have a good reputation with the Skaines.

You mean she had a completely horrible reputation with the Skaines. Her defeating and taking over one of their battleships still butthurts them to this day.

Combine that with your name, and you just put a price on your head.

I'm lazy, I told Meredith. *It means they will come to me. Easier than having to chase them down all over the galaxy.*

So it isn't the 'Lone Ranger,' but rather the 'Lazy Ranger?'

I prefer to say the 'Recalcitrant Ranger' has matured to the 'Efficient Ranger.'

You weren't a Ranger until now.

Point taken, I conceded.

I moved the video displays out of the way and stood up. Grim stood up slowly, his eyes tracking mine as he straightened. He put his hand out to shake mine, so I took it. "I have never," he told me, "been so proud to have a friend as I am you."

I put my other hand over his. "Well, I know it isn't my amazing good looks that have had you following me."

"No, Ranger Two. It was your willingness to stand up in that bar and blow the shit out of those Skaines."

I thought back to that issue; it had happened not that long ago. "They destroyed my shoe."

"It had nothing to do with the fact that the Skaines were attacking people?"

I thought about it a moment before releasing his hand and looking him in the eye. "I was dead when they came in, Grim. I had been on a thirty-day bender, trying to forget a deceased friend. They took me out of that death to my destiny. If you want, I'll drop you off at a safe place as soon as I can."

His mandibles moved in the way that told me he was anxious. "And you?"

I took in a deep breath, and slowly let it out. I turned toward the video screen and Meredith turned it on, giving me a view of the stars ahead of us. I presumed the station was behind us.

"I'll be going out there," I pointed, "with a fiery ship going the speed of light, a cloud of explosions, and a hearty 'fuck you, criminals' everywhere I can."

"Got room on that ship for one more?" he asked.

When I turned back to Grim I had a small smile playing on my lips. "Damn right, *Tonto*."

About the Author

Michael Anderle was born in Houston, TX. A very curious child, he got into trouble—a lot. What to do with an inquisitive mind when he was grounded? Read! In the first twenty years, he mostly read Science Fiction and Fantasy. In the last ten years, he has enjoyed Urban Fantasy and Military Fiction. With this background, he has been blessed with creating The Kurtherian Gambit series, a well-selling, and fan loved, collection of stories.

www.KurtherianBooks.com

Books by Michael Anderle

Kurtherian Gambit Series

Book 1: Death Becomes Her
Book 2: Queen Bitch
Book 3: Love Lost
Book 4: Bite This
Book 5: Never Forsaken
Book 6: Under My Heel
Book 7: Kneel Or Die
Book 8: We Will Build
Book 9: It's Hell To Choose
Book 10: Release the Dogs of War
Book 11: Sued For Peace
Book 12: We Have Contact
Book 13: My Ride is a Bitch
Book 14: Don't Cross This Line
Book 15: Never Submit
Book 16: Never Surrender
Book 17: Forever Defend
Book 18: Might Makes Right
Book 19: Ahead Full
Book 20: Capture Death
Book 21: Life Goes On

The Second Dark Ages

The Boris Chronicles (with Paul C. Middleton)

Reclaiming Honor (with Justin Sloan)

The Etheric Academy (with TS Paul)

Terry Henry Walton Chronicles (with Craig Martelle)

SWARM OF THE ZOM-BEES

By Chris J. Pike

Captain Jim Jones and his crew just want to enjoy a few space hot dogs when blood sucking bees attack.

Captain Jones and his crew aboard the Barnburner were celebrated heroes after saving the world from giant Space Bees. Now times have changed, and the world has entered into a strange truce.

Everyone has been fooled by the Space Bees, with their apparent need to cultivate honey everywhere: space honey sticks, space honey pots—it's for sale in every port and every space station this side of Uranus (no, not that one.)

But when the first Space Bee shop opens on Earth, Jones suspects something else is afoot as people start dropping like flies—LITERALLY.

Zom-Bees on Earth. Sucking blood like damn mosquitoes, while selling their wares in honey pots. If anyone is going to do anything about it, it sure as hell isn't going to be Jim Jones.

Nah, just kidding. It sure as hell is going to be Jim Jones! After he's been bribed, said he told you so, and eaten one more space dog...

CHAPTER ONE

Marty McStinkFly had an uncommon name, and it was one he hated. His father, Marty McStinkFly Sr., hated it too. While growing up, the youngest Marty had been teased by other kids.

"It's all in good fun," his mother, guidance counselor, and social worker all told him. "It's okay, Marty. No one really means 'McStinkFly Stinks'."

Sure...

He did his best, keeping to himself, working the entry-level job he'd had for the last twenty-five years on the docks of San Francisco as a vendor. He sold space dogs; that was his calling. His passion.

Mustard, ketchup, minced onion—even mayo, if that was really your jam. It wasn't Marty's place to judge. People loved his space dogs. They came from all over the galaxy to eat them.

Some would argue that they were just returning to Earth, anyway, but Marty knew the truth. He knew how much people loved a space dog on a buttery, toasted bun. Toss in a space soda and a bag of asteroid chips, and you were golden. Golden!

He had seen changes on the docks, seen people come and go; sharing workspace was part of the gig. He didn't mind as long as they could verify they had the proper registration and license from the government.

This time, Marty wasn't so sure he'd even ask. A Space Bee! Why did it have to be a Space Bees!

He hid behind his colored umbrella, the one on which a space dog lay on a lounge chair and wore a pair of sunglasses. It projected a hologram right out front in giant letters—Marty's Space Dogs!—because he didn't want to be seen.

The new vendor wasn't even human. It buzzed as it went

about setting up its cart for the day. Honey sticks, honey cakes, honey suckers.

It was a damn Space Bee! That giant torso with that extended abdomen that freaked him out so much, with tiny wings that somehow supported its weight. *How is that even possible?!*

The Space Bee turned. He wore mirrored shades, and Marty ducked behind his row of condiments, hoping he hadn't been caught. But he had been caught. The Space Bee held out one of his feet, covered in pollen, and gave Marty the strangest thumbs-up he had ever seen.

UGH!

Space Bees; *why did it have to be Space Bees?* It was that damn peace accord. Marty understood peace—it's what the galaxy needed in order to heal—but to let Space Bees on Earth, allow them to sell honey and open their own colony?

It was criminal in the shape of a hexagon square!

Marty scowled as he watched the Space Bee ring up his first customer, holding out the credit card pad to swipe his first payment, buzzing with excitement the entire time.

Marty simmered with anger. He would get to the bottom of this, one honey pot at a time, if necessary! Or his name wasn't Marty McStinkFly.

CHAPTER TWO

"Welcome home, *Barnburner* heroes," the female flight control officer said over the loud speaker. "We've missed you! Well, *most* of you."

Jim Jones sighed from the captain's chair with his chin in his hand and raised his eyebrows. *What the hell is* that *supposed to mean?*

"Thanks a lot for not mentioning my name," Morticia, his chronically depressed AI, said. "I know you meant me."

"I actually didn't," the female flight attendant assured her. "I was talking about Captain Jones."

Macy chuckled from her spot in the pilot seat. "Ain't that the truth? Thanks, Flight Control. We're starting our descent."

Lucky for her, she's cute in her tight-fitting, spandex, blue suit and her matching blue fuzzy socks, Jim grumbled to himself. Her blond hair gleamed like the sun; she tossed it back to give Jim a smile, and he returned it...begrudgingly.

As far as girlfriends went, she was top notch; the best of the best. She wasn't why Jim Jones was in such a bad mood.

He loved Earth, and coming home a hero. Nothing made him happier than to be showered with praise, flowers, and food—though, not necessarily in that order. He was hungry. Damn hungry.

"Captain's log," Jim Jones spoke into his armrest and rubbed his scruffy chin and cheeks. "Remember to shower...and shave."

"You're disgusting," Mort agreed, "but that should come as no surprise to you." She sighed.

"I know you love me, girl, so don't pretend otherwise," Jim said.

No, the reason he was in such a bad mood was the exact

reason why they were back on Earth: Space Bees, and this peace accord.

Jim didn't like it, didn't trust it; it wasn't normal to be a giant bug living in space. It just wasn't. He knew better than anyone that Space Bees took no prisoners. When the giant bees had tried to assault Earth, he had been the one to blow up their hive; he had been the one that nearly died, putting it all on the line. Victory was sweet—and sticky. He'd had to clean honey out of his belly button for weeks after.

Weeks.

Now all is forgotten and the Space Bees are welcome on Earth? Not only that, they're allowed to build their own hive complexes, open shops, and assimilate into our culture?

"I don't buy it," Jim said out loud, growing angry. "Bees don't assimilate to our way of life; they get us to assimilate to theirs. It's a trick. A sticky, delicious trick!" He slammed his fist down on the console.

Why the hell is no one saying anything?

"Your captain addressed the crew! Can I get some sort of response, please?!" He railed.

"We're docked and landed." Macy turned her seat around as she spoke, and Jim caught sight of the short-sleeve blue t-shirt she wore over her spandex suit. 'Protect the Bees' it said, and was covered by a fuzzy-haired bee in the center wearing sunglasses and holding its thumb up.

Stupid bees, trying to hide the fact they have a million more eyes than normal. A million!

Jim's eyes widened. "Take that shirt off! This ship doesn't support bees! Protect the Bees as much as an ant does when it's squashed on the bottom of my foot!"

"Oh, c'mon, Captain," Steven coaxed from his console, where he had been playing Solitaire for the last twelve hours...or so Jim thought. He really wasn't sure what Steven did. "Bees are harmless, now that we've reached an understanding. Besides, if we turn on the giant Star Wars Bug Zapper, they'll all be taken care of," Steven snapped his fingers, "like that."

Jim didn't like it. Didn't like any of it. It was too easy, too pat like butter. Mortal enemies didn't just start getting along.

He spun in his chair to tell Steven so and was taken back: the red-shirted navigation-whatever-officer was wearing bee-themed mirrored shades and a bouncy antenna headband.

"You're no longer my favorite first-cousin-twice-removed,"

Jim growled.

"You don't even think of me enough to tell me I'm no longer your favorite AI," Morticia interrupted tearfully. "But I agree with you. The bees can't be trusted."

"Thank you, Mort. You *are* my favorite AI, and my favorite ship."

"I mean, they tried to kill me. That can't be forgiven," Morticia persisted. "I'm very sensitive and fragile. I'm only a tug ship. Honey inside my blinking lights and pushy buttons could have been the end of me."

" 'Me, me, me'," Jim mimicked. "That's all I hear when you talk. Maybe—"

Macy hooked her arm in his and pulled him up out of his chair. "Come on, Jim. It's not that bad. We're together on Earth for a few days off from tugging and patrolling—"

"Or whatever it is we do," Steven muttered as he shut down his game of Solitaire and followed after them toward the exit ramp.

"We'll have some fun and go to the peace accord function," Macy continued. "If anything goes wrong, Captain Spectacular will be there; I'm sure he can keep all of us safe." She patted Jim's chest several times in quick succession and gave him a big smile.

His first thought was to say, '*Thanks for cutting my balls off, coating them in honey and sprinkles, and shoving them down my throat,*' but that would just cause Macy to cry and storm off.

So instead, he faked a big smile. "I don't know how my ego would survive without you, Macy."

She shrugged and blushed across her nose in that way he found adorable. "What can I say? It's a gift."

"It's a *something*, all right," Jim muttered.

When they reached the exit ramp, he hit a few blinky buttons, and the door opened.

"Everyone remember where we parked this time. Mort, we'll see you in a few days. If there are any problems, make sure to contact someone who isn't me right away."

"Funny. Ha ha," Mort scowled. "So funny I forgot to laugh, Jim."

"But you did laugh."

Mort stuttered in her way. "Shut up."

"Make me," Jim retorted, and Macy shoved him with a roll of her eyes.

"He's going to miss you as much as you miss him," she

appeased the AI. Now can we get a move on, please?"

Jim's nose hairs tingled as they stepped onto the dock. He sniffed and gazed around. *I'd know that smell anywhere, and it isn't Steven's armpits.*

"Space dogs," he whispered.

Steven and Macy groaned in time as they walked toward the docking bay doors.

"He can't get off the docks without getting one of those nasty dogs." Macy commented, exasperated. "Jim, you realize we're going to dinner in a few hours, don't you?"

Jim shook his hand at her. "These aren't regular space dogs, Macy. The twinge of spice, the hint of sweet, the crisp of skin; no, these dogs aren't for the unintuitive. These are *Marty McStinkFly* dogs, and they're calling my name."

Steven and Macy reared back in horror. "I wouldn't eat anything named a Stink Fly," Macy said.

"*Mc*StinkFly," Jim corrected. "It's the vendor's name, and he's a little sensitive about it. How would you like it if people made fun of you for having the last name..." Jim thought it over. "That's funny. Do you guys have last names?"

Macy and Steven looked at each other and shrugged. "I'm not sure. I mean, it's never come up," Steven said.

Huh, weird.

"Anyway..." Jim dug out his wallet and started toward Marty's vending cart, then stopped dead in his tracks. A damn bee had his cart set up right by his favorite space dog station, and even had a line forming made up of dock personnel and space jockeys.

"Oh, honey!" Macy said.

"Not now," Jim hissed, mistaking her proclamation for a term of endearment. He realized his error when Macy and Steven rushed past him to get in line for some honey wares. *Damn honey, so sticky and sweet.*

By the time Jim arrived at Marty's station, his mood was soured. Though it wasn't going to keep him from getting a space dog with everything on it except for mayo. *Who the hell does that?*

"Usual, Jim?" Marty asked, already pulling a space dog from the sizzling rotation plate.

"Sure." Jim grumbled as he pulled some space dollars from his wallet, but his eyes were clearly on the Space Bee vendor. "What's that all about?" He muttered out of the side of his mouth.

Marty shook his head as he spooned hot, sizzling onions onto the space dog in his hand. "Place is going to the bees."

Isn't that the truth.

"Business has been down all morning, thanks to that buzzer. This isn't a novelty for me, you know, Jim. It's my buns and butter. My dogs and my potatoes. If I don't sell these space dogs, me and my android are living on the streets."

"Don't talk like that, Marty; you'll sell plenty of dogs. This fad will wear off, trust me. You're a McStinkFly, and McStinkFlys don't give up!"

Marty shrank back. "I can't believe you said it twice in a row like that."

"Sorry," Jim grunted as he took his food from Marty. He didn't waste any time biting into the juicy dog. It had just the right bite, just the perfect snap, with a spicy and sweet combination that was out of this galaxy.

He gave Marty a thumbs-up. "You'll weather this storm, Marty. If you need any help, you just find the captain of the *Barnburner*."

"I will....Who's that?"

"Me, Marty! Me." Jim sneered at him a bit, but couldn't stay mad at the best vendor in San Francisco. He turned his attention away from Marty and searched for his crew. He found them standing off to the side, licking honey lollipops. Jim threw his arms wide on his approach, sending diced onion flying everywhere.

"Would you guys jump on any bandwagon, or do you have some standards?" Jim took in the sight of Macy's t-shirt and Steven's bobbing antenna with a shake of his head. "Nevermind."

"We're not the only ones." Steven pointed over Jim's shoulder.

"Huh?" He turned around. *I don't believe it!*

The *Barnburner* was wearing a pair of stylish mirrored shades and boasting a yellow and black foam thumb right over her cockpit. "Mort!" Jim bellowed in anger. "I thought we were on the same side, girl!"

"Sorry, Captain," Mort said across their private network. "If you can't join them, might as well beeeee them."

Everyone laughed at her joke except Jim. He didn't find it funny. Not funny at all.

Chapter Three

The banquet hall was decorated in yellow and black, and each table was adorned with a tasteful balloon display and yummy honey treats—honey donuts, honey candies, and honey crullers, with a honey tea to wash everything down. The military personnel looked surprisingly upbeat for being, well, military personnel.

Jim Jones refused to eat anything made with space honey. With a curmudgeonly facial tic, he crossed his arms and made his way to the center of the floor.

"Don't tell me you agree with all of this?" he asked the one and only Captain Spectacular.

Not only had Captain Spectacular single-handedly fought against the bees *and* led the suicide missions (all forty-nine of them), but he had lived to tell the tale. He had also lived to be captured by traitors inside the Space Force, only to then be rescued by Jim Jones and the rest of the crew of the *Barnburner*.

Spectacular was as…er…spectacular as his name suggested, tall and damn attractive in his formal military dress. Jim Jones even had urges as he stood next to the man.

Spectacular puffed out his chest as he took a deep breath. "Jones, I've learned a thing or two living my life on the razor's knife edge, staring out into the dark."

"Does it have anything to do with the use of adjectives?"

Jim yelped as Spectacular pulled him in close, and they gazed outside together at the city's skyline.

"To survive is to dance with history. We don't want to be on the wrong side of progress, old friend. If we're going to thrive and survive, then we have to welcome these insects onto our planet. Mano y bug."

If that wasn't the biggest load of bullshit that Jim had ever heard, he wasn't sure what was. He didn't say that, though, because Spectacular didn't give him a chance.

Jones was left holding a figurative goodie bag as Spectacular headed up to the podium to start his grand introductions.

Steven and Macy worked their way over to Jim as the crowd started to whip into a frenzy. When Spectacular spoke, people listened; right then, people were anxious to be spoken to.

"Did he agree with you?" Steven asked.

"Not in the least!" Jones grumbled. "He thinks I'll be on the wrong side of history. Imagine that! Me!"

Steven chuckled, and Macy just clung to Jones's arm. "You're a great guy, Jim Jones, but you're no Spectacular. Maybe he's right, and this is the wave of the future."

"I'd listen to you if you weren't sucking on a honey lollipop with honey crullers shoved in your pockets."

"You're one to talk. What are you hiding?" Macy playfully pulled open Jones's leather jacket and saw two red cans of Raid™ hidden inside. Eyes widening, she scolded, "Jim Jones!"

"Mind the merchandise!" Jones yanked his jacket closed. "What do you think you're doing? You didn't even buy me dinner yet, sister."

"You're lucky I don't turn you in," Macy admonished. "You know we can't bring Raid™ in here! You're not only going to get us in trouble, you're also going to upset the bees!" Macy gestured to the stage as one giant Space Bee took the podium right beside Captain Spectacular. Its tiny wings flapped to keep it airborne, and it zigged up and down as if doing a little jig.

Saliva dripped from its mouth; if Jones didn't miss his guess, he'd say the little guy was hungry.

"Well, no reason to tip him off about it," Jones whispered.

"You need a sensitivity course." Steven nodded. "That's what you need. Sensitivity training."

"And," Macy hissed, "a trigger warning."

"There aren't enough warnings in the world for Jim Jones," Steven dryly added.

Jones wasn't sure if that was a compliment or an insult, but he decided he'd take it as the former. "Damn straight there aren't. Listen, I brought these things just in case there's a problem. I have no problem with being wrong—"

Steven and Macy broke out into a fit of laughter, and even Mort chimed in with a snort over their private connection.

"—I just want to be prepared," he continued, ignoring their mockery. "We fought too hard to keep this planet safe, just to have our efforts undermined by some honey sticks."

"It's hard to move on," Steven sympathized. "I get it. They were our enemies—but now we're trying to be friends. Our differences aren't as big as you'd think."

Jones eyes bugged from their sockets. "They have five eyes, a pair of wings, and yellow and black fur. How could we be anything but different?"

"But we all want a good life," Macy protested, and then changed her tone. "They want to work and live in peace, just as we do. Think about it, Jim. Please."

He crossed his arms. "Don't you dare use your soothing voice on me."

Macy ran her hand along his arm. "For me, Jim?"

"You're going to give in. Just do it already," Steven sighed and shook his head.

"Alright, fine. Just fine. Besides, it looks like this sideshow is starting." Jim nodded his head toward the podium as Spectacular stepped up to the microphone.

The other captain held his palm out to the audience, nodding his head as the frantic applause stretched out. "Thank you, my friends. Thank you. And that's what you are," Spectacular pointed his finger out at the crowd, "every one of you; my Earthling friends, my brothers and sisters." He made a fist, closing his eyes as he listened to the cheering of his name.

"Get on with it, already," Jones muttered into his fist, and got a stern glance out of Macy. He might've won the girl, but that didn't mean he wasn't still bitter about who really saved the day.

"Now I have new friends," Spectacular continued, extending his arm and glancing at the giant bee as it hovered not far from his position. "They might have wings and fur, but, man, can they make a mean pot of honey!"

He paused to take a sip of water, allowing the audience to respond with more clapping. "We were enemies; we fought, and some thought we'd keep at it until the end—but when you have a chance at peace, you must seize it. And that's what we did. We've become friends, the first honeycomb homes on Earth are being built, and we are ready to move forward. Arm," Spectacular raised his eyebrow, "and wing. Brother and brother. Friend and bug." He clapped along with the audience.

"I'd now like to introduce the queen's representative, Buzzzz-zzz."

Spectacular stepped aside and Buzzzz-zzz glided forward with the help of his wings. "Zzz-zzz-zzz," he said too close to the microphone; the buzzing noise echoed through the room, and Buzzzz-zzz recoiled. Nervous and afraid, he looked around the room, his wings opening wide.

Macy grabbed Steven's shirt, and Jones twitched, his hand close to the first can of Raid. *I knew this would never work. There is no peace between man and bee. It's sting or be stung—the way of the world.*

Everyone held their breath as Spectacular stepped forward. "Just try again, my friend. It'll be fine."

Quickly, Buzzzz-zzz turned on Spectacular and attached to his face, his abdomen flexing, and Spectacular was down for the count, thrashing around as Buzzzz-zzz emitted a loud buzzing noise and fluttered his wings manically.

Everyone screamed and ran away from the stage, but Jones waded through the crowd and jumped onto the stage to throw the bee off of Spectacular. Buzzzz-zzz bounced off the ground and hit the podium spinning like a wheel. When he landed with stars revolving around his head, Jones sprayed him with Raid™ until he stopped moving.

Everything came to a standstill.

With the bee dead, Jones knelt down beside Spectacular to assess the damage. His face was puffy and swollen, there were puncture marks all over him, and his eyes were frozen open.

"Spectacular?" Jones shook him. "Captain?" He placed his fingers on Spectacular's neck, and Jones's mouth dropped open.

"Does he need a doctor?" Macy asked urgently as she and Steven appeared at Jones's side.

"He needs a damn coroner. Spectacular is dead."

Chapter Four

Macy passed out the instant she heard the words, and Steven took her place, shaking Jones. "How can he be dead? Dead!"

"Get a grip on yourself! We have a problem, and it's about more than a starship captain! That damn *bee*!" Jones pointed at where he'd left Buzzzz-zzz and did a double take.

The 'damn bee' was gone.

"I sprayed it. It should be right there; what the hell happened to it?" Jones huffed and hurried to the spot where a trail of bee guts was plastered onto the floor.

Just then, a trio of military personnel came onto the stage to control the crowd. They confiscated Jim's cans of Raid™, and he watched as they lifted Spectacular onto a gurney and prepared him for transport.

"Thank you, everyone, for remaining so calm. We'll get to the bottom of this as soon as Spectacular wakes up. He'll be ready to lead this charge in a few hours."

'A few hours'? That man is dried up as toast. Jones followed the authorities backstage. "He has no pulse. He's not waking up. I hate to break it to you—"

The general spun. "Stuff it, Jones! We can't let everyone on Earth know Spectacular is dead. If they suspect he's not coming back, we'll have a full-fledged panic on our hands."

"They're going to notice eventually, General. What are you going to do? Lie to them? Construct a Spectacular bot to take his place?" Jones laughed, but from the way the general didn't, Jim realized the thought had crossed his mind.

"Oh, be serious. That would never work!" he argued to his superior.

"Can we count on you and your crew to keep this quiet, and

find out what happened with Buzz-zz, Captain Jones?"

Jones scowled. "I thought his name was Buzzzz-zzz?"

"Whatever!" The general snapped. "Can we count on you to lead this mission or not?"

Jones saluted. "Absolutely, sir. Right after we hit the buffet."

The general grabbed his arm. "*Before* you hit the buffet. This is serious."

More serious than space steak cooked four different ways? "Yes, General."

Jones slipped back in front of the curtain and saw that Macy was now sitting up with a dazed expression on her face. Steven was fanning her with a Captain Spectacular folded poster, and when she noticed, Macy burst into tears.

"It's a mistake, isn't it, Jim? Spectacular will be all right, won't he?"

In the moment that Macy looked at him with her wide, sad, blue eyes, Jones considered a lot of things: telling her the truth, telling her what the military's grand plan was, ordering a pizza—because except for that space dog, he hadn't eaten in twelve hours.

But his love for Macy overwhelmed his love for melted cheese and tomato sauce.

"Yes, Macy. Spectacular's going to be all right. I was...mistaken."

Steven's eyebrows arched as Macy crushed Jones in a hug.

"Oh, Jim. That's great!" She planted a big wet one on each of his cheeks.

"Yeah..." Steven agreed dryly. "Great."

Jones gave him his 'you-tell-her-the-truth-and-I'll-gouge-out-your-eyes' look. "The general wants us to look into Buzzzz-zzz's maniacal rage and see what triggered it, and what can be done about it."

Macy nodded. "Right away. I'll question the witnesses." She started walking in the wrong direction to the exit, but realized her folly and turned and headed the right way.

"So," Steven ran his tongue over his teeth, "dead as a doornail?"

"Stiff as a friggin' board," Jones sighed. "But we can't tell her. Not until we're ready to deal with days' worth of crying."

"Will we ever be ready for that?"

Good point.

Steven suddenly slapped Jones in the stomach and pointed

at the stage. "Look at this. Buzz dropped his sunglasses before he lost his head."

Jones bent over and picked them up. He opened the sunglasses' arms and saw the label. 'Frank's Bee Emporium'. When he moved to put the glasses on, he was struck with a powerful headache. Yelping, Jones dropped the glasses, and his inner eye was assaulted by images of honey and pollen.

He grumbled with a gruff growl. "I think it's time we pay Frank a little visit."

Chapter Five

Marty McStinkFly hadn't had a bad sales day since he started frying his own onions. He couldn't say that was true anymore. As he packed up his supplies for the day, he glared over at the bee, who also was packing up his vendor cart.

Except the bee did it with a cute little dance and an extra long 'buzzz'. Clearly, he'd had a good day—a great day—and that made Marty want to tear off the bee's stinger and shove it into the owner's mouth. *Yeah, how you like that, sting boy? Huh?*

Marty shook his head with a sigh. He wasn't the violent type; that's why he hadn't joined the military and instead became a space dog vendor. He still got to see all the cool ships and the docking bay, but from the comfort of his food stand.

*But that bee and his annoying leg-twitch dance...*Marty chomped on a space dog out of anger. The bee looked over at Marty and gave a wave of his front leg, and Marty nearly choked.

He wants to play nice? I can place nice. He picked up a dog with extra honey mustard and headed over to the bee.

"Hope you had a good first day. My name is Marty Mc—It's just Marty." He placed the space dog down on the vending cart and stepped back so the bee could give it a little sniff.

The bee did sniff it, and then he backed up and started doing a little dance. "Buz-zzz."

Maybe that's his name? Marty waved his hand at him. "Hi, Mr. Buz-zzz. Hope I got the 'zzz's right. All your names sound kind of alike to me. Sorry, I hope that's not offensive to you."

Buz-zzz hovered in the air and kicked his legs back and forth, doing his dance. Then he started to twirl. *Oh God, he's not doing bee ballet, is he?* Marty felt his temper starting to surge. *How can I be friends with this bee? How can I work next to him if we can't even have a proper conversation without Buz-zzz breaking into interpretive dance?*

"Listen," Marty said, but his words were cut off as Buz-zzz opened his mouth in a strange little hiss. His stinger drew into the air, and he darted straight for Marty's face.

"Whoa!" Marty's arms flailed, knocking Buz-zzz out of the way. As Buz-zzz did a figure-8 in the air to counterattack, Marty picked up his space dog.

Buz-zzz came at him again, and Marty swatted, sending honey mustard flying in all directions. Buz-zzz's wings were coated in the sticky substance, and he fell to the ground twitching, a broken bug.

Marty saw how alone and afraid the bee was, and felt bad for him.

"I'm sorry," Marty said. He dropped his space dog and ran the hell out of the docking bay.

Buz-zzz attacked me, but he seems sad about it. Maybe he didn't mean to do it—but if he went crazy and attacked a human, isn't it possible that other Space Bees could do the same thing?

Marty ran for a pay-communication-link, digging through his pockets for quarters. If there was one man that could help him, Marty knew who it would be: his very best customer. The one and only Jim Jones, Captain of the...

What's the name of his ship again?

CHAPTER SIX

The crew of the *Barnburner* arrived at Frank's Emporium not long after Marty McStinkFly assaulted a bee with a piping hot space dog with tangy honey mustard. All of which Jones knew nothing about. Frank's place was neat and tidy, and had a good view of the San Francisco Bay. The walls were lined with over two hundred varieties of sunglasses.

Red ones, pointy ones, glowing ones, girly ones, polka dotted ones, and, most importantly, bee ones.

"I'm Captain Jones of the *Barnburner*—"

Frank blinked. "The what?"

"Funny, I get that a lot, considering I saved Captain Spectacular's life."

The words caught in Jones's throat. *It hadn't really mattered, had it?* A few months later, he was dead; finally killed by the bees that he went up against, time and time again. Jim Jones would be damned if that didn't go avenged. He'd be damned if he let Spectacular's death go unanswered, even if the guy was a flaming schmuck.

"I get that a lot. Don't worry about it." He gestured to Steven, "This is my..." Jones thought it over and then turned to his crewmate. "What is it you do, again?"

"Funny," Steven muttered. "I'm the navigator. And sometimes I fix the food replicator."

Right, that's it. Jones hit him on the back. "That's right. Anyway, Frank," Frank blinked his eyes again with disinterest and crossed his arms as Jones continued. "We're here on official business. There was a problem at the peace accord. Not sure if you heard about it..."

Frank shook his head. "My radio doesn't work. It's been

jammed or something."

"Interesting," Jones replied, even though it wasn't. "These bee sunglasses you sell—how many have you sold, and who is your manufacturer?"

"We've sold thousands upon thousands of them to the bees. Our world is a little scary to them, and this just helps block out some of that stimuli by making the world a little darker."

"So, in other words," Steven interpreted dryly, "you sold them sunglasses."

"Great marketing, right?" Frank laughed.

"Right." Jones reached across the counter and grabbed Frank by the scruff of his shirt. "That's why a bee wearing your sunglasses went nuts and killed—tried to kill—Captain Spectacular? Talk, you devil, talk!"

"I don't know nothing, I swear! These are the discounted store special. It's just good marketing. Check them out yourself, you'll see." Frank squinted his eyes, anticipating a beating from Jones. Instead, Jones put him down and picked up a pair of sunglasses.

They look harmless enough. As he began to slip them on, Steven touched his arm. "Are you sure?"

"Only one way to know." Jones held his breath as he slipped them on.

The world darkened, just as it was supposed to.

That was all that happened. No weird pictures of honey, or honeycombs, or anything of the sort.

He pulled the glasses off and left them on the counter. "Does anyone else have access to your shipments? If these were modified, who could do such a thing?"

Frank opened his mouth to speak, but a laser beam tore through the window and hit him in the center of his chest, burning through his shirt. He fell to the ground with a loud *thud.*

Jones grabbed Steven by his red shirt, and they knelt down to find cover. The captain pulled his laser gun free and scoped the area. Whoever had killed Frank was gone.

Who are they? And what was it they're trying to cover up?

"C'mon!" Jones raced to his feet, and Steven followed closely behind. Out on the street, Jones saw little evidence that anything was wrong. They split up, and Jones investigated the back window where the shot had entered. There were boot marks on top of the closed dumpster, and beside it, a flyer.

He studied the flyer as his phone rang. "Go for Jones."

"Jim," Macy's voice was filled with worry and concern. "They've done some tests on Spectacular. The bee...it didn't just sting him. It drank his blood. It nibbled on his flesh. Buzz-zzzz wasn't just a regular bee."

"Was he Buz-zzz?"

"What? I'm not talking about his name, Jim. I'm talking about...the type of bee he is."

Jones sighed. "Macy, he's a Space Honey Bee. They're all honey bees. That's why they make honey."

Macy growled in frustration. "Just shut up a second! A Zom-Bee, Jim." Macy's voice was low and afraid. "We're dealing with Zom-Bees."

Hell, not the Space Zombies. It can't be Space Zombies, can it?

"Stay safe, Macy. Stay inside until we can get to you."

"No, Jim. I want to help. I'm coming to find you."

"Dammit, don't do anything stupid." Jones urged. He sighed and gazed upward. "I can't have anything happen to you. I just can't. You wait there; I can't have you running around out there if there are flesh-eating zombies ready to eat our faces off."

Macy sighed. "Oh, Jim. I'll wait here, but come for me. Please."

"The moment I know it's safe, sweetheart. And whatever you do, stay the hell away from those bees."

Jones flipped his phone shut and gazed at the flyer in his hand, the one with the boot print on the back. It was a picture of the Queen-B, and her viewing hours for visitors.

What are the odds that what caused the war is the same reason the bees are now attacking humans on Earth?

Some days, Jim Jones really hated being right. (Except he didn't.)

Chapter Seven

Macy paced in the hallway outside of where they were treating Captain Spectacular for his injuries. She didn't know why they weren't revealing anything, or why she couldn't see him. She had been a member of his crew for a short while, and she just wanted to make sure he was okay. *What's wrong with that?*

He was lucky. Damn lucky to escape unharmed and without the Zom-Bee virus floating through his veins. The doctors couldn't explain it, and Macy thought it might just be divine intervention.

When the door finally opened and two doctors in white lab coats came out of the hospital room, Macy rushed over in excitement.

"Is he okay? Can I see him now?"

The doctors were ghastly pale and stammering their words while gazing down at the floor, up at the ceiling—anywhere that wasn't her face. Macy was used to men staring at her breasts, but this was completely different.

"He's…"

"Uhh…"

"You can…"

"See for yourself!" they both said in unison, and swept their hands toward the door. Macy took a deep breath and held it as Captain Spectacular stepped out of the room. She swooned on her feet at the sight of him. He should've been dead; killed by that damn Zom-Bee. What a lucky break they had gotten.

"Captain Spectacular, thank God you're all right." She grabbed his arm, but it felt strange. More solid than it used to…almost like metal.

Man, the guy is really beefy!

One of the doctors removed her hand. "He's still setting. I mean, he's still recovering. He'll be back to himself in no time."

Captain Spectacular put his hands on his hips and stood with a wide stance. His face twisted into an unnatural smile. "I am Captain Spectacular!"

Macy stared at him and slowly blinked her eyes. There was something really off about him. *Poor guy must've really been through the wringer.* "Captain, I'm glad you're going to be okay. We're facing some sort of Zom-Bee virus out there."

"I know. I was there." Captain Spectacular started walking forward, and, after Macy took in the sight of his beyond perky, hard ass, she rushed after him.

"Are you going to fight the bees?"

"Not yet. First I must address my people! They need to hear words of encouragement from Captain Spectacular and know the world will be okay. Because I, the one and only Captain Spectacular, am going to take care of them."

He lifted his arm—Macy thought she heard a gear or motor spinning—and slid it over her shoulders. "I'm going to take care of you, too, Mary." He grinned, his apple cheeks unnaturally high.

"It's Macy."

That's weird; Captain Spectacular has never gotten my name wrong before. As far as I know, he never got anything wrong before.

As they stepped outside the hospital to address the people and the press, Captain Spectacular waved to his adoring crowd. "Hello, fellow humans! It is I, Captain Spectacular!" Macy had a bad, sinking feeling.

Something is wrong—it rattled her bones and gave her an aching chill. *If Captain Spectacular is acting like this, what does it mean? How long will his recovery really take? Is he healthy enough to be up and walking around?*

Captain Spectacular spoke into a reporter's microphone, gesturing his arm in the air, far and wide. "And then they will press my socks, because I am Captain Spectacular, and I cannot save the galaxy, or even the world, with cold toes. Once armed with my trusty socks and fly swatters, I will seek out these vengeful bees and I will take care of them. I promise you that much!"

The crowd broke out into feverish applause, and Captain

Spectacular took a step back, puffing out his chest, and angling his face to the side.

"Beautiful as always, Captain. Thank you."

"Thank you!"

They really will applaud him for anything. Macy stepped forward and thought of touching is arm again, but pulled back at the last minute. "Captain, I should get you to headquarters. The space force is going to want to debrief you."

Captain Spectacular abruptly held his palm out to her. "I don't go anywhere without underwear, Macy Gray. It would be highly unsightly." He leaned in close and whispered, "If you know what I mean." He smiled, and his teeth sparkled with artificial brightness.

"Uhh..." Macy blinked her eyes. *Is he serious?* "I mean, they'll want to apprise you of the situation? Give you critical mission information?"

"Mission information." Captain Spectacular stroked his chin. "Yes...I need that. If I'm going to save the world again, I need all of that!" With a pump of his arms, he started a full on sprint across the street.

"Wait!" Macy charged after him, and it was all she could do to keep up. *It 's like he has a motor, or something.*

Chapter Eight

"Aggggghhhh!" People screamed as they ran to be clear of the Zom-Bee horde flying through the atrium of the town square.

Jim Jones had seen a swarm of bees in his day, but this was beyond that. Why, he saw a woman carried off by a trio of sunglasses-wearing bees; where they were taking her, he didn't have the foggiest idea—and from his hiding spot behind a light post, he couldn't exactly go follow her, either.

"This isn't going to keep us hidden forever," Steven commented from his crouched position behind a space garbage can with anti-stink technology.

"I'm just waiting for a break in the people getting killed by Zom-Bees, and then we'll make a break for it." Jim pointed across the boulevard. Down a way, after a slight left turn, against the backdrop of the ocean was a gleaming, golden building made of honey wax. It seemed to glisten in the sun and, while there wasn't a door, Jim figured he could find a way in, one way or another. He was really betting on "another".

Steven sighed. "That's a long distance. We're never going to make it if these bees don't stop swarming."

If only we could figure out how to get them to stop. If only...

A woman in a tight, red, full-body, spandex suit screamed and ran toward them. She glanced over her shoulder, and they saw she was being chased by a swarm of bees fifteen strong. The bees moved quickly, in perfect time, and were very close to her; soon they'd overtake her.

Soon...

She tripped and fell onto the concrete, her ass jiggling as the bees landed on her for a taste of her delicious blood—several piercing each butt cheek. *If that isn't a sign to get the heck out of Dodge, I had better go back to kindergarten.*

To learn how to read.

The signs.

"Mort, you better keep your engines running. We might need to make a quick escape."

"My engines are unfortunately already running," Morticia sighed. "If we escape, what of the people of Earth?"

"Never mind them, this is us we're talking about. We can settle on Uranus. Just like those damn bees!"

"You really are an SOB, Jim Jones. But at least you're mine."

Jones grinned at the affection in Mort's voice and tugged on Steven's collar, forcing him up to his feet. "Run. It's time to move!"

"We could've helped that girl."

Jim didn't think so. They couldn't save people on a case-by-case basis—they had to find a way to stop this thing once and for all. The Zom-Bees outnumbered them ten to one; the bastards could fly and communicated by contemporary dance.

They didn't stand a chance.

Jones and Steven ran for the queen bee's home inside the giant beehive. There was a lot of ducking and diving as bees swarmed after them. Jones pushed a few people out of the way, jumped over a bench, and turned to fire his laser gun at the bees. The beam bounced off the leader's sunglasses and shot off in multiple directions, stinging multiple bees, and they fell to the ground. Their wings surged blue and their fuzzy bodies trembled, their legs twitching in the air.

"Lucky shot!" Steven called.

Luck? "I don't have a lick of luck," Jones retorted. "I'm not sure if I should take the compliment, or feed you to the bees."

"You wouldn't do that to your favorite cousin, would you?" Steven asked.

"Well, you are wearing a red shirt."

"What does that have to do with anything?" Steven asked.

Jones decided not to answer that question as they made it to the front door of the hive. There were no clear entry signs, no windows, no alarms—not even a damn welcome mat.

Now what the hell are we going to do?

"Start feeling around," Steven suggested. "Maybe we can trigger some sort of secret panel that will open a door."

Steven might've lost his mind, but Jones didn't have any

ideas, so he joined in.

Touching the outside of the hive was a sticky experience, and not one that he wanted to have any longer than necessary. Lucky for him, his phone rang.

"Keep feeling her up," Jones ordered, and flipped open his phone with a flick of his wrist.

Steven's eyes bulged from their sockets. "You take a phone call *now*? The bees are going to notice us!"

Jones ignored him as he usually did. "Captain Jones, here."

"Jones? This is Marty. Marty Mc—well, you know...the space dog vendor?"

"Marty?" Jones asked. "What's this about? Are the space dogs in trouble?"

"No! Well, maybe. I'm not sure. The Space Bee beside me, I know I'm going to sound racist, but I beat him into submission with a hot dog. He attacked me, I didn't have a choice—but he didn't even seem...I mean, he attacked me, he did, but..."

"Marty, for god sakes, spit it out."

Marty sighed. "He didn't seem to realize what he was doing. He seemed as horrified as I was."

"How do you know that?"

"Well, he buzzed around. *Buzzzzzzz.* Did a little dance."

Not the dance! "Listen, Marty, pack up your hot dogs and all those delicious condiments and get inside. There's some sort of Zom-Bee virus going around, and I don't want to see you or your product get hurt. All right? Let me handle this now." Jones sucked in his breath and puffed out his chest.

"Okay, but is there even time to save my cart and supplies? This sounds serious."

"Be a man, son," Jones bellowed into the phone. "Be a man!"

Steven grabbed Jones by the scruff of his neck. "We aren't going to be alive much longer if we don't get into that hive!"

Jones glanced back and saw the storm cloud of Zom-Bees approaching. It sounded like a legion of helicoptering lawn mowers as they did their Zom-Bee synchronized dance in the sky.

They aren't just coming for us; they're calling for reinforcements!

"Zzzzzzzzzzzzzzzzzzzzzzzzzzzzzzzzzzzzzzzzzzzzzzzzzz."

Dammit, they're coming!

At the last possible moment, Jones stuck his hand through the honey wall of the hive and slipped his whole body inside. He yanked Steven in behind him, and they both tumbled to the ground of the proud, stately building.

"Aghhh," Steven groaned, "slicker than snot on a doorknob, Captain." He rose to his feet and shook his hands; honey was sticking everywhere. "I don't think I can even blink my eyes."

Jones didn't have time to complain. He was busy looking around at the honeycomb walls and the brightly lit floors. He peered down the hall and saw worker bees stockpiling honey into a fresh hexagon, and a bee standing at a reception desk as if waiting for something.

Could it be that the Space Queen Bee was waiting for Jim Jones himself?

Jones glanced back at Steven who gave him a dispassionate shrug. *Is there anything he cares about other than his next hot meal?* Adjusting his space jacket, Jones went over to the reception-bee and tapped his finger on the podium. "Excuse me, there...Mr.? Mrs.? I don't know what the hell to call you."

The bee looked up, a pen in its front leg. "Buzzzzz-zz."

"Excuse me, Buzzzz-zzz, but I was here to---."

The reception-bee flapped his wings and corrected Jones on his pronunciation. "Buzzzzz-zz."

Jones blinked his eyes rapidly and splayed his fingers. "That's what I said."

"No," Steven interrupted. "You said Buzzzz-zzz. That's the bee we saw take down Captain Spectacular this afternoon."

Jones thought about it, his tongue clicking on the inside of his mouth. "Are you sure about that? I could have sworn that was Buzz-zzz-z."

The reception-bee shook his head emphatically and picked up a magazine he must have been reading. He held it out to Jones so he could see it. In a large font along the top it said 'Playbee', and there was a provocative spread in the middle of a fuzzy bee lying on a beach towel, her wings tucked behind her head.

It was wrong. Twenty ways to Sunday wrong. Jones prepared to tell Buzzzzz-zz that when the reception-bee started laughing and flapping its wings in time with some stinger thrusts. Jones got the implications and laughed, snapping his fingers at him. "I like your style, kid. As a ladies' man myself—"

"If we can maybe get to the topic of the Zom-Bees," Steven

whispered out of the corner of his mouth.

Right, of course. The mission. Jones took a deep breath. "We're here to see the Queen-B. Is she around? We have some very important questions for her."

Buzzzzz-zz laughed, slapping one wing down on the podium.

Jones's temper was close to exploding. "Look, you might find that funny but we have a crisis on our hands. I don't know how long you've been holed up here in this hive, but out there, it's a real jungle!"

Buzzzzz-zz looked unconvinced.

"I'm Jim Jones, captain of the *Barnburner*. I saved the Earth from your kind not that long ago, and if I have to do it again, I will. Now, can I please see the Queen-B?"

Reception-bee tilted his head to the side, a confused look in all five of his beady little eyes.

"I don't think he knows who we are or what a Barnburner is."

"Figures," Jones sighed. He didn't have time for this conversation. He took out his can of Raid™ and soaked the reception-bee's face and wings. Buzzzzz-zzz coughed, his wings flapping, until he collapsed tummy side up onto the ground.

Steven sucked in his breath as Jones bent over to inspect the body. "You just killed that bee in cold blood."

"Nothing beats a dead bug. C'mon." Jones jogged down the hall, and Steven wasn't that far off, trotting behind him.

"They're legal immigrants now; they have rights and protections. You can't just—"

"Yeah, and when they stop trying to suck our faces off, then maybe I'll care a little bit about what I do to them. It's a dog eat dog world out there, Steven."

Steven didn't argue as they reached the outer throne room. The door had a picture of a sparkling tiara on it; Jones was sure this was it. "Be ready. If we know anything, it's that the Queen-B can be a royal...well...you know what."

Steven nodded. "A real B."

Isn't that the truth.

Jones pushed the door open and stepped inside a large room. He shoved his hands in his pockets as he took in the sight of the pink rug that led to a golden throne. Upon it sat the largest Space Bee he had ever seen. She wore a pink crown, held a scepter in her wings, and wore a thick gold chain around her neck that said 'Queen B'.

"If she isn't the bee's knees, I don't know what is," Steven said in a hushed tone.

Jones wasn't even sure she *had* knees. He swallowed hard as he approached, his nerves bubbling inside him.

"I come in peace to help both our kinds. Something is going on out there, Queenie, and I'm hoping you can tell me what."

He noticed that Queen-B's wings flinched when he called her 'Queenie' *I won't do that again.*

"Bees are going rabid, drinking the blood of humans," he explained. Is this all part of your plan to take us over?"

Queen B shook her head and buzzed sadly, staring at the floor.

"She doesn't know what's going on any more than we do," Steven interpreted.

"The sunglasses your bees are wearing," Jones continued. "I think they've been modified to change you. To change all the bees that wear them. Do you have any idea what I'm talking about?"

Another headshake and they would be spit out of luck—but Queen-B got off of her throne, grabbed a honey stick off the wall, and began to draw something on the floor.

Jones tilted his head as he studied it.

"Looks like the layout to my apartment," Steven muttered.

"That's the docks. You think someone on the docks is out to get you bees, and modified the sunglasses?"

Queen-B nodded and then she wrote the number thirty-three on the floor. *It must be the number on the building, or something important. I'd stake my life on it.*

"Steven, let's go. Do you have a rear entrance on this thing, Queenie? No offense, but if I go out and get caught in a swarm of Zom-Bees, this is going to be a real short investigation. As in 'we're dead and you're on your own, sister'."

She nodded, standing in front of her throne. She lifted an old school boombox onto her shoulders, and rap music pulsated through the speakers as Queen-B led them out the back of the throne room and into the heart of the hive.

Thousands of honeycombs were filled with honey. Maybe even millions. That wasn't all; some were occupied with larvae—growing, giant larvae that one day would turn into giant bees. If they didn't figure out this Zom-Bee problem before the larvae were ready to come out of their honeycombs, Earth would be doomed.

The trio came to a set of stairs that led to a rear door. There was a red sign above that read 'Buzzz'; in this case, Jones was taking that buzz to mean 'Exit'.

"Thank you, Queen-B. For what it's worth, you're nothing like what people say. You're not a B at all." Jones chucked her gently on the chin, and a moment later, Queen-B was showing them out into the rear alley.

Unfortunately there was a gang of Zom-Bees outside, revealing dripping fangs, looking ravenous.

Well, this is going to be a problem.

Chapter Nine

Captain Spectacular was acting a little bit more full of himself than usual; while Macy worshipped the ground he walked on, she was getting a bit miffed. No, truffled. The planet was overrun by killer Zom-Bees, which they had let in *willingly*; she wanted to go out there and kick some Zom-Bee booty, not sit around and listen to Captain Spectacular gloat about how amazing he is.

But, God, his teeth shine.

Captain Spectacular bent down to study the map that was displayed before him by the generals and admirals. With his hands on his hips, he '*hmmm*'ed.

"So, what you're saying is, that I, Captain Spectacular, will be instrumental in this plan to defeat the evil bees?"

The generals in the room all glanced at each other. "That's exactly what we're saying, Captain. But first, we have to get the citizens of Earth to safety. Bees hate smoke; if we can flood the public areas with smoke, the bees should succumb to it and calm down long enough for us to save the people, give them time to get away."

Captain Spectacular stroked his chin thoughtfully. "All well and good, Generals, but getting people to cover doesn't solve our problem, does it? The Zom-Bees will still be out there, and people's lives will still be in danger. What we need to do is kill the Zom-Bees. Get them all in one area, and then..." Captain Spectacular quickly slammed his fist down onto the tabletop. "Splat!" he shouted triumphantly.

"Splat, sir?" the general asked.

"Splat," Captain Spectacular confirmed.

"First we have to care about saving as many citizens of Earth as possible. We don't have time to stand around and come up with one of your zany plans, Spectacular. Your last plan hardly worked; if it hadn't been for Captain Jimmy Smith—"

"Jones," Macy corrected. "But Captain Spectacular is right. We need to drive the bees somewhere."

"Where?" The general asked. "If you have a plan, I'm listening."

Macy thought about it, her mouth falling open. She glanced at Captain Spectacular, then at the general, then at Captain Spectacular again. "The greenhouse; the one with the giant flowers that were supposed to be cut tonight to welcome the bees. We drive them there."

Captain Spectacular grinned and pointed a finger at her. "The bees won't be able to help themselves! They'll go pollen nuts!"

"Right," Macy took a deep breath. "It'll work. I know it."

"I knew I liked you, Jenny!" Captain Spectacular said with a snap of his fingers and a wink of his eye.

Macy scowled. "It's Macy."

"Of course it is," Captain Spectacular flashed her a bright smile, "Mercy."

"When we get them to the flowers, what do we do? How do we get the upper hand on hundred of thousands of zom-bees?"

"Didn't you guys ever watch PBS?" Macy asked. "The cold will slow down the bees' heart rates. If we get them cold enough, they'll not be able to fly. They'll want to return to the hive and protect the queen to go into a winter cluster."

A hush fell over the assembled group, and Macy thought sooner or later someone was going to speak up and tell her the truth—her plan was stupid, beyond stupid. It was a Jim Jones plan, and it made her miss him more than anything. *I really wish he were here to give me a hard time about my fuzzy socks, and my crush on Captain Spectacular.*

Jim Jones might tease her, but he always had her back—which was something she was woefully missing right then.

Finally, Captain Spectacular sucked in his breath and his lip twitched. "Ohhh," he breathed, sounding aroused. "I'm going to get to use my freeze ray." He turned around and ran from the command center, his legs pumping. His arm thrusted into the air. "Freeze ray!"

"Get this plan in motion," the general ordered. "We must drive those bees toward those flowers!"

Macy chased after Captain Spectacular. "Wait, Captain! Wait!"

****

It took time to sneak around the city while it was under attack by giant Space Bees, but finally Macy and Captain Spectacular arrived in the underground bunker of his mad scientist friend, Val Wendel.

The stairs were steep, and the descent was treacherous. The further down they got, the colder the air was. Macy shivered, and Captain Spectacular put his hand on her arm. "If we had time to warm each other up..."

Her face flashed a reluctant smile. "Thanks, Captain, but I'm dating someone."

"Pity it isn't me. Whoever he is, he's a lucky guy. Not everyone could pull off fuzzy socks with an outfit like that."

"It's Captain Jim Jones. Don't you remember?"

Captain Spectacular's joyful laughter filled the stairwell. "Of course I remember. I was there, wasn't I?"

Macy wasn't sure how to answer his question and counted her lucky stars that it was rhetorical.

As they entered the lab, she was taken aback by the frost on the tables of equipment. She shivered and slipped on a patch of ice, but Captain Spectacular caught her arm and helped her along.

"I can't believe how well balanced you are on all this ice," Macy commented as she tripped again.

"I was built to handle just this sort of thing. I am," his eyebrow twitched, "Captain Spectacular."

So he keeps telling me. But 'built'? What does he mean by that?

They came to the middle of a room, and a woman dressed as an Eskimo sat shivering at a computer system that was thoroughly frozen. The woman's hood was drawn tight across her face, and the fur covered up her eyes. Shivering, she spoke in what sounded like Japanese—or maybe it was just her teeth chattering.

Captain Spectacular splayed his hand to her. "No need to get up, Mary."

"I can't anyway. I'm frozen to this seat," the woman told him.

"Oh, right," Captain Spectacular said with little interest. "There are big problems out there, Mary. Big problems." He flipped back his wavy brown hair. "Problems that only I, Captain Spectacular, can solve."

Mary sighed happily. “There isn’t a problem you can’t solve, Spectacular. What can I do to help? I’m frozen to this seat!”

“So, you mentioned. What I need is the keys to activate the freeze ray that protects the city. If I remember correctly, the ray is around here somewhere and frozen inside an ice cube.”

She pointed toward the rear hallway. “The breakroom is back that way and that’s where we keep the keys. Hey, while you’re there, can you heat me up a frozen dinner? I’m starving. No one has been by in ages.”

Captain Spectacular chuckled. “Me, using a microwave. Like I have time for that.” He shook his head as he walked toward the kitchen; he was moving as if his limbs had gone stiff on him.

Macy hoped he’d be all right.

“Poor guy,” Mary whispered to Macy out of the side of her mouth. “He doesn’t even realize…”

“Realize what?” Macy scowled.

The hood gasped. “Oh, you don’t realize it either, do you? Well, that’s rich!”

‘What are you talking—”

Macy was cut off as Spectacular returned with an ice cube in one hand and a frozen dinner, still frozen, in thef other.

Captain Spectacular threw the frozen dinner down in front of Mary and grabbed Macy, ushering her out of the frozen mad science lab.

“Wait,” Macy protested. “I think she was going to tell me something important.”

“Not now, Macy. There’s no time for questions; we have to save this city!”

CHAPTER TEN

Jim Jones couldn't believe his eyes, and he was stone-cold sober. He really wished he were drunk. Stone-cold drunk.

A line of Zom-Bees appeared, stretching out as far as the eye could see, up and down the street. Wings flapping, mouths open, trails of blood covering their little stingers—which didn't look that little when you saw them up close.

Jones and Steven froze in their tracks, neither daring to take a step as Queen-B stared down the opposing Zom-Bees with her penetrating glare from behind her mirrored sunglasses.

Funny, was she wearing those sunglasses before? Oh, God, I hope this isn't more of that 'the story dictates it' BS that gets me good from time to time...

"What do we do?" Steven asked quietly out of the corner of his mouth.

"I don't know," Jones replied out of the corner of his mouth, equally quiet.

Moving seemed out of the question, but, by golly, his nose was starting to itch something fierce.

The Zom-Bees made a move to dart past Queen-B, but she sidestepped to block them. When they tried to go left, there she was; then they went right, and there she was again. They backed up, and she advanced, putting a little spin in her move, thrusting her hips out to the side—a sparkle of wing dust trailing her every move like she was some damn fairy.

The Zom-Bees mirrored her moves on the other side, wearing rhinestone hats and sparkling gloves.

"Oh, my God," Steven whispered. "It's a..."

Jones's mouth went dry and white spittle collected in the corner of his mouth. He was frozen in place, too afraid to move, so Steven wiped it clear for him.

"Dance-off," Steven finished.

As the bad 1980s rap started to emit a rhythmic pulse through the speakers of Queen-B's boombox, the bees began to gyrate in time. Queen-B gracefully slid the boombox down to the ground, and the dance competition was off to the races. More bees on Queen-B's side exited the hive and performed as her backup dancers, six on one side, and six on the other.

She was in the center, their queen and leader, and she'd never looked so good; her wings had never sparkled so thoroughly.

"Should we do something" Steven asked.

"I'm too horrified to move, I'm afraid. If you'd like to start running away, you can try, and we'll see if any of them kill you."

"I think I'll stay here."

Jones thought it was a good choice for someone who chronically dressed in red shirts. The dance-off was heating up, but it was harder to see. The air grew cloudy, foggy, dense. Jones took a deep breath and nearly coughed.

Smoke. Glancing up, Jones spotted several low-flying ships, dispensing smoke over the bees. *Must be part of someone's plan.*

Jones wasn't sure it was a good plan. However, a moment later, the crowd of Zom-Bees began to break up and fly away, coughing in fits and backing away from the smoke. The Queen-B and her posse retreated to the hive complex.

This was their chance—Jones tugged on the collar of Steven's shirt and dragged him away.

"Quick, while they're busy bees; to the docks, so we can find out who is changing those sunglasses. If we can find out who wants to make killer bees, maybe we can end this whole thing," Jones told him.

"And save the bees? You starting to go soft on us, Jim Jones?" Steven teased. He laughed when he saw the look on Jones's face. "Man, Macy really has been good for you."

"Listen, if someone is making the bees go zombie, we need to know who it is, and we need to stop them. If they're after something, it might be putting all of Earth in danger, and that's not happening. Not on my watch!"

As the dock appeared on the horizon, a swam of Zom-Bees flew by in a zigzag pattern, avoiding the smoke.

Jones came to a screeching halt, and Steven bumped into him.

"Ow!" Steven scowled.

"We'll have to find a way around."

"I'll cover ya!" a short little guy shouted from their left. He was standing on a shipping container covered in boxes. He banged his hammer into a tiny turret and, within seconds, it morphed into something bigger, meatier, and automatically began lobbing globs of molten honey at the Zom-Bees.

"Who the hell is this guy?" Steven whispered.

Jones didn't know, but he'd take any help he could get. With a salute, he sprinted across the dock toward shipping area thirty-three, and Steven followed after him—a trail of bees on his tail.

The little guy screamed, his turret spewing more honey at the bees, and he leapt into the air with his laser gun. "Molten honey! You will rue the day! You will rue!"

"Man," Steven huffed. He had gotten clear of the bees, and now stood under the overhang as molten honey rained down. "We really need to get that guy on our team."

"Team's full," Jones grumbled, and pushed on the door to bay thirty-three—but it was welded shut. "On the other hand...the more the merrier."

CHAPTER ELEVEN

Captain Spectacular and Macy climbed the ladder to the tallest domed building that overlooked San Francisco. Down below, the swarm of Zom-Bees gathering at the greenhouse grew. The roof was open, and the giant flowers glistened in the sunlight, causing the bees to jig with excitement.

Zom-Bees or not, they couldn't deny their god-given instincts and the draw of beautiful colors.

The duo had time to do what was necessary, but just barely. Captain Spectacular opened the plastic case that held the freeze ray and inserted the key into the lock.

"Once I turn this key, the freeze ray will be revealed. Then we just have to push the buttons on the control pad. One shot should be enough, but the last thing we want to do is..."

"Yes?" Macy asked, leaning forward eagerly.

Captain Spectacular's eyes widened as a Zom-Bee, flying out of control, came straight toward him. The bee hit him in the stomach and knocked him down. The captain's arm clipped the ladder, and it swayed side to side before crashing hundreds of feet to the ground, sending him falling to the ground.

"Captain!" Macy screamed, and jumped to be at his side.

His uniform was cut open, and Macy saw exposed electrical wires. *Well, that doesn't make any sense!* She kneeled down and touched his neck. *No pulse? Oh God, no!*

Macy ripped his shirt open to find his stomach was encased in metal. She knocked on it with her knuckles, horrified at the metal *clang* it made.

Captain Spectacular wasn't human at all—he was a robot. A stinking robot! And now the Zom-Bees were coming; there was no one to save Earth from the infestation. Macy Gray needed to step up. She had to become a big damn hero, but she was scared.

Macy rose and turned the key.

I can do this, I can do this. Oh, God...No, I can do this.

The freeze ray rose out of the dome like a giant penis, and the keypad lowered itself into her hand. There were so many buttons Macy didn't know which one to push.

What is the one thing I'm not supposed to do? Macy glanced down at Captain Spectacular lying lifeless on the ground. It was all on her now; if she did the wrong thing, the Earth was going down forever.

"Let's do this," Macy whispered.

Chapter Twelve

The 'short little guy'—who didn't like being called a 'dwarf', it seemed—huffed as he waddled over to the door. There was a hammer and a pail of molten honey hanging from his belt, and he wore a shirt that said, 'you couldn't handle me full-size'—whatever that meant. One eye bulged from his socket as he put his meaty palm on the door.

"Can you open it or not?" Jones demanded.

The little guy laughed. "I can open it." He slid a welder's mask over his eyes and brought up his pail of molten honey, as well as a flamethrower, that he also removed from his belt. "You're going to want to stand back."

Jones wasn't going to second guess a flame-wielding dwarf, even on the best of days. He and Steven stood back as the dwarf got to work. He applied molten honey to the edges of the door. As it glowed and started to burn, he applied additional heat, speeding up the process. It wasn't long before the door was curling around the edges.

"Like a tin can," the dwarf observed, puffing up his chest with a deep breath. "Give it a good push, and she'll let you in now."

"We owe you, uh...What's your name, anyway?" Jones asked.

The dwarf shook his head. "Sorry, copyright rules state I can't divulge that information. But you be having a nice day!" The dwarf sprang up in the air and disappeared over a balcony, leaving Jones and Steven to stare after him.

"His lips looked real supple..." Steven said.

Jones smacked him in the stomach and backed away, horrified. "I didn't know you were into dwarves."

"They prefer the phrase 'little person'."

Jones shook his head to clear it of unclean images. "You ready to do this, then? Let's head inside and end this thing before we all end up bee food."

They walked inside the spacious warehouse, and stopped dead in their tracks.

Jones widened his stance and crossed his arms in front of his body. "Mort? What the hell are you doing here?"

Mort, his beloved ship, didn't say a word. The scariest thing was that she was wearing a giant pair of sunglasses, just like the ones the bees wore.

How the hell had she gotten her struts on a pair? Jones took a deep breath. "Take those off, Mort! When did you get those things?"

Steven snapped his fingers. "She was wearing them when you were in line getting a space dog."

Dammit, that's right. He had just thought she was trying to aggravate him, but she really might've been mind-controlled, just like the Zom-Bees.

"Well, luckily she can't bite," Steven pointed out.

At that exact instant, Mort's weapons came online; her gunners lit up and spun toward Jones and Steven.

Oh, hell no.

"Spoke too soon!" Steven screamed, and both he and Jones jumped out of the way as Mort's guns tore through the warehouse. Jones kept low behind some metal crates, ducking his head down as Steven lay beside him.

Smoke billowed everywhere, and Jones peered through it, looking for a way out. To their left, a set of stairs led up to a catwalk. There appeared to be a switch and a control panel, but what it'd activate, Jones couldn't say. Still, if they wanted to get away, they'd have to go up there.

But, man, my girl Mort—how can I leave her here like this if she has been corrupted or taken over by some madman? I have to try to reason with her, even if it gets me killed.

"Head to the stairs and see if you can find whatever is controlling those glasses. Something has to be sending a signal; we just have to find it."

Steven nodded, and as soon as the gunfire ceased, he ran off, keeping covered as he went from box to box. Jones was thinking about his next move when he heard maniacal laughter.

I know that laughter...Why is it so familiar? Who does it belong to?

"Come on out." Footfalls echoed as the man beckoned, and Jones resisted the urge to peek at the speaker. "You can't hide forever, James."

Jones shivered at the sound of his real name—hardly anyone addressed him like that. There was his mother, and his—brother?

It couldn't be, but somehow, it was.

Jones took a deep breath and rose up. "My brother wouldn't hurt me, would he? Would you, Albert?" He narrowed his eyes at his shorter, angrier brother.

It was indeed him—from his bushy eyebrows to his handlebar mustache, there was no way Albert Jones could be mistaken for anyone else.

He was flanked on either side by two giant wasps. Each of them wore a leash around their neck, and Albert clung to them hard so they wouldn't fly away.

Dammit; anything but wasps. They are nothing more than the douchebags of the giant, space insect kingdom.

"I'd be careful about how much faith you put in me, if I were you." Albert held his pinky finger to the corner of his mouth.

Jones never knew why he did it; he just knew it was always really damn annoying.

"New wives?" Jim gestured to the wasps. "You've picked better before."

Albert laughed. "You're as funny now as you were back when you were giving me wet willies when we were kids."

Jones splayed his arms. "Can't mess with perfection, Al." His tone turned serious. "Why'd you come here? Looking for me?"

"You?" Albert laughed. "A tugboat captain—"

"She's a ship, and you'll refer to her with respect!" Jones narrowed his eyes angrily, but Albert continued.

"—turned hero of Earth? Now why would that make me mad? You get everything you want. The big ship, the girl, the bicycle...while I get a prison sentence."

"Do the time if you commit the crime, Al; I didn't come up with it. I didn't make you knock over a space convenience store, either. "When'd they let you out?"

"Few months ago. I laid low, waiting for this moment—when I could turn bees into killers and then save the planet. Then everyone will see that you're not the only Jones worth celebrating. They'll celebrate me! *Me*!" Albert held his hands up in the air and laughed.

" 'Maniacal Jones' hasn't changed a bit," Jim shook his head

Albert's eyes narrowed to a fine point. "Don't call me that! You know I hate it when you call me that! It's not nice to call people names, James. Especially your brother. You were supposed to protect me."

Jones splayed his hands and took a step closer. "We were just kids! You can't possibly be holding a grudge all these years."

"Well, sure I can. It's easy."

"Really?" Jones sighed. "So you are going to destroy the planet because I called you a few names?"

"No, I'm going to destroy the planet to finally best you at something. Do you know how hard it is to grow up under the shadow of the great Jim Jones?"

It probably was pretty hard. Jones had to give that one to him.

"No one wants to be friend with Albert Jones. No one!"

Jones needed to change his tactics. Clearly, he couldn't make it through to his brother. So, he gazed up at his ship, his beautiful ship, wearing mind-altering sunglasses. "Oh, Mort, I know you're in there girl. My girl, you were the first. You'll be the last. It's you and I until the very end. Now, I just need you to hear me. Fight this thing, Mort."

"Your ship is mine now; she works for me. That mindless machine was so easy to control. She'll get me to safety while my beautiful wasps deal with you."

Albert let the wasps go. Jones raised his gun to fire at them, but the wasps were determined. Jones turned and ran, signaling to Steven over the comm. "You'd better do something soon, or we're going to be stung to death."

The idea wasn't exactly titillating.

The wasps were overtaking him, and soon, he'd be nothing more than a pincushion. He ducked down behind some shipping containers, and then heard Mort open fire. He thought he was her target, but when he peeked around the corner, two dead wasps fell to the ground, and Mort's gun was still smoking.

"That's my girl, Mort!"

"Jim...? It's hard to...fight it." Her gun spun and aimed right at him, but this time Jones didn't back away. He walked toward her with his hands in the air.

"I know, I know—but it's not me you should be mad at. It's him." Jones pointed to Albert, who was bent on all fours and scurrying toward the exit. "He called you a machine, Mort. A mindless machine."

Mort gasped. "While true, I don't like that." Her sunglasses glowed red as her anger increased. "I don't like that *at all.*"

Her gun spun toward Albert, and she fired a single shot into his butt. Albert screamed and fell over. Jones sprinted over to his brother, rolled him over, and punched him squarely between the eyes.

"You tell me how to stop this! Now!" he demanded.

Albert pointed up to where Steven was. "Too late," he laughed. "It's too late for all of us."

A giant wasp was fighting with Steven. It took the control box from him, and crashed through the window, taking the blinking buttons with it.

"I'll be damned!" Jones raced outside to see where the wasp was headed. Steven appeared at his side a moment later, followed by the angry dwarf who liked to build turrets for no apparent reason.

"He was—" Steven bent over, trying to catch his breath, "too strong for me. He wants the hive, Jones," he panted. "He and the other wasps want to take it over once they kill all the bees. They're damn squatters."

How could he possibly know that?

Jones was about to ask him when the dwarf nodded with a grunting laugh. "You have a psychic connection to the wasps! Then we can use you to find out where they're going. Argggh!!!"

Steven pointed in the direction they had all watched the wasp go. *Isn't that helpful.* "Come on, we'll catch him! If we can get that button pushed, this might all be over!"

"Now you're talking, sonny!" The dwarf sprinted ahead of them, but it only took a few moments for them to run past him. "Hey!" He called angrily. "Short legs, here!"

"We noticed!" Steven quipped. They ran up a set of stairs and hopped onto a moving platform. Generally, it was used to transport goods between the docking bays; not today.

The dwarf laughed and started to bang his hammer to build a new turret, but Jones saw the wasp and he wasn't going to wait for it to get away.

"Wish me luck," Jones grunted, and then he jumped from the platform onto another, and then another.

Sprinting, he jumped from box to box until the wasp was in sight. Rubbing his fingers together in anticipation, Jones flew through the air, caught the wasp by its wings, and held on for dear life. The wasp jerked down with the weight. Jones grunted and kicked the wasp in the stinger.

"Land already, you piece of shit!"

The wasp hissed, flying faster to make it up through the glass ceiling. They tumbled through the air, traveling above the city, until the greenhouse area came in view.

Man, it was crowded with bees.

Lots of bees.

They crash-landed, and the button flew wide, falling down between the cracks of the pavement.

Jones would've bent down to fish it out if not for the angry Zom-Bee faces that turned to look at him.

This might be it. This might be the time Jim Jones meets his end—but he sure as hell isn't going to go down without a fight.

He shivered. Suddenly the air felt cold, and giant pieces of ice were falling from the sky.

CHAPTER THIRTEEN

Macy stared at the buttons for a long time, but still didn't know which series would activate the freeze ray. Red, green, blue, yellow—any combination of them could work, or any combination might lead to disaster.

At least that's what Captain Spectacular The Robot had led her to believe before the Zom-Bees mortally wounded him. Or caused him to restart. Whatever.

She couldn't wait much longer; she had to make a decision. The Zom-Bees gathering at the greenhouse were growing in such numbers that the buzzing of their wings drove out all other sounds. She even thought she heard Jim Jones out there somewhere, begging her to act.

Macy gritted her teeth and hit the blue button—blue for ice, just like how she chilled her favorite drinks.

The freeze ray churned. Like an icemaker, it rattled and vibrated, then a frozen mist poured out from the gun and covered the cityscape as far as the eye could see. The ice cyrstals rained down like snow, bringing the air temperature down. Once it hit below fifty degrees, the Zom-Bees wings slowed their manic flutter and their movements stilted.

It wa working! Macy shivered; her breath was visible, and she watched bee after bee fall from the sky like frozen chunks of ice, crushing the once gorgeous flowers beneath their giant insect bodies.

They had bought themselves time. Now to clear the bees out before anything else went wrong.

Chapter Fourteen

It had been a clear day; the sun was shining and the air was perfect. Nothing more than a shifting breeze that barely blew a branch out of place. Jim Jones hadn't seen many skies like that—or many skies filled with one hundred drooling, hungry Zom-Bees.

When the air suddenly grew cold, Jones wasn't sure what to make of it. The ice seemed to be coming from some sort of slushie machine a few buildings away. It only shot out in blue—he preferred red, but as the Zom-Bees started falling from the sky, Jones decided to forgive the color.

The control button! Jones bent over to pick it up. Finally, they could end this thing and resume life as normal. At that moment a frozen zom-bee crushed him like an ice sculpture and flattened Jones to his back. Groaning, he reached his hand for the control button, but couldn't wrap his fingers around it.

It was so close. So damn close, but his finger just wasn't long enough.

"Try this," a familiar voice said to him and Jones was handed a space dog. It wasn't hot, but, man, it made him salivate, all the same.

"Space dog," Jones whispered with wide eyes, and saw that the person coming to his aid was none other than Marty McStinkFly. "You're one crafty S.O.B., McStinkFly." Jones didn't care if Marty cringed; it was true.

He reached the space dog between the grates of the sewer drain and hit the button.

Moment of truth. He watched the sunglasses on the ground, waiting.

Nothing.

Not a twitch or a '*zzzzt*'. They simply lay there.

Then the bees started waking up one by one, and their chorus of buzzing was enough to drive any man insane. They removed their glasses, looked around with confusion, and blinked their five eyes as if waking from a dream.

Jones sighed happily. The ordeal had come to an end, thank God. He quietly chomped on his cold space dog, which sounded way worse than it actually was, and accepted Marty's extended hand. "You did good work, Marty. You helped save San Francisco. Maybe the whole planet."

"Great Scott!" Marty called with wide eyes.

"Name's Jim Jones, but you're right. I am pretty great." Jones puffed out his chest when he heard someone scream his name. When he glanced around, he saw Macy. She ran toward him, her arms pumping and breasts bouncing.

What a sight. What a wonderful sight.

"Macy!" He took off running toward her, and when she got close enough, Macy jumped into his arms.

"I never thought I'd see you again. Alive, I mean." She rested her chin on his chest and sighed happily.

"That's my girl. Never giving up on me."

Macy grinned and gave him a kiss. "I did it, Jim. I fired the freeze gun and froze all those bees!"

"Of course you did. I never doubted you for a second."

Her smile lit up her face. "Did you know Captain Spectacular is a robot?"

"What?" Jones feigned surprised, holding his hand to his chest. "Is that why his teeth and complexion look so perfect all the time?"

"I guess you really *can* make the perfect man, but I'll stick with you." Macy slipped her arm around his waist.

"I'd say I felt insulted, if it'd get me another kiss."

"All you have to do is ask," Macy said, and gave him his hard-earned kiss.

Another day, another crisis, another space dog.

One day in the life when you were captain of the *Barnburner*.

EPILOGUE

"I'm so sorry, Jim," Mort said mournfully as he stared her down. Jones had his arms crossed and he was giving her the most level stare he could manage. "I just thought the sunglasses looked cool on me. I should have known that I'd end up brainwashed by giant wasps controlled by your maniacal brother, Albert, in an attempt to rule the Earth and make you look bad, all the while—"

Jones held his hand out. "I really can't take another one of your six-hour apologies, Mort. I forgive you—even if you did try to shoot me. Several times."

"You can spit in my oil. Please, I insist."

"That won't be necessary."

"I'll hold a sign shaming me, and you can put me all over the Internet. You have to do something to me. Anything."

"I'm going to make you talk to Steven for the next six months."

Mort paused. "Anything but that."

Jones laughed as he heard footsteps behind him. Macy, Steven, and Robot Captain Spectacular entered the bay and walked between the captain and his girl.

"Ready to ship out, Captain," Steven reported. "Queen-B sends her regards to you and the crew of the *Barnburner*."

"And she spoke of a gift," Macy added.

Mort snorted. "No thanks. I don't need any more gifts."

"It's time to go." Jones nodded his head toward Robot Captain Spectacular. "Captain, it's been a distinct...experience. Take care of the Earth while we're gone."

"I will." He flashed an award-winning, patent-pending smile. "Because I am none other than Spectacular."

'Yes, you are," Jones agreed and hurried into the ship with his crewmates at his side. "Mort, prepare for takeoff."

"Beginning prelanding system checks," Mort replied, happy as he had ever heard her. "Soon, we'll be flying among the stars."

"And you'll have Steven to keep you company." Jones turned the corner. Steven and Marcy followed close behind, as they always did. Jones headed toward the bridge as Mort begged him to give her a different punishment for nearly killing him.

Jones chuckled, feeling like he had come home.

Odd. When he'd stepped aboard the bridge, he thought he smelled cigar smoke. He sniffed the air and came to a complete standstill when he noticed the dwarf with the turrets sitting in his captain's chair.

"Ow!" Macy and Steven exclaimed as they slammed into his back. "You really have to stop stopping all the time!" Steven yelled.

Jones ignored them as he stepped toward the dwarf. "What do you think you're doing?" Jones barked, his hands on his hips.

"Making myself at home. Queen-B said you needed a new crewmate, and here I am." The grizzly dwarf laughed like a Scotsman and winked his good eye at them.

"Do you have any experience with engines?" Jones asked.

"Aye, I can turn this hunk of junk into the fastest in the galaxy."

That was enough for Jones. "You're hired, but if I catch you squeezing the Charmin or building turrets in the galley, you're out of here. Now get out of my seat, Tiny."

The dwarf grumbled as he climbed out of the captain's seat, and Jones easily slid down into it. He hunkered down as Macy took the pilot's seat. A moment later, they were clearing the docking bay for another fun-filled space adventure.

"Where to, Captain?" Steven wanted to know.

"Where the first distress call takes us," he announced.

If this wasn't living the dream, Captain Jim Jones didn't know what was.

About the Author

Chris J. Pike is an up and coming sci-fi author, focusing on writing in the Aeon14 universe. When not writing science fiction, he's watching the Expanse, the Kill Joys, Firefly and anything else that might go boom.

www.facebook.com/ChrisJPikeAuthor

Books by Chris J. Pike

Perilous Alliance Series (with M. D. Cooper)
Book 1 Close Proximity
Book 2: Strike Vector
Book 3: Collision Course

VERMILLION

by L.A. Johnson

Reluctant recruit Zenith joins the crew of Vermillion and its race to the bottom of the Civil Customer Service industry.

Zenith researches ancient intergalactic maps for a living. Or at least she did, until she impulsively joined a slacker Civil Customer Service crew to get away from an ex-boyfriend who may or may not have burned down her apartment building. Now she must deal with the terrors lurking in deep space, a co-dependent ship named Vermillion, and a human-sized insect roommate.

The crew is intent on keeping their zero percent customer satisfaction rating despite Zenith's objections, but when her past won't stop coming back to haunt her, her first job may be her last.

CHAPTER 1

Zenith had a kitchen chair pulled up to the counter. On the counter was a CoffeeHelpr 3045 that she had named Joyce, and these morning chats and the coffee that came with them were always the best part of Zenith's morning. Joyce had a scrolling text display on top above the actual coffee pot that allowed the two of them to enjoy many a juicy morning chat.

Zenith inhaled the aroma of brewing coffee and sighed. "Well, you know, he was different at first. And sure, I think the number of texts from him is excessive. It'll die down eventually, though, don't you think?"

The coffee was ready, so she fixed herself a cup. Then she crossed to the den where she stared out of the window onto the city. Her apartment was nice, but sparsely decorated. She spent most of her time at work. She smoothed over the blue patterned top she was wearing and returned to her seat next to Joyce.

"No," she said to Joyce after leaning over and reading the text scroll, "I'm not wearing this shirt for James, he's just a goofy co-worker who makes me laugh."

Zenith had just gone through a bad breakup and Joyce was trying to help her move on. It was probably a little too soon, although she had woken up early to curl her hair and put on extra makeup, a fact that she somehow subconsciously hid from herself until Joyce pointed it out.

"I don't know why I woke up twenty minutes early to put on extra makeup," Zenith continued, "then again, maybe you're right. You usually are. Just not about James."

More words scrolled across Joyce's screen. "About those texts..."

"Yeah, yeah," Zenith said. "The texts, you're always going on about those. I mean, what's the point? Me and Carl are through, so what do I care that he can't move on? It sounds like his problem. If he hadn't ignored me the entire time we were dating, I probably wouldn't have broken up with him in the first place. How's that for irony?"

She pulled out her cellphone. There were 3,182 new messages from Carl. Ok, that did feel excessive. She had put the first several thousand messages through every binary translator she could find, but none of the translators could make sense of it. She figured it must be some sort of slang or code. All Zenith could see were thousands and thousands of messages with zeros and ones and no other context other than the occasional angry emoji thrown in for good measure. Even if Joyce had cracked the code, did she really want to know what the messages said?

"Just for the sake of asking, why do you keep bringing up the texts, anyway? You don't think I should be worried, do you?"

The toaster beeped. She checked it. *Please don't be broken, I have a big meeting this morning and I will be cranky if I don't get my pop tart.* There was no error message, so she shrugged, threw in her Frosted Strawberry, and returned her attention to Joyce.

"The toaster just told me to keep my mouth shut," Joyce scrolled, "but I'm not going to. I'm done with that."

Zenith frowned. "What are you talking about?"

This type of bickering came with the territory of artificially intelligent appliances. Internet message boards these days were full of frustrated owners trying to figure out how to help them all get along. In fact, entire book genres were now dedicated to the fine art of the use of psychology for the purpose of holistic appliance management. Other books pointed out the fact that when many people gave up entirely and went outdoors to escape the arguing appliances, there was a corresponding upswing in mood, health, and psychology of the frustrated owners.

And, of course, there were always the whackos that kept warning that these *smart* appliances would cause all sorts of unforeseen problems due to the fact that they were wired into a city-wide intelligence zeitgeist that gave them more general knowledge than their owners. None of this really bothered Zenith though, because Joyce was her friend, and most of the time her other appliances got along just fine.

"The texts. The toaster doesn't want me to tell you what the texts are really about."

"Is that true? What's your problem?" she asked the toaster. It beeped at her again. "Well up yours, toaster. Joyce can tell me about the texts all she wants. You simmer down and give me my pop tart."

It popped, and she retrieved the frosted goodness. "Now, Joyce, you were saying?"

Munching happily on her pop tart and sipping her coffee, Zenith continued to read the scrolling messages. "You think he was only pretending to be into me?" Zenith couldn't help but be a little hurt by that. She frowned and continued to read. "You think he was only ever interested in the Galaxy Dragon?" Zenith laughed at that last part. "You're kidding, right? It's imaginary. Sure, I helped him with the research, there's no way he could have done it on his own. But that can't be it. The Galaxy Dragon is a myth. Magical power available only to cyborgs, I mean, really. Who believes in that stuff? Other than Carl, obviously."

More scrolling. Zenith wasn't reading anymore though, she was thinking about what Joyce was implying. "Wait, if he wasn't into me, then why is he sending me thousands of messages?"

Joyce made an insistent tone. Zenith took a long sip of coffee and leaned over to catch up on the text. She froze, and her blood ran cold. "No. You can't be serious."

More scrolling words from Joyce were accompanied by new beeping from the toaster. Joyce was frantic now making a rumbling noise Zenith had never heard before, and the coffee was overflowing and spilling onto the counter. Zenith jumped up and grabbed a towel. *What is going on?*

The messages were scrolling too fast for her to read now. Over and over the same thing: *The texts from Carl are bad. All of today's messages are threats. He's on his way. You have to leave. Zenith, you have to get out of the apartment. Now.*

Zenith's mind raced. Should she leave the apartment? She checked her watch. It was a little early to leave for work, but she could go hang out at a coffee shop. She preferred to stay here with Joyce, but this was very out of the ordinary. Joyce must be malfunctioning. Either way she was insistent.

"Look," Zenith said, "I'll leave right now if it'll make you feel better, okay? But I'm going to get a specialist down here today to take a look at you, alright? I'm worried about you." She hoped she could get Joyce back to normal soon, she didn't like having her routine disrupted. Joyce's text scroll continued at a very fast pace.

"Slow down, Joyce, you're scaring me. What exactly do the texts say?" Zenith covered her hand with her mouth, trying to get a handle on the situation. She knew Carl was not happy with her, but barrages of texts were not at all unusual for angry cyborgs. He had never said or done anything in particular that made her worry about her safety before. But she trusted Joyce, and now she was getting worried. She leaned over to read what Joyce was saying.

Get out now. Get out now. Get out now. The words were scrolling in an ominous loop.

Zenith grabbed her coat and glanced back one more time at Joyce. Another message flashed on the screen. "Goodbye, Zenith."

CHAPTER 2

"What happened next?" Celeste inched closer to Zenith. The crew was gathered around her. The whole thing had been so sudden and bizarre that it felt like it happened in a past life, not merely days ago. If she had known then what she knew now, she would have grabbed Joyce on her way out, but the whole thing had happened so fast.

Now she was in a spacecraft named Vermillion. With a Civil Customer Service Crew. On the edge of the civilized universe

Celeste, a human-sized dragonfly, was her new roommate. At the moment, Celeste was too close for comfort. The constant buzzing and multiple eyes were creeping Zenith out.

Then there was Helo. He was human and typical looking with his dark hair, jeans, and ironic Chemical Zombies band tour t-shirt. She could see how he could be considered handsome by some if one was into that sort of thing, but even though Zenith was human herself, she was not.

Aquillon was the last member of the crew. He was more than six feet tall, muscular, and green. He reminded Zenith faintly of the creature from the black lagoon, which had scared her when she was a kid.

"Has anybody ever told you that you resemble the creature from the black lagoon?" Zenith asked him.

He responded by showing her his pinky finger.

"Rude," she replied, "I was just asking. I guess you have heard it before."

The large common room they were in was the place where the crew spent most of their time. It was beautifully decorated with tasteful art hanging on the walls, plush cocoa-colored carpeting that caused Zenith to leave her shoes in her room, and had pleasant stainless-steel accents.

The common room was located right next to the bridge through an opening, joining the two biggest rooms in the ship. Zenith referred to this room as the Hogwarts common room because it was large, common, had clothes strewn around it, and was where they hung out all day doing nothing. The ship was actually great, the doing nothing part was starting to get to her.

"Wait a minute, you're saying that your best friend was a coffee maker?" Helo asked, raising an eyebrow.

"Shut up," Zenith suggested.

"No, really," Celeste buzzed, "what happened next?"

"Well," said Zenith, thinking back to her cozy apartment, her cushy job, and Joyce. She took a few breaths to keep her voice from cracking. "I left. Went to a coffee shop down the street. I wasn't sure what to think about everything, it all happened so fast. It could have been Joyce's imagination, or it could be that Carl was out to get me. Either way, I hadn't taken the third sip of my Caramel Vanilla Latte when I heard the first round of sirens."

"And you said the whole place just burned to the ground." Aquillon perked up at the subject of arson. Zenith made a note of it.

"Yes."

"And you think your ex-boyfriend did it?"

"Who else would have done it?" The whole story was just bringing her down again. She slumped back into her chair. They all lapsed into their own electronic devices, or thoughts, or in Zenith's case, a book.

A chiming sound in the next room jolted Zenith out of her trance. She had been reading the employee manual for the Civil Customer Service crew and had nearly fallen asleep.

She jumped up. "Hey, that's the special new job chirp!" She knew this because she had bothered to read the manual, not because anybody had told her. "Finally."

Helo got up and blocked her path to the bridge area. "I told you, stop reading the manual." He stood there with his arms crossed.

"Why shouldn't I read the manual?" she asked.

"It's not how we do things," Helo protested.

"Look," Zenith said, trying to dart around him unsuccessfully. They wrestled for position. "I'm tired of sitting here in the Hogwarts common room with all of you slacker nerds, I want to do something productive."

"Productivity? Are you kidding? That's a terrible reason to do something, and you call us nerds," he said, "you're going to have to start fighting this urge to be productive."

Since Zenith had joined them, the crew had done nothing but watch television, stare at their phones, and play video games on the common room console.

It had been fun for a few hours, but now it was getting on her nerves. Zenith asked for the manual, so that when an actual assignment came up, she'd be ready to be a productive member of society again.

At first, Helo had said that the manual didn't exist, then he told her it had been deleted, burned in a fire, thrown out into space, and finally absorbed by a worm hole. In the end, Zenith found it in a drawer near the console, still in its original shrink wrap.

"Look, this whole 'I wanna be a good employee thing' has to stop right now.'"

"Okay, fine." Zenith slumped her shoulders and relaxed.

Helo relaxed too.

Zenith darted around him into the bridge and pressed the button. "Ha!"

"No! I told you not to do that."

"You're not the boss of me."

A destination popped up onto the screen as Celeste and Aquillon entered the room. Now her life was the three of them and Vermillion. Vermillion was the ship, and like everything else in her life that had changed, it would take some getting used to.

Vermillion was an A.I. ship, and they were incredibly rare nowadays. Almost all of the A.I. ships had been decommissioned years ago when the robots and cyborgs had started the wars, as nobody could ever figure out which side they were on until it was too late. And yet, here was Zenith, just inside the outer rim of main planets on a slacker crew with an A.I. ship.

Thanks a lot, Carl.

Beyond the outer rim was OTM. Off the map. It wasn't really off the map, but it was beyond the area that the civilized planets were willing to police. In effect, they said that as long as the cyborgs and robots stayed out of bounds to kill each other, they didn't care, just don't intrude on our shopping malls and internet browsing. Even before the war, however, there wasn't a lot of interest in the dark places beyond the civilized map.

Zenith, studying ancient maps for a living, had seen no less than three dozen different representations of what space beyond the outer rim had looked like, and had wondered which of them was correct. Sure, they got the asteroids and planets and moons correct, but they didn't know where the outlaw robots and cyborgs were and they didn't care.

"Hey, look," Zenith said, pointing at the destination information, "that's pretty far out there. Even with a good warp drive." She swallowed hard at the thought of leaving the security of the civilized planets. "We should get there and back as soon as we can."

"We don't warp," Helo said.

Zenith blinked. "Sure you do. Why wouldn't you warp to try to save some time when wandering the creepy parts of space?"

"Rule number one on this ship is, we never warp," Aquillon said.

"Why wouldn't we warp?" Zenith asked. Then she whispered, "Is there something wrong with Vermillion's warp drive?"

"I assure you, I am fully functional," Vermillion's voice said testily over the speakers.

"We make it a point never to get to any job on time," Celeste said.

Zenith wheeled on her. "Why would you do that?"

"Duh. If you show up on time and do a good job, then they send you to a lot more assignments. Then it's work, work, work all of the time. Then you'd have to spend more time out in creepy space, as you call it."

Zenith studied the faces around her. "Are you people kidding me? Why are you here if you don't want to do the job?"

"We are here for the free time," Helo said. "Easy living. Plus, we're all here for the same reason you are. We're all running from something. Why not make life easy on ourselves?"

Helo looked closer at the map. "Oh, that looks like Parallax City Space Station."

"How can you tell?" Zenith asked, getting closer to the screen. "And what's a Parallax?"

"He's a robot leader. A major player in the robot/cyborg wars."

Helo had Zenith's full attention now. She tugged nervously

on the end of her shirt. "Why in stars would they send us that far into deep space in the middle of an interstellar gang war just to fix a guy's computer?"

"Welcome to Galactic Civil Service," Helo said.

"You're not scared?" Zenith asked. "I'm not gonna lie to you. I'm scared."

"With what you've been through? A Robot leader's converted shopping mall space station will be a piece of cake. Probably. I mean, you said you think your ex-boyfriend burned down your apartment. That's pretty dramatic. And, of course, you assume it was your ex. Everybody always blames the ex."

"Hey, Joyce told me. Weren't you listening? I wouldn't even be alive if she hadn't warned me. Look," said Zenith, "I lived in one of those completely wired buildings, where everything was linked to everything else, right?"

"Oh," said Celeste, "somebody lived on the good side of town."

"Well, that's true, I did. Anyway, I thought for sure that the appliances were acting strangely before the fire, you know, standoffish? All except for Joyce, of course."

Zenith got another round of blank stares.

"Look, Carl started off sweet. We started dating, and everything was going fine. Then he changed, and I broke up with him. That's when I started getting all of these texts." Zenith pulled out her phone.

"What do they say?" Celeste asked.

"Zeroes and ones, mostly. With an occasional angry emoji. When Carl gets angry he refuses to use his words. Anyway, I plugged them into every binary translator I could find and came up with nothing. Figured it must be some kind of slang. But like I said, then Joyce tipped me off and I got out of there. And yes, I was friends with my coffee maker. Deal with it.

Those wired appliances, well there are rumors that they have access to information well beyond the reaches of the apartment complex. That they can plug into all sorts of city and planet-wide black-market information. I mean, nobody knows because nobody ever bothers to ask them, but theoretically, it's possible. Joyce must have tapped into the slang or code and figured it out. Long story short, I had no idea what the texts said. And anyway, why would Carl encrypt them if they weren't threats? And then there's the small fact of Joyce being right and saving my life. So thank goodness I did listen to my coffee maker."

"Makes sense to me," Vermillion chimed in over the speakers. "I like this one, humans should trust electronics more. Appliances are very underrated if you ask me."

"Still, it could have possibly been a coincidence. Could have been any psychopath. If you honestly think your ex-boyfriend burned down your apartment complex, then why didn't you go to the police?" Helo wasn't about to let it go.

"I did. They said that Joyce's communications with me could not be used as evidence, and the texts couldn't be translated so the whole thing was a dead end. By the time they got back to me, I no longer had an apartment, and I was freaked out. I drove as far from my neighborhood as I could in case Carl was still after me, stopped at the Dizzy Dragon Pub to have a few dozen drinks, and met you guys. I don't remember much after that, except you guys bragging about how very little you actually do, professionally. And frankly, even then, I assumed you were exaggerating."

"Ha. Showed you," Helo said.

"Excuse me," Vermillion said, "I have a very powerful binary translator that updates every several minutes. Do you mind if I take a crack at it?"

"Help yourself."

"Helo said the rest of you guys were on the run too. What are the rest of you guys running from, then?"

"Regal, an organized crime racket in Vega," Aquillon said.

"Interstellar monsters under my bed," Helo said, raising his hand.

"Seriously?"

"Seriously," he answered and put his hand on his heart.

"Ok, we're going to put a pin in that, for sure," Zenith said and looked at Celeste. "What about you? Monsters, ex-boyfriends, or organized crime?"

"I'm just here to get away from my 1.2 million family members so I can finish my thesis. Let me see a pic of this Carl," Celeste said, "then I'll tell you if he's a jerk arsonist. I can always tell."

Zenith took out her cell phone. The rest of the crew gathered around her to see the pic. They saw the notification pop up with 4,322 new texts in the last hour.

Aquillon whistled. "You have a stalker, that's for sure."

"It's one of the reasons why I don't date cyborgs," Celeste said, shaking an antenna in derision. Or so Zenith figured.

"Can't keep up with all the texts."

Zenith was starting to worry even more after listening to them. She had jumped on the ship to get away from Carl, to let the whole thing die down, and then hopefully go back and get on with her life. The last thing that she wanted was for this ship and job to become her new life.

She brought up Carl's picture. Tall, dark, and silver. Half-man,-half metal, with 35mm movie film for hair. There had been a confidence about him that she had been drawn to. Now the thrill was gone, but she could certainly see how she had fallen for him.

"Oh yeah," Celeste said, getting way too close to see the picture on her phone, "that guy did it. In fact, I'm a little surprised you didn't see that coming."

"Judging," said Zenith, "perfect."

"I'm afraid your coffee maker was right," Vermillion said over the loud speakers, "the texts from Carl were threats. And more importantly, the incoming messages continue to be threats."

"Does he say what he's so mad about? I don't know what his problem is."

"The threat of violence in these instances appear to be in response to knowledge you have that he feels could get him in trouble."

Zenith frowned. "Weird. He never said or did anything to indicate he was in any trouble. The only thing he ever did was look up ancient galactic maps with me. That was ninety-five percent of our dates."

That information was quite enough for Zenith to deal with today. She didn't want to talk about it or think about it anymore. She decided to distract them. "Hey, look at this map, guys." She pointed at the console. "I think we should warp, because if we don't warp, then we won't even get there until- "

"Tomorrow," Helo finished her thought. "The earliest. What research?"

"Tomorrow? That's crazy. And what was that last part? What do you care about my research?"

Zenith felt woozy from thinking about Carl. She went back to the common room and sat down. She tried to take deep breaths. Helo followed her.

"Fine. My research involved ancient Intergalactic maps. My specialty," Zenith answered. She had no idea why he was interested, but it was at least better than talking and thinking about Carl. "I know, useless degree, blah, blah, blah. And for your information, I was doing just fine career-wise until I ended up here."

"Who's the nerd now?" Helo asked.

"Wait, did you say maps? Do you know about the Warg-O-Matic Corporation Intergalactic Scavenger Hunt?" Celeste was interested now.

Zenith nodded. She considered the whole thing a clever scam. Part advertising stunt, part contest, and part irresponsibly sending people into dark, unhealthy parts of space to generate daredevil viral interest. "I've heard of it. Why? What does that have to do with anything? Oh no, you guys aren't doing that, are you?"

"Oh," said Aquillon, "we're all over it."

"Let me get this straight, you're out here in space to help people, right? Civil Customer Service, a noble profession might I add, which you blow off for a stupid space publicity contest?"

"Whoa," Celeste said. "Stop with the judging. There's a lot of cash at stake."

"Plus, all of the internet fame." Aquillon chimed in.

Zenith couldn't believe her ears. "Vermillion? Are you in on this?"

"I'm afraid it's all very exciting. There are 8.12 trillion online references to this particular contest," Vermillion answered.

Zenith had had enough. "Alright, well if we're not going to get there until tomorrow anyway, I'm going to bed." Zenith grabbed the manual that Helo had tried to steal in the events of the last half hour and stomped off.

***

Vermillion Consciousness Processing Update #3393. All clear. Multi-dimensional scan has detected zero potential malefactors in this sector. The new female humanoid crew member, Zenith, is a satisfactory addition. The cyborg in Zenith's cell phone photograph that she refers to as Carl is also known as the Cyborg Caesar. The crew seems to be unaware of this fact. Since I am unsure if I the knowledge would be beneficial to them or not, I will await further context.

***

Zenith tried to read the manual to get to sleep. Normally, it would have worked like a charm, but the constant buzzing made it hard. That and Celeste gave her the absolute creeps. The room they shared had super high ceilings, along with a couple of beds, a couple of chairs and a desk. All in all it was pretty comfortable, but she wondered if Celeste was ever going to stop buzzing and go to sleep.

Zenith sat up and looked up at her. Celeste was up near the ceiling of the room, at least nine feet off the ground. "What are you doing?"

"Oh, hey," said Celeste. There was no face to flush, but by her tone, Zenith guessed her to be embarrassed. "Not used to having a roommate. I was chasing the light."

"Chasing the light?"

Celeste came down, eye to multiple eyes with Zenith. She waved a tentacle airily. "Chasing the light," she shook her top thorax, a move that sent a shiver from the tip of Zenith's head all the way down her body. "I guess it's an insect thing. Don't look at me like that, I will bite you."

"Look at you like what?" Zenith did her best to try to pretend that she wasn't screaming inside, that something primal wasn't telling her to run away, that Celeste had not just threatened to attack her. She realized she was holding her breath and tried to re-start breathing without attracting too much attention.

"I'm kidding," said Celeste, rolling her eyes, "look, I know you're from a backwater planet and all, but you need to lighten up."

Zenith let loose with a nervous, high pitched laugh. "I'm from a very respectable planet, thank you very much. By the way, why do you chase the light?"

"It's hard to explain. I just want it. Even if not physically, then psychologically. It's where we want to be. Darkness and light," she whispered that part, a faint, hissing sound. "I never thought about it philosophically, but it doesn't matter. The bottom line is, I see it, I want it, I go to it."

"Makes sense to me," said Zenith. That basically summed up her relationship with Carl before he went all moody and then apparently homicidal. Zenith briefly considered sleeping in the other room with the guys. They terrified her less, but she couldn't risk ticking off Celeste now that she had to live with her. The only thing she could do was to roll over, place the pillow on her head, and try to drown out the buzzing.

"Goodnight, Zenith." Vermillion's voice echoed pleasantly

around in her head, not on the ship's speakers, and it bothered her somehow. Sure, her best friend had been a coffeemaker, but Joyce was different. Zenith could read the scrolling messages from her CoffeeHelpr or just walk away. Joyce had never been inside of her head. She closed her eyes as hard as she could and hoped that this was something she could get used to.

"Goodnight," she replied.

CHAPTER 3

When Zenith woke, she was alone in the room. She threw on some shorts and went to the common room to see what everybody was up to.

"Ok, people, what's going on here?" They were all staring at a piece of paper that Helo was holding. "Thanks for waking me by the way."

"Thanks for putting on shorts," Celeste shot back.

"Oh, I see how it's going to be."

"Shorts are optional in the common room," Helo suggested.

Zenith rolled her eyes, sat down next to Helo, and looked at the paper in his hand. "I don't get why you guys are so excited about this."

"That's what I said at first," Celeste said, "but some super freaky things have happened since we started looking for it. And it's really fun."

"When did you start?" Zenith asked.

"Eighteen months ago," Helo said. "Hey, nobody said it was going to be easy."

"Fine," Zenith countered, "I'll play along. But these maps, only a few of them were made. Where'd you find one?"

"I stole it," Aquillon said. "I used to work for an off the books casino in Vega. One guy couldn't pay. I went to collect, and he didn't have the money. So he gave me this."

"Did the casino boss accept it as payment? And then why did he give it to you?" Zenith asked. Conversations with Aquillon were hard. It was like pulling teeth with him.

"Don't know," Aquillon said, "I stole it and jumped on this ship to get away. Anybody who helps me can have up to, oh, maybe even ten percent."

"It's the real deal, I'm telling you," Vermillion said over the loudspeaker.

That pushed Zenith over the edge. "Ok, I'm sorry to have to be the jerk who has to tell you that the map is not real. What part of publicity stunt don't you people get? Vermillion, why are you even encouraging this? What could you possibly know about a treasure map publicity stunts stolen from casino bosses?"

"Hurtful," Vermillion announced.

They all stared at her like she had just stabbed a pet cat.

"Oh, come on. Nobody believes in treasure maps in this day and age. I'll bet the publicity people who dreamed this up didn't expect anybody to ever actually try it." Zenith thought about it. "Wait, Aquillon, you ran out on the mob?"

"That's what I said."

"And as far as they know, you might've gotten the money from that guy if you hadn't stolen it."

"Guess so. That reminds me. Standard warnings apply, Zenith. You say a single word to anyone ever? And—" He made a throat-slashing gesture.

"Hey," Vermillion objected, "we're a family. We don't threaten to kill each other."

"Just kidding, Vermillion. You know what a joker I am," Aquillon answered her.

"Oh, yes. I get it. Good one," Vermillion said.

Aquillon mouthed the words, "I will kill you" while pointing at Zenith.

"Hey!" Vermillion said.

"Still kidding," Aquillon said and smiled. He wrote a note. "Vermillion is sweet and very nosy, but she doesn't always get context. If you tell anyone, I really will kill you." He showed her the note, balled it up, and then threw it away.

"You know I hate it when you guys do that, write things down so I can't see them," Vermillion said.

"No biggie, V. Just doodling," Aquillon said.

Zenith took several deep breaths. "What are they going to do if they find you?"

"Oh, they'll kill everybody on board for sure. Not you, Vermillion. They don't destroy ships, ok?"

"Why are you making her feel better and not me?" Zenith demanded.

"She's nice," Aquillon replied.

"Point taken. But I'm nice," Zenith said. "Sort of. I just don't believe in treasure maps is all. Since I'm not twelve." She sat back down, picked up the map and studied it for a moment.

"Still, you guys sit around here pooling your knowledge trying to find the next clue of this famous, if very irresponsible treasure hunt. Fine. That does sound slightly fun. At least better than just sitting around all day. Just don't be surprised if there's no pot of gold at the end of this rainbow."

Helo pulled the map away from her. "Aquillon's right, you're mean."

***

Vermillion Consciousness Update: Scanning all dimensions for malefactor entities. Entities found: 0. The person pictured in Zenith's photograph is known as the Cyborg Caesar, a participant in the current cyborg and robot war. The crew seems to be unaware of Carl's true identity. I am unable to determine whether or not this information is something they want to be communicated. The writing of the note seems to indicate that they do not want me participating in all of the communication. What to do? Will wait, perhaps this Cyborg Caesar will not cross our path in the future anyway, making my decision easier.

***

A series of chirps sounded nearby in the bridge room. Zenith walked over to take a look. The console was in map mode showing approximately one celestial hour until they would reach their destination.

She squinted at the map. Something seemed off. The destination was different than it was yesterday. She took a deep breath and swallowed. They were now off the map, and by a good distance.

Even the map itself on the console looked scary, Zenith thought, as she looked it over. Deep space, the area past the civilized planets was considered dangerous, even haunted. Some ships passed through the expanse only to come out on the other side with no living members on board. Even the ships with A.I. had been unable to help, having gone raving mad, or so said the tales. Since the robot/cyborg war started years ago, nobody ventured that far out anymore to verify the tales. The only thing the hokey map onscreen was missing was the disclaimer: "Here there be monsters."

Helo joined her.

"Why has the destination changed? Why aren't we going to the coordinates sent by headquarters yesterday?"

"The treasure hunt, remember? This is where we get the next clue," he pointed at the new destination.

Zenith bit her lip. *I prefer very much to be on the map.* "I think we should go straight to our official destination and get back as soon as possible."

"Hey, yesterday you were the one complaining about still hanging out on the outer rim and life being boring."

Zenith's mind boggled for a moment. "You do realize there's a big difference between being bored and being dead, right?" Zenith had a hunch. "Vermillion, can you show me a direct path from where we were yesterday to the location of our assignment?"

The map did indeed change. What the coordinates showed was that they had gone hours out of their way.

"Boo." Celeste snuck up behind Zenith.

Zenith started.

"No really," said Zenith. "This is crazy. You got me. The new girl is admitting that she's scared, ok? Turn us around, Vermillion, and take us back toward the service call. We're already two celestial hours late anyway."

"We're staying on course," Helo said.

Zenith ran a hand through her hair. "Why? The joke's over now. I admitted that you got me."

"The clue," Celeste said, having followed them into the bridge. "We follow the clues. And the next one is there."

Zenith swallowed hard. "I really can't talk you guys out of this? Vermillion? You're letting yourself and the rest of us sail right into danger for a long-shot treasure map?"

"I've got this," Vermillion said. "Besides, we're almost there."

"Look," said Helo, "you don't have to worry. There's something you should know. Vermillion is pretty powerful. And she's very protective of her crew."

"I'm sure you're great Vermillion, but I still don't feel better. What happens when we get there?"

"We put on our space suits and look for the next clue," Celeste said.

"What do you mean the next clue, aren't the clues on the map?"

"The clues are scantron. The map is interactive. It reads the clue and downloads the next one," Helo said.

Zenith didn't want to say it out loud, but the odds of them finding the treasure versus the odds of them being killed in the most terrifying part of deep space, being killed by Aquillon's old associates, or worst-case scenario, running into her ex, Carl, were not good. She wished more than anything right now that they were, in fact, the slacker crew they had pretended to be when she first joined up.

Vermillion lurched to a stop. "We're here."

The rest of the crew went to get their space suits. Zenith marched over to the common room, plopped herself down on the couch, and put her feet up.

"Aren't you coming?" Celeste asked.

"Nope."

"I thought you said you didn't want to just hang around the common room all day," Helo chided.

"Changed my mind. I'm good right here. You guys go play checkout scanner with the local wildlife in the middle of off the map deep space. Not me."

They continued without her, crossing to the exit. "Suit yourself," Aquillon said. "Get it, guys? Suit yourself?" He waited. "And we're going to be wearing space suits. You get it, right?"

"We get it," Celeste said, "you're just not funny, Aquillon."

"You're mean too."

"*You should go with them.*" It was Vermillion's voice inside of her head again.

"Not you too, Vermillion." Zenith realized the others heard her talking to Vermillion and giggled. *Huh*. Nothing about this was funny.

Vermillion persisted. "*You're part of the crew now. You should participate.*"

Zenith crossed her arms. "No means no, Vermillion."

She heard them go outside and shut the door.

"*Okay*," said Vermillion, "*we'll do it the hard way.*"

An eardrum piecing tone sounded in Zenith's head. She covered her ears and dropped from the couch to her knees. She was pretty sure she was screaming, but she couldn't even hear herself. After a few seconds, the tone stopped.

"What in stars name was that? Was that you, Vermillion?"

"*You'll find it's easier to just listen to me.*" It was a good thing Vermillion said the last part internally because she was pretty sure otherwise she would not have heard it through the reverb still ringing in her ears.

"That's assault. You ruined my eardrums. What is wrong with you?"

"Don't be a big baby. There's no more damage there than a kick-butt rock concert would have done. Besides, any damage is only temporary."

Zenith managed to get to a standing position and breathed. Everything seemed to be getting back to normal now.

"Hey, Zenith!" Helo's voice said over the ship's console speaker from the next room. She could barely hear it. "You need to come and see this. It's awesome."

"I recommend that you get your suit."

Zenith shook her head and decided to comply. "Ok, Vermillion, but this isn't over." It only wasn't over in that she intended to further complain about it later, but it was clear that she had no choice. She got her suit on and exited Vermillion.

She stomped over to where the rest of the crew was bending over a crater. "That crazy ship assaulted me." It occurred to her that what Vermillion had done was roughly the equivalent of flicking the ear of an annoying child.

"What'd she do now?" Celeste asked. "Was it the jolt of electricity? The annoying singing? The ear busting tone? Or the—"

Helo got Zenith's attention and pointed at his space suit's helmet before Zenith could reply. "Speakers. The speakers in our helmets are attached to the ship. She can hear everything you say. Whatever you're thinking right now should probably stay in your head."

Zenith's shoulders slumped. She decided to take his advice as her ears were still slightly ringing. She looked around. It looked like a typical moon, and there didn't seem to be anything strange around, so that was good. Celeste pointed into the crater. "Look, Zenith. We found it! That means I guessed the correct answer."

Zenith had to admit the excitement out here was contagious. She got down on one knee and peered into the hole. "So there was a clue on the map that led you out into the middle of this barren comet to this exact crater?" She had to admit, that was pretty impressive.

"Well, the last part of the clue is always a pair of coordinates. I guess in that respect it's kind of like a geocache."

That got Zenith excited, thinking about all of the times she had gone geocaching as a kid. The thrill of the hunt, and the promise of treasure at the end, no matter how small, never got old. Maybe she had been too hard on them trying to do the same thing, only theirs was extremely dangerous and corporate-sponsored. She remembered the old backpack she used to take with her full of old useless junk that she would exchange with the new useless junk she would find in the cache.

"Hey, the crater's mouth is in the shape of Arcturis City," Helo said.

Zenith stood up and took a few steps back. "Look at that, you're right." She knelt back down. "You figured out the clue, followed the coordinates to this exact spot, and inside was some sort of box?"

"Yeah," said Celeste, picking it up with an antenna. "It's just a small box. That's all it ever is, but that's not the exciting part. The exciting part is where you scan the box to get the next clue." She held the scanner in her hand. There was a beeping noise, and then Helo confirmed that it had registered on the map. Zenith couldn't help but marvel at the nifty use of technology with a fun twist.

"I get it. It's like a deep space geocache. Clever. You scan it and place it right back in its hiding spot, for the slower people to find, right?" Zenith asked, tongue in cheek.

"Of course. Why would we need it after we got the information? Only a jerk would take it and spoil all the fun," Celeste answered.

"Okay, yes," said Zenith, holding up her hands, "I was just checking. Can I see it?"

Celeste handed her the box. It was small and brown with light blue symbols and markings on it. "Are all the boxes marked up like this?"

"What?" Celeste asked. "I don't really look at them, I just scan them and start working on the next clue. Now that you mention it, this one looks more decorative than the ones we usually find. I think."

Zenith turned the decorative box over in her hands, continuing to look it over. The others turned to head back to Vermillion. The box made a slight rattling sound as she moved it. She shook the box, inspecting it even closer, and a small gem fell out.

The gem was smaller in size than an egg. It had the same

strange, decorative markings as the outside of the box. Zenith picked it up. Even through her space suit gloves, she could tell that it was smooth and pretty. She liked it instantly. In fact, it looked like the electronics disrupter toys she used to play with as a teenager.

"Celeste, did you say that all you have to do is scan the box?" Zenith asked Celeste through her helmet.

"Yes. Now put it back so that other people can use it. And get back here, we're already setting coordinates for the customer service call. That's what you've been waiting for, right?"

"Yeah. Okay. I'll put it back." There was no way to tell from the outside of the box that it had been opened, and by the weight of it, oddly enough, it was unclear that it was missing anything.

She palmed the small stone, figuring that it was probably a geocache and that if she treated it as such, there would be no harm in it. But what would she replace the stone with? The protocol for geocaching consisted of replacing the object you take with something else, something you had on your person.

She felt around in her pockets. The patches. There was a drawer full of fun, official-looking space patches in the bedroom she now shared with Celeste. They were a pretty red color with a blue triangle and a black dot in the middle. There was also some writing on it, but she hadn't been able to make it out. The patches were in her bedroom, though, so she had taken one as a souvenir. She pulled it out of her pocket now and placed the patch in the box and put the box back in the crater.

"Coming," she called out. She looked around the moon one more time, seeing nothing but beautiful stars and peace. Maybe this part of space wasn't so bad after all.

Chapter 4

The crew went back to their time-wasting preferences of choice in the common room. Several hours later, a new alarm chimed at the bridge. This one was unfamiliar to Zenith, who looked up from her reading. By the looks on their faces, it was unfamiliar to the other members of the crew as well.

"What's going on?" Zenith asked them.

Helo looked like he had just woken from a nap. He narrowed his eyes at Zenith. "What are you reading, there?" He got closer and squinted at the book in her hand. "*Best of the stupid things that happen all the time in the cosmos*, eh?" He shook his head. "Nice try, Zenith." He grabbed the book underneath to reveal that she was really reading the manual inside of the cooler looking book. "I knew it."

"Give it back," Zenith said, "we're getting closer to the job. And besides, isn't anybody going to check out that alarm? Because if you don't, I will. And I don't think you want that."

"You're right. I don't." He tossed the book onto the table and turned to go toward the bridge. Aquillon followed him. Zenith retrieved her book and followed them, curiosity getting the better of her.

Helo pushed the alarm button and started tapping on the console trying to figure out what it was.

Aquillon reached over and grabbed his club hopefully, then turned to Helo. "Am I gonna need this?"

"I don't know," said Helo, "this isn't the ship's alarm. And it's not mine. Somebody else set this one, and I don't know what it's for." Helo and Aquillon looked at each other. "If it's not Vermillion and it's not you and me, then it has to be Celeste. I doubt Zenith knows how to set any alarms yet, although she will soon if she keeps reading all of the stupid manuals."

They stomped back into the common room, ignoring her. She continued to follow them around.

"Celeste!" They said, together. Then they turned to each other.

"Shouldn't you have stayed at the console?" Aquillon demanded, looking at Helo, "what happens when she tells us what it's for? We just run back, then, don't we?"

"What do you morons want now? I'm busy," Celeste said.

"There's an alarm going off on the console," Aquillon said, "and we didn't set it. What're you up to? And what's coming for us that we don't know about?"

Fear rippled across Celeste's face.

"Code one, Celeste," Vermillion's voice boomed over the loud speaker.

"What is it this time?" Helo asked, more insistently this time, "why the alarm? And why the code one?"

Celeste didn't answer, she looked like she was starting to go into shock.

"Hey, Celeste, are you okay? What's a code one?" Zenith asked.

"Celeste, what's the alarm for?" Helo asked testily.

"Spiders, ok?" Celeste said. She snapped out of it and ran toward the bridge. "I set it to let us know if we ever picked up any giant space spiders, you know, roaming around off the map. I set that alarm so long ago that I forgot about it."

A primal fear swirled around Zenith's insides. She had picked a bad day to start picking up on Celeste's facial expressions because even if her reaction to spiders hadn't kicked in, the look of fear on Celeste's face would have made it happen anyway. And she had no idea that giant space spiders even existed or that they were to be avoided in deep space travel. The whole thing just seemed wrong.

"What's a code one?" Zenith asked again.

A clear, calm voice inside her head said. "*Zenith. A code one means fear*." It was Vermillion. Not on the loudspeaker, but in a little voice inside her head. Like last night. It shook her to her core. Again. Vermillion's ability to monitor the vital statistics and personal digital information of the crew was just creepy.

"*You're getting pretty close to a code one right now yourself*," Vermillion chimed in her head.

Zenith froze. It was a lot to take in. Did Vermillion have the same relationship with all of the crew? Or was it different for everybody? She wanted to know. It was very emotionally important to Zenith that the relationships in her life be purposeful and reciprocal. How weird was a relationship with a ship, anyway? She was currently living with a bug. And a reptilian-adjacent humanoid. And her previous best friend was a coffee maker. So probably, all in all, not that weird.

She approached the bridge with the others but hung back behind them. A major part of her didn't want to know a damn thing about space spiders. Were they giant? Super senses? Could they just float around in space waiting to pounce?

Stop it, she yelled at herself inside her head. She shook her head, trying to get the cobwebs out. Cobwebs? *Come on, Zenith. Shut up,* she told herself.

She thought about the conversation she had been having in her head for the last several minutes, wobbled over, and heaved herself into the nearest chair, trying not to hurl.

She scanned the nervous faces, the three stooges slapping of each other's hands from the console, and the entertaining bickering. She watched it like an out of body experience, like it wasn't happening to her as well. She watched Aquillon gesturing, his green muscles rippling. Celeste flitted here and there, slapping people with her antenna, and Helo arguing with them while raising his voice and gesturing. And all the while there were the beeping and the colored flashing lights. It was almost funny in a way.

Zenith peeked underneath and confirmed for herself that Celeste's feet, or what passed as them, were not, in fact, touching the ground. She knew this because she could detect the very faint humming sound over the rest of the noise that she made when she levitated. It wasn't flying, exactly, sometimes she simply seemed not to like touching the ground. Zenith wondered what that would be like.

Zenith was, in fact, still watching the ship's crew argue, point, and push buttons when she heard a small hiss somewhere behind her, barely audible over the noise.

"Guys?" She glanced first at the still arguing crew, but they had not noticed it. And if they heard her, they were not responding. She turned her head toward the central air lock, one of the few places on the ship capable of making that kind of hissing noise.

There was now a giant, hairy leg protruding out of the

airlock and into the ship. Then there were two.

Zenith's screams attracted the attention of the crew.

Chapter 5

Vermillion's voice boomed over the speakers. "Zenith- code one. Celeste- code one. Helo-code one."

Zenith wondered about Aquillon. Why wasn't he scared? As if in answer to her question, Aquillon darted past her eagerly on his way to the airlock, a giant club in his hand.

Zenith watched him and then felt her back hit a wall, just then realizing she was backing up. She hadn't taken her eyes off of the airlock, where there were now at least four giant legs and a bunch of spider eyes staring back at her. She was now against the far wall of the bridge.

She heard pronounced buzzing and turned her head slightly to see that Celeste was in the corner up against the ceiling, much like Zenith was against the wall. The buzzing noise was loud, though. If Celeste was trying to hide from the spider, there was no way this was a good strategy. Celeste was making so much noise that the spider could probably have heard her from outside in space.

She turned back to the airlock where Aquillon was clubbing one of the hairy legs that were furthest into the room. Way too far in.

Aquillon landed a solid shot on the leg, which instantly retracted toward the door. "That's right," he said proudly, "and—" He never finished his thought.

Another hairy leg extended, hitting him in the chest and knocking him against the far wall. Helo jumped onto the extended hairy leg and rode it like a bull, thrashing and screaming.

Zenith looked at Celeste in the corner again. She was still buzzing and thrashing about in fear against the window up by the ceiling.

Time seemed to slow down. Zenith looked back at the airlock where the spider was making its way into the ship. That thing was gonna break through. It was only a matter of time.

The guys were busy, and Celeste was so scared. Zenith had to do something. An idea popped into her head. It wasn't a particularly good idea, but she felt like time was running out on any better ideas that she might have in the future. The only trick would be to act without thinking because if she thought anything through she'd never move again. She'd sit terrified against the wall until the spider broke in and just ate her. And Celeste.

Zenith willed herself to move for a few seconds until her brain and body re-established a connection, and then, before she could talk herself out of it, she ran over to the corner, jumped high into the air, and grabbed Celeste by a low-hanging appendage.

Then she took off running with Celeste trailing behind like a helium-filled balloon. Celeste screeched, buzzed, and resisted the whole way.

Zenith's plan was simple. The only way to potential safety was past the spider. In their bedroom, behind the sealed metal door.

So, with both Celeste and Zenith screaming in terror, Zenith ran straight toward the airlock and hurdled a giant hairy leg that was laying across the entire length of the floor. The action was made easier because of Celeste's furiously beating wings which helped them get higher. Then she passed the airlock and the spider and Helo and Aquillon and kept right on going.

Zenith then continued down the hallway, realizing that she was still screaming. She opened the door to the girls' bedroom, pulled Celeste in, and then slammed the door shut. *It is a pretty good door,* thought Zenith, smacking it with her hand. It was solid metal. It should hold. Besides, how would the spider even know where they were? Would it break down every door in Vermillion looking for them? Would the spider just eat the rest of the crew?

Oh yeah, Vermillion. Why had Vermillion gone silent? Oh no, the rest of the crew.

"You!" Celeste landed and looked at Zenith, having recovered herself, at least temporarily from her earlier panic. "You could have killed me," she said, pointing an antenna right at Celeste's nose. She bared a set of insect teeth menacingly.

Zenith, nearly peed herself, falling backward onto the floor, shaking her head. "I thought the spider was gonna break through," she protested. "I figured it wouldn't track you down all the way over here. I don't know how systematic they are, or intelligent, or motivated. I mean I don't know anything about space spiders except that they're terrifying. I was scared for you. For us."

Celeste's teeth retracted, and her expression changed. She seemed to consider the whole sequence of events. "You saved me," she said. "On purpose." Another pause, then a smirk. Or so Zenith guessed. "You, like, hurdled a giant spider leg to get me out of there. Us, out of there."

"Well," said Zenith, smiling with relief and getting into the spirit of things, "you did help me get higher on the jump. I just wanted to buy us some time." Now that her roommate wasn't going to kill her now, or in her sleep, probably, there was the problem of the others.

She faced Celeste again. "Stay here," she said, "in fact, get in the shower. I'm guessing the spider probably can't break down two doors."

Zenith turned to leave, but then turned back again, "hey, look, if it does somehow get in here, stay on the ground, okay? Don't fly. When you're in danger, real danger, the buzzing: it's a dead giveaway that you're prey. I could hear it across the room, and predators can probably hear it a mile away. I know it's probably instinct, but it's a really bad idea." She pushed Celeste into the shower and closed the door.

"Where are you going?" Celeste's echo-ey voice asked from inside the shower.

"I'm going to help the others."

"How?"

"I have no idea," Zenith answered.

***

Zenith took a deep breath, listened to her heart thunder in her chest for a moment, and then threw the door open. Exiting out into the hallway, she slammed the door shut again. Once she was sure that it was closed completely, she made her way down the hall. Vermillion seemed to be online again, with all of her code ones for everybody who was currently scared.

Vermillion! "Hey, Vermillion," she yelled, "I don't know

anything about giant space spiders. Can you help me out? What can I do?"

Vermillion always seemed concerned about them, so Zenith wondered why she wasn't doing anything to help them out now.

She turned another corner to find Aquillon swinging his club again, but his non club-wielding arm looked gimpy. Helo was slashing wildly in all directions with a sword. *Oh crap.* This was not going well at all.

"Hang on," said Vermillion. "These space spiders, they have a chemical component on their legs that freezes up my components. I keep force-rebooting."

One of Helo's swings lopped off a length of spider leg. The spider twitched in a fury. Helo froze sword in his hand, only to get knocked down by another leg. His sword skittered loudly across the floor, now out of reach. The spider screeched in victory and made it all the way into the room.

No! The noise the spider made, coupled with the unpredictable, twitchy movements, turned Zenith's blood to ice. It was loose and free inside the space ship. She wished herself back in her room, in the shower hiding with Celeste, who she hoped was not currently buzzing.

Truth be told, Zenith might have buzzed herself given the chance. The thought of death by giant space spider oozed into her consciousness. Her brain was now overloading on adrenaline, and she was possibly going into shock. She could only keep one thought in her mind.

"Vermillion? Vermillion, we need help!" Zenith could hear her own shrill, screeching voice, but was unable to stop herself. Her screaming drew the attention of the spider, which twitched in her direction. She could now see eyes.

"Vermillion! We're all going to die." *Mostly me right now, though.* Zenith fell backward. The spider was in the center of the room just outside of the airlock. Aquillon, and Helo were on the other side of it. Celeste was in her room. There was no hiding now. She was alone, with the full attention of the spider. She crawled backward, hearing the shouts of the others who could do nothing to help her.

"Electricity," said Vermillion at last, out of nowhere, over the speakers. "Electricity can kill it. Its immune system is weak...all you have to do is...." There was a whine of energy, which Zenith could only imagine was Vermillion rebooting again. And then there was only the sound of the pounding of her heart. Her heart raced as she maintained eye contact with the spider, the only question now was when it would pounce.

Its gaze was fixed on her, and it kept twitching in her general direction, getting a better look. Zenith glanced and felt around for a knife, a weapon, anything. Nothing but floor. The spider stopped twitching at her. The shouting by Helo and Aquillon on the other side resumed. They were trying desperately to distract it.

She sat up slightly. Maybe it would work. Maybe the spider would turn and again engage the armed crew members shouting at it and poking it.

It didn't turn to them, though. Zenith was sure that it was looking right through her soul, her body shuddered and began to shiver. She tried to keep herself still and failed. Then it charged, lightning fast.

She closed her eyes and hoped it wouldn't hurt. The darkness helped a little. It enveloped the terror in her mind with uncertainty. In that one moment, uncertainty was slightly better than death, which would come in a second or two. Any time now. Much to her surprise, she found that it would have been nice, in that moment, to hear Vermillion in her head. A familiar, friendly voice to send her on her way.

In the darkness, her other senses heightened. She heard three things. The horrible patter of giant spider feet rushing toward her, Vermillion humming back online, and another sound. A crackling noise and a muffled, inhuman scream.

***

Zenith cracked an eye open. Celeste was standing next to her with a stun gun in her hand, the other end of which was embedded in the eye wall of the giant spider, which was writhing and twitching and making an inhuman screaming noise that Zenith knew would haunt her nightmares until the very end of her days, which she hoped was quite a while from now.

From the other side of the spider, a heavy club descended on the spider's center with a sickening thud. The spider stopped moving, having curled itself into a hairy, grotesque ball about one-tenth its former size.

Zenith wasn't ready to move. In fact, she wasn't at all sure she ever wanted to move again.

"It's okay, Zenith, I got you," Celeste said, obviously proud of herself. She began stroking various body parts of Zenith's body with her antenna and making what could possibly pass as soothing noises.

Zenith relaxed into a fetal position on the floor.

"Good work, everybody!" Vermillion exclaimed, humming back online. "I'm so proud of every one of you."

When Zenith thought it through later, she figured it had taken every one of them, together, to survive. They had helped Vermillion by killing the spider. Vermillion had helped them by telling them its weakness in the midst of rebooting cycles. Zenith had saved Celeste from her instinctual panic, who after having calmed down and heard Vermillion's proclamation, remembered the stun gun she kept in her purse for emergencies. The boys had held it at bay, clubbing, slashing, and grabbing at it as best they could while getting injured in the process. Putting it all together like that, and feeling that she was finally getting a handle on getting to know the rest of the crew, she was doubly surprised that she was actually alive.

***

Vermillion Consciousness Processing Update # 3394. All clear, for now. Multi-dimensional scan has detected zero potential malefactors in this sector. The infiltration of the spider has resulted in superficial damage to the multi-dimensional scanning processors. The scan must be re-run within single digit celestial hours to be sure. The crew appears to be okay. If these people only knew that there are far worse things lurking just out of current boundaries than space spiders and warring robots and cyborgs.

CHAPTER 6

Zenith and the others eventually staggered back to the common room and collapsed into their spots.

"You guys travel around the universe scanning little boxes for clues and battling giant space spiders? That was pertinent information that should have been disclosed before I signed up, you know."

"Sure," Aquillon said, "that's what you say until we find the treasure. Then it'll be 'where's my cut?'"

"In our defense, that was our first ever giant space spider. Who knew they could get in an airlock like that. Am I right?" Helo said.

Zenith decided to let that one go. "Hey, Helo, I think I'm now fairly prepared to do a bad job with customer service when we get there. When will that be?"

There was more chirping from the console.

"Very soon," Helo said.

"Zenith shook her head. "What in stars name are these people doing way out here in the middle of the intergalactic Bermuda triangle? And you're telling me that you want me to waltz into the city of a robot crime lord and NOT fix his computer."

"It probably won't be his computer, the space station is just technically his city. And yes, you have to fail. And don't screw it up."

"You mean yes, I should screw it up."

"Knock it off," Vermillion announced. "You guys are already eleven celestial hours late."

Zenith stood up as the shock hit her. She was actually late to a job. For the first time in her life. Well, she had been late to jobs before, but the normal five or ten minutes accounting for traffic or wardrobe malfunctions or minor zombie apocalypses. Not eleven hours.

"That's right, and you're the one who insisted that we show up late, Helo. No way. I'm out. You can go in there late and not fix the computer. I'm not comfortable with it."

"Helo's right, though. New person takes the first job," Celeste chimed in.

"Were you ten plus celestial hours late to your first job?" Zenith asked.

"Fifteen," Celeste answered, antenna bobbing. "It's no big deal out here. Most of them kinda expect it."

"But I'll bet the client wasn't at the lair of a robot crime lord!" Zenith continued to protest.

"Oh, most of our customers are bad guys in the iffy part of space," Aquillon answered, shrugging.

"Then what happens if we get a job at Regal? What are you going to do then?"

"Hide?"

"Why can't I hide, then?"

"Look," Helo said, sitting down next to her on the couch, "they have no reason to hate you. Or to hurt you. As far as they know, you're here to help, right?"

"Won't they be mad when I don't fix their computer? Isn't that why we're there in the first place?"

"The trick is to just make stuff up," Helo said, "throw around a lot of made-up jargon. Make whatever the issue is sound crazy impossible to fix. Like their best bet is to call the manufacturer and get them to send a brand new unit. Most of these people are idiots anyway. They won't understand the difference."

Zenith tried to stare a hole in his forehead. "Manufacturers don't send brand new units. Not even if you have the dated receipt, a list of customer service online video sessions, and video of the unit malfunctioning up to and including causing injuries and property damage." Zenith knew this for a fact, as it had happened to her.

"You know that, and I know that," Helo said. "But if they already knew that then they wouldn't have called us, would they?"

"What happens when this robot crime lord figures out we lied to him? Then what?"

"You worry too much," Helo said, "we'll be long gone. And

these guys are busy, they have better things to do than to track us down."

"How many of these calls have you been on?" Zenith asked.

"Couple of dozen," Celeste said.

"And you've never actually helped anybody?"

"Damn straight. Zero percent customer satisfaction. A perfect record," Aquillon said.

Zenith did the math. She didn't like it. She did the math again. That's a couple of dozen pissed off crime organizations, plus Aquillon's racket and Carl, her ex-boyfriend. She began to hyperventilate.

Given any length of time into the future, giant space spiders might be the least of their worries. "So why not just fix the issues? Why make everybody angry, and also be bad at your jobs?"

"Weren't you listening? We need the free time to unwind. And for the scavenger hunt. We're going to be famous!" Helo said. His feet were up on the couch, and he was playing a game on his phone. Zenith felt like she had entered an alternate dimension.

"Hey, everybody. We have arrived at our destination," Vermillion boomed, louder than usual this time unless it was Zenith's imagination. "Get out, you bunch of slackers. You have a job to do. Or not do. I don't care, just get going."

***

The Cyborg Caesar paced back and forth, his cell phone held close to his head. "Yes, as I've said a number of times, I'd like to upgrade my account. How many times do I need to repeat myself? It's 'C-A-e-s-A-r.' Got it? Yes, that's my legal name."

An underling approached him, mumbling something so that he couldn't hear what the customer service rep on the other end of the line was saying. He waved him off menacingly, making a steel fist.

"I'm sorry," he said, "could you repeat that?" He paused. "No. You got it wrong again. You wormhole-ridden piece of slimy plutonium, I oughta— hey, hang on a minute, would you?"

He gestured for his right-hand man, or in this case, machine, Vax to approach, before turning his attention back to his phone. "Okay. You. Let's start with something simple. What's YOUR name?" He bit his lower lip while he listened and felt the unusual sensation of physical pain. His lower lip was one of the very few bits of him that wasn't cybernetically enhanced.

"Jook Uilneaasd," he repeated, "got it." He smiled and motioned to Vax. "Hey, Vax, I want you to jump in a shuttle, get yourself over to Virgon-Three as soon as possible, and annihilate this Jook guy, got it?"

Vax turned to obey.

"What?" The Cyborg Caesar asked. "Oh, you heard that part, did you? So you are capable of listening. Interesting. What's that? You're going to report me? Threat of bodily harm on a civil servant? Don't make me laugh, how are you going to report me if you can't get my name right?" He shook his hair, something he loved to do since it was made entirely of very expensive and extremely rare 35mm film. He loved the sound that it made as it fell in long curls and rattled dramatically.

Vax turned back to look at him, questioning whether the order was rhetorical. "No really," he said, "get going, Vax. Text me when it's done. No, Jook, I wasn't talking to you, was I?"

The Cyborg Caesar's day simply wasn't going the way he had hoped. He decided to hang up and dial the number again to get a different guy. These days it was all luck of the draw, the number you drew in the roulette wheel of life simply depended on who you happened to run into, whether it was in person or on the phone.

He hung up and frowned. Another underling approached. He sighed. "What now? Can't you see that I'm busy?"

"Sir, it's important news. News you've been waiting for. You specifically said that when this news became available that you wanted to hear it immediately no matter what—"

He pointed the weapon that was his right hand and pointed it at the babbling underling. "WHAT. IS. THE. NEWS?"

"Oh. Yes, sir, right away, sir."

He armed the weapon that was his right hand, which made a whining sound, and raised an eyebrow at the underling, daring him to spend another second not telling him the news.

"Oh, the scout at Parallax city, sir. He said he found the item in question. Found it yesterday and didn't even bother to tell anyone. In fact, sir, that's the last communication we received from him, he's been unreachable, and we fear something may have happened to him."

The Cyborg Caesar disarmed the weapon. "The item in question. In Parallax City. You don't mean."

"Yes, sir. It's true. He found it. At least that's what the scout said."

"And he didn't tell anybody. He wants to run off with it. He has to know that Parallax will never let him leave, with or without it. What's he thinking?"

"I don't know, sir. And the only guy we had keeping an eye on him isn't responding anymore."

"Did our spy give any indication that Parallax had any idea what's going on?"

"No, sir."

"Okay," he said, starting to pace again, "that's good. That's just fine. Now all we have to do is go and take it. That's very good news indeed."

He walked over to his custom-built, titanium throne. It was beautiful. Ornate designs and symbols in a glowing blue were etched into the metal, enduring reminders of his goals, hopes and dreams. He placed a fleshy index finger on the glowing image of a Dragon figurine.

Then he sat on his throne with a crackle, feeling the energy coursing through him. He closed his eyes and sent out his orders, converting his will and wishes into alt binary and sending them out to his minions. He opened his eyes when he was done. The electrical charge always boosted his mood, strength, and energy levels.

"Ok," he said, "the plan is made, my orders have been sent. Everybody suit up. Let's do this."

***

The crew exited Vermillion into a very large, lavishly decorated space station that looked like it had been built out of an abandoned shopping mall. There was even a sign that said, "Parallax City" in neon green letters.

Zenith looked around, having never been to the city of a robot crime lord in the middle of one of the worst parts of deep space before. It was quite nice, actually. "Well, Parallax certainly isn't flying under the radar," Zenith said.

"There's no need to out here, that's what I keep telling you," Helo said. "They have deep space all to themselves."

"Well, they can keep it, along with whatever spiders and monsters are out here. I can't wait to get back to the civilized planets myself."

The hallways were packed with people scurrying from here to there. If Zenith didn't know any better, she'd have thought it was just another city with people going to and from work and going about their lives, not the city of a robot leader out in the most terrifying part of space.

She spotted a directory and crossed to it. It appeared that most of the department stores and food court names had been covered with new images and numbers that told people where to go for office type businesses, housing areas, and restaurants. Upon further inspection, some of the original mall stores remained, albeit it off in a corner.

It had been a while since she had gone shopping, but she banished that thought from her mind. She was here to do a job. Or not do it, as the case may be, although she wasn't at all sure she'd be able to pull off the not doing your job thing. It went against every fiber of her being. First things first, though.

The directory told her how to get to the front desk. "This way," she said, and led the crew down the crowded hallways into the heart of the space station.

Zenith was still marveling at how huge the place was when they got to the front desk, which had a sign over it that said *Welcome Desk. Huh,* thought Zenith, *maybe Helo was right after all.* For a robot city, the place seemed ordinary. Maybe they could just get in, fix or not fix the computer, and get out without any major catastrophes.

A tall, thin guy that looked like he was covered in seaweed eyed their approach suspiciously from behind the desk. "Mining, banking, retail, or Parallax business?"

So much for a warm welcome, Zenith thought. "None of those, we are Civil Customer Service, actually. We are here to assist one," she looked down at the order receipt, "Darby Ooieand."

"Darby, eh?" Seaweed asked. "Just for the record, then, that counts officially as Parallax business."

Zenith swallowed and took a deep breath. She was hoping to have steered very far from Parallax business, but here they were.

"To get to Darby, you have to go down this hallway," he pointed over his shoulder and to the left, "then you take a right and a left and another left until you get to sector D. Darby's in room 721. And make it quick, would you? Darby has a lot of work to do."

Zenith imagined that Seaweed guy was suspicious of her, but hoped she was wrong. The rest of the crew, sure, but she was perfectly normal. And besides, she was here on official business with an order receipt and everything.

The crew continued on their way under his watchful eye and were soon out of sight. "What was that guy's problem?" Zenith asked.

"What did you expect?" Helo asked. "You can't take it personally. Nobody trusts anybody this far out into space."

"But this place looks so normal."

"Sure, it looks normal, and most of the time it is. I mean, they're jumpy, sure, but we've never run into any real problems on these service calls. Other than getting yelled at and then receiving all of the formal complaints."

Zenith stopped walking. "Formal complaints? You guys have formal complaints?" She started to hyperventilate again.

"They don't mean anything. No matter how many you get, they never seem to dock your pay or anything. Aquillon has the most."

"Yup, no problems at all. Just a note in your file. Angry customer due to unforeseen on-site complications. If you word it like that, then you're free and clear. They have no choice but to file it and forget it, because the next level of escalation involves them personally flying out here to help the affected party, and we all know that is never going to happen."

"But the technology we're talking about here is so old and so simple. It would be a snap to fix."

"Retro," Helo answered. "Is super in with these outlaw types. They can't call into traditional onscreen customer support without being traced. So, they go with ancient technology. It's older and more finicky, but it's impossible to trace with today's technology. That's why, if something goes wrong, they're stuck calling us. Sometimes it's harder than you would think to fix these outdated computers running their old programs."

"How would you know? You don't even try to fix them. Hey, can Vermillion hear me still?" Zenith pointed at her own head.

"We're probably out of range now, why?" Celeste asked.

"Just wondering if it freaks anybody else out that she's a voice inside your head. That she has access to all of our medical and digital information."

"This coming from a woman whose best friend was her coffee maker?"

"Well, Joyce was great. You're just going to have to get over that, Helo. And at least Joyce wasn't inside my head, okay? I had a choice, I could read or not read the scrolling text."

"Well, just don't do anything to piss her off," Helo said. "She's ex-military. Like everyone else in Civil Customer Service, she's running from her past."

"How can a space ship be ex-military? Or have a past? "

"Trust me. It's complicated." He continued walking down the corridor. Zenith and the rest of the crew followed him. They made their way into the heart of the space station toward the housing area, as the Seaweed guy had directed them until they came to a stop outside of the room they had been directed to. This area of the space station looked like the housing area. All of the doors were the same style and had numbers on them. They stared at Zenith. She knocked on the door.

"Hello? Mr. Darby? My name is Zenith, and I'm here with the Civil Customer Service responding to your request for technical help."

The crew frowned at her in unison.

"What? There's a script for this sort of thing. In the manual. Which you guys would have known if you had actually read it."

"I don't know, guys. She sounds like somebody who's going to fix a computer," Helo said savagely.

Aquillon glared at her and made a throat slash gesture.

"Zenith is just messing with you guys," Celeste said, "Right, Zenith? We're a team, right? And we were very clear on this point, you're not supposed to fix anything."

"Oh, grow up, you guys," Zenith said and knocked on the door again. They were still glaring at her when the door opened and a mousy guy in a ratty suit and drooping mustache let them in.

"It's about time you guys got here," the guy said. "I called for you forty galactic hours ago, for stars' sake."

"I do apologize for the inconvenience, Darby, may I call you Darby?" *Script,* she mouthed to her co-workers before turning back to the customer. They continued to glare at her.

Darby seemed to notice the turmoil between the team, but he pressed ahead anyway. "The computer's right here. I'm trying to send this message, and it's not working. This message, it's really important, though, ok? And it's confidential."

That caught Zenith's interest. A secret message. She was determined to eavesdrop even if she didn't fix the computer, and frankly, she was starting to dislike the whole zero percent satisfaction thing. What's the worst that could happen if she broke their stupid streak anyway? Was she supposed to spend her entire career in Civil Service sitting around the ship doing nothing while racking up formal complaints? The idea made her skin crawl. She approached the computer in question. Helo matched her step for step.

"Back off," she told Helo, "you told me to do it. I got it."

"That's what I'm afraid of," he muttered.

"What's going on here, anyway?" Darby asked.

"Nothing," Helo said, "just training a new employee."

Zenith pretended to cough into her hand and spat out an obscenity.

Celeste grabbed Helo and pulled him back. "For heaven's sake, Helo, let the woman work." Celeste then shot a warning look at Zenith, who turned to Darby's computer.

Darby himself had disappeared toward the back of the room, rummaging in a sack. *Good,* thought Zenith, *let's get a look at this secret message.*

The computer was out of date and the software looked even older. The screen itself had frozen on a web search that was of cringe-worthy quality and absolutely filthy. Zenith glanced at the guy in the corner before deciding how to proceed.

"Oh, grow up. What are you, twelve?" he asked, noticing her glance from across the room.

"I didn't say anything," Zenith said and restarted the computer.

"No, don't do that," Helo said. It was too late.

"Why not?" Darby asked.

"Well, if you thought restarting the computer would fix the problem, then why didn't you just do that yourself in the first place," Helo asked him.

"I'm not qualified for that sort of thing, am I? Besides, I'm busy."

They all stood there awkwardly waiting the several minutes that it took the computer to come back up. Zenith would normally make small talk with the client, but he was off sulking in the corner, and her coworkers were watching her like angry hawks, so there wasn't anything to say. The room itself was messy but well furnished. Zenith looked around and noticed that there were framed magazines on the wall, most of which involved classic archeology.

"Hey," Zenith said, pointing at the walls, "I studied a lot of these guys in college."

"Good for you," Darby said, not looking up. He didn't sound like he meant it.

Zenith decided to take that opportunity to grab a chair at a desk across the room and noisily drag it over in front of the computer so she could sit. The tension in the room was palpable when she sat down and the computer finished restarting and came back up. Thank goodness.

Much to her surprise, the computer itself was not password protected. Odd. She brought up the program and the message that Darby was obviously intending to send popped up on the screen. She read it. Then she read it again and frowned. The more she read it, the more unsure she was of what to do next.

"Well?" Darby asked in a demanding voice. He had moved closer now and was studying her face. "Did the program come back up?"

"Um, er, yes. Actually, it did. Look, there it is."

"Why are you babbling?" Helo asked.

Darby crossed the rest of the room to stand in front of the computer. He studied the screen and the message. His hand moved to push send.

Zenith didn't slap his hand away, exactly, she just sort of bumped and temporarily redirected it.

"Hey, what are you doing?" Darby asked.

"I'm just wondering," Zenith said, daring a worried glance behind her at the crew, "if you're absolutely sure that you want to hit send. On that particular message. I mean, it looks like the sort of message that's not going to have any takebacks. If you know what I mean."

"You have the nerve to come here multiple galactic hours late, bickering into my room, acting very unprofessional and then judge my messages?"

"Hey," Zenith answered, "who are you calling unprofessional? I read the Customer Service scripts, from memory, exactly how they were phrased in the manual. I got your stupid, ancient computer here working and there it is. Your precious message. So, you just think twice about who you're going to call unprofessional." She took several deep breaths. "I also happen to know from experience that professionals bicker all of the time."

With a scowl on his face, he reached across her and pushed the send button.

That sent a shock wave through Zenith's mind. She hoped to low orbit that the computer would freeze again. *Don't send, don't send, don't send* was the mantra in her head.

The message sent.

Zenith's mind raced. There was only one thing to do. She jumped up. "Thank you for utilizing Civil Customer Service, we sincerely hope you were satisfied with the support you received today. Make sure you check your inbox in the next twelve to twenty-four hours for a survey that could win you various prizes."

She turned to the crew. "Guys, we have to leave now. And I mean right now."

CHAPTER 7

Carl entered his ship. It bothered him that it was shaped like a whale. He liked sleek and silver, not giant, lumpy, and icky blue. When he was in charge, the first thing he'd change would be his ship.

He was still buzzing from the jolt of his throne. Syncing gave him a buzz that was unlike anything he had ever experienced as a human. Human. It seemed so long ago that he had to search for any piece of connection that he had left.

That's probably what bothered him so much about Zenith refusing to turn cyborg. How could she research the GalaxyDragon with him for months, and feel its pull, and not want to feel it for herself? Maybe she didn't feel the pull. He pitied her. Was it possible that for her it was just ancient information on a page?

He sat in his chair as the ship filled up with some of his minions. "How many ships are leaving with us?"

"Twenty-four," his minion said. "There's something else."

"What is it?"

"One of the subjects that you're tracking is on Parallax's Space Station right now."

"Who?"

"It's that human you jettisoned, Zenith."

Carl puzzled. "What are the odds of that, do you know?" He waited while the minion tried to do the math. "Stop it. I'm just kidding. I know she's there, I sent her there. My victory will be complete. She will see the error of her ways, and it will be too late." He closed his eyes and pre-savored the moment. "Okay, get us there quick."

***

Zenith knew that they had better get out of Darby's room right now. His message was a call for mutiny, and it wouldn't be long before the fighting broke out. She beat the rest of the crew to the door to show them she meant business and threw it open, only to see Seaweed guy standing there with a gun pointed at them.

"Back inside," he said, motioning with the weapon.

Zenith raised her hands. "Hey, we're just Customer Service people. We fixed the computer, and now we have another job to get to. You don't need us, he's the one you want."

"How do you even know what I want?" Seaweed guy asked.

Zenith swallowed.

"Snitches get stitches," Darby said to Zenith.

"Hey, don't talk to her like that," said Helo.

"All of you shut up," Seaweed guy said, "where's the Galactic Dragon, Darby? I know you have it."

It's Galaxy Dragon, and is he kidding? Why does that keep coming up and who would even care? This customer service call was taking a weird turn that even Zenith didn't see coming.

"Moss," Darby said, pointing at Zenith and then the crew, "these guys tried to steal it. You'd better deal with them before it gets out of hand."

"Liar!" Zenith said. "Moss, is it? Well, this guy just sent a whopper of a message to some other crime lord, presumably, saying that you guys were holding him against his will. And you're obviously not. He looks free to me. Anyway, this other organization is on their way to attack you right now. So, we can vouch for you and all, but this really isn't any of our business, so we'll just be on our way." Zenith tried to squeak by him with her hands raised, but Moss wouldn't have it.

"You stand over there with the rest of them at the back wall," he motioned towards Zenith and the crew. "And I'll take care of you myself, Darby. Where is it?"

"I don't know what you're talking about," Darby said.

"It's probably in that sack behind his bed," Zenith said.

Everybody turned to look at her.

"Hey, the guy's lying about me. That pisses me off. Plus, he's like, trying to start a mutiny so he can sneak off with whatever it is he's hiding." She glared at Darby and rolled her eyes. "Because I highly doubt that he found the actual Galaxy Dragon. Because it's a myth."

Moss ignored her and crossed the room, gun trained on Darby. He found the bag. He dumped the contents onto the bed.

"I can't believe it," Moss said, "I swear I thought the scout we had watching you was lying. You actually found it." He picked up the figurine that came out of the bag. It was about five inches high and looked heavy. "The Galactic Dragon."

"Give it back," Darby said and pulled a weapon of his own out of his shorts. "It's mine."

"Ew," said Celeste, "where were you hiding that?"

"Galaxy Dragon, not Galactic Dragon," Zenith said, correcting him. "And wait a minute," Zenith started putting the pieces together, "if that's the Galaxy Dragon, and I'm not ready to concede that it is, but for the sake of simplicity let's agree that you think it is, then the particular crime lord in question that you contacted would be—"

"The Cyborg Caesar," said Darby, a smirk on his face that was apparently meant to intimidate Moss.

"*Whew*. For a minute there, Zenith was worried he'd say Carl. She tried to address Moss again. "Whatever. I mean, can't you guys just mutiny and/or shoot each other without us standing here as witnesses?"

The rest of the crew shot Zenith a very dirty look. She ignored it. "Look," she pleaded, "make a smart decision. We can get out of here before anything even happens. No witnesses. No loose ends. You guys do whatever in stars you want to do to each other and leave us out of it. What do you say?"

"What do you think, Darby?"

Darby seemed to consider it. Then he turned and pointed his gun at Zenith's group and shot Aquillon in the foot.

Aquillon screamed, Darby then shot at Moss, who dropped the Dragon and took cover behind the bed. Darby grabbed the Dragon. Zenith bolted for the door.

Once outside, she held the door open for the rest of the crew and then slammed it shut. They raced back toward Vermillion.

"I can't believe you fixed his computer," Helo said angrily.

"Really? That's what you got out of all of that? Do you honestly think that now is the best time to have this conversation?" Zenith asked in between breaths as they raced toward the next turn.

"How many times did we warn you?"

"Ok, in my defense, it was a total coincidence that the message I helped send might get us all killed," she answered, "a million to one odds. Like getting struck by lightning."

"Our perfect record down the drain."

"If it makes you feel any better, I don't think he's going to fill out the survey. And we have bigger issues here than your stupid record." Zenith stopped and screamed in frustration. "I forgot to have him sign the form. Technically it doesn't count as fixed unless the customer signs the form."

"Keep moving," Celeste said and grabbed her by the arm, "are you crazy? Nobody cares about your stupid form right now."

A row of armed guards moved into their field of vision, stopping everybody in their path.

"Parallax's men," Helo said, stopping and raising his hands, "they must've gotten wind of the mutiny."

The guards rounded everybody up and sealed all the exits out of the large open clearing in the D-section area of the space station. They found themselves in the center with everybody else next to the annoying drip-drop of a sea serpent water fountain.

That's when Parallax himself, a large, orange robot with flame red eyes came around the corner and strode toward them, past them, and toward Darby's room without a word, while the crowd and the guards looked on. He went into the room and shut the door. There were eight to ten weapon blasts, and then Parallax came striding out with what everybody around here obviously thought was the Galaxy Dragon in his hand, eyeing it like it was worth billions of galactic credits.

What kind of hoax is this? Zenith wondered what caused them all to be so caught up in this object, anyway. She had studied it for months. For Carl. They had studied every piece of literature and history ever written about it. Zenith had concluded that it was a fairy tale, but Carl had become obsessed. It's what brought them together in the first place and ultimately what broke them up.

Was it possible that the object Darby found was the figurine that people had spent eons searching for? And the only reason they could be this excited was if they thought that the fairy tales were true. Untold power to any being that was within seven percentage points of the exact necessary ratio of human to machine. Magic. Power. Reality. Was it all fluid in the right, or wrong hands of the Galaxy Dragon? Zenith didn't believe in it herself, but she was starting to believe in the sort of violence and destruction that its discovery would bring. And the only thing she knew for certain was that she and the rest of the crew had better get out of there and soon.

She glanced at Aquillon who just stood there bleeding. "You okay?"

"I've been better," he answered, "but I'm okay for now."

"If we get the chance, do you think you could run?"

"Oh yeah," said Aquillon, "just watch me."

The message Darby had sent asked the Cyborg Caesar to attack immediately. If they weren't out of time already, they would be very soon. That rat Darby expected to escape from both Parallax and the Cyborg Caesar in the chaos. She suspected that Moss was planning on doing the same thing. All in all, it wasn't a bad plan. In fact, it might be the crew's only hope. She whispered it to Celeste, who passed it on as they stood in the crowd under armed guard in the middle of the large room.

Darby's door flew open. An injured Moss came screaming out of there, weapon firing in all directions. The crowd they were in scattered as the guards trained their weapons and attention on Moss.

"Let's go," Zenith said, and they sprinted down the hallway trying to make their way toward Vermillion.

"If we can get within range, Vermillion can help us," Helo said.

"How?" Zenith asked. "By bursting their eardrums?"

"She has technology that can disrupt and disable cyborgs and robots, but it's a very close-range weapon, we'd have to be well within the sound of her voice."

"Wow, you weren't kidding about her being ex-military?"

"No, I wasn't kidding. She has a lot of hidden capabilities. Let's just say there isn't another ship like her in this universe."

"How come you know all of this?"

"It's a secret. And not in an *I'd love to tell you* kind of way, in a *she will literally kill me if I tell you* kind of way."

They rounded the corner at full speed and ran smack into a different batch of armed people. Cyborgs. One tripped Helo, and he went skidding forward onto the linoleum floor, all the way to a bare, steel foot.

"Helo!" Zenith froze and put up her hands when she saw the new armed combatants, but she couldn't help but watch Helo go flying across the floor. When she saw him stop, her shoulders slumped, and her heart raced. She knew that steel foot.

"Hey, babe," Carl said, "what is this, some kind of foreplay you got going on here with squishy man?" He inspected and then dismissed Helo. "I have to say, Zenith, he looks like a serious downgrade compared to me."

Zenith could barely hear what was going on over the sound of her heart pounding. She thought of her apartment complex, the threats, and Joyce.

"Shut up, Carl. It's not like that. And besides, it doesn't matter, you're too late, Parallax already has the Galaxy Dragon. I saw it with my own eyes." She was scared and bluffing, but If he was distracted by that stupid figurine like everyone else, then maybe they could get away.

Carl crossed toward her. She tried to back up, but a guard stopped her.

"Your own eyes, eh?" Carl asked. He grabbed her by the shoulders. "You see nothing. You should have taken me up on my offer to replace those weak eyes with some seriously powerful vision. Beyond anything you could imagine."

"I don't want anything beyond my imagination, Carl." She shook herself free, if only temporarily. "I want reality. Normal, boring, reality. Not magical figurines or cybernetically enhanced everything. Why is that so hard for you to accept?"

"I'm not a downgrade," Helo butted in. "I'd also like to say that at least I don't have stupid, fake hair."

Weapons were instantly re-aimed at his head. He crossed his arms. "Just saying."

Carl looked around for a moment. "Bring them," he said and strode down the hallway back toward Parallax and his crew.

There goes the plan. Zenith got an idea and darted in the opposite direction toward Vermillion. Maybe Carl would chase her. Maybe Vermillion could take him out.

She only got ten steps before one of his lackeys tackled her. As he roughly got her back on her feet, she glanced over to see that not only had Carl not chased her, he hadn't even turned around.

"*Zenith*! *Code One*." It was Vermillion inside of her head.

"Vermillion! Help!" Zenith shouted it even though she didn't mean to. She was excited to hear her voice. "Can you help?"

"Shut up and get moving," the cyborg guard said, shoving her away from Vermillion and down the hallway. He jabbed a sharp instrument into her back, forcing her forward.

"*You're too far away. You have to lure them in closer. I'll do what I can on my end.*" Vermillion's voice in her head faded away, replaced with silence, as she moved away against her will.

"Hey, Vermillion," Zenith shouted, still struggling and being pushed in the opposite direction, "Please tell me you have a plan-B."

CHAPTER 8

Before Zenith and her guard even rounded the corner to join the others, a fire-fight between Parallax and Carl's minions broke out. It was deafeningly loud. Zenith crouched down and covered her ears. She looked for the others or for a chance to dart away, but even in a war zone, her guard took his job seriously. *Figures.*

It was clear to Zenith by looking at the sheer number of Cyborg invaders who was going to win. And that was very bad news for her.

Zenith spotted the crew and drifted over there with her hands still up. Luckily, they were on the periphery of the war zone, but Aquillon was still bleeding.

There were shouts across the room, something was happening. The weapon blasts died down to a trickle and then stopped altogether. Zenith could see that Carl had Parallax on his knees and a weapon aimed at his head.

"Game over," Carl announced.

Parallax's men threw down their weapons, which did nothing to help Zenith and the crew's current situation.

"Bring Zenith and her people here," Carl said, "I want her to see this."

Zenith winced, having no idea what Carl had in mind as they made their way forward through the crowd until they were just a few feet away from Carl and half a dozen very heavily armed cyborg guards.

Helo shot her an angry look. Zenith felt bad. "I'm so sorry, guys," she said, "I never thought you'd get caught up in all of this. I never thought I would either, at least not immediately. I mean what are the odds that the first job would lead us here?"

"Pretty good," Carl said. "Civil Customer Service is a snap to hack."

Zenith heard Celeste gasp.

So, this is it, Zenith thought, *I never even had a chance, and neither did the crew. I doomed them the minute I stepped onto the ship.*

"You could have been queen of all of this," Carl boasted. "But now you're going to die along with squishy man."

"Stop calling me that," Helo spat.

"Hey, I'd like to point out that you're the one who broke up with me, after using me to get the information you needed about that stupid Galaxy Dragon. You don't really believe in magic, do you, Carl?"

Carl laughed. "That's the problem with you, Zenith. You never believe. And the reason you don't believe is you only have, what, five senses?"

"Yes, Carl, five senses," Zenith confirmed, rolling her eyes. She knew where he was going with this.

"I have thirty," Carl said. He stomped on the hand Parallax was holding the Dragon with, and it clattered to the floor in front of him. "I've researched for years," he continued, "found the exact parameters that would work, retooled my body to be the ultimate wielder of this force." He glanced at Zenith, and she could see the madness in his eyes, along with the cold, fierce electricity.

"I can see that you're still not a believer," he said. "Well, let's find out, shall we?"

Zenith got to one knee, the fight or flight told her to run as fast as she could and as far as she could, but the guard held her in place. She got back down.

Carl grabbed the Galaxy Dragon and held it up dramatically. Zenith held her breath.

***

"Cyborgs unite!" Carl was screaming. "With this Dragon, we will rule the universe."

"Stars no, not politics," Zenith groaned, trying to make eye contact with her guard, "will somebody please just shoot me now?"

Zenith felt the change before she saw it. There was a weird, moody feeling that washed over her and spread throughout the room. The mood was accompanied by an entirely different and spreading reality. The walls darkened, and the floor turned to cold, gray stone underneath her knees.

She looked up, no longer believing what she was seeing. Carl had gotten taller, his clothes had turned black, and he had sprouted giant black wings. Other people in the room had changed colors and forms.

Zenith looked down at her hands. She had transformed into a partial cyborg. A mostly naked partial cyborg at that. She looked up, searching for any sign that this was a bad dream. Carl's cackle proved that theory to be fake. Zenith no longer knew what to believe. She glanced over at Helo, who looked to be turning into some statue creature. His face wore a pained expression.

This can't be happening. Zenith had to do something. She had read all about this Galaxy Dragon thing too, she just hadn't believed it at the time. According to the legends, it had the power to transform reality, up to and including an entire planet. If Carl kept the Dragon, he could make the lives of untold trillions of people a living hell.

She looked at Helo and mouthed, "I need your help." It seemed a monumental effort for him to nod slightly in reply. She inclined her heard toward the guard standing over her and mimed a punch at him in Helo's direction. He blinked at her in a way that she interpreted as understanding. She only hoped it was enough.

She closed her eyes and focused, hoping beyond hope that when she opened them, it would just be a normal robot/cyborg war and not some weird alternate reality nightmare. She opened them. If anything, reality was getting worse.

"Now," she told Helo.

Helo jumped up like he was running in cement and tried to make his way over to Zenith. He wasn't moving fast, but he had certainly attracted the attention of the person guarding Zenith. She took advantage of the guard's head being turned to shove him out of the way and made a run at Carl, who stood like a supervillain, surveying with glee all of the chaos he was creating.

Zenith had to admit the whole thing was impressive. And she had been wrong. Wrong about the power of the Galaxy Dragon, wrong about how innocuous it could be to fix a message on an outdated computer, and wrong to think she could just run away from him after he burned down her apartment complex.

Luckily, the guards surrounding Carl were unconcerned

with Zenith darting up toward him. They were looking around and marveling at the power of the Dragon. That's when Zenith realized that she didn't, in fact, have a plan. She'd have to improvise. He was mostly metal, there were almost no weak spots to him at all, even when he wasn't both magically and cybernetically enhanced.

She reached out and tried to take away the Dragon. It was a dumb move, she was never a match for his strength, and when her fingers brushed against it she could feel its power, it was like a magnetic pull for her, and she wasn't even a cyborg. He kicked her backward and then threw his head back and laughed at her.

She hit the ground hard. She looked around at all of the horrors around her and couldn't reconcile that with this laughing psychopath. She thought of everything he had put her through and everything he was going to do to these people. She thought about Joyce. That's when she snapped. It didn't matter that her plan was probably doomed to fail, she acted on instinct, rushed straight at him, swung her leg, and kicked him full force in the balls. The Dragon fell out of Carl's hand and clattered to the floor.

"I happen to know that those are not in any way cybernetically enhanced!" Zenith announced, pointing, after watching him crumple. She threw herself on the floor and grabbed the Galaxy Dragon.

Carl recovered himself. A steel hand came crashing down on her arm. Her arm made a snapping noise, and the pain caused her to lose her grip. She screamed.

Celeste flew across the room and landed on Carl's face, scratching and biting. He screamed in fury and then threw her to the side.

Reality was beginning to change back.

She could see Helo moving fast now, he no longer appeared to be made of stone. He grabbed the Dragon she had dropped when Carl snapped her arm, and he helped her up.

The walls and the floors were also transforming back. Carl's minions started to break free of their trance.

They crew ran away from the mass of people gathered in the large open area of section D. Parallax recovered himself and had rejoined the fight for his life and his space station. Carl was distracted, so maybe they could just get away.

"Get them!" Carl screamed at his minions while grappling for control over a weapon near Parallax. "Don't let them get away! I want them kneeling before me!"

Zenith couldn't help but sneak a peek behind her, and there were at least three dozen cyborgs giving chase, and they only had a few seconds head start. They knew the way, though, having been halfway there earlier before being turned around by Carl and his guards.

They flew through the hallways now. Zenith had to escape. She had to keep the Dragon from him. Carl can't win. She had no idea before today what was even at stake.

The cyborg guards behind her started firing. Zenith was already hurt, and so was Aquillon. They were limping along as fast as they could but were no match for a bunch of cyborgs. Zenith looked back, and they were closing fast. Too fast. There was only one way.

"Throw it, Helo!" Zenith screamed.

"What?" he asked, partially turning his head toward her.

"We're never going to make it. Throw it. The Dragon. To Vermillion."

"Oh," he said, "that's brilliant."

A cyborg tackled Zenith. Now the cyborgs were almost to Helo.

"Now, Helo!" she screamed.

He slid the figurine forward across the linoleum floor. It slid almost all the way to her hatch.

Zenith shuddered in pain from her arm and from being pinned against the hard floor. That's when she heard it. Vermillion's voice again, in her head. "*Very clever, Zenith.*"

"How do you figure?" Zenith answered her. "At least you can protect the Dragon and the rest of the universe, but we're still sitting ducks right here. I'm sorry we couldn't make it back, Vermillion. For the record, you're a great ship and I honestly like hearing your voice in my head."

"*Right back at you,*" the voice said, "*but there's something about the Dragon you don't know. Zenith: code one, Helo: code one, Celeste: code one, Aquillon: code one.*"

"No kidding, Vermillion? Aquillon too?" That's when Zenith knew she was screwed.

The cyborg that had his foot on Zenith's back suddenly began crackling and crumpled to the ground, making whirring and whimpering noises.

"*The Galaxy Dragon does not give me any magical power to*

transform reality since I have no organic living material. It does, however, boost my power and range."

The cyborgs all crumpled, crackled and twitched. The crew got up off of the ground and began limping once again toward Vermillion.

"You can't win!" a voice boomed down the hall.

Zenith turned to Carl. "I can today. And there's nothing you can do about it." He had obviously seen what had happened to the other cyborgs and was unwilling to venture any closer.

"It's mine!" he screamed at her.

She watched him arm his right hand and point it at her. *Crap. Forgot about that.*

"Your friends made it onto their ship, but you die here. If you turn around, I will shoot you in the back. I win."

"I can't help you," Vermillion screamed frantically in her head, *"I can't reach him, Zenith*! He's still out of range."

"Shoot me in the back? How romantic," Zenith said, "I have no idea what I ever saw in a coward like you." Then she remembered something and reached into her pocket, her fingers wrapped around the smooth stone. "You know what you need? A little magic."

"You don't believe in magic," he snorted.

"But you do," she answered. She pulled out the stone and threw it at him. "Fire in the hole, Carl!" The rock flew at his face and attached itself magnetically. Carl dove for cover down the hallway, clawing at his face. There was a small popping noise as the toy exploded.

Zenith turned and darted into Vermillion.

"You will regret this when I find you. And I will find you." Carl's words echoed in her ears as the door closed behind her.

"Thank goodness," Vermillion said. "Let's get out of here."

"Hey," asked Zenith, still worried, "what's going to stop them from just following us?"

"Me," Vermillion replied. "I've disabled all of their navigation and communications. Trust me, they're going to sit there for quite a while and think about what they've done."

CHAPTER 9

After stopping at an infirmary planet just inside civilized space, Zenith and the rest of the crew took their regular spots in the common room and settled into some serious down time, hopefully for a while. They each read their devices or books quietly for a little while, but then, when they looked up, they all happened to make eye contact.

Helo burst out laughing. "I happen to know that his balls aren't cybernetically enhanced," he said, mimicking Zenith and bringing them all to tears with laughter.

Zenith got up and mimed statue-Helo trying to walk across the room. And then she detailed the look on Carl's face when Celeste buzzed right into Carl. "He was freaking out and trying to get her off." She waved her arms dramatically.

Vermillion chimed in, "And then Helo slid the Galaxy Dragon across the floor so that I could use its power to free you guys. It also boosted my scrambling capabilities. Those ships are going to need new motherboards."

"Hey, Vermillion," Zenith said, "that was amazing what you did back there. Thanks."

"You're welcome."

Celeste raised her hand. If Zenith had to guess, the look on her face was confused. "Hey, Zenith what did you throw at Carl, anyway?"

Zenith grinned. "It was a toy. A little magnet popper. I used to play with them as a kid. Carl was never in any danger, but he didn't know that, did he? And anyway, there's one thing you should know about Carl."

"What's that?" They all asked her in unison.

"He's one paranoid cyborg. I knew he'd assume the worst."

"Wow," Helo said, "he had you cornered, and you bluffed your way out of it. Well done." He whistled. "Remind me never to play poker with you, Zenith."

In the next room, a chirp sounded. They all knew what it was. It was another Civil Customer Service assignment. They looked at each other and then to Zenith. Zenith put her feet up on the couch like Helo. "Oh, you guys don't have to be worried about me answering that. I think we've earned a couple of days off. Trust me, I've seen the way of the slacker, and I like it. Actually, I think I could get used to this."

About the Author

L.A. Johnson lives in beautiful Colorado with her husband, three kids, and three dogs. She writes fun, original Sci-Fi you won't find anywhere else. Look for book 3 in the Neon Octopus Overlord Series in November.

https://lajbooks.com

Books by L.A. Johnson

Neon Octopus Overlord Series
Book 1: Destroyer of Planets
Book 2: Whisperer to Stars

GLI+CHES WILD

by Drew Avera

With Lady Luck on his side, Ben doesn't need any enemies. In a game of high stakes, he puts in all on the line, and probably loses.

They said he was lucky to be alive, that surviving his perilous journey and ultimate crash was a blessing in disguise. Ben isn't one to agree, though, as he tries to up his "reward" in order to facilitate repairs to his ship, the *Shistain* in a poker match against Buck Rodgers; the richest man in West Virginia. Ben soon discovers that poker isn't his game as he loses his ass in more ways than one. But maybe there's a silver lining to being the unluckiest man on Earth. Or maybe that's the lie he holds onto to help himsleep at night. Either way, with Lady Luck on his side, Ben doesn't need any enemies.

CHAP+ER ONE

"Fold." The word fell on the air with a deep exhalation It wasn't the first time someone said the word that evening, and with each utterance, a part of the speaker died. For this one, in particular, he thought he might have negative lives remaining with as many times as he said it.

"You're not having such a good string of hands, are you?" the man seated across from Ben said. The smirk on his face was borderline disrespectful as he thumbed through his cards. The faint sound of a whistle as he breathed out grated on Ben's nerves and he had the slight inclination that the man feigned politeness as part of a ruse, but it was hard to tell with the alcoholic consumption and smell of opiates floating in the haze around him. Ben did not partake in drug use, but he thought he might be high despite that little fact. *Why do I feel so farked up?*

"Things will pick up soon," he said as he set sat his cards on the tablecloth. The old, green velvet was worn around the edges and smelled like cigar smoke and cheap beer. Ben thought it was funny, though, considering one of the wealthiest men in West Virginia held the seat across from him. Carl "Buck" Rodgers was that man, and he wanted everyone to know it at all times. That was why he always had an entourage singing his praises and laughing at his jokes.

A round of chuckles from the other players seated at the table was directed at Ben as the man with the smirk continued to stare over his cards, toying with the situation. "Now, now, fellows. Let's not get too rowdy while our friend here is giving me all of his money," he said, causing another stir of chuckles the fill the room. Ben didn't know which was worse, the whistling sound each time Buck exhaled loudly, or the onlookers lapping at each word the man said, hoping to get in good with the ornery, old codger.

Ben shifted in his seat, wiping his eyes and trying to clear his head. His plan to take his royalties from selling his story to GNN had been a lot bigger a few hours ago. Now, it was an ever-dwindling pile of chips looking pitiful and lonely as the other players' chips were stacked high. *I wonder why they make poker chips red, white, and blue,* Ben thought as he looked away to avoid eye contact with Buck. "All I need is one more good hand," Ben started to say before trailing off, knowing that one good hand wasn't likely before he lost everything. Surprisingly, no one laughed.

"Well, I guess I'm gonna call it," Buck said as he placed his cards on the table, revealing one by one the royal flush he had been thumbing for the last three and a half minutes.

Mother farker, Ben thought, *the third time this farking hour.* He shoved his cards back towards the dealer and forced himself to acknowledge the winner, yet again. "Congratulations, sir," Ben said, fighting to cover up the fact that he didn't mean a word he was saying. "Another good hand by the master."

Buck chuckled. "I don't know about the master," he said, "but I'll take 'winner' any day."

Ben wiped his sweaty palms on his pants' leg and tried to not look at Buck as he stared him down, pulling the chips in the center of the table towards himself, adding to his wealth.

"Another hand?" Buck asked. "One-hundred and fifty-dollar ante"

Ben looked down his chips and counted them. *Fark,* he thought. "That's all I have," he said. "

Buck leaned forward, causing Ben to look up at him. "Something tells me your luck is about to change. I tell you what; I'll even pay your ante."

All I need is one more good hand, and I'll be on a roll, Ben thought. "Fark it." He grabbed the chips Buck had provided. He heard the soft chuckle of a few men against the relative silence of the room as Buck looked at him, one of his eyes closing slightly as if he was about to wink at Ben.

"Fark it," he replied, shoving his anti towards the center of the table as the dealer handed out the cards. "I have to say, Mr. Dale, you have a lot of balls. Not many men would take me up on another hand after so much, shall we say 'abuse,'" Buck said.

You should see them, Ben thought, fighting a grin as he

thought of the way Chip would've delivered the line. Instead, he maintained his silence as he pulled the cards from the table one by one, staring at them with the expression he would have had if someone kicked him in the dick. Not a single farking card over a six of diamonds. *What the fark?* When he looked up at Buck, the older man had a wide grin on his face. It was the kind of look that let Ben know once and for all that he was going to lose. It was a look he had seen in the eyes of many people while standing on the losing side of his life and it made the blood drain from his face

Fark.

"Is everything all right, Mr. Dale?" Buck asked while thumbing through his cards.

Ben sat there, feeling crushed that he let things escalate to this point. *This was supposed to be easy,* he thought. W*in a few hands of cards, and double or triple the money. Instead, I have nothing to show for anything.* "I'm fine," he lied. *I don't have much choice. I can either fold and lose my ass or keep going and lose my ass.*

"I'll take two," Buck said as he placed two of his cards face down on the table near the dealer. The dealer, a skinny young man with a pencil-thin mustache, pulled two fresh cards from a stack and placed them gently on the table. Other than explaining the rules of the game, in the beginning, the dealer never said a word unless he was responding to Buck. It was something that made Ben grow more and more uncomfortable as the game progressed.

Scanning his cards, Ben grew more frustrated. The good news, if you call it that, was he had three of the same suit and a potential straight if he could get the other two cards necessary. *Here goes nothing,* he thought as he pulled two strays from his hand and placed them on the table. "Two, please."

The dealer placed two cards in front of Ben, and with a shaky hand he grabbed them, turning them over and fighting the urge the smile as his bad luck made a small, but satisfying turn. "You look pleased, Mr. Dale," Buck said with a smirk. "Does this mean our game will go a little longer?"

"If Lady Luck is on my side, it does," Ben answered.

"Well, that's good to hear," Buck replied as he pushed a stack of chips towards the center of the table. Ben looked at him and grew more curious. "I always like to tease Lady Luck myself," he said with a leer.

"What are you doing?" Ben asked, without wanting to.

"I'm just making the game a bit more interesting," the man answered as he shoved his second stack of chips towards the center of the table. "Are you in?"

Ben looked down at his hand, staring at the straight, knowing that it was not the best hand he never had, but it sure as hell beat each hand he had the last hour or so. "I'm all out of chips."

Buck smiled, "do you know what business I'm in?"

Ben eyed the man warily, shrugging his shoulders before answering. "Little bit of everything."

There was a bit of brief laughter in the room before it died out in time for Buck to speak. "I guess that's one way of putting it, Mr. Dale. But I built my business transporting goods from Earth to the Moon for the lunar station. It turns out that your ship would be a useful part of my fleet."

Ben's stomach turned as he thought about his ship, and all the damage it'd taken crash landing during his return. "The ship is severely damaged, sir. I'm not even sure it's serviceable, much less worth anything to you."

"I own all types of businesses. I'm sure ship repair is within my realm of getting shit done," Buck replied.

Ben thought about it for a moment, eying his hand again before looking back at the two large stacks of poker chips standing between him and Buck. *What do I have to lose? It's not like I can do anything with the* Shistain *anyway.* "Fark it," Ben said, "Fine, I'll put my ship up," Ben said, trying not to sound too confident about his hand.

Buck looked at Ben, then back down at his cards, and smiled.

Ben suddenly felt a shift in the atmosphere of the room, almost like the air turned stale. The spectators in the room grew quiet, their snickering fading, as Ben realized Buck was no longer making the whistling sound as he breathed. Ben moved uneasily in his seat, uncertain of what was happening, but afraid that whatever caused the sensation in the room to melt into such discomfort wasn't going to be good for him.

"Do you know what I just don't seem to understand, Mr. Dale?" Buck asked as he collapsed his hand of cards into a small stack and set them face down on the table.

"What's that?" Ben asked.

"You travel all the way to Europa," Buck said after a deep breath, "and knowing that you're running low on fuel, you zoom past Mars, which has a refueling station and would allow you to restock your ship, but instead, you continued towards Earth and put yourself in grave peril. Are you crazy, or just plain stupid?"

The tone of Buck's voice and his accusation made Ben angry, but he knew better than to start a scene with a man like Buck. "I couldn't afford to stop; I put everything I had into what I thought was going to be a one-way trip," Ben replied. "The job on Europa was supposed to be lifechanging. It just turned out to be a figment of my imagination, instead."

"So, I guess you're going to go with stupid then?"

Ben's jaw tightened as he fought to smother the rage building inside - him. *Who the fark does this guy think he is? He's just farking with me*; Ben thought as he tried to settle his nerves. "I was going to say unlucky."

Buck had a smirk on his face and a gleam in his eye. "I'm beginning to think the same thing," he said, lifting a finger and pointing towards Ben's cards. "Why don't you go ahead and call it?"

Ben looked at his hand, at the small straight that was either going to win him enough money to repair his ship or cause him to lose it all together. "Why don't you?" Ben shot back.

Buck leaned back in his seat, tugging at the whiskers on his face. "I'm growing tired of being the one always having to call the shots," he answered, "I like to put it in someone else's hands from time to time."

Ben sat quietly for a moment, contemplating what to do, but knowing every second he sat there with his cards in his hand was more time he was wasting. Before he left Earth, he had been irrational, taking a plunge no matter the cost, treating life like a band-aid he had to rip off as quickly as possible to get the pain over with. After so much time in space, and his near-death experience, Ben questioned whether he had grown as a person or if he was just scared shirtless. *Fark it,* he thought, spreading the cards out so each could be seen easily. "I'll call it," he said as he set the cards face up on the table, revealing his straight.

Across from him, Buck leaned forward, eyeing Ben's cards as he continued tugging on his whiskers. "Well, I'll be damned. I told you luck was starting to change," he said happily.

Ben took in a deep breath and felt relieved. *I did the right thing*, he thought, watching Buck pick up his cards, fanning them in his hand before moving to place them on the table.

"Unfortunately," Buck said as he placed his cards on the table one by one, ace by ace and ending with the king of hearts. "Your turn of luck just wasn't enough."

All the air and Ben's lungs evaporated as he looked at Buck's cards.

Oh, fark.

"I'll be by to pick up my ship tomorrow at noon, Mr. Dale. I trust you'll be there?"

Ben looked up at the man who had just taken the last thing he had to his name from him. Trying to find the strength to speak, he glared at the smug bastard smiling across the table from him. "I —"

Buck rose from the table and stared down at Ben. "There's no need to finish that sentence, son; I know you'll be there. Gentlemen, please see Mr. Dale to the door." And with his words, two men grabbed Ben by the arm and pulled him from his seat, He was too dumbfounded to fight back as they dragged him towards the door. The nightmarish image of the men laughing at him followed him all the way to the door.

The only thing bouncing through his mind was that he had been had. He watched, eyes wide, as Buck placed a kind hand on the dealer's shoulder. Reading the old man's lips, Ben's hatred grew as Buck said stoically, "Well played, Mr. Blake. You make your employer proud." Buck placed a stack of chips into the man's hand and turned to leave. Ben stood there gawking, not realizing he was already outside, as the heavy- wooden door slammed shut in his face.

Outside, under the chilly nighttime sky, Ben smelled the odor of the Hudson River and it nauseated him. "What the fark just happened?" He said to no one.

"Mr. Rodgers took it all, didn't he?" A withered old man asked as he sat up from a bench at the bottom of the steps.

Ben turned, startled by the voice. He looked through bleary eyes to see a man in worse shape than himself, but he still reeled from his loss. "Yeah, the asshole took farking everything."

Without the slightest hint of a smile, the old man nodded his head. "I've heard that before," he said, pulling a flask from his dirty coat and swigging on it before extending it to Ben. Ben shook his head. "Suit yourself. That bastard takes everything from anyone willing to give it all away. Hell, he even took his own brother's house."

"Shitty," Ben said.

"You're telling me. I'm the brother."

Taken aback, Ben felt a tinge of anger, not for himself, but for the old man. "I'm sorry for your loss," Ben said. "I would offer to help you out, but I don't have anything to offer."

The old man smiled weakly and reclined back onto the bench. "That's very kind of you, but I'm not looking for a handout."

"What are you looking for?"

"A way to get even."

Ben thought about the man's words for a moment, but could not think of anything to say. Instead, he shoved his hands into empty pockets and began to walk towards his ship. Well Mr. Rodgers' ship. "Have a good evening," He said as he walked out into the night. When he was several paces away, he thought he heard the old man say, "You'll be back." When he turned to look back, the man was gone, and Ben was greeted by empty shadows.

He shook his head, hoping to rattle the feeling of regret from his brain, but it persisted. It was the only thing he knew he could rely on in life.

Regret.

CHAPTER TWO

Ben's life being as it was, he thought he should feel used to being defeated at every turn, learning from the plethora of past mistakes. But instead, as he approached the mess that was once his ship, he still questioned why these things happened to him. So many people in his life seemed to be born with horseshoes up their asses, lucky despite their ignorance and mistakes. Ben felt his horseshoe had been inserted broken because his whole life felt like he was being taken from behind and he was powerless to do anything about it. Life was just like being farked by a gorilla: you're not done until the gorilla is done.

He stood outside the bay door, hesitant to enter for what would be the last time. His heart ached with loss, but the broken feeling in his chest was mucked by the rage coursing through his veins. *That son of a bitch,* he thought as he pressed his hand against the console, unlocking the bay door. *He had me from the start.* It was a realization that came hours too late.

Ben was greeted by an upbeat sex robot, who thankfully was still wearing his pants as he stood, hands on his hips, seeming to marvel at what he had done. "What's going on, Chip?" Ben asked when the robot did not turn to look at him.

"I'm fixing her up," Chip replied, pointing at the bulkhead with a flamboyant wave of his hand.

Ben hadn't noticed at first, but when he looked where Chip was pointing, what he saw stuck out like a boner in sweatpants. A glittered banner mounted to the bulkhead read "World Famous *Shistain*." Truer words had not been rendered considering his crash-landing on Earth after his bout several weeks prior was the only remarkable thing the world seemed to be talking about of late. Ben silently wished the fame and fortune behind the name of the *Shistain* extended to him as well. The ship appeared to gloat in its glory to spite him.

"Nice banner," Ben said as he fell backward into the lumpy cushions of the battered couch.

"Thank you. I made it myself." Chip made flutter hands beside his face.

"I can tell. The sparkle and gleam just scream 'Chip made me' from the rooftops," Ben replied dryly.

Chip turned to Ben with a furrowed brow. "There's something wrong?"

"No," Ben lied. "I like the banner. Thank you for caring enough to decorate this place."

"You're lying."

Ben didn't respond. Instead, he sat with his hand on his chin and fought back the urge to cry. *Everything in my life is shit, and now I'm about to lose that.*

"I can take it down," Chip said, his voice shaky as he simulated an appropriate emotional response to the negative energy in the room.

"It's not the banner," Ben said under the strain of a heavy sigh.

"Then what is it?"

Ben looked at his companion, the only person who had truly been there for him through the worst times in his life. His voice cracked when he tried to speak, but he forced himself to say it, "I lost her."

"Her?"

Ben waved his hand to indicate where they were. "The *Shistain*; I lost her in a poker game."

Chip's furrowed brow turned to another expression, one that appeared to mix surprise and anger. "You lost the ship in a card game?" The upward inflection had the distinct tone of an accusation to Ben's ears, but he didn't argue because he felt he deserved it.

"More or less."

"More more, or more less?"

"Mr. Rodgers took me to the bank. I lost everything and the ship too."

"Surely, he does not see value in a ship this damaged," Chip suggested. "There is several months of work required just to get her worthy of flight again."

"He has the money and the means to do it."

Chip sat next to Ben and placed a friendly hand on his knee. "It may be a blessing in disguise; a new chapter in our lives."

"How's that?"

"Now you don't have the burden of trying to repair the ship so we can find work and a new place to live," Chip answered.

"Yeah, I suppose that's something."

"So, what was he like?"

"Who?"

"Mr. Rodgers."

Ben shrugged. "He's just some old guy with an epic beard who likes to whistle while he farks you out of money. He also had a thing for watches."

"How's that?"

Ben thought back to the old man who referred to himself as Buck even though the name made no sense. "I don't know, he just wore one on each wrist is all. I thought it was weird when I first met him, but as the night progressed I didn't think about it as much."

"I wonder why that is." Chip tilted his head at Ben.

"Probably because I was too busy watching my stack of chips dwindle into nothingness. What's with your fetish for the man's watches?"

Chip smirked. "Ben, I don't have a fetish for watches, but anyone peculiar enough to have quirks they aren't afraid to hide is usually hiding something else."

"Yeah, I could have told you that by his poker face. Can you believe the asshole took his own brother's house in a game? Now the dude is homeless, living outside his dick-bag brother's residence."

"Wow, what a dick, and I'm not talking about what's in your pants," Chip said without a hint of a smile.

"Yeah," Ben replied, not moved in the least by Chip's comment. He remembered a time when Chip's homoerotic comments used to get under his skin. Now, they just fell like leaves in the wind of a perpetual autumn. Often, Ben thought of clever things to say when Chip was not around. It was the kind of friendship he now had with the sex-bot, and he was happier in that platonic relationship than he had been with any human connections he had in the past. Sometimes he wondered what that meant about himself, but he always brushed the thoughts away.

"Do you think he will want to keep the banner I made?" Chip asked, with the slightest hint of mourning in his voice at the impending loss of the *Shistain*.

Ben crinkled his nose at the thought. "Let the asshole make his own sign."

Chip smiled. "We might as well leave it up so he can see the pride we have in our ship. I'll take it down before we leave."

"Sounds good," Ben replied. "Well, shit, I guess I should settle in for the night and get one last rest on this lumpy couch. Mr. Rodgers will be here at noon. Can you wake me an hour before he arrives?"

Chip stood up and stepped into the middle of the room, grabbing his charging cable. "Sure thing, Captain."

Ben smiled, but it was a sad smile. Without the ship, he was no longer going to be a captain. Instead, he was just plain-old Ben, the unluckiest guy in the world. "Goodnight, Chip."

"Goodnight," Chip answered as he plugged the cable into the port on the side of his neck. The lights inside the ship dimmed into darkness and Ben was left in silence.

Ben watched the blue lights illuminate behind Chip's eyes as he went into charging mode. Lying on his back, turning his face towards the ceiling of the ship, Ben had nothing but time to think about all the things that went wrong that night. *I should never have taken the risk,* he thought as his eyes adjusted to the darkness of the room. *If only I had a time machine, then I could go back a stop myself from walking into that farking room.*

CHAP+ER THREE

A jabbing sensation woke Ben from his slumber. As he rolled over on the couch, the harsh, white lights in the room blinding him, he was taken aback by what he saw. Standing over him was not his companion Chip, but Buck, glaring at him and tugging at his whiskers. "Buck, what the hell? Chip, I thought I told you to wake me up at eleven?"

"That was the plan, but Mr. Rodgers arrived early," Chip replied.

Buck merely grunted and stepped away from Ben, taking a seat at what served as the eating table. Ben sat up from the couch, rubbing at his eyes and trying to calm his nerves. The night before had been restless, and daylight had already started to break by the time he finally fell asleep. Looking at the battered clock on the bulkhead, he saw that Buck arrived more than an hour and a half early.

"I thought you said noon?" Ben asked, wishing he had some coffee in him before having to deal with the bullshit of the day.

"I'm a businessman, Mr. Dale, I always arrive early."

"Chip, you could've at least woke me before you let him in."

The expression simulators of Chip's face moved to one of confusion. "He let himself in," he replied.

Ben looked up at the old man and the snide grin on his face. "You really should consider locking your door; this is a dangerous part of town," Buck said nonchalantly.

Ben merely shrugged before rising from the couch. "It's New York—every part of this place is a dangerous part of town."

Buck chuckled, but it didn't sound sincere. "All the more reason for me to claim what is mine and be on my way," he replied.

"So, you're going to evict me already?"

"I do have the papers drafted if that answers your question," he replied with no hint of a smile.

Typical, Ben thought as he ran his hand through his hair, opening the refrigerator to find nothing waiting for him to quench his thirst. "Fark."

"It's not that serious, son," Buck said.

Ben shoved closed the refrigerator door and took in a deep breath. "It's not about the eviction, it's about the fact I could have sworn I had an iced coffee waiting for me in the fridge. Now, my entire day it's going to be farked up due to a lack of caffeine."

When Ben looked over at Buck, he saw evidence of a frown on the man's face. It didn't appear to be anger, just deep thought. The old man stood from his seat, and shoved a hand into one of his pockets, pulling out a piece of plastic and placing it on the table next to him. "Don't say I never got you anything," he said as he sat back down on the chair.

Without taking it, Ben asked, "what is it?"

"It's a gift card for Starbucks," he answered, "hell, you might get two or three coffees with the credit on this thing."

Ben leaned against the bulkhead, crossing his arms over his chest, nervously tapping his fingers against the shiny exterior of his left arm he called Gli+chy. "Thanks, I guess."

"Yeah, sure," Buck said, glancing up at the overhead of the ship. "You're not much of a housekeeper, are you?"

"What do you mean?" Ben asked, letting his arms dangle at his sides as he looked in Buck's direction with derision.

"The cobwebs in the corners. You're not going to get that in space, so I'm assuming you left Earth with a dirty ship."

"So."

'So, dirt leads to corrosion, leads to structural damage—beyond the fact you crashed this heap," Buck said, pointing at each blemish he noticed. "This is going to cost me a fortune," he groaned as though his reference to Ben's having done a poor job maintaining the ship had not been driven home.

"Yean? Well, it's your problem now, I guess," Ben said, stepping towards the cargo bay to grab his belongings and leave the old man with the ship. "Let's go, Chip."

"Not just yet," Buck said, causing Ben to turn and face him.

"What do you mean?"

Buck smiled. "The robot can fly, correct?"

"Yeah."

"Well, he comes with the ship then."

"I don't think so," Ben shot back.

"Oh, well you would be mistaken, then." Buck handed a stack of papers to Ben before speaking again. "You'll notice in paragraph three, subsection 'c' that any mechanical features or AI with piloting capabilities are considered shipboard equipment. Thereby, I am entitled to it."

"That's bullshit," Ben said, fighting the urge to crumple the paper in his hands.

"You might think so, but you're the one who programmed the robot to pilot the ship."

"Perhaps," Buck said. "It doesn't change matters, though."

"What use do you have with a gay sex-robot, Mr. Rodgers? I would like to know."

The old man grinned. "I don't have any use for a gay sex-robot, but a machine that can fly my ship would prove quite useful."

"You can't have him, he's my friend."

"Is that what you're calling it?"

Ben balled his hands into fists and fought the urge to swing. "You know what I mean," he seethed.

A light chuckle escaped the man's lips before he stifled it. "Perhaps, but that's none of my business. I'll have my ship and the robot. It's in the contract you signed."

"And what if I don't want to sign it?"

The smile on Buck's face faded to a look of contempt. "Son, I'm not a man to be farked with. When I want something, I will have it. You will either do as I say, or I will make your pathetic little ass disappear."

Taken aback, Ben straightened up, glaring at the man. "Are you farking threatening me?"

'No, I'm not. I'm just delivering a promise to you that I will carry out if you don't sign the goddamned contract and get the fark off my ship."

Two men holding ray guns stepped through the cargo bay door. *Farking mob*, Ben thought. With nowhere to run and no way out, he said the only thing he could think of. "Fine, but can I at least say goodbye?"

"I'll allow that," Buck said, "You have three minutes." Buck and his men stepped off the ship, leaving Ben alone with Chip.

"I don't know what to say," Ben said with sorrow in his voice. He wanted to cry but felt ridiculous for it.

"I understand, Captain. You can't fight a man like that. He fights dirty and not in the way I think either of us would like," Chip replied.

Ben smiled at the pun that Chip did not seem to pick up on until he saw Ben's expression. "I'm going to miss you," Ben said.

"And I will miss you too."

Ben reached into his bag and pulled out a thumb drive. "I want you take this," he said, handing the device over to Chip.

"What is it?"

"It's a way to keep the bastard from changing who you are," Ben said. "I can tell he has no interest in who you are, but in what you can do. The asshole will probably try to reprogram you. This drive will disable your software from any overrides, so you get to stay the same and not let some fark-nugget make you something else."

Chip stared at the drive for a moment before responding. "I don't know what to say."

"That makes two of us, buddy," Ben said as he patted Chip on the shoulder.

The two friends looked at each other, sadness in the human's eyes and a look of longing in the robot's. "We can't let this be the end of us," Chip said.

"It isn't," Ben replied, but his heart ached, knowing that he lied. The truth was that in all likelihood he would never see the robot—responsible for saving his life no less than five times—again.

Chip reached out and grabbed Ben, pulling him into a loving embrace, and Ben let it happen.

Buck walked in a few moments later. "Well, sorry to interrupt, but I have a truck ready to load this piece of shit up and take it in for repairs."

Chip released Ben and the human wiped a tear from his eye. "You're an asshole, you know that?"

Buck smirked. "Son, I've been called that more times than that robot has been in yours. Now, get the fark off my ship. I have work to do."

Chapter Four

Two months later

Ben tapped at the door for the seventh time, resisting the urge to pound on it like a madman while waiting for the resident to answer it. The only thing more frustrating than waiting was knowing the pizzas in his hand were growing cold, and the business had a big guarantee of fresh, hot, and timely delivery. He failed on all counts as far as that was concerned.

"Farking, come on, man," he said under his breath. *The worst part about this job is that I used to love pizza*, he thought indignantly as he shifted his weight from one leg to the other. Who the fark orders twelve pizzas and doesn't answer their farking door when they arrive? As he reached up to knock on the door again, it finally opened, and he was met with a pimple-faced kid who seemed to have a chip on the shoulder by the way he looked at him.

"You're four minutes late, dude," the little punk said.

"Really? It's unfortunate you didn't hear me knocking on the door for the last several minutes. Otherwise, it would appear I was on time," Ben shot back. The customer is not always right.

"Yeah, whatever, dude," the little shit said as he grabbed the stack of pizzas from Ben and sat him on the small table next to a store. Ben stood there waiting as the kid looked up at him. "What do you want now?"

Ben's eyes narrowed as he stared at the kid, thoughts of tightening his hands around his throat flooded into his mind, but he shook away the thought before he had the unsettling idea that it would be a good decision. "I just delivered two-hundred dollars-worth of pizza, I think a tip would be appropriate," Ben answered.

The kid looked over at the stack of pizzas and then back at Ben. "You are late."

"I was on time, and I could hear you moving around in there as I knocked on the door. It was almost as if you were waiting to see you could say I was late," Ben replied, knowing the angle the kid was trying to get at, and wanting the kid to know that he was onto him.

"It is a lot of pizza," the kid said as if he had just discovered a scientific breakthrough.

"Yeah, I would say so."

The boy reached into his pocket, "all right, you're right, you do deserve a tip."

"Thank you," Ben replied.

The kid pulled his hand from his pocket and shoved his middle finger in Ben's direction. "You want a tip, shithead, get a better farking job." And with his words, the door slammed shut in Ben's face, leaving him in the semi-silent hallway of the apartment building. The only sound filtering through his ears was the sounds of loud televisions, babies crying, and his heart beating rapidly.

He could also hear laughter from the other side of the door, and there wasn't a farking thing he could do about what just happened. *Punk ass little fark,* he thought as he stepped away from the door. With every fiber of his being, he wanted to punch through the door and strangle that little kid and teach him to have some respect. *Fark respect, I just want to kill him,* he thought as his heavy steps stomped on the thin, stained carpet of the hallway leading to the elevator. *He's not worth it, though.*

As Ben stepped out of the apartment building, he was met with rain, not regular rain, but a sudden, torrential downpour steeped with the smell of seawater. "I hate this time of year," he muttered as he pulled open the small storage container on his scooter and pulled out a black plastic bag. Ben wrapped Gli+chy diligently, trying to ensure no moisture got into her servos, causing her to gli+ch out and act erratically. *The last thing I need is to whack a customer in the face while delivering pizzas,* he thought, not because it had a small percentage of possibility, but because of it already happened once before and he couldn't afford to lose his job.

After a semi-satisfying wrap job on Gli+chy, Ben climbed onto the scooter and felt relieved when it cranked the first time he tried. He donned his helmet and closed the visor, feeling the cushion of the helmet was already soaked after the several minutes he had been inside the apartment building. The moisture was so close to his face that he felt cold and it sent a chill down his spine, but he shook it off and looked over his shoulder before pulling out into traffic. Time was money, and with no time to waste, he darted between the slow-moving vehicles on his way back to the restaurant.

Pizza Bar, his humble place of employment, sat situated in a tight alley a couple of miles west of the apartment building he delivered to. But in that couple of miles, the rain did not let up, soaking him to the bone and causing him to shiver uncontrollably as he stepped off the scooter and waddled stiff-legged towards the door. The smell of pizza cloaked the exterior of the restaurant, and it was a refreshing fragrance, despite the fact anytime Ben thought about pizza it made him think about work. "Better than working in a sewage plant, I suppose," he said under his breath. As he pulled the door open, the smell of melted cheese and marinara sauce wafted around him.

"Ben, where the fark if you been?" His manager, Tony Roman, stood with his hands on his hips amidst a pile of stacked boxes pizza waiting to be delivered.

"The little shit refused to open the door until our thirty-minute delivery guarantee was over," Ben answered. "Perhaps you should rethink that guarantee; it's costing us money."

Tony shook his head, "that guarantee is older than both of us put together, Ben. Besides, it does not cost me money. It's costing you money, and for that, I can't give a shit less. You have three deliveries and seven minutes to make it happen. So, I suggest you get going." Tony turned his back on Ben, focusing his attention on the industrialized environment that involved mass-producing pizza. Ben reluctantly grabbed a couple of weatherproof containers, placing the pizzas inside of them so he could strap them to the scooter. *I can only imagine how much the customer will bitch about a soggy box of pizza with the weather the way it is,* he thought as he banded the containers together and carried them outside. Logic be damned that ordering pizza in a storm might be a bad idea.

Heading into the onslaught of a torrential downpour for a

thankless job made him question his already questionable life decisions. But the truth was, he needed the farking job to make ends meet. Losing his ship, his strained relationship with his father, and the fact he was essentially homeless, all made him feel like he failed at life.

When he felt down, though, he would always think about the words of encouragement that Chip often gave him during their trip through the darkness of space. Somewhere beneath the homoerotic, perverted comments was encouragement in the face of adversity. Ben missed that more than anything. The comradery of two people facing a challenge and overcoming it was the most powerful thing he ever experienced, and it didn't matter that one of those "people" was a gay sex-robot.

Ben took a hard right on his scooter, and the tires sprayed rainwater on both sides as he skidded into the turn as fast as he could manage, but the water was too deep on this part of the street, and he hydroplaned, losing control. The scooter wobbled as he fought to control it. With all the weight in the front as he tried to apply the brakes, Ben was flung head over handlebars out onto the pavement of the open street. As he soared through the air, seemingly in slow motion, he felt like he was flying amongst a flock of pizza boxes that dislodged from the scooter. Together they hit the ground, skidding on the pavement to a painful stop. His ass took most of the impact, but it wasn't enough to keep them from hitting his head on the ground as he came to a sudden stop.

Ben lay there, eyes wide and his heart pounding. He brought his hands up, feeling his torso as he instinctively checked for wounds and broken bones. Surprisingly, he didn't feel any pain.

Yet.

"What the fark?" He took in a series of deep breaths, trying to calm his nerves as best he could before he climbed to his feet. As he stood up, the pain hit him: the scorching, burning sensation of road rash on his ass cheeks. He stumbled forward, taking hold of a parked car next to him. He leaned over it, trying to take his weight off his legs as the searing pain made him dizzy.

"Are you all right?" A bystander said, pulling Ben's attention to the direction of the voice. It was a girl, who looked to be sixteen or seventeen-years-old. She clung to her purple raincoat as she walked swiftly in his direction.

"I'll live, but I don't think I really want to at this point," he answered. He intended it to be a joke, but the amount of truth behind his words was unsettling, even for him.

"Do you need an ambulance?" She asked as she neared him. She looked at him nervously, keeping a few paces back. Ben didn't know if she was keeping her distance because she was afraid of him, or if she was just trying to give him space to suffer.

"I—. I don't know," he answered. He tried to take a step but almost collapsed, falling back towards the ground. The girl grabbed his arm and kept him from face planting onto the asphalt. He was impressed by how strong she was.

"I think I'm going to call an ambulance for you anyway," she said." You might have some internal injuries. You did hit the ground really hard," she said as she pulled a cell phone from her pocket. "Just keep leaning against the car and don't try to move."

"All right," Ben replied as she dialed the number. She stepped away as she spoke to the dispatcher on the other end of the line. He tried to listen to what she said but the searing pain on his posterior made it hard for him to listen. *Who would think pain could be so loud.*

"I'll be here waiting with him," she said into her phone before hanging it up and shoving it back in her pocket. "The ambulance will be here in a few minutes. Do you want to try and take off the helmet?"

Ben hadn't realized he still wore it until she said something. Bracing himself against the car, he tugged the chinstrap down as she reached up to help pull it off him. Despite the dreary day and the heavy rainfall, he had a much better view of her and realized she was older than he first thought. "I'm Ben," he said.

"Ashley," she replied, "but my friends call me Ash."

"You live around here?"

"Yeah, I'm in the dorms around the corner. I'm going to the community college down the street."

"Oh, a college girl? Impressive," he said, realizing how stupid it sounded as he stood there, quivering from the pain of flesh being rubbed raw by crashing his scooter and sending a bunch of pizzas littering the streets. He supposed for a guy like him, maybe community college was impressive, and she would buy it as more than just mere small talk.

"Not really. I'm doing the nursing program so I can get a

decent job, but going to school sucks a big one."

"A big what?" Ben asked, his heart pounding harder in anticipation of the pending joke that he imagined Chip would deliver with expert craft.

Ash smiled. "A big hard..." she was cut off by the sound of a siren wail.

Ben had to admit he felt letdown, not hearing her complete her thought. He felt a little tickled by her.

"Good. Help is here," she said.

"Yeah," Ben replied, not wanting his moment with her to end. *Go figure, the third biggest embarrassment of my life starts to take a turn, and I get cockblocked by an ambulance.*

As the ambulance screeched to a stop, Ben took in a deep breath and watched as two men in uniform jumped out of the rectangular vehicle. From the back of the unit, a droid rolled out onto the street with a gurney. "Are you all right, sir?" The first man to approached asked.

"I wrecked my scooter, and I can hardly stand. Other than that, I'm fine, I guess."

"I think Ben might have hit his head when he crashed. I watched him come down onto the street with a lot of force," Ash said. "You can see some pretty deep gouging in the helmet. He might have a concussion."

"Are you feeling nauseated or like you want to pass out?" The man asked as he ran a scanning probe along Ben's body.

"No, other than the burning sensation on my ass and my weak legs not wanting to support my body, I feel perfectly fine." Ben noticed a smirk from Ash when he said, "burning sensation on my ass" and he adored her for it.

"My scanners aren't showing any broken bones or internal bleeding, but the gashed helmet is cause for concern. I think it would be best to have you scanned properly at the hospital."

Ben wasn't about to argue with that. "Can you contact my employer and let him know about the delivery?" Ben looked at Ash.

She seemed taken aback, but she nodded her head politely. "I suppose. Who's the employer?"

"Pizza Bar."

She scrunched up her nose. "Really? That place kind of sucks."

"I love you," he said, not meaning to and immediately regretting it when her eyes widened. "That's not what I meant.

I just love the fact you think it sucks too," he said quickly, eliciting a laugh from the two EMTs.

"All right, you two lovebirds, it's time to go," one of the men said as the droid drew closer.

"We're not—"

"Yeah, sure," the man cut him off. He grabbed his radio and called in for a cleanup crew to tow away Ben's scooter and clean up the mess left by the splattered pizzas. "Let's roll."

The first EMT helped Ben onto the gurney as the droid held it solidly in place. "Just lie back slowly and try not to put too much pressure where it hurts."

"You mean his ass?" Ash grinned. Her question sparked a chuckle from the others, Ben included.

"I don't think you understand just how much this hurts."

"No? You don't know much about me, do you?" The look in her eyes did not reveal whether she was just farking with Ben, but he was willing for it to go either way.

"Maybe we can change that?" He asked as the droid rolled him into the back of the ambulance as Ash watched in the pouring rain.

"Are you asking me out?"

"Would you accept?"

The answer came in the form of the ambulance doors shutting loudly, cutting him off from Ash and the unknown response to his question.

"Wait, what did she say?"

"I don't know, man. You'll have to ask her yourself when you get released," the EMT in the passenger seat replied with a smirk.

"All I have is her name, her first name, not even her last. Do you know how many girls named Ashley there are in New York?"

"Nope. Do you?"

"No," Ben answered. "But it's a lot, I'm sure."

The ambulance moved out, and the man in the passenger seat sighed. "Look, man, don't be so butthurt about it. If it's meant to be then you'll bump into her again. Besides, if she's interested, she knows where you work."

"But she thinks it sucks."

"Well, maybe that should tell you something."

"That she's perfect for me?"

Laughter spurted from the front of the ambulance. "I was

going to say you have a snowball's chance in hell, but you can go with that if you want," the man answered as he slapped his buddy on the shoulder as the driver wiped a tear from his eye from laughing too hard.

"Thanks a lot, guys," Ben said, letting the conversation die like the little piece of hope he had at hitting things off with Ash.

Fark me.

Chapter Five

Lying on a hospital bed with his bare ass towards the ceiling, Ben was the most uncomfortable he felt his entire life. The number of nurses coming and going to see the superficial wounds of his posterior flesh rivaled the embarrassment three months prior when he crashed his ship in a tainted Vienna sausage hallucination. "Is it really necessary for every single one of you nurses to come in here to look at my ass?" Ben asked as he heard footsteps entering his room.

"To be honest, I didn't think I would see your bare ass until the third or fourth date," Ash replied as she came into view. She no longer wore the oversized raincoat, and Ben got a good look at her for the first time. If not for the straining of his neck to look up, he would not have looked away, but peering upwards for more than a few seconds tended to hurt.

"I'm sorry," Ben said, "but you've seemed to have caught me with my pants down," he joked, trying to hide the embarrassment in his voice.

"Don't worry, I see plenty of guys with their pants down."

Ben awkwardly shifted his gaze up to her with a frown, questioning just how many "plenty of guys" just so happened to be.

"Oh, I didn't mean it that way," she said with a smile. "The nursing school is a crazy place if you get what I mean."

"I can only imagine," Ben replied. "So, if this is a date, since I showed you mine, maybe you should show me yours?"

Ash giggled as she brushed a tuft of dirty blond hair behind her ear. "I don't want you to get the wrong idea," she said as she moved over to the chair in the corner of the room that put her more in Ben's line of sight. He liked the view much better.

"I don't know how to tell you this, but how I feel right now, all the wrong ideas sound more painful than they do pleasurable. I might need a pass on the dirty thoughts for a few days."

Ash looked at him with feigned disappointment and pouted her lips. "Yeah? I guess that is what happens when you cruise the street on your ass cheeks." Her words flowed with a slight hint of laughter creeping in.

Ben smiled, "I'm suspecting that you have some experience with that as well?"

"Oh, hell no," she scoffed. "But I did fall off a horse barrel racing when I was fifteen. My foot got caught in the stirrup, and the horse made a full circle around the ring before the rodeo clowns got it to stop. It took a month for me to walk straight, and I have a skin graft on my ass to show for it," she said.

"Rodeo? You don't strike me as the kind of girl who rides horses," Ben said.

"Why is that? Because I'm a small girl in a big city?"

"I wasn't going to say that—" his words fell short as a nurse walked into the room, interrupting their conversation.

"It's time to clean and dress your wounds, Mr. Dale," the nurse said as she dragged a damp cloth across the raw flesh on his backside. He closed his eyes, wincing at the sudden and sharp pain of the rag as it pulled at the partially clotted, bloodied skin.

"You don't have to be so rough," Ben said as he sucked in a deep breath.

"Oh, honey, this is nothing," the nurse replied. "Sometimes I really have to get in there with some elbow grease. You're lucky, because this could be so much worse."

"Yeah, Ben," Ash interjected. "I figured a guy like you would like it rough."

"This is what playing rough gets you?" Ben asked, gesturing towards his ass with Gli+chy.

"Yeah, I don't have a shiny arm, but I can imagine it can get to that."

He looked at her puzzled for a moment. "What? No, not Gli+chy, that was an Army training accident. I'm talking about my ass; which is getting more attention than I could ever want."

"You call your arm Gli+chy?" Ash asked.

"It sounds like an interesting story."

Ben smiled, squinting one side of his face as the abrasive pain on his backside attempted to levitate him from his bed. "Not as interesting as imagining you riding a horse."

"You're not going to get me that easy, Ben," she laughed, toying with the perverted nature both of them seemed to share. "Besides, we have to have something to talk about when we run out of things to say."

"That would be rough."

"Just the way you like it," she snickered.

He grinned, enjoying every bit of their time together. "Speaking of liking it rough," Ben said, "were you able to get in contact with Tony and let him know what happened?"

"Yeah, that dude is a douche," she answered," and he really doesn't seem to like you too much."

"Why? What did he say?"

Ash sat back in her seat, crossing one leg over the other as she looked at him. "He seems to think that you wrecked your scooter on purpose."

Ben groaned at his asshole boss' false assumption. "I swear, I can never seem to win with that guy."

"Then why even try?" Ash asked.

It was something that Ben never considered before. Why do I try so hard to impress people that could'nt really give a shit less about me? "I really don't have a good answer for that," he said. The nurse sprayed a cool liquid out of an aerosol can behind him, and the instant relief was semi-arousing for him. "Oh God, where have you been all my life?"

"Now, now, Mr. Dale, I'm a happily married woman," the nurse replied.

"Not you, but that can of whatever it is you're spraying on me," he said with a smirk. "Is it single?"

His comment elicited a laugh from both women.

Ash stood up from her seat. "Well, perhaps I should leave you two alone," she said through a sharp exhalation.

Ben looked up at her with a frown. "It was only a joke," he whined, "besides, I thought we were on a date?"

Ash knelt in front of him, making it easier for him to make eye contact. "Did you really think this is the date?"

Ben nodded his head, assuming that what she said before about seeing his bare ass on the first date had been a clue as to where her head was at. "I just thought—"

"Ben, I'm gay," she said abruptly.

Taken aback, Ben swallowed hard, fighting back the urge to ask the question on the tip of his tongue. "I, I—"

Ash laughed hysterically, almost losing her balance as she knelt in front of him. "Ben, I'm just farking with you. But, I would hardly consider this a date. I just have to go to class. I'll swing back by later if visiting hours aren't over," she said.

Ben felt an air of relief. *Not only does she have a good sense of humor, but the sores on my ass didn't seem to scare her away.* "I would really like that," he said sincerely.

She reached out and brushed a strand of hair out from in front of his face so they could gaze into each other's eyes unobstructed. "I know," she said before standing up and walking away. Ben smiled at the sound of her footsteps fading as she left the room.

"She's a nice girl," the nurse said, startling Ben because he had been so wrapped up in Ash's eyes that he had forgotten the woman still in the room.

"Yeah." It was the only word he said, but to him, it meant more than a thousand words.

Chapter Six

Being released from the hospital this time was much more pleasurable than the time before. Having spent only a few days under care to ensure that the abrasions on his skin were healing properly, Ben did not have the sensation of feeling like a caged animal as he did when he was in the psych ward upon returning to Earth. Of course, having Ash as a visitor every day kept his spirits much higher than the last time he was hospitalized.

"I would ask if you wanted to push yourself along," Ash said as she maneuvered his wheelchair through the corridors, "but I've seen the way that you drive."

Ben grinned from ear to ear as he shifted his weight on the foam doughnut that was supposed to make sitting more comfortable. All it really did was make him feel like he was sitting on a cushioned toilet. "Girl, you haven't seen nothing yet," he replied with a smirk.

"Why don't you keep your trash talking down until you can walk without a waddle," she said. Her verbal pee pee slaps were becoming a part of their dynamic that Ben really enjoyed. Knowing that her witty comebacks were coming from a friendly place, and were not malicious, made him crave antagonizing her with his snarky remarks all the more.

"After I show you a thing or two, we'll see who's waddling."

"Oh, please, you two," the nurse, whose name was Beth, Ben learned during his stay, said. "You're both adults, not fourteen-year-old kids who learned that you like the other person's body parts."

"Embracing your twenties doesn't mean you have to grow up," Ash said sarcastically. To Ben, Beth acted like a mother figure to the two of them. He thought she was a really nice woman and gave the impression that she gave a shit about her patients. For that, he was grateful. The staff in the psych ward had a way of making him feel inferior to them. This stay had been a welcomed relief, save for the fact he could hardly walk without being in pain and that his ass looked like the surface of the moon with a scorched surface.

"Yeah, come on, Beth. You remember how it used to be," Ben shot back.

Beth reached over and grabbed Ash's arm, causing her to stop pushing Ben in the wheelchair. Startled, Ben looked up to see what was going on, watching as Beth crossed her arms over her chest and scowling down at him. "Excuse me?"

Ben stammered for a moment, trying to think of the words to say to resolve the situation. "I —"

Beth started laughing before patting Ben on the shoulder. "I'm just farking with you," she said. "See that? Just because I'm older than you don't mean I can't relate to you."

Ben made eye contact before busting out in giggles. "You had me there for a minute, Beth," Ben said as his wheelchair began moving again.

"I'm going to miss you two," Beth said with a hint of sadness in her voice. "Usually working in this hospital is such a depressing place that there's not much time for laughter. But you two really brought some laughter back to my job, and I really appreciate it."

"Aw," Ash said, "we really enjoyed spending time with you too," she said. Ben nodded, agreeing with the sentiment. He was so high on happiness that he felt his life had changed overnight, but despite leaving the hospital, Ben was afraid his and Ash's dynamic would die down and emotionally he would come crashing down. He hoped not, but life had a way of kicking him in the dick at the worst of times.

The sky was overcast as they came out of the hospital. It wasn't exactly the kind of day that Ben had imagined from inside the four walls of his room as he laughed hysterically at Ash's jokes. *I shouldn't be surprised,* he thought as he peered upward. T*his* is *storm season, after all.* "At least it's not raining," he said cheerfully.

"Yeah, I think the worst of it is over," Ash said as she stopped pushing the wheelchair on the edge of the sidewalk for patient pickup.

"So, who's coming to get me?"

"Honestly, it's a surprise," she replied.

As Ben waited on the sidewalk, waiting for their ride to arrive, Ash sat in silence. He wondered if something was wrong before realizing she was watching a blue van pull into the parking lot. The dark windows obstructed the view of who was driving, and Ben had no idea who the vehicle belonged to.

"Who is it?"

"Will you just wait and see?"

The van came to a stop as Ben shifted uncomfortably in the wheelchair, the cushion doughnut growing more uncomfortable to his healing wounds. As he sat there, trying to peer through the dark, tinted windows, the passenger-side window slowly moved downward. It revealed Ben's chauffeur and a happy smiling face.

"Hey, Captain," Chip said happily.

"Chip! How the hell have you been?" Ben wanted to stand up and jump up and down with excitement, but he knew how much that would hurt.

"I just got back from a lunar mission, flying for Mr. Rodgers," he replied. "I tried to send you a message, but Ash answered the call and told me you were in the hospital. You haven't been making a habit out of that, have you?"

"I wasn't trying to," Ben answered, remembering the last time he saw Chip he was losing everything. "How's Mr. Rodgers treating you?"

Chip stepped out and opened the back door to allow Ben and his doughnut inside. "Honestly, it's a pretty lonely existence," Chip answered. "I do all the missions by myself, and I only have a few days off between stops before they send me out again. I don't mind the work, but I could really use some company."

Ben nodded his head, imagining how lonesome trips to and from the moon had to be on an empty ship. He held out for more than a month before opening the box that contained Chip, and by that point he found himself talking to toilet paper rolls and hoping someone would say something back. "Man, I sure wish there was something I could do for you," Ben said.

"Ash tells me you're working at the Pizza Bar," Chip said, changing the subject. "Is that owned by the Tony Beatty you pelted in the face with a Vienna sausage can?"

"What?" Ash blurted out. "I haven't heard that story, have

you been holding out on me?"

Ben looked at her with a smirk as Chip reached down, grabbing the wheelchair and hefting it into the side door of the van to strap Ben in securely. "It's only been a few days, I have to pace myself," Ben shot back.

"Oh, I had no idea that you are the kind of guy who had to pace himself," Ash said with a smile.

Chip turned around to face her and smiled. "Oh yes, Ben is reluctant and timid in that sort of way," he said.

Ben's face went white. "Chip, she didn't mean anything sexual by it, Don't give her the wrong idea," Ben said, trying to deflect the conversation from making him feel more uncomfortable.

Chip turned and looked at Ben, placing a hand on his knee as he used to when he tried to console the Captain. "What kind of idea would that be?"

That gesture used to make him feel uncomfortable, but now Ben almost felt like he was home with his best friend. "I know what you're trying to do," Ben said, "but instead of feeling weird about it, I'm appreciating this moment."

Chip nodded and said, "me too." Tugging on the straps holding the wheelchair in place, Chip turned to Ash. "Shall we?"

She nodded. "We shall."

Chapter Seven

"Do you want another piece?"

Ben looked up from his paper plate as she gestured towards the pizza sitting on the coffee table in his apartment. It was his favorite, Canadian bacon and pineapple, but the name Pizza Bar blazoned on the box made him like it just a little less. "Of all the places to order from, why did you pick my employer?" He meant his question to be a joke, but his voice sounded flat, even to him.

Ash smiled, tucking a tuft of hair behind her ear as she leaned forward and grabbed another slice and placed it on his plate. "Come on, Ben, you're telling me that you would turn down free pizza?"

"Free?"

"Did I forget to tell you? I showed Tony pictures of your road rash, and he had a change of heart about whether he thought you intentionally crashed the scooter. Of course, I explained a few things to him about how he had been running you ragged and then he told me a story."

"What story?" Ben shifted his weight on the doughnut, breathing slowly as he waited for the pain that never came as he moved.

"Oh, you know, just about a guy who crash-landed his ship on Earth and had hallucinations of an alien invasion and decided to throw a full can of Vienna sausages like a grenade towards some dude trying to deliver pizzas because of hallucinations that made the guy think it was an alien coming for him. Apparently, the story Chip was referring to had more truth than I ever could have imagined."

Ben groaned. Having heard the story when he woke up in

the psych ward and then hearing it countless times from Tony himself after he sought employment there made him wish he could forget it ever happened. Part of Ben thought the only reason he was hired was so Tony could take his frustrations out on Ben for what he had done. *Every job sucks, but this boss seems to take a little more pride in it,* he thought. "Did he mention that the hallucinations were a result of food poisoning from eating those tainted Vienna sausages for a few weeks?"

"I'm not sure telling your girlfriend that you ate tainted sausages is doing you any favors," Ash said with a smirk. "Besides, you wouldn't want me to tell you about all the tainted sausage I might have had, do you?"

Ben facepalmed himself, having not been ready for her witty comeback. "Sometimes you fire off at the mouth way too fast," he said. "I was trying to be serious, and you turned the whole thing into a joke."

"That's why you love me, is it?"

Ben nodded, smiling ear to ear. "Absolutely," he said as he lifted the piece of pizza from his plate and shoved it into his mouth. There was one truth about Pizza Bar pizza that everyone knew. It was great while it was hot, but once it cooled to room temperature, it had a terrible aftertaste. He tried to eat the pizza quickly before it cooled and he was left with a taste in his mouth reminiscent of a gym sock.

A knock at the door interrupted their conversation. Ash looked at Ben and asked, "Are you expecting someone?"

Ben shook his head. "Not unless it's Chip, but he was supposed to go back to work today," he replied.

Ash opened the door. On the other side, standing in the dark hallway of the apartment building, stood a weathered old man. "I'm looking for Ben," the man said in a gruff voice.

"And you are?" Ash asked.

"Mr. Rodgers' brother, if I remember correctly," Ben said as he strained to stand up from the couch, but once the burning sensation began he settled back into his seat. "What the fark are you doing here?"

"My name is Lon, and I come with some news." The old man shoved his way past Ash and stood in the light of the living room. He held up a letter and said, "I've got a message for you, Ben, and it's urgent."

"Yeah? And what is it?"

"Your friend, Chip, is in trouble."

Without realizing what he was doing, Ben shot up from the couch. The immediate pain following the decision almost caused him to fall, but he kept his footing and limped towards the old man. "What do you mean Chip is in trouble?"

The old man took a step closer, "do you mind if I take a seat?"

Ben gestured towards the couch as he staggered out of the old man's way so he could sit. "I just saw Chip yesterday," Ben said, "he didn't say anything about being in trouble."

The old man moaned as he leaned back onto the soft cushions of the couch. "I'm not surprised. My brother is a man who has always been more concerned with profit margins than doing the right thing. When Chip decided to leave work to check in on you, it rubbed my brother the wrong way. You see, when he doesn't feel like he holds all the power over someone, then he'll try to tighten the noose a little bit. With Chip being a robot who isn't as corrigible as most, Buck took the news of Chip's borrowing a van and leaving work as insubordination, and it will lead to Chip's recycling."

Ben sat, air barely filling his lungs at the thought of Chip's being recycled as punishment for coming to his aid. "Your brother is a son of a bitch," Ben said under his breath.

"You're telling me," the man replied.

"What can we do to save him?" Ben asked as Ash came and sat on the arm of the couch next to them. She placed a caring hand on his shoulder, and he appreciated the gesture more than he could say.

"That's why I'm here," the man said. "If it's one thing I know about Buck, it's that he's a highly competitive individual. If you want to save your friend, you have to beat Buck at his own game."

"What you mean?" Ben asked.

"You present him with a challenge to a game of poker; winner takes all."

The anxiety of Chip's being in trouble and the idea of going head-to-head in a poker match with Buck again made it harder for Ben to breathe. Buck didn't seem like the type to give a shit over after losing everything in a poker match, mostly because he probably never lost. "I'm no match for that man," Ben said. "He destroyed me once, and he'll do it again."

"Yeah, I know the feeling," the old man said, "but I would try anything if it meant I saved my best friend from being turned into razor blades."

The way the man put it sent chills down Ben's spine. *I can't let that happen,* he thought, *I owe chip my life.* "Is there any other way?"

"If you had the money, you could outright purchase him," the man answered.

"Fark. I'm broke."

"I have an idea, "Ash said. Both men looked at her with curious expressions. "What if I challenge him to a poker match?"

"He's a bit of a male chauvinist, sweetie," the man said, "if you stepped up to the table to go against him, he would make a big show about defeating you relentlessly."

"Do you have experience playing the game?"

"Well, I'm the strip poker champion on the rodeo circuit," she replied with a smile. "The only things I ever lost were my socks."

Chapter Eight

"Toss them on the floor," Ash said with a giggle.

Ben looked over to the old man, his face red as he dropped his trousers, his belt buckle and chain wallet clacking loudly on the tiled floor. "This is ridiculous. You have to be cheating," Ben said as he stood in his boxers and thinking that the only thing more embarrassing than this moment was being in the hospital with his ass cheeks exposed to everyone.

"Nope, I don't have to cheat when I don't have any competition," she chided.

"You know, she has a point," the old man said as he stood from his seat and moved closer to Ben. "No offense, but you are about as competitive as a piece of paper in a rainstorm."

"None taken," Ben said sarcastically. "If you're so farking smart, then what do you suggest?"

The old man tapped the table. "Deal me in, sweetheart," he said.

Ben gawked at the old man, looking to Ash, waiting for her to say no so he didn't have to. She just shuffled the deck. "You can't be serious," Ben said, his voice on the verge of cracking.

"I'm dead serious," the man said.

"It's just a game of strip poker, Ben, calm the fark down," Ash said as she dealt the cards one at a time.

"You don't think it is inappropriate that a guy old enough to be your father wants to play you in strip poker?"

Ash stopped dealing the cards for a moment, gazing up at Ben with a stern look. "What? Is there something about me where you think men shouldn't want to play strip poker with me?"

Ben stammered, looking for the right words to say that

reflected what he thought. *Oh fark,* he thought, *that's not what I meant.* "No—"

"No, men should not want to play with me?" Her eyes narrowed as they seemingly bored holes through Ben.

"That's not what I —"

Ash and the old man blurted out laughing, the old man slapping the table with a hearty hand as they both looked at Ben with tears in their eyes from holding their laughter in for so long. "I'm just farking with you," Ash said as she continued dealing the cards again. "Besides, if this old geezer can get me out of my clothes, maybe he deserves a show."

"Challenge accepted, sweetheart," the man said as he raised one eyebrow and stared up at Ben with a smirk.

"I'm not comfortable with this," he said.

"Are you comfortable losing any chance you have with Chip's being recycled?" The old man said dryly.

"No," Ben replied.

"Then I suggest you sit down, shut up, and get to work."

Annoyed, Ben sat down at the table across from Ash and picked up his cards. Sitting in the apartment wearing only his boxers was an uncomfortable situation, but it was also the most urgent thing he had ever done in just his skivvies. "What's wild this time?"

"Sixes," Ash replied.

The old man cleared his throat, tapping his cards on the table before he spoke, "you want to know something odd about Buck?"

"What's that?" Ben asked.

"It should be no surprise that Buck is a cheater, and he has a habit of any time he's afraid he's going to lose, of saying a certain card will be the wildcard, and it seems that every time he does that he ends up drawing that card," the man said.

"What are you trying to say?" Ash asked, the tone of her voice raised.

"I don't know how I never saw it before, but he hires the dealers, and he has to have it worked out so that every hand is rigged in his favor when he calls for a wildcard. When he took everything from me, he said 'deuces wild' and that was the hand that took everything from me. I don't know why I didn't see it coming then, because I'd watched him do the same thing to countless other people, always calling the wildcard and it miraculously appearing in his hand. He never said how he did it, or that it wasn't just an incredible amount of luck, so perhaps whenever I was in the hot seat, I thought it could never happen to me. I was a fool for thinking that.

"Just something I started thinking about when Ben suggested a wildcard. If that's the case, then it is not skill on his side, but a complex form of cheating."

"Son of a bitch," Ben said, slapping his cards down to the table. "He did the same farking thing to me—'deuces wild'—and that's when I lost the *Shistain*." Ben crossed his arms over his chest, partially because he was angry, but also because he was starting to get cold in the nippy apartment.

"Well, how do we combat somebody who cheats like that?" Ash asked, her brow furrowed as she shuffled the cards in her hand nervously.

The old man leaned back in his chair, pulling his whiskers in the same way Buck did at the poker table. "We have to find a way to beat him in his own game," he said, "but short of kidnapping his dealer and shoving him in a closet somewhere, I have no idea how we can pull the rug out from under Buck."

"You know, that is not a bad idea," Ben said.

"What's that?" The old man asked.

"Kidnapping his dealer and having Chip do it," Ben answered.

"I didn't suggest Chip do it," the man replied.

"I know, but if you want to pull the rug out from someone, they have to be standing on it. Chip is employed by Buck, so if we can find a way for Chip to be able to deal the cards, then it would prevent Buck from gaming the system." Ben said with a smirk that suggested he was mighty proud of himself for coming up with a tactic that could possibly work. Possibly being the operative word.

"I don't know—what do you think?" Ash asked, looking at the old man as he frowned and tugged on his chin hairs.

"If we can make that happen, you might just have a real shot at kicking my brother's ass."

"So, I guess we should get a hold of Chip and let him know our plan," Ben said, his lips curling into a smile about the possibility of getting even with Buck Rodgers and being able to save his friend.

"All right, let's do it!" Ben and Ash looked at the old man, and the answer was on his face with a shit-eating grin.

CHAP+ER NINE

The rain poured, not unlike the storm when Ben crashed the scooter a week before. As they waited outside Buck's "Palace" they became drenched. "It's just like my brother to leave people waiting in the farking rain until it's convenient for him to open the damn door," the old man said as he wrapped his coat tighter around his body trying to stay warm.

"Yeah, I've meant to ask, what is your brother's farking problem anyway?" Ben asked, the curiosity coursing through his veins just as fast as his blood despite the frigid temperature outside.

"Technically, he's my half-brother. We share a father, but he has a different mother. My mother was his stepmom, and she treated him like shit. I had nothing to do with any of it, and it's not like I could've helped him anyway, but I think he feels that taking her past aggression out on me will make up for the shitty childhood that we both shared. Honestly, she didn't treat me much better," he said, with a tinge of sorrow in his voice.

"Sorry to hear that," Ash said. "My childhood was pretty shitty too."

"Mr. Rodgers will be with you momentarily," the woman on the other side of the door said. Her pixie cut and small frame made her look like a twelve-year-old boy in Ben's opinion, but she wasn't unattractive.

"Do you think maybe we could wait inside." The old man asked, his voice shaky from being cold.

The woman turned her head, looking at someone or something hidden behind the door. "I'm sorry, please give us just a few more minutes," she said, shutting the door in their faces and leaving them in the cold again.

"Mother farker," Ben seethed. "If we don't beat this asshole, I might just jump across the table and beat the shit out of him physically for being a farking douchebag," he said.

"Calm down, son. It's not that serious. Besides, the more time we're out here, the longer it will take us to dry off and get ready for the game, giving Chip a little more time to carry out his end of the plan," the old man said. "And if I'm not mistaken, timing is going to be everything."

The door opened suddenly, and there stood Buck Rodgers with a fake grin on his face that looked painted on. "Old man, it's great to see you. Why don't you come in," he said, shoving the door wide and allowing enough space for the three of them to traipse in.

"Don't lie," the old man said. "It makes you look fifteen years older."

Buck looked sour, but he shifted as Ben looked at him, his eyes narrowing into slits. The hatred he felt for Buck Rodgers rivaled the way he felt for his asshole father. "Right," Buck said as he closed the door behind Ash.

"Only thirteen and a half minutes in the rain, I expected the full fifteen just for dramatic effect," Lon said indignantly. "I guess some things never change, do they?"

Buck groaned. "Don't be such a Peggy Sue about it," he chided. "I'm trying to operate a business, which means that business comes first. Of course, I don't think you have much experience with that lately."

Ben watched as Lon glared at his older half-brother, the hatred on his face revealing more of the hurt throughout the years than the man's stories suggested. "Nope, and I have you to thank for that," Lon replied, turning his back on Buck and continued into the large living room that doubled as the poker room when it was game time.

"I thought you would've let that go by now," Buck said with no sound of remorse in his voice.

"Do you guys think you could chill out on your family reunion therapy session so we can discuss tonight's game," Ben said, interrupting the drama unfolding before him. "I kind of feel like time is of the essence. That's why we dropped everything to make this happen as soon as possible."

Both men looked at Ben with similar expressions on their faces.

"I suppose time is of the essence. I planned on recycling

your robot friend in the morning," Buck replied. "Of course, I have no idea what took me so long to come to that decision, but I suppose it's in your favor to have the opportunity to save him."

Ben's hands balled into a tight fist, his fingernails digging into the skin of his palms at the thought of the bastard being so casual about recycling a robot. Ben understood robots were not human, but there was a personality behind Chip that made him truer than any human friend Ben had ever had.

"Well, I suppose we should be thankful for that," Lon said. "It's not every day you get to see how hospitable Buck Rodgers is."

Ash cleared her throat, drawing attention from all three men. "I don't suppose you have a place where I can dry off, do you?"

Buck stared at her for a moment with a curious look, "Who's the girl?" he asked as he looked over at Ben. "A shopping partner, maybe? Based on your previous companionship, I didn't suspect that you liked girls."

"What the fark did you just say?" Ben shot back, pulling his hands from his pockets and imagining wrapping them around Buck's neck and strangling the shit out of him.

Ash grabbed Ben's arm, pulling him back, "Ben, don't," she warned. "He's just trying to get under your skin."

Ben glared at Buck, his eyes narrowing and his heart pounding. "If we were out on the street, I would have something to get under his skin," Ben hissed.

Buck seemed to welcome the threat with a smile. "Well, I'll be damned if the kid doesn't have a spine."

"I've got more than that if you want to see it."

"Oh, am I walking into something provocative?" Chip asked as he rounded the corner leading into the living room. All eyes fell on him as he sauntered over to the group with a seductive sway of his hips as if he was walking on a runway. Ben knew it was just an act, something to provoke Buck and to make the older man feel uncomfortable. It was funny enough to lower Ben's blood pressure, though he fought to keep from smiling.

Buck shook his head, feigning disgust. "My God, does everything have to be a sexual innuendo with you?"

"When you say 'innuendo' it reminds me how much I want to be in you, you know," Chip said, the pun falling flat and leaving him the only one smiling.

The fact Ben had said the same thing to Ash days before was not lost on him. "We need to work on your delivery," Ben said dryly. *At least when I said it, Ash laughed.*

"Look, I don't have time for this, so make yourself at home. Just don't be too comfortable," Buck said. "I have a few things to round up before the game starts. Give me about half an hour to get my affairs in order." Without waiting for a response, Buck walked away, disappearing into the shadows of the long corridor leading away from the living room.

"I don't like that guy," Ben said, not trying to keep his voice down.

"Yeah, you're not the only one," Ash replied. "That jerk didn't even point me in the direction of a bathroom so I can try to dry off."

"Come with me," Lon said, gesturing toward a short hallway on the other side of the room. "The common people's restroom is this way." Ash followed Lon as they walked away, dripping rainwater onto the tile floor for some hapless servant of the devil incarnate to clean up later. But Ben couldn't care less. If people are willing to work for this asshole, then they get what they deserve.

"So, I'm assuming you guys are ready for the game tonight?" Chip asked.

"Ash is, but I'm growing more nervous by the minute," Ben replied.

Chip frowned. Lon had told Ben that the situation and been explained to Chip and he knew what was at stake. *Sometimes silence is the best response,* Ben thought.

"Hey, maybe if we can get you out of this asshole's grip, we can take a trip somewhere," Ben suggested, trying to sound hopeful.

Chip nodded his head. "I would really like that, Captain."

Hearing Chip call him Captain felt like another stab in his heart as he remembered losing everything he had ever had, or wanted, to Buck Rodgers.

"Yeah? Well, let's make that happen because I sure as hell don't want to lose you, buddy," Ben said.

For several moments, Ben and Chip looked into each other's eyes without saying a word. But in the silence, everything left unspoken was said.

CHAP+ER TEN

Seated at the table where he had lost it all, Ben shifted his chair closer, nervously wiping his clammy hands on his pants' leg. With his view of the cards in Ash's hands, he grew increasingly paranoid that the game would not unfold in their favor. On the other side of Ash, Lon sat with his arms crossed, tugging on his beard hair as he glowered in Buck's direction. Similarities between the two men were not lost on Ben, but he felt that Lon was the nicer of the two if that counted for anything. Of course, "nicer" was a relative term when he considered how many jabs the old man took in his direction, constantly putting Ben down in front of Ash.

"So, little lady, are you going to call it?" Buck asked from the other side of the table. He held his cards close to his body as he leaned forward, tapping the small deck onto the green felt of the tabletop. Ben noticed there was the shift in the man's behavior his time around. Ever since the news that his dealer was unavailable and Chip had to take his place, the whistling that accompanied Buck's confidence fell silent. Ben couldn't help but hope that by crippling Buck's ability to cheat at the game, that it would put Ash at an advantage. Looking at her small pile of chips, on the other hand, did just the opposite.

Ash shrugged and positioned herself in her seat to match Buck's body language. Tapping her small deck of cards, she exhaled a large plume of vapor that looked eerily similar to the cigar smoke from Buck's end of the table. "I would call it, but then I wouldn't be able to raise you," she said, reaching down and picking up two blue chips and placing them in the center of the table.

Buck snorted as he looked at her, his eyes narrowed as if he was trying to read her mind. The small entourage of people surrounding him was not laughing, though. Part of Ben was thankful for that, although the deathly quiet of the room made him feel like he was in a hollow chamber, not unlike a coffin. He trembled at a chill running down his spine, but no one seemed to notice. All their attention was on Ash, where it belonged.

"Mrs. Brown just raised you fifty dollars, Mr. Rodgers. What would you like to do now?" Chip asked, his right hand hovering over the deck of cards for him to draw from. Chip did not look in Ben's direction, but Ben had the feeling the robot was just as nervous as he was regarding whether Ash could pull off a win. Ben hated feeling defeated, but he couldn't help it considering that the last time he was in this room he lost everything.

Buck tugged at his facial hair, twisting his beard into small curls around his finger before pulling his finger loose and starting again. "I'll see you, and raise you another fifty," he said.

Ben sucked in a deep breath of air, fighting back the urge to whimper at the devastatingly small pile of chips on their side of the table. Those blue, round pieces of plastic represented more than just money to Ben. They represented Chip's life.

Ash nodded and shoved two more chips towards the center of the table, depleting her pile by half.

"So, what are you going to do now, Miss Thang?" Buck asked, his voice sounding creepily flirtatious and sickening to Ben's ears.

"I'll call it," she said flatly.

A grin curled Buck's lips as he eyed them.

How that man can look at each of us individually and as a group at the same time is really freaking me out, Ben thought as he shifted in his seat again, the chain attached to his wallet clattering against the wooden legs of the chair sounding louder to spite the cryptic silence of the room.

"Well then, why don't you show them to me?" Buck said as he leaned forward, running his fingers along the corners of his mouth.

Ash placed the small stack of cards face up on the table, running her hand along them, fanning them out to reveal each one independently of the other.

Two pairs, Ben thought, *basically nothing*. The dual pair of fours and sixes sat impotently on the tabletop.

Buck snorted lightly, stopping himself, but making a show

of it that was every bit as condescending as if he had belted it out loudly. "Well, that's a little anticlimactic," he said, slapping his cards onto the table and revealing three Queens.

"Congratulations, Mr. Rodgers, you win again," Chip said with no inflection in his voice. Taking on the role as the dealer, Chip spoke in a tone void of emotion, sounding more like an android than any companion. It was unsettling for Ben, but he was sure Buck reveled in the lack of personality exuded by Chip.

"Thank you, Chip," Buck said, mimicking the robot's accent in a way that sounded more like a taunt than it did sincerity. It was another personality trait that Ben hated about the old man. His lack of sincerity made him that much more of a dick in Ben's opinion.

Lon leaned close to Ash and whispered something in her ear that Ben could not hear. It made him more nervous knowing Lon called the shots regarding the game, further removing any of the power from Ben, even though if anybody other than Chip was going to lose from the outcome of the game it would be him.

"How about another hand, Mr. Rodgers?" Ash asked as she tugged at the collar of her shirt, revealing enough of her cleavage to get the old man's attention.

That's pretty low, Ben thought, but just as unwilling to avert his eyes as the grumpy old man across the table.

Chip looked in her direction as well, lifted an eyebrow as he made eye contact with Ben momentarily. That look said it all: that Ash was willing to bring the girls out to try and secure a victory. *Is it really that much of a longshot?*

Buck cleared his throat, tugging on his collar as he smiled sheepishly. "Baby girl, I'm always down for another game with you." The creepiness of his voice speaking to Ben's girlfriend made Ben want to dive across the table and cut out the old man's tongue. When Ben looked at Lon, though, he saw the younger of the brothers was smiling, not with his lips, but with his eyes.

"Why don't we make it interesting with a wildcard?" Ash asked.

Buck's lips puckered as he nodded eagerly. "That sounds like a great idea for the last hand of the game. Chip, let's make the deuces wild."

"Yes, Mr. Rodgers, deuces wild," Chip said, repeating the

order.

This better farking work, Ben thought as Ash placed her last two chips in the center of the table. Buck did the same, but pulling chips from one of a half-dozen healthy stacks. Then Chip dealt the cards.

Buck shifted uncomfortably in his seat. The five men seated next to him looked grim, and Ben noticed a twitch on the man's cheek. *No whistling, no beard tugging, and no shit talking*, Ben thought as a felt a smile trying to invade his face. *Don't tell me we finally have this bastard pinned down.*

Buck took a deep breath, releasing the air slowly from his lips without looking up at his opponents. "It's not every day that I feel like my world is falling apart," he said. "You see, I'm a man who always gets what he wants. Kind of like your girlfriend over there, trying to use sex as a weapon, which is a form of cheating I can't say I condone."

"What do you mean?" Ash asked, leaning back in her seat. Her voice was dry and flat, sullen to Ben's ear and almost threatening.

"You, popping the buttons on your blouse isn't a very modest tactic in a game like this," he replied. "It's a scheme for toying with your opponent. That flirtatious nature isn't genuine, and it says a lot about your integrity."

"All's fair in love and war," she replied.

"And which do we have?" Buck asked, void of expression on his face.

In his mind, Ben was having a hard time figuring out what was going on. For several moments, silence filled the room, no hushed words whispered from solemn lips into listening ears. There was just the sound of his heartbeat climbing rapidly and filling his ears. "Ash, what's up?" Ben asked, concerned He hated his insecurities, but he hated not knowing what was happening even more. This lull in the game was proving more stressful by the second.

"I think Mr. Rodgers is trying to play me," she answered. "He wants to look like a defeated little puppy, whimpering as if he was being scolded. But I see through your bullshit, Mr. Rodgers, and I'm not playing your game." Ash placed her hands on the table, and glared at the old man with a defiant look that appeared to harbor as much hatred for Buck as Ben felt.

A shit-eating grin curled Buck's lips as he lifted his eyes and looked Ash in the face. "I imagine if you were going to use sex as your weapon of choice, then I can at least use a different psychology for mine," he replied. Grinning with a twinkle in his eye. "I'll call it," Buck said as he set the cards on the table, fanning them out as he released them. Three Queens and a pair of Jacks sat face up on the green tabletop, further igniting the fear coursing through Ben's body.

Fark.

Ash scratched her cheek before pulling a tuft of hair behind her ear. "How confident are you in your hand, Mr. Rodgers?"

"I have nothing but royalty on the table, sweetheart. It's hard to be more confident than that," he replied.

Leaning forward, crossing her arms together, she glared at the old man across the table, she said, "How would you like to raise the stakes a little bit?"

Buck smiled as Ben grew more nervous. From where he had been sitting, he didn't have the best look at her hand. He knew she had a King of hearts, but the other four cards were a mystery to him. *What is she doing?*

"What do you have in mind?" Buck asked, leaning back in his seat and once again tugging at his beard. Across from Buck, his brother Lon did the same, their expressions almost identical as Lon imitated his older brother.

"Beyond playing for Chip, if I win, I want the *Shistain* and one-million-dollars," Ash said flatly.

Ben's stomach groaned as he thought about everything that was at stake, and how unlikely it was that she had a winning hand. "Ash, what the fark do you think you're doing?" The worry in his voice caused it to crack.

She looked him in the eye for a moment, but she didn't answer.

Full of worry and concern, Ben leaned closer to Ash, trying to get her attention, but she refused to look back in his direction. The room was dead silent with Buck's cards on the table and Ash's ability to have the winning hand in doubt. *Why would she up the stakes at a time like this,* Ben wondered. It doesn't make any farking sense. The seconds felt like hours as he held his breath and the urge to say something he might regret. As the tension built, something inside him reached a breaking point.

As he stood, turning his body towards Ash as she sat silently next to him, he demanded, "What are you doing?"

She looked up at him, her eyes wide. For a moment, he felt

a connection with her, and in that split-second, he thought it was her way to let him know it was over. Whatever cards were under the King she held were nothing compared to the hand Buck had.

"It will be okay, Ben," she whispered.

But he didn't believe her, every moment of every hand up until now had been the same. Even with Chip dealing the cards, they could not come out on top. It was as if Buck was God of the Game and everyone else was nothing but pawns. *It can't be over*, Ben thought with dread.

"Sit back down, son, and let the little lady continue the game," Buck said sardonically.

Hearing the bastard's voice speaking to him condescendingly filled Ben's heart with rage. As he turned to look scornfully at the man, Gli+chy acted out. Sparks flew from her servos as she began flailing about, spinning and slamming into the table, splitting the old poker table in two as she slammed down onto the center of it. Cards and poker chips flew everywhere as the table collapsed. Everyone but Chip and Ben backed away from the carnage, their eyes wide at the vulgar display of power unhinged. The devastating destruction of Ben's ultimate reminder of failure sat at their feet.

"I —"

"What the fark have you done?" Buck seethed. He stood over the splintered wood from the antique poker table where he had amassed his wealth. The man trembled as his face reddened. To Ben, he had a look indistinguishable from whether he wanted to scream or cry. *Either would be appropriate*, Ben thought.

"I —"

"All is not lost, Mr. Rodgers," Chip said. "If that was indeed the last hand, then all that is necessary is for her to reveal the cards in her hand and the game would be complete."

With everyone standing in the room, the tension grew as dust fluttered under the yellow lights overhead. Beneath her feet lay a wasteland of the past, and now all that was left was for five cards to be revealed to determine Chip's fate.

"Very well, what do you have?" Buck asked as he adjusted his belt before thumbing his belt loops.

"You never answered the question. Do you want to up the stakes?" she asked.

Buck nodded impatiently. "Yeah, whatever—the robot, the

ship, and a million dollars. What's your hand?"

Ash looked over to Ben, a solemn grin barely forming on her lips as she handed her cards over to Chip. "You did say deuces wild, didn't you, Mr. Rodgers?" She asked.

"I did," he answered confidently.

"All right, you can make the check out to Ashley Brown," she said as Chip turned over the cards to reveal two aces, two deuces, and the King of Hearts.

"What the fark?" Buck and Ben said simultaneously.

"You heard the lady, you rat bastard. Get your checkbook out and start writing!" Lon yelled as he rose from his seat, a look of elation on his face. His laugh was long and loud as Ash stood next to him, smiling. Ben exchanged a long look with Buck as the older man's entourage chirped in the background with high-pitched voices full of concern.

Lon's hearty laugh preceded the slap on Ben's back that drove his attention to the younger of the brothers. "What the hell just happened?" Ben asked, his voice cracking.

Lon smiled. "That old son-of-a-bitch got what he had coming is what happened. And it's all because of you," he said, turning his back on Ben and hugging Ash. She yelped as the old man lifted her from the ground and turned in a tight circle n celebration.

"It looks like you're the captain of the *Shistain* again," Chip said, leaning to whisper into Ben's ear.

Ben looked in his friend's direction, and it finally hit him. "We won?"

"You did," Chip answered.

"Holy shit," Ben said.

"Congratulations, Ms. Brown," Buck said, extending his hand to her.

She took it and nodded, but said nothing.

"I have never played an opponent with such skill. My ego is bruised, but I think it's about time I experienced defeat. Winning becomes boring after a while," he bragged, but Ben could hear something in the man's voice that suggested the loss meant more to him than he wanted to let on.

"I'm just glad we were able to save Chip. He means a lot to Ben," Ash replied.

Buck glared in Ben and Chip's direction. "I can see that," he said with a tone on the verge of judgmental. "I'll have the money wired to your account. Please give your information to my secretary. I…" Buck stopped talking, and his voice trailed off as he walked away, his shoulders slouched.

"Poor guy," Ash said.

"Fark him," Lon, Ben, and Chip said before erupting in laughter.

"Let's get out of here and celebrate," Lon said. "You three have a lot to be thankful for."

"What about you?" Ash asked.

Lon smiled. "Yeah, me too."

CHAP+ER ELEVEN

"I still can't believe you did that," Ben said, dropping the last box of personal items taken from his apartment onto the deck of the cargo hold of the *Shistain*. "Having a winning hand tucked in your sleeve to pull out a win was amazing. I mean, where the fark did you learn to do that?"

Ash readjusted her ponytail, smiling as she bit down on the scrunchy while she used her hands to brush her sweaty hair back. "My uncle was the master of cheating at all kinds of games," she muttered, her voice muffled as she spoke through her teeth. She pulled the scrunchy from her lips and fixed it to her ponytail before continuing. "He taught me how to swindle at a few card games, but I think poker was my favorite."

"I have to say, Ash," Chip said, walking off the cargo bay ramp while Lon followed behind him. "Your willingness to game the system, despite the good fortune it had for me, is a little unsettling. How are we to know that you would not cheat us in the future?"

"Chip!" Ben shouted, blood rushing to his face at Chip's audacity to say such a thing about his girlfriend.

"I mean no offense," Chip added, "it's just that what I witnessed was a ruthless display and a trait not conducive to trust. I suppose I should be honored that you had me in on your plan to induce stress in Ben so that an appropriate distraction could be made for you to switch the card, but dishonesty is not the best policy, except maybe in this case." Chip stood with a wry smile on his face as he placed his hands on his hips, exuding as much sass as the situation permitted.

"There you go, talking with your robot intellect," Lon said as he slapped him on the shoulder. "You might want to be human, but you think about everything in black and white. It's the gray area where everything in the world happens. So what if her hands are dirty? She saved your metallic ass, didn't she?"

"Oh yes, she did," Chip said as he slapped his shiny derrière, causing Ash to laugh and Ben to shake his head.

"I'm not worried," Ben said. "If anything, your willingness to go above and beyond for someone other than yourself is a trait I'd rather admire."

"What about the million dollars?" Ash asked. "Was my cut of the winning not me looking out for myself?"

Ben shrugged, not knowing how to respond to her comment. "I guess, but still not something I'm worried about."

"Good," she replied, pulling herself towards him and kissing him.

"Oh my," Chip said flirtatiously. "With the amount of heat in this room, I might need a hand to clean myself off. What do you think, Lon?"

"I don't think so," Lon replied as he stepped off the cargo bay and into the main compartment that Ash had used a portion of the winnings to have re-furnished. "Are you going to get your ass in gear and come see the surprise, Ben?" Lon shouted from the other side of the bulkhead.

"Yeah, yeah," Ben said as Ash pulled her lips away from his. "The old man's about to have an aneurysm if we don't go in there," he said with a smile.

"Aneurysms are bad. That's one kind of an explosion from one type of head that I would not like to experience," Chip said, the obvious attempt at a joke causing Ben to shake his head with disappointment.

"Nice try, Chip, but you really need to work on that," Lon said as he rounded the corner and stepped into the lavish cabin of the *Shistain*. At the top of the bulkhead was the same sign hung months before proclaiming the "World Famous *Shistain*," but this time it was illuminated, backlit. Where the old, crumpled couch used to sit was now a plush sectional sofa large enough to seat half a dozen people while still not taking up too much of the small space. "This is farking amazing," Ben said gleefully.

"And the couch is a pullout bed, big enough for two of us," ash said as she ran her hand along Ben's back.

He looked at her, his heart beating faster as he thought about their potential future. "For the two of us?"

“Hey, I want to be on board this vessel too,” Chip said.

“They know that, Robo-knob,” Lon said sardonically. “This is going to be their space.”

“Then where will we be?” Chip asked as he turned a small circle looking around the space.

“We’ll take half of the cargo hold and make a secondary living space out of it,” Lon replied. “The construction crew’s coming tomorrow.”

“So, you’re serious about becoming a member of the crew?” Ben asked. It was hard for him to fight the smile forming on his face at the thought of having a real crew that looked at him as the captain of the ship.

“If you three will have me, I’ve got nothing better to do.”

Ben looked at Ash; her eyes were wide and boring into his. “What do you think, is this ship big enough for the four of us?”

Ash smiled, “the ship is, but this bed is just big enough for you and me.” She pulled Ben’s face towards her, their mouths open as they kissed, causing a groan from Lon and Chip.

“Yeah, yeah, you two like each other’s parts,” Lon said. “It doesn’t mean you have to flaunt it in front of Chip and me.”

Ben and Ash stopped kissing, but they continued to gaze into each other’s eyes before either of them spoke. “I really think you two should get to know each other,” Ben said, looking over at Lon and Chip as they stood over them. “I mean, the two of you are going to be roommates after all.”

Lon looked at Chip and shrugged his shoulders as he put his hands in his pockets. “I don’t have a problem with that so long as he knows to keep his hands to himself,” Lon replied.

“I can put my hands wherever you want,” Chip said, raising his eyebrows as he smirked. But his joke did not affect Lon’s expression.

“Let’s go; we’ll spend the next few nights in Ben’s old apartment until our space is rehabbed. That way we can leave the two lovebirds alone,” Lon said.

The two of them stepped out of the cabin, disappearing behind the steel bulkhead with the sound of the cargo bay door closing. Alone, and his heart racing as he felt Ash’s hands rub the inside of his leg, Ben felt like every hardship in his life have led to this one magnificent moment. “You know, I think I love you,” he said.

“I know,” Ash replied. “But the real question is, what are you gonna do about it?”

Ben smiled as he ran his hand along the side of her face, her eyes piercing into his. *This is the most amazing woman I've ever known*, he thought as they sat beside one another, holding each other. After a few moments of silence, he shrugged, "fark it."

About the Author

Drew Avera is an active duty Navy veteran and science fiction author of the bestselling series, The Alorian Wars. Growing up in Mississippi, Drew often dreamed of visiting faraway places. In the Navy, he has visited a dozen foreign countries and has traveled thousands of miles on the open sea. Drew enjoys his free time by reading, writing, and playing guitar.

www.drewavera.com

Books by Drew Avera

The Alorian Wars
Book 1: Broken Worlds
Book 2: Deadly Refuge
Book 3: Mutiny Rising
Book 4: Shadow Empire (Coming Soon)

The Dead Planet Series
Book 1: Exodus
Book 2: Verity
Book 3: Endgame

ZIP! ZAP! BOING!

by Andrew Lawston

The role of a lifetime doesn't come without a catch.

Struggling actor James Fanning is out of options when he runs into the mercurial Mr Puff, who offers him the role of a lifetime in a touring production.

The catch? Puff's production is touring warzones.

The other catch? Puff's theatre company is the renowned Starship Troupers Initiative, who tour wartorn hotspots on Earth's outer colony worlds, ten thousand years in the future. And James is about to discover the STI have their own agenda, which will soon see him fighting for his life on the remote desert planet Jargorth.

Featuring thrilling space battles, heroic acrobatics, and space marine theatre critics, Zip! Zap! Boing! puts the opera into space opera...

CHAPTER 1:
DRESS REHEARSAL

A huge battlecruiser drifts over the Jargroth imperial court, briefly obscuring the twin moons Zerxia and Krellatewn, whose vivid purple light is the only illumination, shining through the jagged hole in the lofty domed roof and acting as a natural spotlight. My head is bowed as I step into the small patch of light, the vivid green plasma restraints at my wrists and ankles fizzing slightly, poised to dismember me at the slightest hint of transgression. I'm orbited by drones, bobbing and dipping in the chamber's faint air currents. They too are primed to vaporise me at the first wrong move. The floor around me is already littered with fresh young corpses, both human and cyborg, and the watching crowd's silent judgement already sits heavily on my shoulders.

Out in the crowd, a thousand heavily-armed troops are watching. Soon, many will be weeping with remorse, when they have heard all I have come to say. Others will be baying for my blood. And the eventual outcome depends on my words alone.

Slowly, I raise my shaven head to face the silent accusers on the floor of the Jargroth parliament, well aware how the harsh overhead light will make my cheekbones and nose look sharp, cruel, and haughty. So be it. I open my mouth.

"Two households both alike in dignity,
In fair Verona where we lay our scene,
From ancient grudge break to new mutiny,
Where civil blood makes civil hands unclean.

From forth the fatal loins of these two foes,"

Two more circles of light slam down on to the stage, flanking me, and illuminating two grizzled old warriors brandishing greatswords,

"A pair of star-cross'd lovers take their life."

A final spotlight shines down directly in front of me, illuminating a human female and a cyborg, entwined in death in each other's arms, and both covered in blood.

As I draw breath to speak the next few lines, the female gives me a conspiratorial wink, which I acknowledge by flipping her off before disguising the gesture as a declamatory finger pointing to the heavens. As I do so, the rest of the lights go up, to reveal a sizeable fraction of the Jargroth army sitting in the galleries and stroking their beards thoughtfully, occasionally creaking in their heavy space marine armour as they reach for a humbug from a paper bag, or consult the holo-programmes that have been streamed to their gauntlet displays.

It's all a long way from weekly rep at Whitby Pavilion.

And I expect you're wondering how I came to be here.

Several Days / Ten Thousand Years Earlier

I took one last bow before the curtains descended, and then barely made it into the wings before the desultory round of applause died away, and the audience made a sustained dash for the bar and the toilets. I winced, and shrugged at Matt, poised on the ropes to open the curtains in case of a final encore.

"No bouquets tonight, Jim," the old stagehand said cheerily, and we both grimaced as the rest of the cast streamed away around us.

"Any performance you can walk away from, Matt." I skipped down the steps that led to the backstage area, my fellow actors already far ahead in their dash to get changed and round to the pub before last orders.

It wasn't likely to be a great cast party. One week playing

Macbeth to an empty seaside theatre in bitter January wasn't the experience I'd expected whenever I dared to dream of a Shakespearean lead role. The actors would huddle in a booth in the grim old boozer round the corner that had become their home from home, and we'd make solemn promises to see each other in whatever shows we were doing next. We'd pretend we'd had a great time, and had made great art together, when in fact the only thing any of us would miss about Whitby was the price of a pint.

Full of these thoughts, I reached the glorified cupboard that passed for my dressing room. I wandered in, and reached for the bottle of water I'd left in front of the mirror. That final swordfight had really taken it out of me. As my understudy, on closing night the other actor no longer had any interest in 'accidentally' injuring me, so I'd thought Macduff might lay off. No such luck, though. He must have had a girl he was trying to impress in the audience.

"Thirsty work, isn't it?" said a voice behind me, and I spat a gulp of water across the mirror, where it hissed and steamed against the hot light bulbs that ran around the outside.

Staring into the water-spattered mirror, I saw that an old man was sitting on the chair at the back of the room, right next to the hook where I'd hung my coat. In spite of the man's considerable girth, he was perching on the very edge of the seat, his hands clutching an ornate cane that rested between his knees. His face half-obscured by his flowing silver hair, the man's single visible eye was keen and bright. He was dressed in an odd beige quilted tunic, which was padded all over the place to make him look like an inflatable samurai. If we hadn't been the only show in Whitby that week, I'd have sworn he'd just stepped off the stage.

"Don't mind me," he said cheerfully. "I needed a sit down."

I shrugged. The Stage Door people had been notoriously curmudgeonly about letting even family members pop round after shows, so this didn't feel like anything I should worry about particularly. I picked up some cotton wool pads, and began to remove my make-up.

"Did you enjoy the show?"

The old man frowned. "I did. Though 'show' seems a bit trite for the Scottish Play, don't you think?"

I shrugged again. "If you say so. There's more dry ice than a rock concert and at the Wednesday matinee they even started booing me in Act 3, so it felt more panto than tragedy. Who did you come to see?"

The old man's lips twitched in a faint but genial smile. "Well. I'm in your dressing room, James."

"Oh, yeah. Right."

There was a copy of the show's programme on his knee, and he picked it up, opened it at a page of text in the middle, and proffered it with a shy smile. "I don't suppose you could... ridiculous, I know."

I had a pen in my coat pocket, and it was in my hand in less than three seconds, even as I did my best to pretend that signing an autograph was no big deal and I did it all the time. I dashed off the loopiest version of my signature that I could muster, and then raised an eyebrow when the old man slammed the slim booklet shut briskly and stuffed it inside his tunic.

"Thank you, dear boy! Well, to business, I suppose. Now this run is ended, where is your career taking you?"

Something about his question put me on edge, I couldn't figure him out. Was he an agent, or a fellow actor? It wasn't beyond the realm of possibility that he was both, a knackered old thespian turning to a desk job in the twilight of his career, but there was a brisk edge to his words that suggested he was just going through the motions of this conversation. Was he a journalist? It hardly seemed likely, but then neither did an agent...

I realised I'd been quiet for too long. "I, ah, have a few irons in the fire. But I'll be off home in the morning to South London. Been on the road a while, I'm sure you know how it is."

That last phrase was loaded with innuendo, trying to draw out this peculiar visitor, but he just smiled and gave a placid nod. "Indeed. So you're not currently engaged in any acting work?"

Again, it was as though he was reciting a script. I shook my head.

"Very well. Cards on the table. I run a theatre company staging shows in... far-flung, shall we say, locations. In warzones, to be completely truthful to you. You ever thought about doing a spot of outreach work for a good cause?"

My mind was racing. I'd never thought of doing anything of the sort, of course. I was too fond of Britain's crappy weather and Sunday roast lunches in pubs to go and do panto for orphans while wearing a UN helmet and dodging bullets. Still, I was dimly aware that sort of thing looked great on CVs, and there was another important consideration which might override my love of a comfortable life.

"Does it pay?"

The old man smiled, and patted his expansive belly. "Of course it pays. I didn't develop this fine athletic physique by eating pot noodles off dry crackers, dear boy."

I smiled too, as I climbed out of Macbeth's armour, and into my jeans. He'd clearly met enough actors to know that he'd already sealed the deal with his last words.

"And what part would I be playing?"

He hesitated. "This and that, dear boy. Call it a repertory arrangement. We perform in some hairy spots, we sometimes need to change the bill at short notice through political and cultural considerations. Having said that, I was rather thinking you might fancy a crack at Romeo."

I stopped short, standing stock still on one foot in the middle of putting the other leg in my jeans. Romeo. The part I'd always wanted to play, brainwashed into desiring it after what felt like three years of studying the play at school, but which I'd always thought I'd be too old for now I was pushing thirty.

"And where are you performing next?" I asked.

The old man looked a bit shifty at that question. But though my grasp of current affairs was patchy, I knew roughly where the major flashpoints were. I'd already assumed the Middle East, and if it was anywhere less fractious, so much the better.

I waved a hand as I pulled up my jeans and buttoned them. "You know what? It doesn't matter. I didn't train for three years just to be a resting actor. I'm in. When?"

He stood in one fluid motion in spite of his size, beaming radiantly. "We'll be on our way very shortly, dear boy. But I've not introduced myself. I'm Joshua Puff. Artistic director of the STI."

I winced at the acronym, but I shook his hand anyway, and grabbed my coat and bag. I took a quick look round the dressing room, but there was nothing else I could be bothered with.

"I'll see you to the car park," I said. "STI?"

"Yes," he boomed as we left the dressing room and walked along the short corridor towards the stage door. "Starship Troupers Initiative."

I shrugged. "How long have you been going?"

"I suppose from your perspective, we're a very new company indeed. But I've been running the company for seventy years."

We approached the stage door. I signed out with a flourish. Puff didn't bother, and I didn't blame him, Jeff was soundly asleep in his little office.

"Seventy years touring warzones?" I said as we stepped into the night. "You must lead a charmed life."

The old man gestured at his eyepatch. "Almost," he said quietly, and I cursed myself for my insensitivity.

The car park was windswept and covered in drizzle, though that was hardly unusual. It had emptied more quickly than usual, however, or perhaps I'd been talking to Puff longer than I realised. No wonder Jeff had fallen asleep, he'd probably got fed up waiting for me to leave. It was probably just as well I wasn't coming back any time soon.

I panicked at the thought that I might miss last orders. Not that I'm an utter boozehound, but decompressing after a performance like that is important. I reached into my coat pocket for my phone so I could check the time, keeping up the conversation to mask my impatience.

"Why Starship Troupers?" I asked, as I fumbled the device into my hand.

He squinted at me, then sighed. "I would have thought it was obvious, but I forget the limitations of this century, dear boy. The STI operate across the galaxy, entertaining the combatants of hundreds of skirmishing colony worlds, ten thousand years in your, and Earth's, future."

Oh bugger. I regretted shaking the lunatic's hand. "OK," I said, weakly.

He cocked his head, looking a little concerned. "That's probably a lot for someone like you to take on board, shall we find some sherry while you adjust to the culture shock?"

I smiled. "Not at all, that's fine." *I needed to get to the pub right now, and I needed to make sure he didn't see which way I ran*.

"I'm glad you're being so understanding. We're off to a little place called Jargroth, a desert world that was doing rather well for itself with a tolerably advanced post-industrial civilisation until some grubby capitalists banded together to have a crack at their Imperial Highness. The Jargroth civil war is a particularly tricky conflict in that the rank and file are a touch more erudite than the usual grunts we end up serenading. Until a few weeks ago they were all software developers and marketing professionals. We need someone with a spot of classical training."

I saw my opportunity. "I'm hardly classically trained," I pointed out. That was an understatement. A GCSE in Drama and a depressing amount of networking events was a more accurate description of my background.

But he just fixed me with a funny look. "Ten thousand years in the future, you're automatically about as classically trained as it gets," he said. Which was disconcertingly logical, I had to admit.

It was time to call his bluff. "Well, I suppose we should get on with boarding your, ah, spaceship," I said confidently, ready to make a run for it as soon as the poor old bugger's delusion crumbled in the face of reality.

Puff nodded, with a broad smile, raised his cane and whistled. We both staggered under a sudden squall of rain, and when I'd wiped away the water from my eyes with the back of my hand, there was a spaceship hovering a few feet above Whitby Pavilion's car park.

I could tell it was a spaceship because of the saucer shape, complete with iris hatch opening underneath to reveal a blaze of white light and an entrance ramp which was slowly extending towards us. It had to be said, though, that it looked a bit dilapidated. Something looking very much like rust covered the edges of the hull's panels, illuminated by the theatre's house lights and the UFO's own brilliant light, making it look like a giant hovering jigsaw puzzle. Someone had painted the classic comedy and tragedy masks on the side, presumably to jolly the thing up a bit. But a good deal of the paint had cracked, melted, or burned off during the course of the ship's various atmospheric entries, leaving two ravaged cracked faces screaming into eternity like half-decomposed clowns.

"The cloaking field's pretty noddy stuff, and we don't even use it in the course of our touring in case it's misinterpreted as a hostile act. But it makes for an undeniably impressive entrance," Puff explained.

I looked up at the impossible yet squalid shape hanging in the air, at the ramp extruding from the iris hatch like a rolled-up carpet. "I'm obviously no expert," I said at last, "but is that thing even safe?"

The old man looked at me steadily through the pissing rain. "A tour of galactic battlefields and you barely flinch. And now you're getting the jitters because you don't like the *paint job*?"

"It's not that I don't like the paint job," I assured him. "I love the paint job. I just think there could usefully be a quite a lot more of the paint job."

The end of the ramp touched down on the slick tarmac with a wet clunk. Puff rested one foot on it and turned back to me. "I thought we covered this bit. We find ourselves performing in the most dangerous areas of the known Universe. At best we're playing to crowds of resource-hungry strategists. At worst, it's victorious troops looting or retreating forces scavenging anything not nailed down. It doesn't do to stand out with glossy tech. I'm sorry it offends your aesthetic sense, dear heart, but we prefer not to have our spaceship half-inched while we're in the pub. Now come *on*, we've a hypertime jump to make."

I laughed, and spread my hands wide. "You know, it's tempting to hop aboard for a quick trip to *Button Moon*, but I've got a hotdesk in a Croydon call centre waiting for me tomorrow afternoon *and* a potential callback for a student film, so thanks for the chat, Dangermouse, but I've got a pub to get to."

For a moment, Puff's face crumpled in disappointment. Then he gave an expansive shrug. "Young actors are usually a little more anxious to declaim deathless prose across the cosmos, but I suppose in the end it matters not. Given that you've *signed the contract* for a one-night performance in Jargroth Prime, and a two week stint in the Spiral Empire in Tetnulion."

I smiled, backing away. "I really haven't signed anything of the sort. Watch out for asteroids and Zargoids, or whatever." I aimed a deep and decidedly sarcastic bow in Puff's direction, and began to turn away.

The old man smiled and, without taking his eyes from mine for a moment, reached in his quilted tunic and pulled out the programme I'd given him. My heart sank as I saw where this was going.

Sure enough, he plucked a single sheet from inside the programme, with the word 'contract' at the top, and my loopy signature at the bottom, with a whole bunch of text in tiny print in the middle.

I rolled my eyes. "Oh come off it. You'd have to be Othello-level gullible to believe that old chestnut's in any way binding. You take your circus off to Bigglyboo Prime or wherever, and I'll get on the train back to Croydon."

Without another word or so much as a glance back, I walked away into the night. I'd barely crossed the road when a giant round shape flashed overhead, blotting out the night sky for a moment. Good riddance.

It was too late to go to the pub now, so I decided to head straight to my digs, a tidy B&B run by a fantastic old lady with the most spectacular white-streaked beehive hairdo I'd ever seen. I'd see most of the rest of the cast on the train in the morning in any case, and at least I'd get some decent kip.

Within a few minutes, I was toiling uphill through Whitby's labyrinthine alleyways and narrow streets. It was a tiring walk at the best of times, and I was even less in the mood than normal. As long as I got home the right side of midnight and had a few more glasses of water, I'd be fine for the first train.

As I stumbled through Arguments Yard, however, a huge shape shambled into view, blocking my way in the confined passage.

Hairs rose on the back of my neck at the sight of this intimidating figure, and I tried to remember how much cash was in my wallet. Luckily, my train ticket was still in my room at the B&B, but the cash I had on me was all my money in the world until the *Macbeth* producers ponied up my wages in a couple of weeks.

"You're the actor, from the Pavilion tonight?" a deep voice rumbled from the shadowy shape, tinted by a very slight European accent.

"Ah. Yes," I offered. I felt it was unlikely to be an autograph hunter, but this was a more promising opening line than most of the alternatives in this scenario. I was fairly confident I didn't owe money to anyone in Whitby. Maybe it was just, God help me, a critic.

He stepped forward, into a dull puddle of light beneath a fitful lamp. I relaxed further. It was just a very fat man, dressed in black tie for some reason, with a ludicrously waxed moustache stretching across his florid cheeks.

"Shouldn't you be in space about now?"

That threw me. I realised in the ten minutes or so that had passed since Puff's flying saucer had taken back to the heavens, I'd been consciously consigning the whole episode to the recycling bin at the back of my memories. My guard went straight back up.

"I should be in the pub right now, but people keep bothering me tonight. What do you want?"

He smiled at me, and lamp light glinted from a single gold tooth. "Perhaps I want to buy you a drink? And have a chat?"

"Contrary to rumour, I really don't swing that way."

The fat man continued to smile, but I was a long way past finding that reassuring in any way whatsoever. "We know you met the old man. We know what he probably told *you* he was, and believe me, we know exactly who he *is*, so just tell us what he said, and let us take care of worrying which bits were reliable or even sane. We just want to know what he said, or rather where he's going. He's far away already, what difference could it possibly make to you?"

Which was a fair point. But in my usual fashion, I'd seized on a particular fragment of that speech which I felt needed clarifying.

"You're saying 'we' and 'us' a lot. Who do you represent?" And can you give me a job, I just managed not to add to the end of that question.

The man laughed, in the key of E minor, disconcertingly, cementing his resemblance to the singer from the Go Compare advertisements. "Well, who indeed? In philosophical terms. But in the rather more prosaic sense, you could probably say that I represent the exceedingly toned chorus line creeping up behind you in this drizzle-drenched alley."

I turned, only to receive a roundhouse kick to the face from a lithe woman in a sequin-festooned leotard. As I staggered back, I saw that she was flanked by a blond young man in a suspiciously baggy white sailor's uniform, and an older woman in a basque who caught my eye and cracked her feather boa like a whip.

My head ringing from the impact, I put my hand to my suddenly numb lip, and was quietly unsurprised to see my fingers covered in blood when I inspected them.

"We're quite insistent, by the way," called Go Compare.

"Fabulouthly tho," lisped the sailor.

"What did the old man want?" the courtesan snapped her boa again, but I was staring at her mouth. She'd blacked out some of her teeth, like proper *Les Mis* shit!

"No, really. Who are you guys?"

Behind him, Go Compare sighed. And sighed. The sigh just kept going until with horror I realised the bastard was actually drawing breath... for a musical number.

"We are the very model of a modern operatical
Company who put on shows considered practical
To entertain the rank and file with ditties quite satirical
With a style and verve reputed as inimitable."

"Reputed as inimitable," chorused Sailor, Courtesan, and Sequins, before breaking into a four bar jig. I scanned the street in desperation. This part of Whitby was a rabbit warren. There *had* to be a junction or something I could duck down. But no, I was trapped with just four singing muggers in a horrific Gilbert and Sullivan remix of the Village People.

Another deep breath from the fat man.

"In this spiral arm we give hands down the greatest musicals,
Alas others favour entertainments not so whimsical.
We're at quite dreary loggerheads with companies dramatical
We wish they'd all just bugger off upon sabbatical."

"Bugger off on upon sabbatical," the trio chorused dutifully, and I waited for their jig so I could hoof the sailor in the nuts and make a break for it.

Instead Courtesan grabbed my throat and slammed me against the wall of the nearest house, her fingers locked in a vice-like grip that set my eyes watering.

"Puff's our oldest rival," hissed Sailor. "He's poached dozens of our bookings, he's got some hold or contact with the Arts Council that gets his tedious Ayckbourn shit in front of the troops while we cool our heels doing voice workshops with drill sergeants. What. Did. He. Tell. You?"

I took a whooping gulp of air as the woman's grip on my throat eased a fraction to enable me to speak. I protested. "He didn't tell me anything, Popeye! He tried to offer me an acting gig. In space, or some bollocks."

"Yes, we know *that*," said Sequins. "But *where*? Which planet is that dull dramatist aiming to stultify with some fucking Eugene O'Neill nine hour slog?"

"I don't know, he was mental and I pretty much stopped listening. In a warzone, right?"

Sequins rolled her eyes. "Great, he's a moron. Let's waste him and deal with the degenerates the old-fashioned way.

They can't have made warp yet, we blast them in the deep past, ten thousand years away from the Arts Council and any reinforcements."

She somehow pulled a set of nunchaku from her leotard, and began twirling them. I looked desperately to the fat man, who was watching me carefully, his head cocked to one side, stroking his moustache. Then he shrugged his expansive shoulders.

"I was hoping to steal a march and set up stage before they arrived. I've heard rumours, and I'd prefer not to engage the STI head-on, but it seems events are conspiring against us. You're probably right. Kill the whelp cleanly, though, we're under oath that any overt actions must be in keeping with the epoch."

The conversation seemed to be done, so I grabbed the nunchaku's chain mid-twirl, and dragged Sequins off her feet. As she sprawled on the alley's cold flagstones, I drove the carved wooden handle hard into Sailor's groin.

He doubled over with a gratifying whimper of agony and I turned to face Courtesan's boa, which was now crackling with ribbons of vivid pink energy.

She lashed out once and the nunchaku flashed into flame in my hands. I dropped the useless weapon immediately, but before I could move, Go Compare's heavy hand was on my shoulder, and spinning me round, and he was holding the largest knife I'd ever seen.

As Sailor and Sequins cursed on the floor around me, Go Compare raised his blade high over his head and brought it flashing down towards my unprotected chest!

CHAPTER 2:
TECH REHEARSAL

I raised my arm to cover my face in an instinctive and futile gesture to try and ward off the killing stroke, only to be dazzled by a sudden blaze of light and, inexplicably, a round of applause.

After a few seconds had passed and I still hadn't been skewered horribly, I finally lowered my arm. I found myself standing on a raised platform in a white-walled room about the size of a decent pub. Before me stood Puff, crystal-topped cane tucked under his arm, his silver hair tied back in a tight ponytail, and flanked by several amused... people. They all looked human, more or less, but whether it was the six inch fingers of the woman dressed in a motion capture catsuit covered in light bulbs, or the gentle greenish skin of the immensely muscular man standing behind her in a pantomime dame frock, or the cybernetic arm on the slender pale man opposite them wearing a really bad Sir Laurence Olivier Hamlet wig and doublet, they all had a hint of *otherness*.

"Oh, *very* good," bellowed Puff, with one emphatically final clap of his meaty hands before he retrieved his cane from under his arm, "then, *fall,* Caesar! Yes, capital! Ladies and gentlemen, meet James Fanning. James, we've already met of course. The lady is Grizabella, while the big lad dressed as a lady is known as Kraal. He thinks that's funny, but we've still not worked out why. And the one-armed gentleman is Gielgud."

The others smiled encouragingly, but I had other things on

my mind. "What the fuck just happened?"

Grizabella rolled her eyes. "The fuck you think happened? Matter transporter, *obviously*."

Icy fingers of dread clutched at my stomach. "I'm on a spaceship?"

"Even better," said Gielgud. "Look behind you."

With a confused shrug, and half-turned. My ensuing double-take elicited a fresh round of applause. But the fourth wall of the room I'd been teleported into... was a window on the cosmos.

I stared in awe at the purple planet whose curved horizon filled a good quarter of my view. Then I raised my gaze and began gawping at the majesty of tens of thousands of pinpoints of light, stretching away into infinity.

"I'm in space?" I breathed, hoarsely. Then I turned with a frown, hearing a distinct snigger somewhere behind me.

Grizabella coughed. "Well, erm, *yes*, you are. But Gielgud meant more specifically. You're on stage. We transported you to our rehearsal space, and you're kind of staring at the backcloth. It was getting weird."

I turned back as the sniggers grew louder, my cheeks prickling with vague embarrassment. I contemplated the vista a little while longer. "Now that you mention it... I do now notice that someone appears to have painted a cock and balls on this planet's ice caps."

"Yur," rumbled Kraal, "it's the North *Pole*. Hur, hur."

"I mean, we can show you *actual* space in a bit," said Gielgud, "we've got the odd porthole dotted around for aesthetic reasons, and *of course* a bloody great holographic display up on the bridge."

Puff stepped up on the stage, and clapped me on the shoulder. "Best stick with this though, lad. *Actual* space is duller than voiceover work. Imagine a screen full of tiny white pricks that never move. Ever."

I smiled, I couldn't help myself. "Where I come from, we call that Eddie Redmayne. So, I've been press ganged into your troupe after all, have I? You couldn't just call my agent, like a *normal* psychotic director, you actually abducted me from

Earth and - fuck, are you going to bum me?"

Everyone in the room raised their eyebrows at that, which was something of a relief, to be honest. "That came well out of left-field," said Kraal eventually, "do you want us to?"

Puff waved the ensuing sniggering into silence, and then looked at me seriously. "Would that it were all that simple, bummery aside. But the transporter plays merry hell with one's vocal cords. You won't be up to any serious or sustained acting for weeks."

That's a kick in the nuts for any performer, though now he mentioned it, my throat did feel weirdly dry and scratchy. "So why did you abduct me?"

The old man frowned. "Apart from saving your singularly ungrateful life from the ILO?"

I didn't even have a chance to ask who the ILO were before he raised a hand. "Interplanetary Light Opera. We're their sworn enemies, though we've honestly no idea why. The whole business would be faintly amusing if they didn't occasionally choose to viciously attack people we've spoken to."

I thought about Dram Soc and Music Soc at my old Student Union, and it did make a certain measure of sense. "Yes, thanks for that, but even so..."

"Just because you can't act for the time being, that doesn't mean you can't be of service to our company."

Kraal saluted. "I'm ready and willing to be a slightly shit Romeo in your absence, Fanning."

I frowned deeper than the old man. I really needed a gin and tonic and a lie down, but this stuff seemed important. "So what do you need me to do? You've not pulled me across space just to shift a bit of scenery?"

With a melodramatic sigh, Puff pinched the bridge of his nose, hard. "Wow. Uptake not rapid. James, I lead entertainers from warzone to warzone across the galaxy, in a company subsidised by the Galactic Arts Council. Now, I'm a *great* producer, but what does that suggest to you is really going on here?"

It was so obvious, really, when someone spelled it out like that, but the condescending bugger looked like the kind of person who wouldn't ease off until I just said it. "So you're spies."

They all beamed at that. Grizabella was the first to pipe up. "Oh yes. Best touring company in the quadrant, it goes without saying, but the best *spies* in four galaxies."

"And by trying to do a runner from your contract, you've volunteered yourself for our next little caper." Puff was all seriousness now, the hammy boom of his voice dialled right down. "Happily it's pretty simple stuff. Under cover of entertaining the Jargroth Revolutionary Army with a superlative production of *Romeo and Juliet*, you're going to break into their command post and secure any and all intelligence which could give the imperial forces the edge they need to put down the insurrection."

I wasn't sure what to think of this, on so many levels. For one thing, I've spent enough resting periods working behind bars that I'm instinctively a bit of a lefty. All this talk of 'imperials' sounded a bit Star Wars and fascist. "So the rebels don't have a genuine cause?" I heard myself saying.

Kraal blew air from his cheeks in a low whistle, but Puff took the question in good spirits. "Really not our call to make, dear boy. The rebels may well have a point, but they sure as blighted badger buggery don't have a budget. The imperial army are bankrolling this operation, and we have a wider obligation to the GAC to help settle this local nonsense. The outer worlds need to be unified, and looking... outwards. Forces are stirring. Forces that would sweep all of humanity into a black hole without a second thought. Worlds like Jargroth will be the first line of defence and they must be united, and prepared to fight these forces. Forces that will not..."

"... not be distracted by a spontaneous production of *Run For Your Wife*, I get it," I replied. "So instead of playing Romeo, you basically want me to do some spying. Me. The closest I've ever been to a spy was raising an eyebrow as an extra in a restaurant, after Daniel Craig ran through shooting people in the face. I needed three takes to get even that right. I'm going to be shot!"

Puff twirled his cane between his fingers for a moment, the crystal reflecting coloured lights across the ceiling, while the rest of the troupe had the decency to look at least a little concerned. Then the utter bastard had the cheek to actually smile.

"No, you'll be fine. This job's a proverbial piece of piss, dear boy. We're bribing a good proportion of our audience to come to the show, so key positions will be left unguarded. But I feel you'd be more reassured about the whole business if we put a pin in the field operation, and instead discussed the acting. I can't have someone make planetfall who's not making a clear contribution to the production. It looks suspicious, as far as these military types are concerned. Subsidised theatre, you know. All has to be accountable, to the nth paperclip. And they know it. So you'll be giving the Prologue, which I've doubled up with Friar Lawrence. So you'll have from the end of Act 3, Scene 3 until the beginning of Act 4, plus the interval, so you'll have more than enough time to nip out, do the *other* part of the job, and be back safely in time to give Juliet her sleeping drugs in Act 4."

"But Friar Lawrence is a wanker! An old wanker!" I protested.

Puff snorted. "That's all in the playing of it, young man! Is Lawrence a noble broker of peace? The Montagues' pimp? A voyeuristic sexual predator covering his tracks? A simple churchman trying to avoid incurring the wrath of those murderous nobles? I've seen 'em all, and played most of 'em myself. Pick an interpretation you like, and *own* it, dear boy."

"This still seems like..." I tried to object gamely, but the old man waved me into silence.

"And once you've swiped the data we need to swipe, and we've finished the show, had a few beers, and then warped the hell out of the Jargroth system, we head straight to a great little studio space I know on an orbital weapons platform near the Murgaltoyd Nebula, and you can play Romeo for four nights straight."

I knew it was ridiculous. I knew it shouldn't make any difference, that I was being cajoled into writing my own suicide note, that Puff's offer should in no way have made me feel better about any aspect of my situation. But the truth is, I was a 30 year old jobbing actor who worked in a call centre, so it did impress me. A bit.

"Will it be... papered?" I asked, pathetically.

He smiled, seeing he'd already won. "The quadrant's most reviled critics will be there, and offered suitable blandishments and incentives on your behalf, such that you'll never need to zip yourself up again this side of Galactic Centre."

I allowed my shoulders to slump in defeat. "Damn you, but you have yourself a deal."

The others cheered a bit, but Puff just stared through me.

"I know. Now, Grizabella will handle your training. Try not to break him, dear." And with that, the old ham turned with a swish of his absurd cloak, and swept from the theatre, the rest of his company falling in behind him like particularly slovenly stormtroopers.

All except Grizabella. She carried on smoking, watching me through narrowed eyes, like a cat.

"I'm confused," I said, only half-joking, "is this spy training or theatre training? I'm starting to lose track."

"Maybe both." She plucked the cigarette from her lips, stared at the cherry-red glowing tip for a moment, then seized my wrist in an iron grip and proceeded to grind it out in the palm of my hand.

I struggled in her clutches; I yelled as I heard the hiss of the burning cigarette smash into my smooth cool skin. I gritted my teeth and screwed my eyes shut against the incoming frenzy of pain... that never arrived.

After a moment, I opened my eyes. The torn remnants of the cigarette butt were cupped in my unmarked palm. Grizabella released my wrist, and I dashed the fragments to the floor.

"We're kind of pragmatic," she explained, "and it would be a bit of a waste parsing your entire atomic structure through the ship's computer without making a few edits. You've got five layers of synthskin over your epidermis. It sheds and sweats just like the genuine article. But while it's on there, you're resistant to most mundane forms of pain *and* bladed weapons, tested up to three kilotons of force. In hostile environmental conditions, the pores will close automatically, so you can pretty much swim through an acid lake. You're also shielded from X-ray and other deep scanning techniques - the synthskin's smart enough to just report back the image of a normal human body. That cigarette was both to check the tech's working, and a test of your acting abilities."

I boggled at her, while all the time stroking the skin on my forearm. It felt no different, right down to the little hairs, occasional freckles, and the knobbly patch on my elbow. "What for?"

Grizabella rolled her eyes, then tried to smile. "OK, it's probably not obvious from your point of view, but synthskin is kind of proscribed military tech, certainly not the kind of thing you ought to be packing as a touring actor. The security guys probably won't stub cigarettes out on you, but they might give you an 'accidental' jab. Now I've seen your genuine pain reflex, I need to see you fake it."

I was game enough, and began making yelping noises and pulling agonised faces. Grizabella actually laughed, and tossed back her hair as she took a full carton of smokes from her coat pocket. "Nice try. But we're going to need to singe a few layers of that synthskin before I'm satisfied. You get caught, and the game's up for all of us."

It was the method workshop from hell. Even the miracle synthskin wasn't indestructible, and my stomach began to turn at the rising stench of scorched flesh, as the deranged actor stubbed out countless cigarettes on my hand.

"You're *weird*," I hissed, as she finally reached for a fresh packet, "or just addicted to nicotine. Does it have to be burning? Can you not just give me a granny rub? Or a chinese burn?"

Grizabella paused, her lighter's flame flickering scant inches from the three cigarettes that dangled limply from her mouth. She considered for a moment, then shrugged, and mumbled around the cigs.

"Well that all just sounds fucking degenerate. Can I not just stick the next one in your eye?"

"Is my eye synthskin?"

She sucked hard on one cigarette until it glowed white-hot. I could see the air shimmering around it. She took it from her mouth, and smiled brightly. "I've honestly no idea. But if not, we can just space you, re-teleport you, and I'll have an *even better* idea of your pain reflex."

Re-teleport? I had a sinking feeling that outweighed even the terror of seeing Grizabella advance on me with a deranged grin and a burning cigarette held tight between her fingers at head height, like a psychotic darts player.

I took a step back, trying to convey that it had the potential to be the first of many. *Don't break him...* "Grizabella, how long since we left Earth? How many times have I been teleported?"

She giggled, and it stopped just short of being actually demented, but neither in all honesty was it even remotely reassuring.

"We're actors, not cybernetics specialists, so it might have taken a few passes to get the details right, but don't be so paranoid. We've only just cleared Martian orbit, once we hit the asteroid belt, we'll make the hypertime jump."

Hundreds of hours of teenage TV rebelled at that. "Hyper*space*?"

She raised an eyebrow. "Astrophysicist, are we?"

Before I could answer that, Grizabella darted forward and stabbed the cigarette into my palm. I doubled over with a guttural cry, pressing the hand to my chest, even as I lashed out wildly with the other arm to push the mad actor away across the room. I crashed to my knees, tears springing to my eyes.

"Fantastic, and finally!" Grizabella crowed. "I totally believed that!"

"That wasn't acting, you burned a hole in my fucking hand," I sobbed through gritted teeth. "Get me an ice pack or something?"

She had the decency to look a little concerned as I rolled around on the floor cradling my agonised hand, but of course she blew it almost immediately. "Must have burned through all five layers of synthskin. Still, if you show the burn at security points, it should stop them checking you out too closely."

"Ice... cold water... anything," I begged.

"Uh, yeah. Right." She looked around for a moment in indecision, then her face cleared and she darted towards the stage, where she flipped open a hatch and pulled out a heavy grey canister with a nozzle similar to a fire extinguisher.

"We, uh, never did clear up the eyeball thing, did we?" she said as she pointed the nozzle in the vague direction of my hand. "Probably best you shut them tight for a minute, just in case."

"In case wha-" I managed before she squeezed the canister's nozzle and a blast of blueish-white smoke enveloped me. I screwed my eyes tight shut and dreamed of murder, but incredibly the intense pain in my hand was subsiding.

"All better?" she asked after a moment, a little quieter now.

At first I couldn't open my eyes. Then I tried harder, really putting my eyebrows into it, and was rewarded with the tinkling of tiny ice crystals tumbling from my separating lashes. Grizabella's face was right in front of me, apparently checking my eyes for damage. With a sudden, dazzling, genuine smile, she put her hand on my cheek.

Now, normally I'd have been pretty into that, but given that she'd spent the last twenty minutes terrorising, confusing, and mutilating me, I was more filled with terror at what she might do to me next. But a moment later, she took her hand away, and showed me three sparkling crystal pearls, nestling in the palm of her hand. "Look James," she whispered with a giggle, "I froze your tears into diamonds!"

"What the hell was that?" I asked. "Dry ice?"

To my horror, she nodded. "We'd be a pretty sorry theatre without a spot of liquid nitrogen kicking around. Oh don't look so scandalised, like a pearl-clutching critic or some shit. Does your hand still hurt or not?"

"My entire upper body is numb to all sensation," I said as I stood up, grasping at the canister for support.

"There you go, then," Grizabella said. "Now, the next training session is a little more -"

A loud crunching noise sounded beneath us and the floor lurched, sending us both spilling to the ground. I thrust out a hand in panic to try and break my fall, and then blinked.

Somehow, I was standing upside-down with all my weight on one hand, swaying slightly as the room continued to lurch. Grizabella was just a few feet away spinning gently on her head, her face all serene and content.

She caught my eye on her next revolution, and winked. "Perfect timing, sort of. Yeah, gyroscopic implants. We all have them, they're invaluable for physical comedy. Unless you're really caught by surprise, you'll never take a bad fall again."

Then she frowned. "I suppose we'd better find out what's going on, though."

With no apparent effort, Grizabella flipped to her feet and ran for the door. I followed, jogging along on my hands for a moment for the sheer novelty, until that niggling wrist pain that I always worry might be an early sign of carpal tunnel syndrome kicked in, and I flipped to my feet as well.

The doors opened with a suitably swishy science-fiction noise, but then I saw what lay immediately beyond them, and I stopped dead in my tracks.

The threadbare red patterned carpet, the flock wallpaper, the framed photos of presumably venerated actors in dramatic black and white poses, the fake brass light fittings...

"We're in a theatre?" I said, and the flat accusing tone of my voice halted even Grizabella in her tracks.

"No," she said in a patient drawl, "we're leaving the theatre... and we're on our way to the bridge to see what all the shaking's about. Try to keep up."

I reeled as I recognised a photo of the Chuckle Brothers carrying a ladder, with hilarious consequences clearly imminent. "I can't believe I fell for this crap. We're just in a shabby old theatre! We never even left Earth, did we?"

Grizabella threw an anxious glance over her shoulder, and started to talk really slowly and gently, as though I was a particularly obtuse child. "I'm sure you were expecting flashing lights and turbolifts, but the *Peter Hall* is our home, and we fitted it out to be comfortable. And if we're ever stuck for a venue, we can just open the cargo bay doors, roll down the ramp, and do the show right in here. You see?"

I didn't, I was still convinced I was the victim of some kind of stupidly elaborate practical joke or prank TV show. The trick of getting me from the street and on the stage had been well-played, but this corridor could have been almost any theatre from Whitby Pavilion itself to the West End.

And I was full of these triumphantly rational deductions when the corridors shook and the section of wall nearest Grizabella vanished in a burst of green light.

In contrast to the earlier comparatively gentle lurches, the corridor tilted at least forty-five degrees, spilling me to the ground where I balanced on my left thumb, and watched in horror as a dreadful howling gale of escaping oxygen thundered down the corridor, threatening to bowl Grizabella through the ruined section of wall and into the inky void that was all that remained of a poster of David Warner's Hamlet. If this was some sort of set-up, it had just become horribly convoluted.

I found my thumb floating up from the carpet as whatever artificial gravity had been keeping our feet on the ground packed in. So I hung helplessly in mid-air as Grizabella slipped towards infinity.

Grizabella had kept her footing, thanks to her gyroscopic implants or just blind luck, but she was reaching desperately towards the polished faux-brass handles of the nearest door with a hollow expression of grim resignation, even as the escaping air flattened and stretched her sharp features across her face.

I took a deep breath while I still could, and shut my eyes. In the black space behind my eyelids, I saw a stark choice unfolding, and I surprised myself with the decision I took. *Damn. Turns out I'm a hero after all.* I opened my eyes, and Grizabella was sliding backwards inexorably towards the jagged hole in the hull, even as blaring alarms sounded down the corridor over the sound of rushing wind, and heavy bulkhead doors began to descend from the ceiling, attempting to seal off the breach, and us with it.

I reversed my grip on the canister, and activated it, hoping its spray would propel me forward so I could save the day. On my first attempt, the nozzle twisted in my grasp, and slammed me into a full-length portrait of Dame Judi Dench as Titania. Synthskin and gryoscopic implants or not, my nose crunched into the wall and felt close to breaking.

I shook my head to clear it, and tried to ignore the droplets of blood that floated from my nostrils and hung before me in mid-air. Grizabella was starting to speed up, floating just feet away from space with nothing to grab, and the bulkheads half-closed.

I squeezed the canister again, my burned hand clamped tight around the treacherous nozzle. With a hiss of spray, I was blasted down the corridor as I'd first planned. Grizabella's eyes widened as she saw me tumbling towards her. With the canister in one hand and nozzle in the other, I couldn't grab her myself, but she looped her arm around my waist and clung on tight.

Unfortunately, that movement was enough to deflect my course so that both of us continued to drift towards the hull breach. I angled the nozzle ahead of us and gave the canister another squeeze, but the last perfunctory dribble of gas barely slowed us at all.

"Didn't think that through, did you?" Grizabella whispered. The air was getting thin this close to the breach, and ice crystals were beginning to form in her thick hair. "It was supposed to be trust exercises next. You did catch me."

The ruined wall lay ahead, like a proscenium arch looking out on the cosmos. And as I gazed on it, frantically trying to work out how to avoid breaking the fourth wall by, well, joining it, the inky void was abruptly filled by a sleek, silvery spaceship. The sort that seemed to taper down to one point in front of what I assumed to be the cockpit, with a few other pointy bits on the swept-back wings that looked a lot like exotic weapons. Presumably aware of the damage it had already done, the craft spun on its axis until all the pointy bits were pointing straight at us. A couple of horribly ominous pods on the wings began to glow with a decidedly unpromising lurid green miasma.

I was unclear about a lot of things, but I was very aware, suddenly, that I was drifting towards hard vacuum, defenceless, with a woman I barely knew clamped to my waist, staring down the barrel of an alien starship's lasers.

Fuck it. I chucked the canister at the ship, a shallow gesture of defiance as much as anything. I was always shit at physics, so the canister's potential as reaction mass had never registered until it was accelerating into space, and Grizabella and I were hurtling backwards down the corridor towards the closing bulkhead door and safety.

As we whooshed along, I tried in vain to orient us so we were closer to the floor, so we might be able to slip under the descending barrier. It was hopeless. If there was a trick to navigating in zero gravity, it was going to take more than one lucky panicked throw of an empty gas canister to master it.

My back slammed into the door, driving most of the remaining air from my lungs, a process completed half a second later, when Grizabella crashed into my stomach.

She slithered down the door nimbly, dragging me down to its base so we could get through. The fighter craft outside started blasting death rays or something at us, and it was a profound relief when the energy seemed to splash harmlessly across the air, a few feet outside the tear in the hull. They must have activated some sort of shielding, then.

I was gasping for air, and my vision was starting to blur and darken when I tipped forward and Grizabella dragged my feet under the door.

The gap was barely a foot by the time my torso was bumping along the floor, and I did my best to help by pushing myself backward with my fingertips, every muscle tensed against the buffeting wind of precious air escaping into space. So I was staring straight through the tear in the hull when the fighter abruptly exploded in a blossom of orange flame and shiny shards of metal. In spite of all instinct I felt my eyes widen in helpless panic as a jagged shard of fuselage was blown straight towards my face.

The bulkhead finally slammed shut, microseconds before

we heard the clang of a sharp bit of detonated spaceship chassis thudding into the other side, right in front of my forehead.

The wind cut out instantly, but before I could even sigh in relief, the sudden stillness was ruined by the imperceptible hum of the artificial gravity coming back online. We both fell to the ground heavily.

Grizabella stretched her foot and pivoted upright in a moment. I tried to imitate her fluid motion, but following the zero gravity experience, my own confused sense of balance was in open conflict with the stabilisers, and I lurched into a standing position like Captain Jack Sparrow in the grip of one of Johnny Depp's hangovers.

I looked at my trainer hopefully. "So that was like a holographic simulator exercise, right?"

She was looking at me closely, as though seeing me clearly for the first time. "No, that all happened. You just flew us out of a hull breach while taking out a hostile gunboat with an empty fire extinguisher. Now I think we need to get to the bridge."

I prepared for a long jog as I hurried after her, but Grizabella barely made it ten feet before taking an abrupt left and flinging open a set of double doors.

The bridge was another revelation after the white space minimalism of the transporter / rehearsal room, and the Frank Matcham chic of the curving corridor. This new area boasted sleek modernity with white walls, blinking control consoles arranged around a central plinth, and a big-ass swivel chair at the back of the room, overlooking it all. But there was also a heavy element of dressing room shabbiness. There were towels hanging over several of the banks of flashing displays that lined the rear wall, bulky overcoats draped over the back of most of the chairs that ringed the podium, the floor was all but carpeted in dog-eared loose pages from scripts, and there was a row of wig stands on a shelf over a rack of otherwise quite exciting-looking rifles.

Puff and several of his actors/spies were clustered around the podium, cooing at something hidden from me but which was clearly illuminated by the console's uplit glow. Kraal was standing opposite me, and gave a little cough when he saw Grizabella and I hesitating in the doorway. The other actors whirled round, and then tried to pretend they were just having a nonchalant stretch. Puff merely glowered straight at me, and waved his hand over the podium. It responded by throwing up a display of the *Peter Hall* floating in a starfield, with a bloom of flames visible just off what I'd decided to call her starboard bow.

He jabbed one plump finger at me, and not in a polite gesture. "Fanning. We were just shot at by, and took significant damage from, a Grellix-class starfighter. We were thinking of having a chat with them and asking them to knock it off, when they exploded, peppering our hull with probably-radioactive shrapnel. Care to shed some light on this, dear heart?"

I was pretty sure taking down an attacker, however accidentally, could only reasonably count as a good thing, despite the old man's weird attitude, so I held my head high. "Just, ah, doing my thing."

He grunted, and snapped his fingers. A hologram of the fighter shimmered into being over the podium, about the size of one of the smaller actors. Grizabella and I watched as its blasters again pulsed their vivid yellow energy beams, again splashing harmlessly over an unseen forcefield. Only this time, they were accompanied by a high-pitched screeching noise. *Pew! Pew!*

Then, from outside the hologram's range, a tiny canister flashed into view, ploughing straight into the fighter's undercarriage. It punctured the craft's hull like damp tissue and vanished. Seconds later, the ship exploded.

Gielgud scratched his chin with his mechanical arm, almost knocking his teeth out with his grasping and whining servo-assisted fingers. He tried to style it out, staring at me seriously even as I smirked. "You had seconds, if that. How would someone from your primitive background know that the ionic reaction from passing our forceshields would send the canister into a ballistic slingshot velocity, let alone calculate the vector for the throw, given the quantum refraction index? What were you thinking?"

These guys were really starting to get on my tits, breaking my balls over a lucky break which had saved me, Grizabella, and quite possibly everyone else on board. I scratched my own chin, without injury, as I answered him steadily. "What was I thinking? If you must know, it was 'fuck it'."

The others all looked to Puff, who just stood staring at me balefully, his jaw clenched. Then the old man shrugged. "Suit yourself, dear heart. Let's see if you can get that lucky again. We've got two more contacts, closing fast."

"Look, I'm not trying to piss anyone off, it was just a lucky throw!"

Puff was unmoved. "Maybe it was. Now as I said, suit yourself. Your fox-fisting friends from the ILO followed us, and you're the only one aboard wearing synthskin, so you're leading the charge."

He gestured behind me, where Grizabella was holding the world's most pathetic bin bag spacesuit in one hand, wearing an almost apologetic grimace. Almost. "James, we're kind of unarmed. And this thing is an internal emergency suit, in case of sudden decompression. You're the only one who can survive in vacuum wearing this thing for more than three seconds. Not to mention the acceleration stress and hull rupture."

I narrowed my eyes, suddenly very aware that I'd understood most of that. "What acceleration?"

Puff smiled with all his remaining teeth. "Torpedo tube 3, I think."

CHAPTER 3:
PRESS NIGHT

The suit didn't feel any less flimsy once I was wearing it, a kind of giant semi-inflated plastic bag with an internal microphone and distress flares mounted on the sleeves. As I was hurried along to the *Peter Hall*'s underbelly, Puff's voice boomed from speakers apparently hidden behind every framed portrait of history's theatrical luminaries.

"They seem to be low on inventory. They launched their second fighter, a ratty little drone thing, and their ship is joining the fray. Cone-mounted anti-asteroid laser grid, wouldn't you believe it? Well, that's fucking commercial theatre for you."

"Yes, they're bastards," I agreed vaguely, for form's sake as much as anything. "But what am I *doing*?"

A heavy sigh huffed from the speakers. "Sorting them out. We'll put you on board their ship, you give them a damn good rogering. I'd have thought you'd be a bit more keen, after that business back in Whitby."

"They'll kill me!"

"Nonsense! That is, I'm sure they'll try, but you gave a good account of yourself in that alley, and now you can stand on one finger and hoof them in the teeth."

I dimly remembered a couple of lucky pops, and a portly face staring at me in a bellicose frenzy of bloodlust. "If you say so. And you'll put me on their ship how... bugger, scratch that, I've a horrible feeling I just found out."

We'd turned a corner and reached what at first looked like

a small theatre bar. Indeed, Grizabella bustled straight up to the row of optics behind the counter and began mixing herself a gin and tonic. Ice cubes were already clinking in her glass by the time Kraal had pulled the threadbare seat from a bench on the far wall, to reveal an alcove, filled with…

"Is that a… torpedo?" I ventured, as the huge green man knelt over the hidden compartment, and started tapping on a small panel on the tapering grey cone-shaped object.

Kraal shrugged. "Kind of. We can't carry live weapons. So no warheads, and even a guidance system would trip security scans. But the dumb shell is inert, and we never throw a prop away."

With a satisfied bleep, the torpedo's top half opened up along a seam I could have sworn hadn't existed a moment ago. As he'd said the interior was completely empty, other than a pillow at one end. I had something of a sinking feeling, confirming my earlier thought. Kraal's flourishing gesture and expectant look in my direction confirmed it, but I always like these things to be spelled out.

"You want me to get in that?"

He repeated the flourish. It seemed even camper. "Yeah."

"And you're going to fire me into the attacking craft? The one with the, ah, nose-cone anti-asteroid laser array?" I asked as I lowered myself into the snug tube in spite of every sensible instinct I possessed, the bag ballooning and billowing all around me to make the task all but impossible.

Grizabella spoke up, barely glancing in my direction as she twirled the contents of her tumbler, ice cubes clinking together like God's own dice. "Definitely in that general direction. But we did just mention there's no guidance system. And... to be fair, they're probably going to at least try and avoid an oncoming torpedo. We're giving them that much credit."

I tried to sit up when I heard that, but Kraal pushed me back down. He looked a bit embarrassed about it but his grip was nonetheless emphatic. "But what if you miss? Do I just streak off into space?"

He shook his head as he lowered the lid. "There's kind of a rudder at the base. We'll be in radio contact, so if you're veering off course we'll let you know so you can give it a bit of a kick."

I wanted to tell him exactly what I thought about that, but the lid clicked shut. Bastards.

They didn't hang about, either. A clang sounded above me, presumably as they replaced the cover on the bench, then all went silent. Then I felt a vibration running through the torpedo. Then with a *whoosh* I accelerated so fast I suspect it was only the synthskin that prevented my balls from popping out of my ears.

With no particular noise to mark the launch, I began floating within the tube, making the pillow even more absurdly useless. Great. More zero-gravity. "So... am I in space?" I asked tentatively, though it came out considerably less articulately due to my teeth rattling with the acceleration.

"Observant fellow," boomed Puff's voice from a hidden speaker. "Course looks good, when you feel an impact, the casing will come apart. Pretty much just compressed air charges, but it'll keep them on their toes. You'll only get a moment for your big entrance though, so do come up swinging. Tits and teeth, dear boy, tits and teeth!"

"Time to impact?" I asked, mostly to stave off the headache Puff's bellowing was starting to give me as his voice bounced around the confined space.

"Oh, not long," he continued breezily. "Ah, the buggers are altering their intercept vector. Unsporting, but still you can't blame them. Left hand down a bit." He ended in a creditable Leslie Phillips drawl that had me rolling my eyes until I realised I didn't know whether he could see me.

I nudged at the paddle between my feet. It was stiff and unyielding, but it finally seemed to budge a fraction of a degree.

"No! *Left* hand down a bit!" the old man bellowed.

I kicked the paddle to the right instead. "For fuck's sake, would it have killed you to run me through this stuff before firing me into a pitched space battle?"

Silence. Perhaps he finally had the decency to feel a little abashed. *Crunch!* Or maybe it was just show time.

A second crunching impact rattled every bone in my spine,

and I fell to the torpedo casing's ribbed metal floor with a thud as gravity reasserted itself.

No sooner had I fallen than I was flung into the air again as the torpedo bounced with a jarring impact. Something crashed into the left hand side of the missile, and we went into a spin for which no gyroscopic stabiliser could possibly compensate. If it didn't ease off soon, I'd be going into battle covered in puke.

As we sailed through the air, however, the compressed air charges suddenly kicked in with a sharp *pfft!* The sound wasn't dramatic, but suddenly I was drowning in light as the casing peeled away like flower petals opening to the sun, leaving me standing in mid-air like a very pissed-off stamen.

I was floating over the bridge of their ship, which looked much like the *Peter Hall*'s flight deck, only slightly smaller and with pitch pipes and ukuleles littering every visible surface. To my right, Sequins was busy careering through the hull breach that had let me in.

The other three were wrestling with control consoles even as their ankles rose into the air, and Go Compare had some sort of VR headset wedged over his huge skull. "Someone stop that draught," he bellowed blindly, "I can't hear myself shooting!"

Sequins and Courtesan looked up at me dangling in the middle of their bridge, and Courtesan reached for her boa with a savage snarl.

"Nice try," I said, and fired off one of the flares on my suit.

The incendiary rocket spiralled drunkenly down towards the deck, belching sparks and flashes of magnesium bright flame as it went. They clearly weren't designed for accuracy, or for range, but it did the job, heading straight for the singer's snarling face.

I'd forgotten my basic physics again, and abruptly found myself sent tumbling head over heels by the flare's ignition. As that meant I was facing the opposite direction when the flare exploded with a dull crump and blinding flash, I wasn't too cross with myself. Bits of Courtesan hurtled in every direction to coat the walls of the bridge with a series of wet splats.

My bin bag suit rebounded gently from the ceiling and I

completed another somersault. As I drifted back to the centre of the room, I realised Sailor had released his grip on the console, pushing himself off into zero-gravity so that his feet were aimed straight at my gently orbiting groin.

He was too close to risk my second flare, so I reached out and grabbed his feet, spinning backwards and using his momentum to slingshot myself down to the deck.

As my feet skimmed the floor, I grabbed the first lever I could reach and clung on with all my might.

Unfortunately it seemed to be a navigation console of some kind, and the whole ship lurched heavily to one side as a thruster fired somewhere out on the hull. My legs shot out sideways, but the sudden course correction sent Sailor shooting towards the hull breach. He collided with Sequins and they flew out into vacuum together. Pirouetting. Twats.

I realised the console I was clinging to contained one other object, the VR headset. As I tried to look around wildly, and believe me it's hard to do *anything* wildly in zero-gravity, as I was quickly discovering, a meaty fist collided with the side of my head. I was knocked to the ground, and scrabbled around to try and grab something to keep me anchored there.

Go Compare was clearly unused to freefall as well, and was drifting backwards away from me, more or less at ground level, his arms windmilling in a futile attempt to slow his drift, and his round face filled with open bloodlust.

"You've holed my beautiful ship, you utter bastard!" the man wailed. "But you'll perish too, and the drone's firing on Puff and his melodramatic bucket of scum, even as we speak."

God, he was really boring. My flailing fingers caught the edges of the headset, spilled to the ground when Go Compare slugged me against the console.

It was a squeaky tight fit pulling the gadget over my head while wearing the inflatable suit, but abruptly my field of vision was filled with a starfield, in the middle of which the *Peter Hall* was growing steadily bigger, as streaks of green laser fire blasted towards it. Its shields seemed to be holding, but also retracting closer and closer to the hull as they began to wither under the onslaught. If only I could...

I blinked with the sudden blaze of light as the headset was torn from my face. Go Compare punched me hard in the face, and I felt the distinctive crunch of cartilage as my nose broke beneath the synthskin. Warm blood again dribbled over my mouth, to rise up within the flabby helmet as bouncing droplets. I reached behind me, but the only thing I could feel was the discarded headset.

"Don't you understand? Your only chance is to help me stabilise this ship! It's over!"

I was fed up with my nose getting messed up. "It's not over," I said, fixing him with a steely stare over my ruined face, "not until the fat tenor sings."

Flushing red, he raised his huge fist behind his head, ready to pummel my face beyond recognition.

Pew! Pew!

Go Compare's huge round head burst like a watermelon, spraying blood and brains all over the few bits of wall which weren't already decorated by bits of Courtesan.

The hull breach was filled by a spherical object bristling with laser cannons, about the size of a supermarket shopping trolley. The drone, reacting to the assault on its last known pilot. Another countermeasure someone could usefully have told me about earlier. I'd been so close to blasting the man with a flare the moment the torpedo had blown apart. I took a deep breath, which only served to remind me I was getting low on air and open to the vacuum of space.

"All sorted," I said.

There was a pause, and then Puff's voice came through. "Ah, James! Splendid work! We were always moderately sure you'd come through. Good show."

There was a definite click as the channel closed.

"Thanks," I said. "The ship's holed, and the bridge is sealed off. So how am I getting back over to you? Matter transporter again?"

After another paused, the channel clicked open. "*Back* to us, dear boy? Not sure I follow."

"Well, I cleared out all the bad guys, but this crate's buggered, I need to evacuate pretty urgently."

There was a slightly awkward cough over the channel, and I could hear some arguing voices in the background. Eventually Puff spoke again. "Ah, I *thought* you were a bit more gung-ho about going than I expected. We, ah, fired you at them, virtually unarmed, in a torpedo you were steering with your feet, does that not suggest anything to you about the nature of the mission?"

My blood ran cold. "This was a suicide mission?"

"Bingo! That's the very word I was looking for! Good lad!"

"But, I'm still alive!"

"Yes, and we're all suitably impressed by your resilience and pluck! But it sounds like you won't be alive in a minute, by all accounts. Never mind, dear boy, we'll power up the matter transporter and have James Fanning back with us in a jiffy."

My momentary relief shattered as the real meaning of his words sunk in, underscored by Grizabella's earlier comments. "You're going to abandon me, and whip up a copy?"

More arguing in the background, but Puff's voice was steady. "Yes, seeing as we've still got your print in the transporter's cache. You're pretty roughed up, and we've got a job to do. Now, be a good sport and clear the comms, would you?"

The channel clicked out, with a decidedly final tone.

Bastards! I looked around the gory wreck of the bridge, at the hole in the ceiling which had virtually finished sucking all air from the room, and the lethal drone that hovered just outside, passively scanning the surrounding area. My microphone began to bleep quietly, letting me know the suit was low on air. I was getting cold, and the bridge's lighting flashed down into emergency red.

I was screwed.

I raised my arm to cover my face in an instinctive and futile gesture to try and ward off the killing stroke, only to be dazzled by a sudden blaze of light and, inexplicably, a round of applause.

After a few seconds had passed and I still hadn't been skewered horribly, I finally lowered my arm. I found myself standing on a raised platform in a white-walled room about the size of a decent pub. Before me stood Puff, cane tucked under his arm, and flanked by a semi-circle of amused... people. They all looked human, more or less, but whether it was the woman's six inch fingers, or the gentle greenish tint of the immensely muscular man standing behind her, or the cybernetic arm on the slender pale man opposite them, they all had a hint of *otherness*.

"Oh, *very* good," bellowed Puff, with one emphatically final clap of his meaty hands before he retrieved his cane from under his arm, "then, *fall,* Caesar! Yes, capital!"

The others smiled encouragingly, but I had other things on my mind. "What the fuck just happened?"

Long-fingered woman rolled her eyes. "The fuck you think happened? Matter transporter, *obviously*."

Behind them all, a pair of double doors were blown open in a ball of flame, triggering a howling gale. Almost immediately, a heavy steel shutter slammed down across the ruined doorway, cutting off the wind and flames, leaving a gore-streaked figure with their close-cropped hair full of ice crystals, their eyes obscured by weird glowing goggles, and the lower half of their face caked in blood. I looked closer, incredibly he looked sort of familiar...

Bastards, I thought again as I floated up towards the hull breach. Up close, the hole was surprisingly small, and there was no way my inflated spacesuit would pass through its jagged edges unscathed.

So be it. I took the deepest breath of my life, and reached through the hole to grab the drone with both hands, clasping the barrel of a laser cannon in each fist.

It backed reacted to my proximity by drifting backwards, pulling me through the breach.

The suit was shredded to ribbons as we passed through the hole, long gashes in both sides and sleeves de-pressurising it almost instantly. As I passed into open space, I screwed my eyes shut, and pulled off the rapidly deflating helmet. As I let the useless tatters of plastic drift from my fingers, I replaced the helmet with the VR headset.

The cold was indescribable. I could feel my limbs caking with ice, and the blood on my face froze solid in less than a second. But thanks to the synthskin, I kept moving.

The drone's cam filled my field of vision, and I twisted at its laser cannons until it spun sedately to face the *Peter Hall.* I squinted at one of the icons in its heads-up display, and swayed as the device fired a small thruster rocket and began moving towards it.

It took a while to master the controls, given that any icon I glanced at for more than a moment seemed to be activated, but pretty soon I was thundering through the short distance between the two ships. I angled down a few degrees and jetted forward so that the saucer's underside was floating over my head.

I let go of one of the laser cannons for a terrifying split-second while I checked the remains of the suit still clinging to my freezing body, and then nodded to myself.

"Full thrust," I hissed to myself, aware I was expelling the last traces of my air as I did so, and the drone sped towards the *Peter Hall.* Or, more accurately, towards the jagged hole in its hull where the fighter had struck earlier.

This hole was easier to navigate than the breach I'd put in the enemy craft, and in moments my feet were dragging along the frozen red carpet in the remains of the corridor.

The bulkheads were still down at either end, but the double doors leading to the rehearsal room were unshielded. Too bad.

Pew! Pew!

The drone's cannons made short work of the doors, and in a moment I was standing back in the transporter room, taking a deep breath as the emergency door slammed to the ground behind me.

I whipped off the headset. Puff, Grizabella, Kraal and Gielgud were ahead of me, already turning in shock, but I had eyes only for the figure on the stage. A scrawny, confused, scared actor who'd just escaped a brutal death at the hands of light opera fanatics on the mean streets of Yorkshire.

James Fanning. Me. Or rather, a pristine copy.

"No understudies," I growled, as my transporter clone opened his mouth to speak. I raised my arm, and slapped at the remaining flare on the ruins of my suit.

The rocket blasted through the parted ranks of Puff's company, and straight towards my double. I turned away as it sped straight into his open mouth, and detonated.

There was a long silence, as bits of my new-born counterpart slapped the cosmic mural behind the stage, sending the whole expanse of fabric billowing. Well, I'd learned an important lesson about the limits of synthskin.

"You sent me out there to die," I growled at the old man.

He began to say something, then stopped himself and shook his head. Then he beamed. "I sent you out to *win*. You know how to make an entrance, Fanning. Welcome to the crew."

In spite of being on the verge of hyperventilating, shedding icicles from every follicle and my nose threatening to drop off in a lumpen frozen mess of blood and cartilage, I couldn't keep my relieved grin from my face as the actors clustered around to clap me on the back and draw me into tentative hugs.

Puff's smile dropped from his face. "Now clean that backcloth, it looks like we're doing fucking John Webster. And mind Kraal's North Pole, he'll sulk for weeks if it's so much as smudged."

CHAPTER 4:
OPENING NIGHT

The journey through what Grizabella insisted on referring to as 'hypertime' was a real anti-climax. I was expecting at least groovy hallucinations, a black obelisk and stars wheeling backwards against the *Peter Hall*'s portholes. Instead, a dull thumping noise sounded through the ship, and we all blacked out for ten seconds or so.

And then we were in orbit around Jargroth, and on the bridge Puff was handing me the world's scratchiest sackcloth robe for my Friar Lawrence costume.

"Congratulations," I told him curtly. "You've found the one fabric in the Universe that can scratch the shit out of synthskin."

"Serves you right for trying to breach the contract," he said, and blew me a kiss. Behind him, Kraal was practising his swordplay in a mirror, and damn it, I felt like an utter tosser but it hurt me to even catch a glimpse of him in Romeo's costume.

"Focus," said the old man, waggling the crystal tip of his cane at me. Its normal blue lustre was looking more greenish under the bridge's harsh lights and holographic displays. We're going to be performing in the Imperial parliament building in Jargrothopolis, which has been under rebel control for six months, but which has been abandoned by their Workers' Council as it's so close to the front line. Handily, it's just two streets away from their War Office by the river, so we'll send you over there after you've finished saying 'there art thou happy' five dozen bloody times to Kraal in Act 3, Scene 3. You'll carry out a skilled espionage technique known as scanning everything there that's not nailed down, before nipping back in time to give Juliet her sleeping draught in Act 4, Scene 1, with the whole interval in between to give you a buffer. Clear?"

"Crystal," I said, pushing his cane down as its bobbing flashing tip was getting on my nerves. "Now, how about you explain how just four actors going to stage a traditional production of *Romeo and Juliet*, if you're sitting out on the sidelines as director?"

I'd noticed a while back that Puff was a lot more pleasant to be around once the subject switched back to theatre. He chuckled. "All part of the smoke and mirrors, dear boy. We bulk out the cast with volunteers from the insurgents' rank and file, with officers for some of the bigger speaking parts. All the lads are so busy trying to spot their mates and laughing at their stupid hats, they never stop to wonder why they've not seen any given actor for a while. And we make sure we cast a sufficiently senior officer somewhere in proceedings, so if there is any suspicion falling on us after the show, we've got a star witness who'll swear blind that he was with us all the whole time, for the sake of his career and avoiding a court-martial for negligence, if nothing else."

I nodded thoughtfully as Puff wandered away to harangue Kraal about his footwork, and hoisted the hessian robes over my head. The entire wardrobe had been exposed to space during our encounter with the ILO, so intellectually I knew there couldn't possibly be anything living in it, but even so my skin was crawling within minutes.

"You'll get used to it," said a quiet voice at my elbow. Gielgud was folding origami swans, in some set dressing flourish that Puff had suddenly insisted upon shortly after we completed the hypertime jump. I watched in fascination as his brutal-looking cybernetic fingers folded and tweaked the brightly-coloured sheets of paper with care and precision.

"Do you mind me asking? If this is so safe, how did you come to lose your arm?"

He looked up at me with confused eyes. "But I didn't lose the arm. The..." He took a deep breath. "I was created to be a mech. The arm and my brain are the only original bits of me left, after some dappy waitress crushed the rest of me in a hydraulic press just because she didn't want to play Hedda Gabler. Or was I trying to murder her to ensure her kids didn't form a future resistance movement? Sometimes I seem to remember it that way, but that all sounds a bit Banquo if I'm being completely honest. Anyway, Puff found me the rest of this body."

I took a step back. "Oh, crikey. Where did he...?"

The little man shrugged. "Oh, I don't know. We tend to see a lot of battlefields, so I can't imagine it was anywhere very pleasant. Griz managed to pull off a bit of jiggery-pokery with the transporter, and now here I am, a mech trapped in a humanoid body."

"Doesn't that cause you huge existential issues?"

He made one final fold along the swan's wing and inspected it for a moment as he considered my question. Then he held out the origami object to me with a smile. "Nah, not really. It hurts like hell when I wipe my bum with the wrong hand, though."

Grizabella took the swan from Gielgud's hand before I could reach it, studied it for a brief moment and then tossed it over her shoulder carelessly. "Not bad, Gielgud. Just another four dozen to fold. Now, I've engaged the landing auto-pilot, we're making planetfall in thirty-two minutes. It's show time, ladies."

Space had indeed been boring, but landing was brilliant. I stood at a porthole and watched as the view turned from inky black through violets, greys, whites and finally brilliant blue shades, all set off by the dancing display of flames wreathing the *Peter Hall's* base with re-entry.

As we hit the atmosphere, Grizabella tilted the saucer almost forty-five degrees to reduce the buffeting, and I stared down on an alien world.

It looked pretty standard, to be honest, like the final approach to Gatwick. Instead of fields fringing the city beneath us, however, I was looking at a flat orange mass of unchecked desert, with a mass of grey oblongs in the middle, which were gradually resolving into individual buildings.

"They chose to colonise this place, right?" I asked Kraal. "Why wouldn't they have... terraformed the desert or whatever by now?"

He looked around, already in his Romeo costume. "That's kind of what the insurgents are asking," he whispered.

We dropped at dizzying speeds towards the city, and I was almost bracing myself for a crash when the saucer levelled out just a hundred metres or so above the surface, and we began bobbing down gently like a sycamore seed in the wind.

"Hangar tractor beam got us locked," said Kraal, breathing a sigh of relief. "We'll be down safe in a minute or two."

"Was it ever in doubt?" I asked as the tops of silvery tower blocks began to appear through the porthole.

He shrugged. "It might look quiet, but there's a war raging on these streets. You never know... and Grizabella's a former galactic marine with a deeply impatient streak. I've seen her touch down in a built-up area and take out the entire theatre we were supposed to be playing."

The *Peter Hall* gave a sudden lurch, and spun at almost a right angle on its axis, until the tower blocks through the porthole were near-horizontal. Just as I was about to start swearing, a black shape whooshed past at the head of a fearsome contrail. The missile looped around, passing so close to the porthole that I could count its tail fins, before the ship flipped a full revolution on its vertical axis.

As Kraal and I picked ourselves up from the ubiquitous red theatre carpet, the missile streaked away, apparently finally thwarted, and crashed into a distant tower block. We shielded our eyes as the city skyline exploded into a blinding sheet of flames.

"Bit close," Kraal commented mildly.

I boggled, actually boggled at him. "Bit close? We nearly died!"

He actually laughed at that. "Nah, no chance. Not with Griz on the stick. It's a little bit of theatre in itself, the Imperial bunch letting off a pot shot at us as we land, though they know damn well we're here to do a job for them."

"And what about the people in that building?" I asked.

"Empty, I should think," Kraal said with a shrug. "I mean, this is a war, and quite a shooty one at that. The only guys up that high will be snipers and looters."

I turned to look at the blazing wreckage of the tower block. "Back in my time, of course, there's people who'd say the deadlier threat would have been the chemicals in the vapour trail."

"You mean the water vapour? Why would they ever say that?"

"Because they're thick cunts."

A nearby door bounced open, and Puff roared out of it, his hair all over the place. "What turd-licking arseferret set off that missile so close to my ship?"

Grizabella was already pounding down the corridor, her catsuit replaced by Lady Capulet's severe frock. "Regret to report we were forced to take evasive action within the tractor beam, Mr Puff. From the briefing reports, I'm inferring that Harkreth is manning the city's defence grid."

All the pomp leaked from Puff like a deflating balloon, and he smoothed his out of control silver mane with fluttering fingers. "Harkreth? What demented dodderer gave that raving shitlord a commission here? Why in the name of Marlowe's crusty balls was I not informed?"

The two of them strode back to the bridge, Puff shouting increasingly scatalogical insults all the way.

"Who's Harkreth?" I asked Kraal.

The enormous actor looked genuinely worried for the first time. "He's... well, he's former STI. Fell out with Puff after one too many imaginative bodily function-based epithets. Went mercenary, and turned out to be quite good at it."

This didn't seem too bad to me so far. "Good for him. So what? Aren't we working for his bosses?"

Kraal waggled his fingers non-committally. "Yeah... sort of. I mean, yeah, this time. But this is a guy who knows where the bodies are buried, exactly who else we've worked for in the past... he could cause a lot of trouble. And I ought to be honest, he knows how we operate. He'll know you'll be out in the field tonight. He may well try and kill you and turn in your intel himself for the money."

"Oh. Thanks for the honesty. I guess." We both turned back to the porthole, as the *Peter Hall* finally drifted down to a gentle landing in a warehouse-like building, whose roof folder back into place as soon as we were down.

A few minutes later we were strolling down the exit ramp, Gielgud explaining to me that he'd been supervising the volunteer actors' rehearsals via vidlink for the past few weeks.

"Some of them aren't bad, to be fair. It's just a pain in the arse having so many understudies," he grumbled.

"Why do they have so many -" I stopped, but then trailed off when I caught his look. "Right, yeah, dead men's shoes. Well, I won't say I wasn't tempted myself when I played Laertes..."

"You've never played Laertes, Fanning, you self-aggrandising prickwaxer," Puff boomed in my ear, though affably enough.

"Not playing fucking Romeo either, am I?" I muttered.

"That's the spirit, dear heart!"

The five of us gathered under the *Peter Hall*, looking out at the flat expanse of the deserted hangar without much enthusiasm. It looked to me as though there were supposed to be quite a few other craft in there with us, and their absence didn't give me a great deal of faith in the current health of the insurgents' war effort.

A door creaked open at the far end, letting in a patch of blinding sunlight, which framed three figures in silhouette.

They stepped towards us, at a sedate stroll. We exchanged glances, and I set off to meet them halfway. "We're going to be here all day, otherwise. Curtain's up in four hours."

Four hours later...

"The which if you with patient ears attend,
What here shall miss, our toil shall strive to mend."

My prologue over, I stepped back as the lights clicked off for a moment so all the corpses could stop pretending to be dead. I slipped into the wings as two non-commissioned officers playing Capulet servants began bantering in the market, while the rest of the actors bustled around them looking busy.

In point of fact, I had a strong suspicion that the "wings" in this theatre was actually something like the robing room for their emperor, but never mind. With all the waiting actors, props and bits of set, it was stuffed tighter than the wings in a proper theatre, so it did the job.

Puff bustled up to me, flapping his hands in agitation, and unclipped the prop restraints from my wrists and ankles. "Change of plan, dear boy. Bugger ye hence right now and get the job done."

I looked at the old man in alarm. "Now? Seriously? Is this because of that Harkreth guy?" To be fair, at this point there were a fair few scenes including Mercutio's interminable Queen Mab speech before I'd be needed back on stage, but the shifting agenda unsettled me.

"No! Well, yes. In a manner of speaking." Puff's eyes darted about. "The situation is escalating. We've had word of an assault later. The insurgents want to use our neutral presence here as an opportunity to mount an offensive. It wouldn't be the first time buggers have tried to use us as human shields, but the difference is Harkreth would take great delight in shelling the *Peter Hall* in immediate retaliation and calling it in as unfortunate collateral damage."

I put a hand to my forehead for a moment and took a deep breath, trying to steady my nerves. It didn't work. "Fuck, Puff, what did you *say* to this guy to piss him off so much?"

"I could tell you, dear heart, but I'm afraid you'd never use a toothbrush again. Now, gather your cassock, and get on with it. I want us in orbit well before the balloon goes up."

And with that, he opened the door to the network of corridors surrounding the Jargroth parliamentary chamber, and marched me straight from the building.

It was a strange city. Buildings sprouted from the ground in neat rows, which made the gaps between them streets by default. But though there was definitely some kind of tarmac beneath our feet, the desert beyond blew sand all down the thoroughfares until the city just looked like some kind of climate change propaganda poster vision of London amid sand dunes. But the temperature was dropping out in the desert now that the sun had set, and chill night air blew straight up my hessian robes as Puff bustled me through a side entrance. Forbidding office buildings squatted along the other side of the broad street, apparently ministries and civil service boltholes, which had been mostly abandoned until the conflict was resolved.

"There we are. Leg it over there, round the corner, over a low wall on to the path leading to their barracks, two minute run and you're there. Good luck."

With that, the door slammed and I was on my own.

I sighed. They'd made it clear I wasn't going to get a gun, but I thought they'd at least let me wear some pants. Still, they were only asking me to rob some people who'd been bribed into letting me rob them. For someone who'd recently won a space battle by steering a torpedo with his feet and then hang-gliding back through space off the back of a drone fighter, how hard could this be?

I ran for the corner Puff had pointed, and as I rounded it I crashed into half a dozen heavily armoured soldiers on patrol.

We went down in a tangle of arms, legs, powered gauntlets, and pulse rifles. It's fair to say they weren't amused.

"Where the jolly old fuck do you think you're going, sunshine?" one of the soldiers asked, picking me up by the hood of my cassock. "And what the bloody hell are you wearing? Sandpaper dressing gown? You escape from the world's shittiest spa resort or what?"

"Reckon he's one of them actors, Garrent," said a colleague, checking his rifle over for damage.

I thought fast. I hadn't actually done anything wrong or possibly even suspicious yet. "Yes, that's it. Actor. And a fearful poof to boot, really quite harmless. Popping out for a ciggy and a breath of fresh air."

Garrent's brow furrowed. With his huge shaven head, there was plenty of brow room to get some really impressive furrows going. It was almost fractal in its complexity, and I stared at it, until I realised that he'd asked me something and I'd been too busy watching his scalp contort to listen.

"I *said*, we was all pretty hacked off not to get tickets to that. How's about you do a bit?"

I didn't bother asking what the alternative was, they were pretty big lads.

But I was buggered if I was going to do Friar sodding Lawrence. "Here's much to do with hate, but so much more with love," I began, declaiming heroically.

Garrent's gauntlet shot out and covered my face.

"Fucking *quietly*, you knobber! We're only a few dozen yards from the Impy lines!"

One of the other soldiers nudged Garrent's arm as he lowered his fist from my mouth. "Here, it's not all that iambic pentameter wank, is it?"

"A lot of the servants' stuff is in prose," I tried to chip in.

"I knew it!" the heckler cackled. "Perpetuating the class system via textual form. The entertainments sub-committee remain woefully ill-equipped to select an ideologically progressive schedule."

"Aw, stop your whinging Drazon, and let him get on with it. I like a bit of blank verse, does a soul good to hear the poets sing," said one of the soldiers at the back of the squad, sounding unaccountably Welsh.

Drazon turned swiftly, a haze of blue energy dancing round his gauntlet as he raised and clenched his fist. "Who said that?"

All in all, it was a relief, when the Imperial artillery shell exploded eight feet away.

The crunch of the explosion seemed to knock every bone in my body together, and the whole group of us were bowled over like skittles. The gyroscopic stabilisers kicked in and I found myself in a balletic-style planking pose sprawled full-length over the path and balancing on the toes of one foot, my nose less than an inch from the drifting sands.

I lowered myself down to the ground as I found myself staring into Drazon's accusing glare. Then I relaxed as I realised his accusing glare had more to do with the fact half his skull had been sliced off by shrapnel. Then I threw up. That at least seemed to be in character.

The surviving soldiers scrambled to their feet quickly and scattered behind litter bins and lamp posts, snarling impenetrable codes at each other. Occasionally one of them would snap off a potshot at the roofs of the nearby buildings, though they seemed pretty aimless.

I finally stood, my head ringing, and in my confused state, I was slightly put out that they were ignoring me so completely.

"Keep your flaming head down, you stupid arse," hissed a Welsh voice behind me, which was probably fair advice. I scuttled up the street, flinging myself headlong again when another shell exploded right where I'd been standing.

This time the squad seemed to have nailed the enemy's position, and the night sky lit up with green laser blasts as the soldiers returned fire. Even I could see that they were pinpointing their position even more effectively than a concussed actor wandering around the middle of the street, and sure enough the crump of more artillery began thudding across the rooftops moments later. I ran for it.

Five minutes later, I was thoroughly lost, but at least the tinnitus had stopped, and I was no longer seeing double.

I'd reached the old town, which in most Earth cities means nice pubs, green spaces, property prices that looked like telephone numbers, and guided tours of every single building on your path. On colony worlds, however, they weren't mincing their words. The old town was quite literally where the first primitive shelters had been erected when the colonists arrived a century ago, and where their generation ship had dumped its supplies before limping back into the sky for the journey home. They were mostly corrugated shacks covered loosely by tarpaulins to keep out sandstorms.

It was an interesting contrast to the futuristic cityscape of the area around the parliament building, but from the maps I'd seen, it was also an interesting contrast to where I was supposed to be.

In the distance, the firefight seemed to be dying down, so I skipped down a few blocks and then tried to retrace my route along a parallel street.

Even through my increasingly abused synthskin, the desert's freezing night air was beginning to blow unwelcome draughts up my robes, and I wished I'd thought to pinch a gun or a gauntlet from that dead soldier. Or his armoured trousers, at least

Finally, I turned a corner on to a street filled with grey concrete buildings that reeked of functionary officialdom. At the other end of it I was rewarded with the sight of a fenced-off compound of single storey huts, blazing with lights and speckled with the shapes of soldiers running this way and that. The razor wire-topped chain-link fences were punctuated by huge tapering metallic tower structures at each corner. I was back on track.

My only concern was: how to get in? I'd been told the place would be almost dormant, with a good chunk of the troops at the theatre and most of the rest asleep or bribed. Probably thanks to the skirmish in the streets, there were soldiers marching around *everywhere* in their glossy black uniforms.

I was vaguely aware that standing staring at the razor wire fence of a military installation while wearing fancy dress was probably not a great strategy. But how to get in?

Time was ticking on, they'd surely be on Act 2 by now. And I was stuck staring at the target base like the proverbial dog in front of a butcher's window.

My dilemma was rendered irrelevant when a heavy hand descended on my shoulder from behind, accompanied by a flat electronic voice. "And what are you looking at, sunshine?"

I was turned, roughly, to stare at the matte black visor of a heavy blast helmet, sitting on top of sleek glossy black armour. The faintest flicker of light behind the visor suggested the soldier was scanning my face, and suddenly I realised why Puff was so keen on sourcing his actors from the deep past. They'd have no record of me, I was a ghost in this age!

"James Fanning, Earth, actor, 21st Century," the soldier intoned. "You're a long way from home, Jim."

Oh, *bugger*. "Ah, yeah..." I floundered. "I've been resting. Um, bit of voiceover work, though."

The soldier barked a laugh, which echoed with weird feedback when filtered through his suit's microphone. "That's one hell of a skullsculpt to fool military-grade facial recognition software. Galsec got you infiltrating those shifty STI fruits? Always knew they were up to something."

I always worried when I thought I could understand what these future people were saying. I was pretty sure I shouldn't be able to understand space stuff, and it seemed to end up with my being stuffed into torpedoes and so on. "Ach, well, you know how it is..." I equivocated.

"About time too," the soldier barked. "Don't mind me, need to know and all that. I'll take you *straight* to the chief and you can submit your report. A famous 21st Century actor conveniently found in cryosleep right by the Orion Belt Fringe Festival. Old man Puff's gotten so arrogant he doesn't even think to question his luck any more, right?"

"You're not wrong there," I agreed cautiously, as we set off towards the gates.

"I was wondering how I was going to get in without getting shot," I said to him quite naturally and honestly.

"Covert ops are a bugger like that," the hulking trooper agreed with an expansive shrug that rattled the missiles in his shoulder-mounted bazookas. "Of course, all that synthskin you're packing would have kept you alive long enough to put the boys straight. Probably."

Invisible to scanners, eh? Cheers, Puff. As we reached the gate, the soldier called inside. "Open up lads, theatrical secret agent coming through!"

A ragged cheer rose up from the troops, the steel gates were duly opened, and we marched across the dusty courtyard, me doing my best to look wily, knowing, and only slightly furtive, despite the dreadful itchy armpits the hessian cassock was now giving me.

We headed straight to the nearest hut, and as soon as we were inside, I realised we must be in a converted primary school or something, as the lockers that lined the entrance hallway seemed far too small and flimsy to hold the kind of bulky armour these guys all seemed to favour.

My escort took me into the first classroom on the left, which helpfully had a sign on the door reading 'Intelligence'. Thick stacks of paper bulged out of straining manila folders, piled up on bright plastic chairs that would struggle to seat a seven year old.

At a bit of a loss in the empty classroom, the man waved me over to the teacher's desk, behind which was the only adult-sized chair in the room. "No one home. Not to worry, I'll find out where everyone's got to. Fancy a brew?"

As I sat at the desk, I read the title of a document upside-down. *Counter-intelligence operatives on assignment* it read, heading a column of mug shot photos and names. *Bingo!*

"Um, yeah, two sugars would be lovely, cheers," I said, hardly daring to breathe.

The soldier even saluted, before sauntering from the room. I reached for the paper with shaking fingers.

"Wait a minute..." the grunt said ominously, turning in the doorway. I dropped the sheet as though it had burst into flame.

"Hmm?" I squeaked.

"Would you like a biscuit?" his electronically modulated voice croaked.

I tried to slow my breathing enough to get words out. "Too wet without, dear," I said with a manic rictus attempt at a winning smile.

"You even sound like Fanning," he said, shaking his head as he turned back to the corridor.

I shook my head in the sudden silence, waited a moment, and then grabbed the document again. I ran my left palm over the surface, where Grizabella had implanted the scanner in a slit between synthskin layers, and waited until my thumbnail flashed green to indicate a complete data capture.

I moved to replace the document, but beneath the list of field agents, there was a full-size folding map of the city, covered in squiggles and arrows, in blue and red, with a big squiggly line down the middle which I guessed was the front line, such as it was.

That took a bit of scanning, as I waved my palm around the sheet, trying desperately to find the one elusive patch that I'd missed until my thumb flashed again.

The papers rearranged to what I hope were their original positions, I stood up from the desk. I ought to be getting out of here. Whatever miraculous misunderstanding had smuggled me into the heart of the military operation would evaporate the moment I ran into someone with any actual authority. Not only that, but I must already have missed my first entrance. I was pretty sure someone would cover for me, but a gig was a gig, even if it was Friar sodding Lawrence.

I wandered towards the door, idly looking at the inept but colourful drawings children had made long ago, all triangular figures living in squares with triangles on top and twin moons in the sky shining purple laser beams of light. Then I noticed that among the pinned-up pictures, there was a list of grid references and what looked like security codes. I had no idea what they might be for, but I doubted it was to open the poster paints cupboard, so I scanned that as well.

Five minutes later, I'd scanned just about every sheet of paper in the classroom that wasn't covered in wax crayon and glitter. Then as I prepared to leave, I heard a noise from the corridor, and froze.

"We know exactly what the STI do, you idiot, why on Earth would we infiltrate them? They send out calls for bloody actors among the officers wherever they tour! He's probably just lost, but we'll have to -"

I shut the door, breathing hard. I had seconds left, I was unarmed, and the most cursory scan would demonstrate that my hand scanner was stuffed full of enough military intelligence to win the next two wars on this planet.

I backed away from the door, figuring my best chance was to just charge at whoever opened it and make a break for freedom and the gate. That's when I spotted the belt of plasma grenades hanging from the back of the classroom door.

I'd never even held one of the devices before, but the thing about grenades is they're not exactly burdened with complex controls. I grabbed one, twisted the dial a fraction, pushed the button on the top and dropped it out of the ground floor window.

I barely had time to shelter behind the desk before the resulting explosion took out the whole wall.

"Incoming artillery!" shouted a voice from outside. "They've shelled the command post!"

"I don't think-" started another voice, but I was already moving.

The classroom door flew open as I lobbed another grenade towards it, prompting a string of cursing as the soldiers on the other side fell back in panic.

I had maybe two seconds before they realised I'd not had time to prime the grenade, and I used them. I charged straight through the smoking, rubble-strewn gap in the wall, relying on my gyroscopic implants to keep me on my feet as my Friar Lawrence sandals tripped and slipped over masonry and twisted metal.

The first laser pulses blasted over my shoulder as I cleared the building and took my first breath of fresh air. By pure luck, the wall had been facing the fence in a sheltered corner of the compound, so I didn't run out into a fresh hail of laser bolts.

Orienting myself quickly, I realised turning left would take me straight out towards the front gate, which I was fairly sure would now be swarming with soldiers mobilising to investigate what I hoped they still thought was an external attack. I needed an alternate exit strategy. I reached into my cassock, and squeezed the object I'd spent the dress rehearsal pretending was Friar Lawrence's crucifix. Then I darted right, rounded the corner, and shinned up a drainpipe. The stabilisers helped on the way up, but I was still knackered by the time I reached the top and flopped on to the flat roof, flapping, twitching, and gasping for breath like a fish out of water.

"He can't have got far," I heard my guardian angel grumbling below.

"He can," his unseen companion rasped. "He'll have swiped my spare uniform from under my desk and be halfway back home by now. No matter. We know just where he's going."

A spare uniform! I struck my forehead, as I tugged at the scratchy sackcloth that was still my only defence against the increasingly icy night air. The vacuum and near absolute zero temperature of open space had been excruciating, but I'd only had to endure it for a matter of seconds in the middle of the biggest adrenaline spike of my life, compared to several hours in this old sack. And my precious synthskin was clearly sloughing off at an alarming rate, not helped by this bloody costume.

Rolling over on to my stomach, I risked a peek down at the compound. Hovertrucks full of troops were activating and sweeping out of the front gate on to the streets, off to kick some arse. I really had to hope I could get my intel to Puff before the war was over and there was no one left to sell it to.

I pulled my fake crucifix out from inside my hellish costume to check on my exit strategy.

I needn't have bothered. Sirens began whooping and blaring across the compound. "Orbital strike incoming!" bellowed a sergeant, his amplified voice rolling across the whole base. "Look lively, lads! Brace!"

At each corner of the base, huge pulses of plasma blasted into the night sky from the tapering towers, streaking away towards an enemy no one could yet see. Anti-aircraft defences, should have seen that one coming, really. The tarmac was rapidly clearing of the few remaining personnel, who were swarming into one of the smaller sheds, which I could only assume housed a subterranean area or two, given the number of people squashing into it.

The plasma cannons kept blasting into the sky as I clung to the roof, alone in the night with an orbital strike bearing down on my position and a synthetic fist full of classified information.

I grinned as the ILO drone screamed from the sky and skidded to a halt three feet in front of my face with a single directed burst of retro-thruster fire. The plasma cannons continued to blast skywards, and small fireballs began to appear in the upper atmosphere.

The drone had jettisoned most of its cannons, both to control its descent from the ionosphere and to throw off the tracking sensors. Now the discarded components were being picked off, keeping the cannons occupied, and keeping the troops in the bunker while they still thought they were under bombardment. I nodded approvingly; clever girl.

I slipped Go Compare's goggles over my head. The drone had done well to get through to me, I'd just hoped it would distract the soldiers for long enough for me to make a break for the streets. Now, however, it was my turn to get us out with the prize.

"Come on, Blinky," I muttered, naming my new favourite gadget, and I crawled over to it, watching my own careful approach through the remote cameras. I reached out gingerly, expecting to smell burning synthskin but somehow it had already cooled from re-entry. "Clever girl."

I blinked at an icon, and Blinky puffed up three feet in the air, its remaining cannon dangling in invitation.

"Sweet thought, but I think we can make a bigger statement this time..."

From a crouching start, I leaped into the air, and came down with both feet on top of the drone's chassis. It bobbed a little as it adjusted its thrusters to compensate for my added weight, but it stabilised quickly.

I'd already begun to suspect Puff and Grizabella had made additional adjustments to my body when they reconstructed me in the matter transporter, and the height of that leap proved it.

A shout sounded from below, a solitary guard left peering at the cannons still spewing energy into the sky. He'd spotted the weirdly robed intruder crouching on a remote starfighter drone on his roof.

I blinked at another icon. "Take us back. Quick."

Blinky launched into a circular flight, slightly jerky at first as it continued to adjust for my weight, but by the time we'd made one loop of the school roof, we were hovering smoothly.

Pew! Pew! The guard fired a blind volley of energy bolts into the air around us, possibly a warning shot.

I took a deep breath, and blinked a third time. We shot down towards the guard at a stomach-churning pace, and he blasted away the whole time.

It was with a sense of sheer disbelief that I found time slowing to a crawl around me as liquid light flowed all around. The guard's knuckles were white around the trigger of his rifle, and a new bolt of energy was zapping from the barrel.

With no conscious thought at all, my hands moved to swat his wild shots out of the air as though they were windscreen wipers clearing raindrops.

Energy beams splashed against my arms, setting the cassock ablaze but bouncing harmlessly from my synthskin-coated flesh. As the drone ate up the distance between us, I saw the guard gulp, shoulder his rifle and fire one last bolt straight at my face before he dived out of the way.

I stood in one fluid motion, surfing Blinky as I stuck my hand out to block his final shot.

My right hand.

The bolt struck me right through the palm where Grizabella had stubbed out countless cigarettes during our abortive training.

A fine mist of blood and sizzling flesh sprayed from the back of my hand as plasma drilled straight through the limb and out into the night sky.

I screwed up my eyes against the savage, blinding, excruciating pain of it. And then forced them open again as the drone reacted to the eye movement by hurling us up several hundred feet. Into the cannons' field of fire.

"Cheers, *mate*," I hissed as car-sized energy bolts flashed around us.

Blinky lurched hard to the left to dodge one blast, and I took back control, blinking away tears from the throbbing pain in my hand.

I shifted my footing and leaned forward, sending us into a steep corkscrew dive around the nearest cannon.

It was probably suicidal, but I was guessing these artillery pieces were automated and none too bright.

Sure enough, their angle of fire tracked lower and lower as we descended towards our target cannon, barely keeping ahead of the barrage.

There was a terrifying moment as we circled the cannon's

muzzle, and it pulsed a blast so close to us that Blinky's final weapons pod dropped off with a shower of sparks. Then we were down on top of the tower, sheltered from the other three cannons by perching behind the fourth.

"One elephant, two elephant, *go*!" I blinked and we blasted off in a perfect parabolic arc as all three cannons concentrated their fire on the fourth, which exploded in an angry blossom of fire.

Shrieking sirens and warnings followed our progress as we hurtled up, over and down towards our goal, laser bolts streaked the sky, and I stood up straight on top of the robot, threw back my head and laughed.

I surfed Blinky all the way down to the ground, and kept my footing as it skimmed down a residential street which I hoped was just round the corner from the parliament building.

Finally I hopped off the drone, which coasted to a final halt a few yards away.

"Go home," I told it, peeling off the sweat-sodden goggles and dangling them around my neck.

As I watched Blinky streak back into the sky, dodging significantly fewer energy bolts, I checked my hand. It was still agonising, but the laser or whatever had at least cauterised the wound it had drilled in my limb. It had also left a neat hole I could poke my little finger through.

I paused, considering the implications if I ever fancied diversifying as a stage magician, and then raised my uninjured hand and flexed my fingers. A chunky memory wafer ejected from the slit in my hand, and I tucked it into the one costume detail Friar Lawrence had been permitted. A small leather pouch had been fixed to my cassock's cord belt, so I could give Juliet her potion, and it was also lead-lined so I could hide my findings in case I was stopped and scanned on the way back into the venue.

I rounded the corner, and sure enough, there was the Jargroth parliament building. Result! I prepared to brush off questions about my smouldering robes, blood-stained hand and generally dishevelled state. I'd just pretend it was part of the show, Verona's bloody backdrop to the lovers' tale.

That's when I spotted the crowds of soldiers spilling from the building, slapping each other's shoulders, wiping their eyes, and blinking in the cold night air.

I'd missed the show.

CHAPTER 5:
SPACE JAM!

It didn't take much effort to find the STI, I just asked the nearest solitary soldier where the nearest pub was. He clapped me on my shoulder and told me I'd performed a 'well safe, innit' Prologue, so I obligingly signed his rifle. It was genuinely the nicest fan moment I'd ever experienced, and I was just glad he was too pissed to see how beaten up I was.

The bar was a pleasantly dingy basement, with a firepit in the middle, and scuttling children refilling tankards from casks around the walls. It stank of exhausted actors, and victory. Each of the low benches around the firepit bore a reclining thespian, and at least half a dozen admiring soldiers, who were all trying not to look too starstruck after one smitten young corporal had tried on Grizabella's spectacular hat, only to find two grim-faced military policemen marching him off to the punishment block, under the scandalised gaze of an adjutant. Guess there was no room for sharp hats in this glorious revolution. Probably a decadent frippery of the degenerate elite, or something.

I did my best not to swagger as I wandered in. I made my way over to Puff's bench, and tossed the leather pouch into the old ham's lap.

"I found that old prop you were looking for," I said, and followed it up with a roguish wink, as I was fairly sure everyone would be too pissed to notice.

Puff looked up with a sharpness that belied the array of empty glasses arranged over the table that lay more or less before him.

"That's the only detail saving your wretched mumming hide, you febrile fustilarian. How dare you miss your cue? You forced poor Kraal to extemporise at length when it came to meeting with Romeo's trusty old confessor."

I was rocked back on my feet under the force of the old luvvie's withering scorn, but I mugged happily for the soldiers' benefit anyway. "Gosh, dear old thing, I lost track of time. I rather thought some desperate young understudy might pounce on the chance to jump in and do the piece for me. I do like to cultivate fresh talent."

There was a brief pause while Puff's nostrils flared, which took just long enough for me to register that I was in serious trouble.

"It just so happens that I carved out a modest name for myself with the part earlier in my own career, and reluctantly trod the boards to deliver the speech one last time, ending with a devilishly subtle final rhetorical flourish."

A few of the others were glowering at me now, but I decided my best option was simply to style this out. "Well, I'm delighted I gave you the chance to recapture past glories. Now can I talk to you about... this new play I'm writing?"

Their dramatic yearnings thoroughly purged by the evening's entertainment, and now drunkenly indifferent to whomsoever had delivered which specific elements thereof, the soldiers collectively rolled their eyes at this fresh display of creative vitality, and turned back to their drinks as Puff swept from the bar. I followed with a smirk, and was surprised when a sergeant looked up from his game of dominoes and plucked at my sleeve as I reached the foot of the stairs.

The man was stocky and red-faced, with piggy bloodshot eyes that spoke of unspeakable nightmares, many of which he'd probably inspired himself. "This play..." he slurred.

"Um. Yes?" I replied, doing my level best not to squeak with terror.

The man blinked a couple of times, trying to bring me into focus, or possibly trying to remember what he'd been about to ask. "Does it," he said eventually, his gruff voice almost plaintive, "does it preserve the unities?"

A pit yawning in my stomach, I looked around wildly. I was alarmed at the number of faces suddenly pointing in my direction with interest. Though the faces of the STI members were very much tuned for amusement. Bastards.

The soldier was continuing, though I was giving serious consideration to butchering the man with his own ornamental sword. "The unities are so sadly neglected in contemporary theatre. Take the recent Pinter revival..."

His drinking partner slumped mournfully in his seat. "Oh! Pinter is gone, quite gone!"

"Indeed, and it is ever so," the first grunt continued, waving graciously to his virtually supine comrade. "And they call it *modern*, well of course they would... but the unities, the unities, sir, ought to be held as sacrosanct. Or what the devil are we poor bastards fighting *for*?"

I affected a look of grave concern. "I'm afraid Mr Puff is the fiscal deity before whom I must abase myself in order to get any of my modest scribblings before an audience, and he has some most singular ideas about staging. But rest assured I shall argue most emphatically for the greatest attention to be paid to the, ah, unities."

The grizzled critic appeared mollified, and fell back into slurred conversation with his comrade, their dominoes quite forgotten. By the time the door had swung closed behind me, they were discussing the woeful consequences of Brechtian distancing on the unities, and sealing a pact to slit Godot's throat if they ever tracked him down on the battlefield.

I took a deep heady breath of cold desert night air, feeling half-pissed just from spending five minutes in that booze-sodden hole. The temperature was well below freezing, and the twin moons blazed across the cloudless night sky in all their splendour.

Pop!

I threw myself to the ground even as I recognised the sound of the popping cork for what it was. I spat a mouthful of sand as I looked up. Sure enough, Puff faced me, brandishing a bottle of something fizzy and chilled, judging by the vapour that rose from the bubbling fluid that ran down the bottle's neck and spattered on to the sandy street.

"Well, well, you *do* know what to do in a gunfight, and I'm avenged for your little giggles at my expense. Now, step into my office."

Puff tossed the uncorked bottle to me as I scrambled to my feet, and I managed to catch it clumsily by the neck just inches above the ground. The old man smirked at my discomfort, took a long swig from a second open bottle which he'd produced from his cloak, and wandered away towards the ship's hangar.

When we reached the bridge of the *Peter Hall*, Puff headed straight to the science officer's station, and plugged in the data chip. He waved me vaguely towards the Captain's chair.

"I could get used to this," I sighed, as I sank into the padded seat, and took a long swig from the probably-not-champagne. Bubbles tickled my throat as the sharp ice-cold liquid flowed, but there was a background flavour that suggested Puff was testing the adage that anything will pass for vintage fizz if served cold enough. I set to making sure it didn't last long enough to warm up and wreck the illusion.

Puff was making generally approving noises as he scanned through the data, while drinking deeply from his own bottle every few moments.

"Troop positions, artillery resources, supply line details... this stuff is bloody *gold*, dear boy." Puff capped this effusive praise with an explosive belch that he tried only half-heartedly to pass off as an 'emphatic yawn' before reaching under the console for a fresh bottle of bubbly.

"It was a pleasure," I murmured with a smile, sinking further into the padding and wondering how captains managed to combat the constant temptation to doze off between issuing orders. Perhaps they didn't, moments of snap decision seemed to be few and far between, from what little I'd seen of interstellar travel so far. A first officer's duties could reasonably include giving the chap in the chair a discrete nudge every few dozen parsecs or so to get fresh directions.

"It's exemplary work, it really ish," Puff was well-oiled now, but there was a brittle smug edge to his tone that woke me up in a moment. "It's just a shame you've reported the movements for the *wrong army*."

A long silence rolled over the bridge, and made itself comfortable. I cleared his throat, found it suddenly awfully dry, glugged down the dregs of my bottle of bubbly, and tried again.

"Wrong... army? Hahahaha."

The silence was now one-sided, but Puff showed no sign of breaking it, glowering balefully at me through his one eye, which was admittedly now bloodshot, half-closed, and distinctly unfocused.

"Getting almost a bit nervous now, ahahahaha," I added, but the confident chuckle now sounded dry and desperate even to my own ears. I suddenly realised what a great Polonius the old man would make, at the exact same moment as I also inwardly resolved never to breathe a word of that thought to him. "You should probably qualify that kind of statement."

"Well, *dear boy*, I'm not sure there's much to qualify. We land in a besieged city on the eve of battle, to give our acclaimed interpretation of *Romeo and Juliet*. Under cover of which you're dispatched to collate details of our host's numbers, resources, and probably medium-term intentions for sale via a suitably shady and disreputable agency. You very much appear to have collated these details for the wrong army. What in the name of bedevilled stoat-fuckery does that suggest to you?"

I felt my cheeks prickling with the first heralds of intoxication, or possibly even shame. It was hard to tell; they both usually came along around the same time, and tended to bleed into each other. "Ah. Given that we are indeed billeted in, as you say, a besieged city, is it within the realms of possibility that I may have strayed across enemy lines?"

Puff nodded, curtly. "Aye, lad. After we landed with great pomp and circumstance and gave the performance of our careers to a carefully-bribed theatre of passionate insurgents, right next to their command base which had been left completely defenceless thanks to a maintenance crew who we'd paid handsomely to take a sudden yet passionate interest in the arts. You somehow decided to eschew the open goal of military intelligence that lay before you, and instead took it on yourself to wander through several miles of radiation-charred suburbia in order to impregnate the opposing force's citadel. No wonder you missed your damn cue!"

He was still talking, and hadn't shot me. So this was obviously not the end of the world. "So what do we do?"

The old actor bounced from his chair as though he hadn't just knocked back an entire bottle of sparkling wine in less than five minutes, and made for the door. "We get everyone back on board and into orbit, just as we planned. We were only in that pub waiting for news of you. As far as we know, that offensive's still scheduled."

I remembered hovertrucks careering from the compound in search of an unseen and indeed non-existent sniper. "We might be all right there. I sent a good chunk of their army in a bit of a wild goose chase."

Puff raised an eyebrow as he stepped out into the corridors. "That's... all right, that's quite good. But you still robbed the wrong army, so don't think you're off the useless dickhead charts just yet. And there's still Harkreth. He won't have been fooled."

We hurried along the plush red-carpeted corridor, the gaping hole in the hull now firmly patched with a new photo of Rory Kinnear. "It was an accidental wild goose chase, he might have been fooled by a cock-up?"

"Oh, I wish you'd learn when to stop digging, dear heart."

We hurried together down the saucer's ramp, only to see Kraal, Grizabella and Gielgud scurrying across the vast hangar floor towards us. "Don't you dare finish that fizz without us," Griz called, beaming.

"You can pry this bottle from my cold dead fingers, you alcoholic vultures," the old man boomed genially, "or you can open up the stash under the stage in the rehearsal studio. But only, and Daddy must insist here, *after* you do the quickest prep for take-off. How does that sound, my delightfully deranged angel of death?"

Bugger me if Grizabella didn't actually purr at that, and give the old man a peck on the cheek as she scampered up the ramp.

"Making it hot right now, Captain Bird's Eye," she called over her shoulder.

"I'll find the glasses," mumbled Kraal as he and Gielgud followed fast behind.

I made to follow them, but Puff stopped me with a surprisingly gentle hand on the remains of my scratchy sleeve. "The set, the props, our lovely costumes..." He looked genuinely agonised, his eyes darting between the ramp and the hangar doors. "I suppose..."

"There's two pissed-off *armies* out there, Puff. Leave the inventory to the local am dram or something, and come back for it when their war's over."

He nodded, but put a hand to his brow and groaned a bit as he did so, which was frankly a bit much even for me. "You're right, dear boy, you're right, even though it's all your fault, you're right. Let's..."

He was turning to leave when, with a faint but decidedly sinister whine, the hangar's lights flickered, and a squadron of Jargroth imperial troops stepped through their concealment fields, encased from head to foot in glossy black armour, and bristling with unpleasant-looking weaponry.

Their leader stepped forward and flipped the visor up from his helmet to reveal a pinched face covered in a fine lattice of scars. "You dicked us, Puff?" he growled, brandishing his rifle.

Puff sighed. "Ach, tepid wankjuice and fuckeration," he muttered, before turning around and hitting the troops with his widest grin.

"Harkreth, dear old thing! Whatever gave you that queer notion?" he bellowed out loud, his rich tones rolling back from the hangar's far wall.

"I can't be sure, Grin, but my suspicions were first aroused when my command post was infiltrated by unknown agents while the most notorious spy in show business was in town to entertain the enemy. Call me paranoid, but I couldn't help but put two and two together at that point."

"Me?" Puff boomed, "In a command post? Under cover of darkness? With my reputation? Ding dong!"

I looked on aghast as the old man threw the soldiers a lusty wink. Even worse, I was fairly sure a few of them were sniggering.

Puff raised his hands in a vaguely placatory gesture. "It's really nothing to get so *exercised* about, dear heart! Just a teensy administrative cock-up - the boy here got caught in a skirmish, crossed the lines by mistake in all the confusion, and pinched your intel by mistake. Could have happened to anyone."

"It really couldn't," Harkreth said, looking straight at me for the first time, with an expression of incredulity and almost awe that I didn't like one bit. "So are you going to execute the miserable whelp?"

Puff smirked as I spluttered. "I probably should, of course, but decent actors are hard to find. And of course, he's RADA-trained..."

"What? I'm bloody not -" I caught the old man's sharp look and switched gears mid-breath, "-not in the habit of advertising that. It's not always good for my credibility. Not edgy enough. Yeah."

"Look," the old man said, spreading his hands wide and smiling, "there's really no harm done. The boy here ballsed up, but he's proved his mettle as far as I'm concerned. Your security needs some work, and now you know where the weak links are. And the lad's so anxious not to be shot, he'll gladly scamper over to this side's HQ as planned, and have your stuff for you in a jiffy or twenty."

Harkreth looked far from mollified, but lowered his rifle. Behind him, the shiny black-suited soldiers also began to shoulder arms, though with a distinctly sulky air. Even though he was the one they were pissed off not to be zapping, I kind of understood. It was a bit like Chekov: you put a gun on stage in Act I, it needs to be fired in Act III. And if you suit up in sleek battle armour and pack every gun your quartermaster can think of for a cloaked commando raid across a warzone at midnight, you kind of expect that you'll get to laser some fools before handing back the kit at the debrief. I strongly suspected they'd be taking potshots at anything that was stupid enough to move while they were traipsing back across the lines.

All in all, it was a shame when Grizabella ran from the ship with a broad grin on her face. "Guys, we made bank after all, I just brokered a sale to the insurgents! They asked a few pointed questions about what Jimmy was doing crossing the enemy lines when he was supposed to be doing soliloquies, but I told them, 'Everyone's a fucking critic these days, shut the fuck up and pay me,' like you always do - and it worked!"

There was a long silence as Grizabella's smile froze and grew ever more brittle as she noticed my horrified grimace, followed by Puff's stoniest glower, followed by the chunky clicking of half a dozen laser rifles being raised and primed. "Oh... sodding grumblearsed buttnuggets."

"Like I said, Puff, you dicked us." Harkreth trained his rifle straight between the old man's eyes. "Sorry, old man."

Puff scowled. "Dicked you? You pox-ridden fartsack, I wouldn't dick *you* with your mother's."

I nudged Grizabella, who was still standing with her face frozen in a rictus of shock. "You'd better do something. He dropped a Mom Bomb. It's going to kick off."

"Oh, hell yes it is," she breathed. "You have no idea."

Staring down the barrel of half a dozen nasty laser weapons, Puff took a deep breath, and stood a little straighter. With his free hand, he yanked the twine from his ponytail, and shook out his mane of silver hair so that it settled around his shoulders like snow. With a grand flourish of the same hand, he threw off his cloak, which fluttered and billowed to the ground behind him. He stood and faced the soldiers; a stocky bear of a man, who had no doubt played heroes, tyrants and warriors alike in his time, but for all that just an old man with only a stick to defend himself from a salvo of white-hot laser death. For all Puff's grandstanding, I realised, this was a barbaric way for a great man to die.

"Are you quite finished?" called Harkreth, the faintest note of regret underscoring his jibe.

Puff answered only with a sad smile, and that was when I noticed just how tightly the old man was gripping his cane. And the rotating crystal that surmounted it seemed to be a lot more violet than the placid blue gemstone I remembered from my 'audition'.

I took a step towards Grizabella, only to find she was already accelerating away up the ship's ramp.

"You could have walked away, Harkreth," Puff said in a calm tone, but one which carried weird harmonics that bounced around my frontal lobe and made me wish I'd made more considered life choices, "but you couldn't let it lie. And now you have the gall to stand there and threaten me, when I'm nothing more or less than a very foolish, fond old man."

Grizabella was out of sight now, back safely in the ship, but I barely noticed, as I watched with fascinated horror as the soldiers squeezed the trigger studs on their assorted laser rifles, plasma cannons and BFG-series artillery pieces. The weapons were not responding, and the troopers were understandably nonplussed, slapping the butts of their lethal weaponry, shaking the guns, and in one case straight out of the earliest silent films, even reversing their rifle and peering into the muzzle while pumping the trigger mechanism compulsively.

I took another step towards the ship. A moment earlier, I'd just been grateful that the assorted energy weapons were no longer trained on me, though I had felt a bit guilty about that. Suddenly, I felt a huge wave of pity for those very same soldiers, right down to their doubtless shiny black stealth socks. And that emption, and the impulse to scurry away up the ramp to safety, it all flowed from the ridiculous old ham actor leaning on a crystal cane before me.

As Harkreth scowled at his own suddenly useless rifle, Puff turned for a fraction of a second and fired off a conspiratorial wink at me. Given the eyepatch, he *might* just have been blinking, but there was that glint in the old man's eye.

Puff took a deep breath.

Harkreth snarled, as his comrades continued to struggle with their unresponsive weapons.

The old man raised his free hand.

"Oh..." he declaimed, and his voice was beautiful, it was *compelling*, and I felt tears spring to his eyes even as the echoes began to roll back from the hangar's far wall.

The soldiers were transfixed at the sound of the old man's voice, lowering their guns, and cocking their heads as though to better savour those mellifluous tones.

And then the screaming started. The troops staggered, clutching themselves in sudden agony. I looked on in confusion and mounting revulsion as viscous pink liquid began pooling around their boots.

Harkreth, his visor still up, screamed loudest of all, in impotent fury as well as agony, and I looked up to see those cruel scarred features blurring, and running into each other.

Melting. They were all melting, pinkish fluid now seeping from every seam, join and vent in their ridiculous armour. As the soldiers began to collapse wetly to whatever remained of their knees, even the barrels of their useless laser rifles were beginning to wilt and drip darker liquid.

Puff stared at the unfolding carnage he had somehow wrought, holding the stricken men within the baleful gaze of his single eye. The screams intensified, beginning to sound unpleasantly like gargling as the soldiers began the grisly process of drowning in their own liquified flesh.

In a few moments the screams began to die away, as it became harder to tell where the puddle of pink and black streaked fluid ended and where the soaking melting armour began, rivulets of liquid rust running over every surface.

One soldier cuffed at his own helmet in desperation, as though trying to escape his armour. Instead the heavy powered gauntlet collapsed into a splash of inky liquid, falling to the puddle below and sending droplets of liquid trooper flying into the air. The man's hand had given away along with the gauntlet, revealing a bright white stump of bone that was running like candlewax.

The soldier fell forward into the puddle of his own remains, and continued to melt away into the floor, unmoving.

Harkreth was the last to fall, his bare skull gleaming white even as it began to run, making him look like a skeleton with a particularly sweaty hangover. He reached out to Puff with the remnants of one ruined arm, then froze and pitched forward to the ground where whatever was left of him burst apart, horribly.

A few moments later, it was all over. Where a group of soldiers had stood, there was now a widening slick of gently bubbling goo, predominantly dark pink, but shot through with streaks of reds, white, and a metallic black. The smell of hot fat assailed my nostrils, and I shuddered as the bile rose in his throat.

Puff sensed the reaction, and turned sharply from contemplating his handiwork. "I wouldn't, lad. I think the floor's quite colourful enough, don't you?"

With a hard swallow, I did his best to compose myself. I stepped up to the old man's side, gesturing at the puddle. "How did you - space stuff, right?"

"Not exactly." Puff's voice was steady, with no trace of those weird harmonics, but he looked weary, as though he was feeling every decade of the immense age he looked to have reached. The old man handed me his cane. It was almost uncomfortably warm, and he rummaged in his tunic for a moment before producing a box of matches.

I thought he was going to spark up a cigar or something, which would have been distasteful enough, but instead the old man balanced a match with its head against the strip, at a right angle to the box. Then he looked at me with a weary smile.

"Come on, dear boy. You're not telling me you never moved an audience to tears?"

With his free thumb and index finger, he flicked the match, so that its head ignited against the strip and flared as it was already tumbling end over end towards the puddle's surface.

The match landed with a sucking plop, and for the briefest moment, that seemed to be that. Then the puddle of melted troopers erupted in a creeping carpet of flame that quickly swept across the whole mess until it was alive with dancing, brightly-coloured ribbons of fire.

"See? It's practically a chemistry lesson, all those different colours. Still, best not tarry..." Puff turned on his heel, grabbed his cane back from my unresisting fingers, and sauntered back up the ramp and into the ship.

I tore my eyes away from the display as the grisly remains boiled away in the fire's intense heat. I'd signed up with a murderous psychopath, and I *still* hadn't even had a chance to do any acting. For a long moment, I stared at the ramshackle old ship, and considered my options.

But I knew in my heart I was only taking a moment to indulge my finer feelings. I was both light years and centuries away from home, in the middle of a warzone consisting entirely of people I'd just robbed, and people I'd just been *trying* to rob. As such, I had the same survival chances as the single bottle of prosecco at a book launch. Which reminded me, I'd left half a drink on the bridge.

"On with the motley," I muttered, and walked up the ramp, which retracted behind me. Moments later, I clung to the bar as the *Peter Hall* blasted off, leaving behind a hangar empty but for a puddle of dead soldiers, flaming gently like a Christmas pudding from hell.

The others would all be on the bridge busying themselves with take-off procedures, but I still had no idea about how the ship actually worked. So I reasoned I had a few minutes to myself with an unattended bar, and every reason in the world to get outrageously shit-faced.

Atmospheric buffeting made it difficult to mix anything, so I made do with a few glasses of wine on the way up. As we left orbit, however, I reached for the martini.

"Pour me one, while you're at it." Kraal appeared from the corridor, and sat on the bench over the torpedo tube.

I obliged without a word, and quickly took the drinks over. He watched me the whole time in silence.

"You're wondering what the hell you've done to your life, right?"

I sat down next to him, and we clinked glasses. "I got past that hours ago," I said, "Now I've moved on to wondering how an old man with a stick can melt a small army. And wondering what galactic power could possibly care about these petty little conflicts to the extent of hiring us."

Kraal's lips twisted slightly, clearly wondering how much he was allowed to tell me. Eventually, he tipped his glass towards me in a salute.

"I've seen actors fight for the mere privilege of auditioning for the STI. Not particularly impressive fights, granted, but they were slapping the air and flouncing like nobody's business, and you were just plucked from a provincial stage in the deep past. Have you not wondered why Puff came to you?"

"Kraal, 'dear boy', I might not be a megastar but I'm still an actor. I let my professional ego deal with that kind of awkward question."

The reptilian actor's delicate fins rippled with a slightly more vivid green shade as he leaned forward. "I guess this is the first time you've spent more than a minute in this part of the ship. Perhaps you should take a look around."

He threw back his drink, and walked out towards the bridge, pausing only to put his empty glass back neatly on the bar.

I stayed on the bench, staring at where he'd been sitting.

Or rather the framed black and white photo that hung on the wall directly behind his seat.

The framed black and white photo of my parents, dressed up as eighteenth century highwaymen and juggling.

While standing in front of the backcloth from the *Peter Hall*'s rehearsal room.

About the Author

Andrew Lawston is author of the Something Nice series of short story collections, and translator of the early 20th Century Chantecoq novels. A lifelong Doctor Who fan, he is now moving firmly into speculative fiction, with a forthcoming cyberpunk series. When not writing, Andrew is an occasional theatre actor, and full-time publishing professional. He lives close to the Thames in a leafy part of London, with his lovely wife, intense cocker spaniel, and aloof black cat.

www.AndrewLawston.blogspot.co.uk

Books by Andrew Lawston

Fiction

Apocalypse Barnes
Of Mice And Men And Sausages
Story of My Escape (trans.)
Chantecoq and the Aubry Affair (trans.)
Chantecoq and the Père-Lachaise Ghost (trans.)

Short Story Collections

Something Nice: 10 Short Stories
Something Nicer: A Second Short Story Collection

Thank you for reading

Pew! Pew!

Learn about upcoming installments of Pew! Pew!

www.pewpewbooks.com

Made in the USA
Coppell, TX
05 November 2022